Love's Unexpected Journey

"FALLING IN LOVE IS ALWAYS UNEXPECTED." — UNKNOWN

RUSTY LE GRANDE

Contents

Foreword

Love has the extraordinary power to transform our lives in ways we could never anticipate. It can lift us to euphoric heights or plunge us into the depths of despair; it can inspire us to become our best selves or reveal the shadows we hide within. In "Love's Unexpected Journey," we embark on a profound exploration of this complex emotion, one that defies the confines of convention and navigates the unpredictable terrain of human connection.

As you journey through the pages of this book, you will find a narrative that intertwines the joy of love with the challenges it presents. Each chapter serves as a stepping stone, guiding you through the myriad experiences that shape our understanding of intimacy, desire, and the very nature of connection itself. Here, love is not merely a destination; it is a winding road filled with lessons, revelations, and unexpected turns.

I am Rusty Le Grande, the voice behind this exploration, and this story is as much an introspective journey as it is a collective reflection of the human experience. Drawing from personal experiences and the wisdom of those who have traversed the landscape of love, I aim to illuminate the complexities of relationships—the thrill of falling in love, the heartache of loss, and the courage required to embrace vulnerability.

The quotes that punctuate each chapter serve as touchstones, offering insights from thinkers, poets, and philosophers who have grappled with these themes throughout history. They echo the sentiments we all feel at one time or another, reminding us that we are not alone in our struggles and triumphs. Love's many facets are laid bare: the exhilaration of first love, the burn of desire, the pain of secrets, and the triumph of trust.

Throughout this narrative, expect to encounter moments that resonate deeply—reflections of your own experiences and emotions. You may find yourself laughing, crying, or contemplating the choices you've made in your own relationships. This book does not shy away from the discomfort of truth; it embraces it, offering a candid examination of what it means to love and be loved in return.

As we delve into the pages ahead, prepare to be challenged and moved. "Love's Unexpected Journey" is not simply a book; it is an invitation to ponder the depths of your own heart and the connections that shape your life. It is a call to recognize that every relationship we enter, every bond we forge, is a journey of discovery. In love, we find not only joy and fulfillment but also the courage to face our fears and confront the truths we often avoid.

Let this narrative serve as a reminder that love, in all its forms, is an adventure worth embarking on—one that teaches us about ourselves and the world around us. Each chapter offers a glimpse into the intricate dance of trust, desire, and vulnerability, ultimately guiding us to the understanding that it is the journey itself that enriches our lives.

Welcome to "Love's Unexpected Journey." May you find within these pages the courage to embrace your own journey, wherever it may lead. Whether you are currently in love, searching for it, or healing from its loss, remember that every experience is valid, and every heart has a story to tell. As you turn the pages, may you discover not only the depths of desire but also the unyielding strength of love itself.

Chapter 1: A Dangerous Game

"And those who were seen dancing were thought to be insane by those who could not hear the music." — Friedrich Nietzsche

Sydney pulsed with an energy Emma Carter had almost forgotten. The city's heartbeat throbbed beneath the glittering skyline, a siren song of neon lights and whispered promises. The salted air from the harbor carried the hum of possibilities, the kind that made her skin prickle with something dangerously close to anticipation.

She wasn't supposed to be here. Not in this bar, not in this moment, not in this game she had convinced herself she would never play again. And yet, here she was—heels clicking against polished floors, a glass of wine poised between her fingers, red lips curved in a knowing smile.

Emma had spent too long caged inside expectations, drowning in a life that had once felt safe but had become suffocating. The divorce papers had been signed a year ago, yet the ink still felt wet, a lingering ghost of the woman she had been before. At forty-two, she wasn't old, but she wasn't a fresh-faced twenty-something either. And maybe that's what made this all the more intoxicating—because she knew exactly what she wanted, and she had stopped apologizing for it.

Tonight, she wanted danger.

The kind of danger that looked like Jack Kingston.

He was across the room, leaning against the bar with the sort of confidence that wasn't performed but innate, like he belonged there, like the world bent to accommodate his presence. He wasn't beautiful in a conventional sense, but there was something about him—something raw, untamed, magnetic. A man who had tasted life in ways most people only fantasized about.

Their eyes met, and it was electric. A slow, deliberate exchange that sent a shiver curling through her body. Jack's lips tilted into a smirk, dark eyes lingering before he lifted his glass to his mouth. Whiskey. Of course.

A challenge.

Emma had never been one to back down from a challenge.

She moved toward him, each step measured, deliberate, the silk of her dress whispering against her thighs. His gaze followed her every movement, and when she finally reached him, he straightened, his full attention settling on her like a weight. Heavy. Intentional.

"You're staring," she murmured, tilting her head just slightly.

"You walked in here like you owned the place," Jack replied, his voice a low hum, smooth like the whiskey he was nursing. "Hard not to stare."

She smiled. "And you? You look like you've got a story worth hearing."

"That depends," he said, eyes darkening as they flickered over her. "Are you the type who likes to listen, or the type who likes to play?"

The air between them tightened, thick with something neither of them cared to name. It wasn't romance—not yet. It wasn't even attraction in the simple, casual sense. It was an unspoken agreement. A prelude to something dangerous. Something thrilling.

And Emma was ready for it.

She reached for her drink, taking a slow sip before responding. "I suppose that depends on the game."

Jack chuckled, the sound rolling through the space between them. "Then let's see if you can keep up."

Hours passed in a blur of conversation and suggestion. Words laced with hidden meanings, hands that didn't touch but threatened to, breaths that mingled in the small space between them. Emma was drowning in the moment, letting herself be swept under, intoxicated not by the wine but by the man who sat before her.

Jack wasn't like the others. He didn't fawn over her, didn't try to impress her with hollow compliments. He saw her—really saw her—and that was infinitely more dangerous than any flirtation.

At some point, the air in the bar had changed. People had filtered out, leaving the atmosphere quieter, more intimate. Jack leaned in, his fingers tracing the rim of his glass. "Tell me something true, Emma."

She hesitated. Because truth was vulnerability and vulnerability was a risk. But hadn't she come here for this? Hadn't she stepped into the night looking for something more?

"I forgot what it feels like to be wanted," she admitted, voice barely above a whisper.

Jack's expression didn't change, but something in his eyes sharpened. "Then maybe you need a reminder."

A breath. A heartbeat. A choice.

Emma tilted her chin up, her pulse quickening. "And what exactly are you offering?"

Jack smirked, but this time, there was nothing teasing about it. "A dangerous game."

And just like that, she knew she was already playing.

Chapter 2: The Edge of Temptation

"The only way to deal with this life meaningfully is to find one's passion, and follow it without hesitation." — Friedrich Nietzsche

The night after her encounter with Jack Kingston left Emma restless, her mind tangled in the electricity that had sparked between them. Sydney's skyline, bathed in moonlight, seemed to mirror the storm brewing inside her—a chaos of desire and hesitation, a craving for something she hadn't allowed herself to feel in far too long.

Emma had always been practical. Her life had been carefully curated—a well-ordered path of career, relationships, and stability. Until her marriage fell apart. Until everything she thought she knew about herself had crumbled, leaving her standing in a new world where the old rules no longer applied.

She should have stayed away from Jack Kingston. A man like him was trouble. He wasn't the type of man a woman like her could afford to get involved with—not after everything she had been through. But there was something in the way he had looked at her, something dark and irresistible that made it impossible to let go of the encounter.

By morning, Emma was still tangled in thoughts of him. She had a meeting with a potential client, a woman who owned a local fashion label, and the prospect of the deal was supposed to dominate her thoughts. But Jack kept slipping into her mind, uninvited and impossible to ignore. His smirk, the challenge in his eyes, the way he made her feel—alive, dangerous, seen in a way no one had ever seen her before.

As she sat in her office, sipping her coffee, Emma's phone buzzed. It was a message from an unknown number. She hesitated for a moment before opening it.

"We need to finish what we started. Meet me tonight."

The message was simple, but the implications were far from it.

Emma could feel her heart rate quicken. She stared at the screen, wondering if she was imagining the weight of it. Her fingers hovered over the keyboard, the impulse to reply burning in her veins.

It would be so easy to ignore him, to go about her day and pretend the night hadn't happened. But the part of her that had been starved for excitement, for something more than the mundane routine of her life, whispered louder than her rational mind. She had come to Sydney to rediscover herself, to find something beyond the predictable. Could she really let this opportunity slip away?

With a slow breath, she typed a response. *"What if I don't want to?"*

Almost instantly, a reply appeared on her screen.

"Then you're playing a dangerous game, Emma."

A smile curled at the corners of her lips. She had spent too many years in a controlled, orderly world. Jack Kingston was unpredictable, exhilarating—dangerous, yes, but in the most thrilling way. The kind of danger she'd longed for, without even knowing it.

Before she could change her mind, Emma set her phone down and began gathering her things for the meeting. It was time to act. She didn't know where this was leading, but for the first time in a long time, she didn't care.

Later that evening, Emma found herself at a chic rooftop bar overlooking the Sydney Harbour. The lights from the Opera House and Harbour Bridge shimmered like jewels in the night, a stunning backdrop for the tension that pulsed in her veins.

She arrived early, giving her a few moments to adjust, to breathe in the cool evening air, but her mind kept drifting back to Jack.

She glanced at her watch. She was about to make a decision that could change everything, but for once, she wasn't scared. No, she was alive with anticipation, filled with a raw hunger for something she couldn't yet name.

And then, there he was.

Jack Kingston, like a vision out of a dream. Tall, dark, and effortlessly powerful, he walked toward her, his presence filling the space around them. His shirt clung to his broad shoulders, his jeans moulding to his long legs in a way that made her breath catch. He looked like a man who had seen everything, a man who had lived—and enjoyed—every second of his life.

He stopped just in front of her, the slight tilt of his lips making her heart race. "I was starting to think you'd stand me up," he said, his voice low, like a promise waiting to be fulfilled.

Emma stood and met his gaze, her pulse quickening. "Would you have been disappointed?"

Jack's eyes sparkled with amusement. "Maybe. But that would've been a shame, wouldn't it?"

They shared a long look, a silent agreement passing between them. There was no need for words; they both knew what was at stake.

Emma was here now, and whatever came next would be a choice she made, one she couldn't take back.

Jack motioned for her to follow him, leading her to a quiet corner of the bar, away from prying eyes. The city hummed beneath them, a distant lullaby of cars and people, but here, it was just the two of them.

"I'm not the type of man who waits for permission," Jack said suddenly, his voice like velvet, dark and smooth.

"I never asked you to," Emma replied, her heart pounding in her chest.

His gaze softened for a moment, as though considering her words. Then, without another word, Jack leaned in close. His breath was warm against her skin, the scent of whiskey and something deeper, more intoxicating, filling her senses.

Emma's heart raced, her entire body reacting to his proximity. She didn't know what had come over her, but she couldn't pull away.

"Are you ready for the next step?" Jack asked, his lips brushing against her ear, sending a shiver down her spine.

Emma closed her eyes, her body humming with anticipation. "I think I am," she whispered, her voice barely audible, filled with a vulnerability she hadn't allowed herself to show in years.

Jack took her hand, his fingers tracing her palm with a knowing touch. "Good. Then let's begin."

Chapter 3: The Price of Desire

"*In the end, we will remember not the words of our enemies, but the silence of our friends.*" — Martin Luther King Jr.

The next few days after that night were a blur. Emma had returned to her normal routine, trying to focus on work, trying to forget the pull of Jack Kingston. But it was impossible. Every time she closed her eyes, she saw his dark gaze, the way he had leaned in close, his breath warm against her skin.

She hadn't expected this. Hadn't expected to crave him so deeply, so completely. The desire was unlike anything she had ever felt before—untamed, urgent, raw. She had always thought of herself as a woman who kept her emotions in check, who was above such base instincts. But Jack had unlocked something inside her, something wild that she wasn't sure how to control.

It was on the third day after their encounter when Emma received the message. Simple. Direct. Just as he always was.

"I'm not the type to chase. But I'm giving you the chance. I'll be at the same place tomorrow night. I expect you to be there."

Emma stared at the screen, her pulse quickening. She had thought about it, over and over, each time convincing herself she should walk away. He was dangerous. A man like him wasn't someone you got involved with. But the thought of not seeing him again, not knowing where this could lead, gnawed at her.

With a breath, she typed her reply.

"I'll be there."

Her fingers trembled as she sent the message, and she immediately regretted it. She could feel the weight of the decision sinking in. It was one thing to let herself be caught up in the moment, to let the thrill of the chase consume her for a night, but this felt different. This felt like something deeper, something that could change everything.

The following evening, the city felt different to Emma. The air seemed thicker, more charged, as if the universe itself was holding its breath in anticipation. She stood in front of her wardrobe, the delicate fabric of her dress catching the dim light in her bedroom. It was a piece she had worn for special occasions—sexy but refined, with a hint of something dangerous. It was the perfect choice for tonight.

She took her time getting ready, her hands moving with precision as she applied makeup, letting herself feel the weight of the moment. The choice she had made wasn't just about Jack. It was about her. About taking back control, about allowing herself to step into a world she had once feared. A world of passion. A world of risk.

When she finally arrived at the bar, the familiar skyline of Sydney twinkling in the distance, her heart was already racing. Jack was there, just as he had said he would be. He was sitting at the same spot as before, his posture relaxed but his eyes scanning the room, waiting.

He looked even more striking tonight, dressed in a tailored black suit that accentuated the raw masculinity in his frame. He wasn't just a man; he was an enigma, a puzzle she wasn't sure she was ready to solve.

As she approached, Jack's gaze flicked to her, and for a brief moment, the world seemed to fade away. There was no one else in the room. No distractions. Just the intensity between them.

"Emma," Jack greeted her, his voice a deep, seductive drawl. "I was beginning to think you'd change your mind."

"I thought about it," she replied, her voice steady despite the racing of her pulse. "But I didn't."

Jack's lips curled into a small smile, a glint of approval in his eyes. "Good."

He stood and gestured to the seat across from him. As she sat down, Jack's gaze didn't leave her, his intensity never wavering. The air between them was thick with unspoken words, with promises that neither had yet to voice.

"Why did you come?" Jack's question was simple, but there was a weight to it, an expectation that she answer honestly.

Emma swallowed, her mind spinning with the truth. She could tell him she was curious, that she wanted to see where this would go. But the real reason, the one that scared her most, was something she wasn't ready to admit—not even to herself.

"Because I'm tired of playing it safe," she said, her voice low, barely above a whisper. "And I think you're the kind of man who will push me past the things I've been holding onto."

A flicker of something darker passed through Jack's eyes, but it was gone almost as quickly as it appeared. He leaned back in his chair, the slight shift in his posture both casual and commanding. "I'm not a man who's afraid of pushing boundaries. But I won't do it unless you're ready. Completely ready."

Emma felt a rush of heat flood her chest. "I'm ready."

The words were out before she could stop them, but she knew they were the truth. Whatever was happening between them, whatever this was, she couldn't walk away from it. Not now.

Jack regarded her for a long moment, the silence stretching between them like a taut wire. Finally, he leaned in, his voice lowering to a whisper that only she could hear.

"Then let's see if you can keep up."

As the night wore on, Emma found herself drawn deeper into Jack's world. Every glance, every word between them felt like a test, a subtle challenge she was eager to accept. He was relentless, pushing her to confront the parts of herself she had kept buried for so long. She had come here looking for excitement, but what she found was something more dangerous, something she wasn't sure she was ready to face.

But there was no going back now. She was already in the game, and Jack Kingston had made it clear that once you entered, there was no easy way out.

Chapter 4: The Fire Beneath the Surface

"*Desire is a powerful thing. It can consume you whole, if you let it.*" — Unknown

The days that followed were a blur of anticipation, every moment building toward something Emma wasn't sure she was ready to face. Her thoughts kept drifting back to Jack—his eyes, the heat of his touch, the promise of what was to come. She had told herself she wouldn't be one of those women who fell into a whirlwind romance. But Jack wasn't just any man. He was a force, a presence that had woven itself into her every waking moment.

It was another Thursday evening when Jack's message arrived. Simple. To the point. As always.

"*Tonight. I'll be waiting.*"

She didn't hesitate. The decision had already been made. She couldn't stop herself. She found herself in front of her mirror again, the same tension thrumming in her veins as she chose the dress—a soft, silk number that clung to her curves in all the right ways. The deep red colour made her feel dangerous, like something that was meant to be touched, to be devoured.

When she arrived, Jack was already there, waiting for her at a quiet, dimly lit table at the back of the lounge. The air was thick with the scent of expensive cologne and the promise of something wild. He looked up as she entered, and the moment their eyes locked, the world shifted. His gaze was intense, like a predator on the hunt, but there was something more. Something almost possessive.

He stood, his tall frame towering over her, and before she could speak, he pulled her in, his lips capturing hers in a kiss that was soft at first, tentative, but quickly deepening into something far more urgent. His hands slid to her back, pulling her against him as if he couldn't get close enough.

The kiss was everything—everything she had been craving, everything she hadn't known she wanted. His lips were firm, demanding, but there was tenderness in his touch. He was exploring her, claiming her, and every nerve in her body seemed to come alive in response.

When they broke apart, Emma was breathless, her pulse racing. She didn't have to say a word. Jack's gaze told her everything she needed to know. The night was just beginning, and there was no turning back now.

He led her to the elevator, his hand low on her back, guiding her with a sense of purpose. The building was luxurious, everything about it screaming wealth and sophistication. But in that moment, all Emma could focus on was the heat between them, the electricity that sparked whenever their skin brushed together.

They didn't speak as they entered the penthouse. The door clicked shut behind them, and Jack's lips were on hers again, this time more insistent, more demanding. His hands roamed over her body, touching, caressing, as though he was discovering every inch of her for the first time.

Emma let herself be consumed by it. She had never allowed herself to be so vulnerable, to be so completely lost in someone else. But with Jack, it felt natural. It felt right.

He pulled back slightly, his hands moving to the straps of her dress. "You're beautiful," he murmured, his voice low and thick with desire. The words sent a shiver down her spine, and she let him slide the silk off her body, her skin tingling as it came into contact with the cool air.

Jack's eyes darkened as he looked at her, the intensity of his gaze making her stomach tighten with anticipation. "You have no idea how badly I want you," he whispered, his voice gravelly with desire.

Before she could reply, his hands were on her again, this time roaming lower, brushing over the delicate curve of her hips before sliding up to cup her breasts. She gasped as his fingers brushed over her sensitive skin, a tingling heat spreading through her body.

Emma's hands slid to his chest, feeling the solid strength beneath his shirt. Her fingers fumbled with the buttons, eager to get closer, to feel him against her skin. But Jack stopped her, his hands wrapping around her wrists and pulling them above her head, holding her there as he leaned in to kiss her again, his tongue slipping into her mouth with a slow, deliberate exploration.

The kiss deepened, and Emma felt herself becoming lost in him, in the heat of his body against hers, in the overwhelming sensation of being wanted. His hands moved to her thighs, lifting her up effortlessly, as if she weighed nothing at all. He carried her to the bedroom, their lips never parting, his hands continuing their slow journey over her body.

When they reached the bed, he laid her down gently, his body hovering above hers. Jack's eyes were on hers, and for a brief moment,

Emma saw something vulnerable in his gaze—something she hadn't expected from a man like him. It was quickly masked by the heat of his desire, but she knew, deep down, that he was just as consumed by this as she was.

"Are you sure?" he asked, his voice hoarse with need.

Emma nodded, her breath coming in shallow bursts. "Yes," she whispered, her hands reaching up to pull him closer. "I want this. I want you."

Jack's lips returned to hers, his hands exploring her body with a renewed urgency. As he kissed her, his fingers slipped beneath the waistband of her panties, teasing her with a slow, deliberate touch that made her gasp in pleasure.

Every inch of her seemed to ache for him, the anticipation building with each brush of his skin. She wasn't sure how long they had been kissing, how long they had been touching, but time seemed to have lost all meaning. All that mattered was the heat between them, the hunger that burned in both their bodies.

Jack's fingers finally slid inside her, and Emma moaned softly, her back arching off the bed as she felt him stretch her. His touch was skillful, precise, and Emma couldn't hold back the soft cries that escaped her lips as he moved inside her. Each stroke sent waves of pleasure through her, and she could feel herself unraveling with every touch.

She wanted more. Needed more.

Chapter 5: Surrendering to the Darkness

"*The only way to deal with this life meaningfully is to find one's passion, and follow it without hesitation.*" — Friedrich Nietzsche

The sunlight filtering through the curtains was the first thing Emma became aware of when she woke. The soft, golden glow of morning bathed the room in a serene light, but her mind was anything but calm. Her body hummed with the aftershocks of the night—of Jack's touch, his kiss, the sweet violence of their passion that had left her trembling and breathless. But as much as she wanted to surrender to the blissful memories, her thoughts were already tugging at her, pulling her deeper into a place she wasn't sure she was ready to go.

She sat up slowly, her legs tangled in the sheets. Her skin still carried the warmth of his touch, the subtle ache that reminded her of just how much he had consumed her. Her heart beat rapidly, almost erratically, as she replayed every moment from the night before. The fire in Jack's eyes, the quiet but intense way he had touched her, the way he had driven her to places she never thought she would go. Emma had always prided herself on being in control—on not letting anyone overpower her. But Jack was different. He wasn't just a man. He was a force, an irresistible pull that had lured her in, leaving her with no option but to follow.

The bed beside her was empty, and for a fleeting moment, she felt an unexpected pang of emptiness. She pushed the feeling aside, forcing herself to sit up fully, the crisp white sheets slipping from her bare body as she stretched. She wasn't sure what she had expected from Jack—whether it would be a fleeting encounter or something more—but she had never anticipated it to feel like this. He had awakened something in her, something she hadn't even known existed. Something darker. Something thrilling.

Her phone buzzed on the bedside table, breaking her out of her thoughts. She reached for it, her fingers still tingling from the night's touch. Jack's message was short, but the words hit her like a splash of cold water.

"You've never felt anything like this before, have you?"

She stared at the words for a long moment, her heart racing again. How could he know? How could he possibly understand what she was feeling? Her fingers hovered over the screen, and without thinking, she typed her reply.

"No. I haven't."

The reply came almost immediately.

"I told you I'd push you. I meant it."

Emma's chest tightened at the words. She had known Jack was dangerous in the best way, but this—this was different. She had spent so many years burying her desires, pretending that she could live without passion, without risk. But now, everything had changed. She couldn't deny it. Jack had shown her a world where limits didn't exist, where every feeling, every touch, was an invitation to something more.

Her heart thundered in her chest as she typed again.

"I want more."

She sent it before she could stop herself, her fingers trembling slightly as the words left her fingertips. She couldn't take them back now. She didn't want to.

A moment passed before Jack's response appeared.

"I'll see you tonight. Don't be late."

The words were clear. Simple. Commanding. And as Emma read them, something inside her shifted again. She had never been the kind of woman who followed orders. She had always been independent, always in control. But with Jack, that control was slipping through her fingers, one moment at a time. And somehow, she didn't mind.

The day stretched out before her, and yet it passed in a blur. Every minute seemed to drag on, every second filled with a gnawing anticipation that she couldn't shake. It was as though the entire world had shifted beneath her feet, and she was now standing on the edge of something thrilling, something dangerous. She tried to keep herself occupied, tried to focus on work and the mundane tasks that usually filled her day, but her mind kept drifting back to Jack. To the memory of his touch, of his eyes dark with desire. The pull of him was irresistible.

When the evening finally arrived, Emma felt the familiar tension build in her body. She stood in front of her mirror again, the same one she had stared into just days before, but this time, she was different. She was no longer the woman who had walked into Jack's world unsure of what she wanted. Now, she was a woman who was willing to explore it, to surrender to the unknown and let him take her places she had never dreamed of.

Her fingers brushed the fabric of the dress she had chosen. It was black this time, sleek and elegant, hugging her curves in a way that made her feel both powerful and vulnerable. The low-cut neckline revealed just enough, while the tightness of the fabric clung to her body like a second skin. She felt seductive in it—dangerous in a way that was completely new to her.

When she arrived at the same upscale lounge, the one she had been to the night before, the atmosphere felt different this time. There was a palpable energy in the air, a sense of expectation that made her pulse quicken. She was here for Jack, and she knew he would be watching for her. The moment she entered, his gaze locked onto hers across the room, and it was as if the entire world disappeared. The noise, the people, the chaos—everything faded until all she could see was him.

He stood as she approached, his expression unreadable, his body language commanding. There was no trace of the man who had kissed her passionately just days before. This time, he was in control. She could feel it in every muscle in her body, in the way his eyes never left hers as she moved closer.

"You're late," Jack said, his voice low and smooth, but there was an edge to it. A hint of something dark.

Emma's heart skipped a beat. She wasn't late. She had arrived exactly on time. But she didn't correct him. She simply smiled, her lips curling into something that was both playful and seductive. "Am I?"

Jack's lips curled into a smirk, and he stepped closer, his breath warm against her cheek. "You've been keeping me waiting," he murmured, his voice husky with desire. "And now, I'm going to make you regret it."

Without another word, he took her hand and led her toward the elevator, his grip firm and unyielding. The tension between them was palpable, the air thick with anticipation. Emma's mind raced, her pulse hammering in her throat. She had no idea what to expect from him tonight, but she knew one thing for certain—she was going to get lost in this, in him.

As they reached the penthouse, Jack's lips found hers again, fierce and demanding, as though he couldn't get enough. He pushed her against the wall, his hands roaming over her body with a sense of urgency, as if time was running out. She felt her body respond immediately, her own hands sliding up to pull at his shirt, desperate to feel the heat of his skin beneath her fingertips.

"Take it off," she whispered, her voice breathless.

Jack didn't need to be told twice. He was already pulling his shirt over his head, his eyes never leaving hers. Emma's hands found their way to his chest, her fingers tracing the solid muscle, the heat of him intoxicating. His body was everything she had imagined—strong, sculpted, perfect in every way. She wanted to run her hands over every inch of him, to explore him the way he had explored her the night before.

He pushed her back toward the bed, and this time, Emma let herself fall into the surrender, into the rawness of the moment. Her body was on fire with anticipation, every nerve ending alive with need. Jack's lips traveled down her neck, his hands tracing the outline of her body, slipping beneath the fabric of her dress. She gasped as his fingers brushed against her skin, sending a jolt of pleasure through her.

"Tell me what you want," he whispered, his breath warm against her ear.

Emma closed her eyes, her body trembling with desire. "I want you," she whispered, her voice thick with longing. "All of you."

The words were barely out of her mouth before Jack's hands moved to remove the rest of her clothing, his touch both gentle and possessive. Every moment was charged with an intensity that left Emma breathless, her body burning for more. She didn't know how much longer she could hold on. The world outside no longer mattered. All that existed in that moment was Jack, and the wild, uncontrollable fire between them.

Chapter 6: The Game We Play

"The only way to get what you want in life is to first understand what you're willing to lose." — Unknown

The days following the night at Jack's penthouse were a blur of restless anticipation. Emma found herself in a state of perpetual tension, a restless energy coursing through her that she couldn't shake. She was no longer the woman she had been before. Jack had changed something in her, something deep and primal, and now there was no going back.

Her thoughts kept returning to him—his touch, his gaze, the intensity that had marked every moment they shared. Every time her phone buzzed, her heart raced with the possibility that it was him. She was drawn to him in ways she hadn't thought possible. The fear that had once held her back from exploring her desires had dissolved in the heat of his presence. He had unlocked something in her that couldn't be ignored.

It was a Wednesday afternoon when she received his message. It was brief, like all of his messages were, but it made her blood run hot.

"Tonight. 7pm. Don't be late."

There was no ambiguity in his words, no room for hesitation. Emma knew exactly what he wanted. The same thing he always wanted: control, power, and surrender. And as much as she tried to convince herself she wasn't ready, she knew deep down that she was. She was already addicted to the pull of him.

The time between receiving the message and arriving at Jack's was agonizing. The hours seemed to drag on, each one filled with anticipation and uncertainty. Emma spent the time preparing herself, both physically and mentally. She chose her clothes carefully, selecting a soft, deep blue dress that clung to her curves in a way that made her feel both confident and vulnerable. The colour of the dress reminded her of the ocean—deep, mysterious, and endless.

When she arrived at his building, the same rush of excitement flooded her system. This time, however, it was mixed with something else—something darker. There was a part of her that feared the power Jack had over her. But there was another part, a part that was far more dominant, that reveled in it. The thought of surrendering to him, of losing herself completely, was a tantalizing thrill.

Jack was waiting for her in the same private lounge, though this time he was alone, sitting in one of the plush chairs by the window, a glass of whiskey in his hand. He looked up as she entered, his eyes locking onto hers with a predatory intensity that made her heart race. There was something in his gaze that sent a shiver down her spine, a silent promise of what was to come.

"You're late," he said, his voice low and filled with purpose.

Emma's pulse quickened. "I'm not late. I'm right on time," she replied, her tone confident, though she could feel the underlying tension building between them.

Jack raised an eyebrow, a small smirk curling at the corners of his lips. He stood and crossed the room toward her with that same fluid grace, as if he were moving through the air. "No," he said, his voice soft but commanding, "you're late. And that means you'll pay for it."

Before she could react, he stepped closer, his hand sliding around her waist and pulling her to him with surprising force. Emma gasped, her body reacting to his touch before her mind could catch up. His lips found hers with a hunger that was almost frightening, as though he couldn't wait another second. His kiss was demanding, almost bruising, but there was something intoxicating in it—a depth that went far beyond mere physical attraction. He wasn't just kissing her; he was claiming her.

When they broke apart, both of them gasping for breath, Jack's hands slid down her back, his fingers pressing into her skin as he tugged her even closer. His breath was hot against her ear as he whispered, "You have no idea what's about to happen, do you?"

Emma shivered, her body trembling with anticipation. She didn't respond, but she didn't need to. They both knew what was coming.

Jack led her toward the elevator, his grip never leaving her side. The silence between them was thick with tension, each step carrying them closer to something neither of them could resist. When they reached his penthouse, Jack wasted no time. He ushered her inside, his hand at her back, guiding her through the door and into the dimly lit space.

The air was charged, the weight of their shared desire thick in the atmosphere. Jack's eyes locked onto hers, and for a brief moment, Emma saw something in his gaze—a flicker of vulnerability, of raw need—that sent a shiver down her spine. But it was gone almost as quickly as it had appeared, replaced by that same dark intensity that had drawn her to him from the beginning.

"You've been running from this," he said, his voice quiet but filled with meaning. "But now, you don't have a choice."

Emma swallowed hard, her heart pounding in her chest. She wasn't running anymore. She had stopped running the moment she had given in to him, the moment she had allowed herself to be drawn into his orbit. And now, there was no turning back.

Jack moved toward her, his fingers brushing over the fabric of her dress, his touch light but electric. Every nerve in her body seemed to come alive with his touch, and she couldn't help the soft gasp that escaped her lips.

His lips hovered just above hers, his breath warm against her skin. "Are you ready?" he asked, his voice low and thick with desire.

Emma's pulse raced. She nodded, her body responding to the pull of him, to the promise of what was to come.

Jack's hands were on her instantly, his touch rougher now, as though he were losing control. He pulled the dress from her body with ease, revealing the smooth skin beneath. Emma gasped as his fingers skimmed over her curves, each touch sending a wave of heat through her. His eyes darkened as he took in the sight of her, his gaze possessive and filled with hunger.

"You're perfect," he murmured, his voice thick with desire.

Before she could respond, he kissed her again, this time with a fierceness that left her breathless. His hands roamed over her body, tracing every inch of her skin, his touch leaving a trail of fire in its wake. Emma's hands slid to his chest, desperate to feel the solid muscle beneath his shirt. She tugged at the fabric, eager to get closer, to feel him against her.

Jack responded immediately, his shirt discarded in an instant, his bare chest pressed against hers. The heat of his skin was intoxicating, and Emma couldn't help but melt into him, her body arching toward his as their lips collided once more.

His hands moved lower, sliding down her body to cup her hips, pulling her flush against him. Emma moaned softly, the sensation of his hardness against her soft skin sending a flood of warmth through her.

Jack pulled back slightly, his gaze intense as he looked into her eyes. "Tell me what you want," he said, his voice low and demanding.

Emma's breath hitched in her throat. She had never been one to ask for what she wanted, to expose herself so openly. But with Jack, it felt different. She felt exposed, but in a way that was freeing, like she could finally let go of all the walls she had built around herself.

"I want you," she whispered, her voice thick with longing. "I want you more than I've ever wanted anything."

Jack's lips curled into a satisfied smile. "Good," he said, his voice filled with approval. "Then you'll get exactly what you deserve."

Without another word, he lifted her effortlessly, carrying her to the bed, his lips never leaving hers. The moment she hit the mattress, he was on her again, his hands exploring her with a sense of urgency, as though he couldn't get enough.

Every inch of her body was on fire, every touch, every kiss, sending her into a spiral of need. Jack moved with an expertise that had Emma trembling with anticipation, his fingers brushing over her skin in a way that made her ache for more.

He was relentless, pulling her to the edge of something she had never allowed herself to feel—a loss of control, a surrender that was both terrifying and exhilarating.

And as he pushed her further into the abyss, Emma knew one thing for sure: she was completely, utterly, and irrevocably his.

Chapter 7: The Edge of Desire

"*We are what we choose to become.*" — Jean-Paul Sartre

The days after that night at Jack's penthouse were a blur of conflicting emotions for Emma. She couldn't deny the pull he had on her, the way his presence consumed her thoughts, twisting her in ways she never thought possible. The more time they spent together, the more she wanted him, but it was a dangerous game they were playing.

Each time he touched her, each time they shared another intimate moment, it felt as though they were stepping further into an unknown world—a world where nothing was certain except the overwhelming heat between them.

But Jack was a mystery, one she wasn't sure she was ready to solve. His control, his dominance, were like a drug. The way he made her feel—desirable, wanted, needed—was intoxicating, and it was becoming harder and harder to resist. Every touch from him, every kiss, left her with a hunger that only he could satisfy.

But there was something else too. A growing sense of unease that settled in her chest when she was alone. She couldn't help but wonder how much of herself she was losing in the process. She had come into this expecting passion, adventure, but now, there were moments where she questioned whether she was surrendering too much.

It was an internal battle she kept to herself. She couldn't afford to show weakness in front of him, not when he held the reins so firmly. He was the one in control, and she had come to accept that. But that didn't mean it didn't stir something deep inside her, a feeling she hadn't quite figured out yet.

The phone buzzed on her desk at work, pulling her from her thoughts. She glanced down to see a text from Jack.

"Meet me at 8. You'll be mine tonight."

Her stomach fluttered. Even just reading those words made her pulse race, her body responding without hesitation. She had no idea what he had planned, but she knew one thing: he would push her boundaries. And she would let him.

It was a Friday evening when Emma arrived at Jack's penthouse once more. She had dressed carefully, choosing a black satin dress that hugged her figure just right, the soft fabric slipping like water over her curves. Her hair was loosely tied back, a few strands falling to frame her face in soft waves. She felt confident, but beneath that confidence was a simmering excitement, the anticipation of what was to come.

Jack was waiting for her when she arrived, standing in front of the large windows overlooking the city. The lights of Sydney sparkled below, a distant reminder of the world beyond this private bubble they inhabited. His eyes met hers, dark and intense, and for a moment, the air between them was thick with unspoken promises.

"You're late," he said, his voice as commanding as ever, though there was a glint of something softer in his eyes.

Emma tilted her chin up, refusing to let him see how the words affected her. "I'm exactly on time," she replied, her tone confident.

Jack's lips curved into a smile. He took a step forward, closing the distance between them with his usual grace, his presence overwhelming.

"You're always right on time, Emma," he murmured, his breath warm against her ear. His lips brushed her neck, sending a wave of heat through her body. "But tonight, we play a different game."

Emma's pulse quickened. "What kind of game?" she asked, her voice barely above a whisper.

Jack didn't answer immediately. Instead, he placed his hand on her waist, guiding her to the centre of the room. She could feel his touch all the way through to her bones, a steady reminder of his power over her.

"This is a game of trust," Jack said, his voice low and steady. "You trust me, don't you?"

She swallowed, her throat dry. She wanted to say yes, but there was a part of her that hesitated. Did she truly trust him? She wanted to, more than anything. But there was always that nagging feeling at the back of her mind that she was giving up too much, too soon.

"Of course," she said, her voice barely more than a breath.

He smiled again, but this time it was different—more predatory. "Good," he replied, stepping back. "Because tonight, you'll be blind-folded."

Emma's heart skipped a beat. The idea of being so vulnerable, of giving him complete control over her senses, stirred a mixture of excitement and anxiety within her. But she didn't hesitate. She knew that once she agreed to something, she couldn't take it back.

Before she could protest, Jack had already moved behind her, and she felt the cool fabric of the blindfold against her eyes. The world around her went dark.

"Relax," Jack's voice came from directly in front of her, grounding her in the absence of sight. "Trust me."

She inhaled deeply, feeling the steady rhythm of her breath. Her body had already started to respond to him, her heart racing, her skin tingling with anticipation. Without sight, every other sense became heightened—every sound, every touch, every movement.

Jack's hands were on her immediately, guiding her to the soft velvet chaise lounge. He kissed her neck softly, his lips a whisper against her skin, and she shivered in response.

"You're going to experience everything tonight, Emma," he murmured. "Every sensation, every touch, every moment. You'll feel it all."

Emma could only nod, her mouth too dry to speak.

His hands moved lower, slipping beneath the straps of her dress, and she gasped as the fabric slid from her body, leaving her exposed. The cool air against her skin only heightened her sensitivity, and she felt every nerve alive with anticipation.

Jack's fingers traced her collarbone, down the curve of her breast, and lower still. Each touch was measured, deliberate, and full of promise. He took his time, exploring her as though he were learning her all over again, and Emma's breath hitched with every pass of his fingers.

"I want you to remember something, Emma," Jack's voice came again, soft but commanding. "You don't need to speak tonight. All I need from you is to feel."

And feel she did. Every brush of his hands, every kiss, every movement sent waves of heat rushing through her body. Jack had a way of drawing her in, of making her forget everything but him, until there was nothing left but the pure, primal connection between them.

Chapter 8: The Power of Surrender

"*In surrender, there is strength.*" — Unknown

The first rays of morning light crept through the large windows, casting soft golden hues across the room. Emma's eyes fluttered open slowly, her body heavy with the lingering sensations of the night before. The sheets tangled around her were warm and soft, but nothing compared to the warmth she felt in the core of her being, a heat that had burned brightly through the hours they spent together.

She could hear Jack's steady breathing beside her, his chest rising and falling in the quiet rhythm of deep sleep. The silence in the room was a stark contrast to the passion and intensity of the night, but Emma found solace in it. She allowed herself a moment to simply observe him—his features softened in sleep, the dark stubble on his jaw, the chiseled perfection of his body that had left her breathless more times than she could count.

But there was more to him than just the physical. In the moments when they were together, she saw the traces of vulnerability behind his eyes, the flashes of tenderness that surfaced beneath the dominant exterior he wore like a shield. It was these moments that kept her coming back, moments where the power balance shifted just enough for her to see a side of him that not many did.

Her body ached, but it wasn't pain—no, it was a satisfying soreness, a reminder of every touch, every kiss, every moment where Jack had pushed her limits. She smiled softly to herself, the warmth of the memory spreading through her. It wasn't just the physicality of their encounters that left her feeling this way—it was the trust they had built, the intimacy that went beyond the skin.

Turning her head, she found Jack still asleep, his features relaxed, completely at ease for the first time since they had met. There was something beautiful in that peace, and it made Emma's heart flutter unexpectedly. She had never imagined someone like Jack would be capable of such softness, but she was beginning to see how multi-dimensional he truly was.

The soft warmth of the sunlight on her skin made her drowsy, and for a moment, she was content to stay there, nestled in his bed, allowing the calm of the morning to envelope her. But Jack had other plans. He stirred beside her, shifting slightly in the bed, his eyes slowly opening to meet hers.

There was no shock, no hesitation in his gaze—just that steady, calculating look that always made her heart race. It was as though he knew she was awake, knew she was studying him, and yet he wasn't bothered by it. He simply gazed at her with that knowing intensity that had become so familiar.

"Good morning," his voice was husky from sleep, but still, there was an undeniable power in the way he spoke. His words made her pulse race, her body instinctively reacting to the sound of his voice.

"Good morning," she replied, her voice thick with the remnants of sleep and the echoes of the night. She felt something stir deep within her, an urge to reach out to him, to feel him close once more.

Jack's eyes darkened slightly as he studied her, a smirk tugging at the corners of his lips. Without a word, he moved closer, shifting the sheets between them, and placed his hand lightly on her shoulder, his touch sending a jolt of warmth through her body.

"You were amazing last night," he murmured, his lips just inches from her ear. "The way you surrendered to me, the way you trusted me... It was beautiful, Emma."

Her breath hitched at the intensity of his words. He didn't just speak them—he made her feel them. The way he said "surrendered" sent a shiver down her spine, and though she wasn't sure why, it stirred something inside her—a dangerous, thrilling hunger.

"I wanted to," she whispered back, her voice barely audible, though her heart pounded in her chest. "I wanted to be with you, to let go."

Jack's gaze never left hers, his fingers tracing the curve of her neck, down to her collarbone, before gently brushing over the sensitive skin of her breast. He moved with such precision, such intent, as though every touch was planned, every caress meant to unravel her further.

"You're learning, Emma," he said softly, his thumb brushing over her nipple, causing her to gasp softly. "But this is just the beginning. There's so much more to explore, more to discover. With every moment, I'll take you deeper into the things you didn't even know you craved."

She closed her eyes, the sensation of his touch so much more intense with every passing second. Her body responded to him instinctively, the way it always did—her pulse quickened, her breath shallow and uneven. But there was something different today. A shift, perhaps, or maybe it was just the culmination of all the moments they had shared so far, but Emma found herself craving something more—something beyond the physicality, beyond the pleasure that Jack had been so skilled at giving her.

She wanted to let go even more, wanted to lose herself in the moment, to surrender completely and without reservation. But as much as she wanted that, there was a part of her that held back, a quiet, nagging voice that reminded her how much of herself she had already given. Was it too much? Was she losing herself in this intense connection?

Before she could over-think it, Jack's lips were on hers, pulling her back into the moment. His kiss was firm, demanding, but there was a tenderness in it too. A tenderness that she knew was reserved just for her. His hands slid down her body, pushing the sheets aside, exposing her once more to his hungry gaze.

The heat between them ignited instantly. There was no time to second-guess anything. Jack was already moving, pulling her on top of him, guiding her with gentle force, his hands never leaving her body. She followed his lead, her hips grinding slowly against him, teasing them both with the friction that she knew would drive them both mad.

Emma moaned softly as Jack's hands roamed over her body, exploring every inch of her with the familiar possessiveness she had come to crave. She could feel the raw, animalistic desire between them, but there was something else too—a deeper connection that neither of them had yet fully acknowledged.

Jack's lips trailed down her neck, his teeth grazing her sensitive skin, sending a wave of heat surging through her. His hands gripped her hips, urging her to move faster, harder, as he pressed her closer, as though he needed to feel every part of her.

It wasn't just the pleasure, Emma realised. It was the surrender. The way Jack made her feel completely and utterly in his power, but also free. Free to experience every inch of herself, to explore the depths of desire and intimacy she had never known before. With him, she could let go of all the walls she had built around her heart.

His voice broke through her thoughts, low and commanding. "I want you to let go, Emma. Completely. Give yourself to me. All of you."

Her heart raced, and she responded to him without hesitation, moving with him, pushing herself to the edge of everything she had known, allowing herself to fall into the sensation, the pleasure, the power of complete surrender.

And for the first time in her life, Emma felt truly free.

Chapter 9: Unraveling the Layers

"*To know yourself is the beginning of all wisdom.*" — Aristotle

The days that followed were an intoxicating blur of passion, excitement, and quiet moments of reflection. Emma was caught in a whirlwind, unable to distinguish where the thrill of desire ended and where the depth of connection began. She had entered this arrangement expecting adventure and passion, but what she had found was something far more complex—something that challenged every notion she'd ever held about herself, about love, about vulnerability.

Jack was always a mystery, an enigma she couldn't quite decode. In the bedroom, he was a master of control, always knowing just what to say, just where to touch, how to make her feel like she was the only woman in the world. But outside of those walls, he was a different person—cool, calculating, his emotions guarded, hidden behind a carefully constructed mask.

Emma wasn't sure which version of him she craved more—the man who took control in the bedroom or the man who kept himself at arm's length in the light of day. The contrast was confusing, pulling her in two different directions. But she had learned quickly that in Jack's world, things were rarely as they seemed.

It was a Friday evening when Jack invited her to dinner. The invitation had come with a sense of urgency, a whisper of something more than the usual casual affair. There was an air of mystery about the way he had worded it, a promise of something beyond just food and conversation.

Emma dressed carefully for the occasion, choosing a deep red silk dress that clung to her body in all the right ways. Her hair was styled in soft waves, and her makeup was subtle yet alluring, just enough to enhance her features without drawing too much attention. As she applied the final touches to her look, she couldn't help but feel a sense of anticipation bubbling within her.

Tonight felt different. The way Jack had asked her to meet him—there was an edge to it, a tension that hinted at something more. She could almost feel the weight of it, as if they were on the verge of crossing a new threshold in their relationship.

When Emma arrived at Jack's penthouse, the atmosphere was noticeably different. The usual dim lighting and minimalist décor were still there, but there was a sense of intimacy, of careful preparation. The soft glow of candles lit the room, their flickering flames casting shadows against the walls, creating an almost seductive ambiance.

Jack was standing near the window when she entered, his back to her as he gazed out at the city below. He looked every bit the powerful businessman he was, his suit impeccable, his posture regal. But there was something else too, something she couldn't quite put her finger on—something raw in the way he held himself.

"Emma," he said softly, turning to face her as she stepped inside. His eyes locked onto hers, dark and intense, as though he could see straight through her.

"Jack," she replied, her voice steady, though her heart was racing. She could feel the pull between them, the undeniable magnetic force that had only grown stronger with each passing day.

"You look... stunning," he said, his gaze sweeping over her. The compliment was genuine, but it came with a hint of something else, something possessive. It made her stomach flutter in the most dangerous way.

"Thank you," she replied, her lips curling into a soft smile. "You look good yourself."

Jack didn't smile in return, but his eyes gleamed with something more—a silent promise of what was to come. He stepped closer, closing the distance between them, and reached out to touch her cheek. His fingers brushed over her skin with the slightest pressure, a gesture that sent a wave of heat through her body.

"I'm glad you're here," he murmured, his voice low and controlled. "I have something I want to show you tonight. Something important."

Emma's pulse quickened. She didn't know what he had planned, but she knew it would be something that pushed her boundaries further. Jack had a way of unraveling her, of getting under her skin and making her crave things she never thought possible.

"Lead the way," she said, her voice steady despite the wild beating of her heart.

Jack's lips curved into a slight, knowing smile, and he turned to gesture toward the dining table. It was set for two, but there was something different about the meal this time. The atmosphere was intimate, but it was the kind of intimacy that was deliberate, charged with anticipation.

"I've prepared something special for us tonight," he said, his eyes never leaving hers as he pulled out the chair for her. "I thought it was time we moved past the superficial and explored something deeper."

Emma's curiosity piqued, but she didn't ask questions. Instead, she sat, allowing Jack to serve them both. The meal was exquisite, a delicate fusion of flavors that complemented each other perfectly. They ate in relative silence, the occasional murmur of appreciation escaping their lips as they savored the food. But beneath that silence, there was an undercurrent of tension, a building intensity that neither of them acknowledged directly.

It was as if they were both aware that the night was leading to something more, something that would change everything between them.

When they finished eating, Jack stood and moved to the side table, pouring them both glasses of wine. He returned to her side, handing her the glass with a look that was both soft and demanding.

"To new beginnings," he said, his voice quiet but full of meaning.

Emma raised her glass, meeting his gaze, and took a sip. The wine was rich and velvety, a perfect complement to the evening's atmosphere. But as the glass touched her lips, she felt a sense of vulnerability creep in. There was something in the air tonight—something that felt like a turning point.

"Jack," she said, setting the glass down and meeting his eyes, "what are we really doing here?"

Jack paused, his expression unreadable for a moment, and then he placed his glass down as well. He moved closer to her again, his presence overwhelming as he loomed above her.

"What do you mean?" His voice was calm, but there was a hint of something darker behind it.

"I mean..." Emma trailed off, unsure of how to put her thoughts into words. "You and I, this... what we have. It's not just about the physical, is it? There's more to it than that. There's something deeper."

Jack's expression softened for a fraction of a second, and then his hands were on her, pulling her closer. He cupped her face gently, his thumb tracing her lips as he stared into her eyes with an intensity that sent shivers down her spine.

"You're right," he said quietly. "This isn't just about the physical. It never has been."

Emma felt a knot tighten in her chest. She had known there was more, but hearing him admit it out loud made her heart race with uncertainty. She wasn't sure where this would lead, but she couldn't turn back now. She had already crossed a line, let herself be pulled into Jack's world in a way she hadn't planned.

"I'm not sure I can do this," she whispered, the words leaving her lips before she could stop them. "I'm not sure I can keep up with... all of this."

Jack's eyes softened, and he gently pressed his forehead to hers. "You can," he murmured. "You can, because I'm here. And I'll guide you."

His words were both reassuring and terrifying. In that moment, Emma realised just how much power Jack had over her. But for some reason, she didn't mind. She trusted him—perhaps too much. And as much as she feared losing herself, there was a part of her that wanted to surrender completely.

Jack kissed her then, his lips warm and urgent against hers. She responded immediately, her hands threading through his hair as she pulled him closer. The kiss deepened, becoming more desperate, more consuming. The intensity of the moment swept them both up, and Emma's mind spun with desire and confusion.

Jack's hands moved down her back, gripping her firmly as he lifted her effortlessly, guiding her toward the bedroom. Emma's heart raced in her chest, her pulse a frantic rhythm as she felt herself being led into uncharted territory once more.

Chapter 10: Beyond Control

"In the absence of control, there is freedom." — Unknown

The days stretched into weeks, and the tension between Emma and Jack became an undeniable force, palpable in the way they moved around each other, in the silent communication that passed between them with every glance, every touch. There were moments when it felt like the entire world fell away, leaving only the two of them, tangled in a web of desire and connection. But just as often, Emma found herself questioning everything—their connection, her own desires, and the strange feeling that no matter how far she went, there was still a part of Jack that remained untouchable, beyond her reach.

It was a strange dance they had begun, one that had both exhilarated and frightened her in equal measure. Jack had shown her things—passions and pleasures—that had pushed her limits in ways she hadn't thought possible. He had unraveled her, piece by piece, revealing parts of herself she hadn't known existed. Yet despite every-thing they shared, there was still a sense of distance, a wall that Jack had erected between them, one that Emma wasn't sure she could break down.

She sat at the edge of the bed, staring out the large windows of Jack's penthouse. The view of Sydney's skyline stretched before her, but tonight, the city felt distant. Her mind wandered, caught in the whirlwind of emotions that seemed to pull her in all directions. She could still feel the phantom traces of Jack's touch on her skin, the heat of his kiss lingering on her lips. But there was a hollowness now, an ache deep in her chest that hadn't been there before.

The door to the bedroom creaked open, and Emma didn't need to look to know who it was. Jack's presence filled the room as soon as he entered, like an electric charge that set the air humming with tension. He was dressed in his usual tailored suit, looking every bit the part of the enigmatic businessman he was. Yet beneath that polished exterior, Emma could feel the underlying intensity, the force of his desire that was always just below the surface.

"You're deep in thought," Jack's voice was low, and when she finally turned to face him, his gaze was unwavering, searching, as though he were peeling back the layers of her soul.

Emma offered a soft smile, though it didn't quite reach her eyes. "Just thinking," she said quietly, her voice betraying a hint of uncer-tainty.

Jack stepped closer, his movements fluid, deliberate. He reached out, cupping her face with his hands, tilting her head slightly to meet his eyes. The touch was gentle, but there was an intensity in it that made her pulse quicken. It was as though he could see right through her, into the depths of her heart, and for a moment, she felt completely exposed.

"Don't think too much, Emma," he murmured, his thumb brushing over her cheekbone. "Let me take care of that."

Emma swallowed hard, the words stirring something inside her. She wanted to let go, wanted to surrender to him completely, but there was a voice in her head warning her, urging her to be cautious. She had already given so much of herself to Jack, and every time she did, it seemed to pull her deeper into his world, into a space where nothing was as simple as it seemed.

"I don't know if I can keep doing this, Jack," Emma confessed, the words slipping from her lips before she could stop them. "I'm starting to feel like I'm losing myself."

Jack's expression softened for just a moment, but the steely determination in his eyes remained. He gently brushed a strand of hair from her face, his touch tender yet possessive.

"You're not losing yourself," he said firmly. "You're finding parts of yourself you didn't even know existed. Don't be afraid of that. Don't be afraid of the power you have."

Emma's chest tightened, the weight of his words settling over her like a heavy blanket. It wasn't that she feared losing herself—at least, not entirely. It was that she feared how much of herself she was willing to give up in order to stay with him, in order to keep walking this path. She didn't know where it would lead, but every time she stepped closer to the edge, she found herself more and more willing to leap.

"Are you sure?" she asked, her voice barely above a whisper. "Are you sure you won't get bored of me? Of this?"

Jack's hands tightened ever so slightly, as if anchoring her to him. His gaze darkened, and he stepped even closer, his lips hovering just above hers. "I'll never get bored of you, Emma," he breathed. "What we have is something unique, something that can't be replicated. I don't want anything from you except your complete trust."

Complete trust. The words echoed in her mind, and Emma closed her eyes, letting the sound of his voice wash over her. She wanted to trust him. God, she wanted to believe him. But trust had always been something she'd kept in tight reserve. To give it fully, to lay herself bare in front of someone else—especially someone like Jack—felt like a risk she wasn't sure she was ready to take.

"Jack, I..." she started, but the words faltered before they could leave her lips. She didn't know how to explain what she was feeling, the turmoil churning in her chest. Every time she tried to talk to him, it felt like something got lost in translation.

"You don't have to say anything, Emma," he interrupted, his voice smooth and calming. "I know what you need."

Before she could protest, Jack closed the distance between them, his lips crashing against hers in a kiss that was both demanding and reassuring. It was the kiss of someone who knew exactly what they wanted, someone who understood how to make her feel alive, how to make her forget her doubts, her fears. His hands slid down her back, pulling her closer, urging her to respond, to lose herself in the moment.

Emma's body obeyed before her mind could catch up, her hands reaching for him, threading through his hair, pulling him closer. The heat between them intensified, igniting every nerve in her body. She felt the familiar pull, the magnetic force that had brought them together in the first place, and for a moment, she allowed herself to simply feel—feel his touch, feel his need, feel her own desire blooming with each second they were entwined.

Jack's hands slid beneath her shirt, his fingers brushing over her skin, sending a jolt of heat through her. She gasped into the kiss, her body arching into his, needing more, wanting more. He had a way of making her feel like she was the only woman in the world, a goddess, a queen—and she didn't want it to stop.

But just as quickly as it had begun, Jack pulled back, his hands resting on her waist as he looked down at her with a mix of desire and something deeper—something more serious. "I want you to trust me, Emma," he said softly, his breath warm against her lips. "Trust me to guide you, to show you the next step."

Emma's heart skipped a beat at the weight of his words. She felt herself teetering on the edge of something unknown, something that both thrilled and terrified her in equal measure. She wanted to trust him, wanted to dive deeper into this world they had created together, but the fear of losing herself was always there, lurking just beneath the surface.

But Jack's gaze held her, his intensity never wavering. He was giving her the choice—giving her the space to decide what came next. And for once, Emma didn't feel rushed. She didn't feel pressured. She felt something else—something warmer, more genuine.

Slowly, she nodded, her voice barely a whisper. "I'll trust you."

Jack's expression softened, and he pulled her back into his arms, his kiss gentle this time, as if he were savoring the moment. Emma melted into him, her body responding to the tenderness of the gesture, feeling as though she were finally, completely, surrendering to the connection they shared.

Chapter 11: The Art of Surrender

"*True love is not about perfection; it is hidden in vulnerability.*"
— Unknown

The following days passed in a haze of anticipation, each one a mix of longing and quiet contemplation. Emma had given Jack her trust, but it was a trust laced with uncertainty, a fragile thing that she feared could shatter at any moment. He had drawn her in, consumed her with his intensity, but now she was left to navigate the complexity of what had unfolded between them.

The vulnerability she felt after that night—the one where she had given herself to him completely—was both thrilling and terrifying. Jack had never once demanded that she open up, never once forced her to reveal more than she was ready to. But with each touch, each kiss, each whispered promise, he had peeled back her layers, and with every passing day, Emma felt herself becoming more entangled in the web they had woven together.

She stood in front of the mirror, adjusting the silk robe around her waist, the weight of her thoughts pressing down on her. Her reflection looked back at her with an intensity she hadn't seen before, as though the woman staring back was both her and someone else—a woman who had tasted the forbidden, who had surrendered parts of herself to a man she wasn't sure she could fully understand.

Emma reached up to adjust her hair, but her movements faltered when she heard a soft knock at the door.

Her heart skipped a beat. She knew who it was before the knock had even ended. Jack.

She didn't need to be told to open the door. Her body moved instinctively, as if drawn to him by an invisible thread. When she opened it, she was met with the familiar sight of Jack, standing tall and poised, a subtle smile tugging at his lips. But his eyes, dark and intense, told a different story—one of desire, of anticipation, and something deeper, more meaningful than she could put into words.

"Emma," he said, his voice smooth and low, a note of command buried beneath the surface. "I think it's time we take the next step."

She stood there, frozen for a moment, her pulse racing at his words. She had been expecting this, the next step, whatever it might be. Jack had always been one to push boundaries, to test the limits of their connection, and she knew that once again, she would be asked to surrender.

But this time, there was no hesitation. No fear. She had already trusted him once. This time, she would trust herself too.

She stepped aside to let him in, the air between them crackling with unspoken tension. Jack didn't waste time. He closed the door softly behind him, his eyes never leaving hers as he crossed the room. Without a word, he reached for her, his hands brushing gently against her skin as he pulled her toward him.

"You look beautiful," he murmured, his breath warm against her ear as his hands slid down her back, urging her closer. His touch was soft, yet demanding, a contradiction that made Emma's heart race even faster.

"Thank you," she whispered, her voice barely audible as she felt herself drawn into the magnetic pull of his presence.

Jack didn't waste time with words. His lips descended on hers in a kiss that was both gentle and urgent, the pressure building between them as their mouths fused together. His hands roamed over her body, his touch exploring, learning, reminding her of the power he held over her.

But this time, Emma didn't hold back. She responded, her hands sliding up his chest, fingers digging into his shirt as she pulled him closer, her body pressing into his, the heat between them almost unbearable. She wanted him. She needed him. And for the first time in a long while, she didn't question whether or not it was right. She simply let go.

Jack's lips trailed down her neck, and Emma gasped, her head falling back as he kissed the sensitive skin there, his teeth grazing lightly. His touch was both tender and possessive, as though he couldn't get enough of her, as though he were marking her in ways that couldn't be undone.

"Do you trust me?" Jack asked softly, his voice a low growl as he pulled back just enough to look her in the eyes. His hand slid down to her waist, his fingers grazing the fabric of her robe as he waited for her answer.

Emma's heart pounded in her chest, and for a moment, she felt exposed, vulnerable. She had trusted him once, but this—this was different. She had opened herself to him in ways she never had with anyone else, and she was afraid that with each new step, she was losing a part of herself she could never get back.

But then she looked into his eyes, saw the sincerity there, the raw intensity, and something inside her clicked. She had already given him a piece of her soul, and there was no going back. She wasn't afraid anymore.

"I trust you," she whispered, her voice steady, though her body betrayed her, trembling with desire and uncertainty.

Jack's lips curled into a slow smile, and without another word, he guided her toward the bed, his hands never leaving her body. He undid the robe slowly, the fabric slipping off her shoulders as he looked at her with a mix of admiration and hunger. Her skin was warm, her body trembling beneath his touch, and he drank it in as if it were the most precious thing he had ever seen.

"Emma," he breathed, his voice thick with desire. "You have no idea how badly I want you."

His words were a claim, a promise, and they sent a shiver of anticipation through her. She had heard him say similar things before, but tonight, the meaning behind them felt different, heavier, as if this was more than just physical pleasure. As if this was the moment they crossed into something deeper, something unspoken yet undeniable.

Jack's hands moved over her body with deliberate care, each touch sending waves of heat through her. He was patient, allowing her time to respond, to meet him in the moment, but Emma could feel the urgency beneath the surface—an urgency that matched her own.

His lips returned to hers, more fervent this time, as he pushed her gently back onto the bed. Emma's body melted beneath him, her mind overwhelmed by the sensations rushing through her. She let herself go, letting Jack take the lead, trusting him to guide her, to show her what came next.

There was a rawness in their movements, a desperate need to connect on a level that transcended the physical. Every kiss, every touch, every whispered word between them was laced with meaning, a promise of something that was building, deepening.

Jack's hands slid down her sides, his fingers tracing the curves of her body, and Emma's breath hitched as he found the sensitive spots he had learned to worship. His lips trailed over her skin, his tongue dipping to taste her, his hands caressing her as if he were memorizing every inch of her.

"Are you ready?" Jack's voice was barely a whisper, his breath hot against her ear as he positioned himself above her, his body radiating heat.

Emma's heart raced in her chest, her body aching for him, craving him. She could feel the tension building, could feel the edge of something—something wild and untamed—waiting just beyond the horizon.

"I'm ready," she whispered back, her voice shaky but certain.

And with that, everything else faded away. There was only the sensation of their bodies moving together, the rhythm of their breaths, the connection that seemed to transcend everything else. In that moment, Emma realized she wasn't just surrendering to Jack—she was surrendering to herself, to her desires, to the woman she had always been but had never fully embraced.

It was a release—a release from fear, from doubt, from the walls she had spent years building around herself. And as Jack's body pressed against hers, as their connection deepened, Emma felt herself unraveling in the most beautiful way.

Chapter 12: Unspoken Truths

"*The truth is not always what we expect it to be, but it is always what we need it to be.*" — Unknown

The air in the penthouse felt different the next morning, heavy with unspoken words and lingering touches. Emma woke to the soft hum of the city beyond the windows, the faint sound of the waves crashing against the shore echoing through the walls. The sheets were tangled around her body, and she could still feel the warmth of Jack's touch on her skin, the memory of their passion etched into her muscles, into her very soul.

But as the haze of sleep faded, so did the warmth. A quiet unease began to settle in her chest, a growing sense of doubt that she couldn't quite shake. She had trusted Jack—completely, without question—but now, as she lay there, the reality of it all was beginning to catch up with her.

Jack. The man who had made her feel things she hadn't even known were possible, the man who had unlocked parts of her that had been buried for years. He was everything she had never expected—intense, commanding, yet vulnerable in his own way. And yet, for all the connection between them, there were still so many things left unsaid, unspoken truths that hung in the air between them.

She heard the soft sound of footsteps approaching the bedroom, and before she could collect her thoughts, the door opened. Jack stood in the doorway, his posture relaxed but his eyes sharp, as though he could sense the shift in the air, the change in her mood.

"Good morning," he said, his voice low, as if testing the waters.

Emma sat up, pulling the sheets around her to cover her, her fingers fidgeting with the fabric as she tried to find the right words. The truth was, she didn't know what to say. What did you say when everything felt so perfect on the surface but there was a storm brewing underneath?

"Morning," she replied softly, offering a smile that didn't quite reach her eyes. Jack, ever perceptive, noticed the subtle change immediately, but he didn't push. Instead, he walked over to the bed, sitting down beside her, the bed dipping under his weight as he leaned back against the headboard.

"Are you okay?" he asked, his voice gentle, his gaze intent on her face.

Emma hesitated, her fingers stilling in the sheets. She wanted to say something, to tell him how she was feeling, but the words felt like they were trapped inside her, tangled up in the confusion she was trying to sort through. She felt so vulnerable, so exposed. She had given herself to him in ways she had never given anyone else, and now there was a part of her that wasn't sure she could take it all back.

"I don't know, Jack," she admitted, her voice barely above a whisper. "I feel... I don't know what I feel anymore."

His eyes softened as he reached for her, his fingers gently cupping her chin, tilting her head up so she was forced to meet his gaze. The warmth of his touch sent a shiver down her spine, but there was something more in his eyes—a quiet understanding, a patience that Emma hadn't expected.

"You're scared," he said simply, the words not as a question, but as a statement of fact. "And that's okay. You've given me a lot, Emma. And I know it's not easy."

Her chest tightened as she looked at him, and for a moment, it felt as though the room itself had closed in around her. She had been so sure, so certain of what she wanted with Jack, but now that everything had shifted, she found herself unsure of where she stood. The emotional weight of their connection felt almost too much to bear.

"I don't know if I can keep doing this," she whispered, the words slipping out before she could stop them. "I've never trusted anyone like I trust you, Jack. But every time I let myself go, I feel like I'm losing myself. I don't want to lose who I am."

Jack's gaze softened further, and he moved closer, pulling her into his arms. His embrace was warm, comforting, yet the strength of it reminded her that he was not a man who let go easily. And she didn't want him to. Not really. But there was a part of her that feared losing herself in him, in what they had.

"You're not losing yourself, Emma," he murmured into her hair, his fingers trailing soothingly over her back. "You're discovering parts of yourself you didn't even know were there. This is about growth, not surrendering who you are. You don't have to become someone else to be with me."

Emma closed her eyes, allowing the sound of his voice, the feel of his touch, to wash over her. He was right, in a way. She was growing. But it was more than that—it was the depth of feeling, the intensity, that was both exhilarating and terrifying. Jack made her feel things she couldn't explain, things she didn't know how to handle.

She pulled back slightly to look at him, her fingers brushing over his jawline, feeling the roughness of his stubble against her fingertips. "I've never felt like this before, Jack. I don't know how to handle it."

He smiled, a small, knowing smile that made her heart race. "You don't have to handle it, Emma. Just feel it. Let it happen. Let me show you what we can create together."

His words were both a promise and an invitation. And Emma felt the weight of them, sinking into her chest. She had already given him so much, but there was more to be given, more to discover, more to explore. She didn't know where it would all lead, but she was willing to take that step, to allow herself to be carried away by whatever came next.

She nodded slowly, the decision settling in her chest like a weight lifting off her shoulders. "Okay," she whispered. "I'll trust you. I'll trust us."

Jack leaned forward then, his lips brushing against hers, soft at first, as if testing the waters, but then deepening as the heat between them flared. His hands slid to her waist, pulling her closer, his body pressing against hers in a way that made her pulse quicken. There was nothing tentative about the way he kissed her now—there was a rawness to it, a hunger that mirrored her own.

Emma responded eagerly, her hands threading through his hair, tugging him closer, as if she couldn't get enough of him. She could feel the warmth of his body against hers, the heat of their shared desire igniting the space between them. There was no more hesitation now—just the connection, the chemistry that bound them together.

Jack's hands moved over her body, slow and deliberate, as though he were savoring every inch of her, as though he couldn't get enough. She shivered under his touch, her body responding to him in ways she hadn't expected. He made her feel like she was the only woman in the world, and for that moment, she believed it.

They moved together, the rhythm of their bodies matching in perfect harmony, until Emma felt the overwhelming rush of sensation that only Jack could evoke. Her body arched into his, and she gasped as the wave of pleasure washed over her, taking her to the edge and beyond. It was unlike anything she had ever experienced before—the connection, the intimacy, the trust.

As she collapsed against him, her breath coming in ragged gasps, Jack held her close, his hand running through her hair as he kissed the top of her head, his voice soft and reassuring.

"See?" he murmured. "It's not about losing yourself. It's about finding something even more powerful."

Emma closed her eyes, allowing the quiet afterglow of their shared moment to settle over her. She wasn't sure what the future held, but in that moment, she knew one thing for certain: she had found something with Jack that was more than just desire. It was trust, it was connection, it was something deeper.

And for the first time in a long while, Emma felt truly at peace.

Chapter 13: The Weight of Desire

"Love is a force more formidable than any other. It is invisible—its power is not to be understood by the mind, but only by the heart." — Unknown

The days after that morning felt like they were suspended in time. The air was thick with unspoken words and the weight of all that had passed between them, but at the same time, there was a sense of calm—a quiet understanding that settled between Emma and Jack. They were no longer in the early stages of something new. This was no longer just flirtation or curiosity. This was real. This was deep.

Yet despite the undeniable intimacy that had blossomed between them, Emma still felt a subtle tension in the back of her mind. She had given herself to Jack in ways she hadn't anticipated, trusting him more than she had ever trusted anyone, but there was a part of her that wondered if she could continue down this path without losing herself entirely. She didn't regret anything, not in the slightest, but there was a nagging fear that this connection, this all-consuming bond, might begin to overshadow the person she used to be.

She stood in front of the window that overlooked Sydney's bustling streets, watching the people below, the world continuing on without a care. It was strange, really—how something so profound could exist within her life, yet the world outside remained indifferent, unaffected by the emotional storm that raged inside her. She had felt this before, this sense of disconnection—where her own reality felt so separate from the world around her, like she was trapped in a bubble that only Jack could reach.

A soft knock on the door broke her from her thoughts, and before she could move, Jack stepped into the room. His presence was undeniable, a quiet power that filled the space between them without a single word. His eyes locked on hers immediately, and in that moment, Emma felt a wave of vulnerability rush over her. It was as if he could see right through her, as if he knew everything she was thinking, even the things she couldn't articulate.

"Hey," he said softly, his voice low, almost tentative. "Can we talk?"

Emma swallowed, nodding slowly. Her heart beat a little faster, and she couldn't help but wonder if this was the moment when everything would shift again. Was he ready to take things further? Or was this the beginning of something else, a conversation that would force her to confront the doubts that had been quietly festering inside her?

"Of course," she said, her voice steady, though she could feel the flutter of nervous energy in her stomach.

Jack walked over to her, his steps measured, his eyes never leaving hers. He reached out to touch her, his fingers brushing against the back of her neck, sending a shiver down her spine. The touch was light, intimate, and the warmth of his skin against hers made her feel safe in a way she hadn't quite expected.

"I've been thinking about us," he said, his thumb tracing a gentle circle on the skin of her neck. "About everything that's happened between us."

Emma's heart skipped a beat. She had been thinking about it too. About him. About what they were, about what they could become. But she hadn't said anything, hadn't allowed herself to voice those questions because she was afraid of what the answers might be.

"Jack, I—" She stopped herself, unsure of how to proceed, unsure if she even wanted to ask the questions that were forming in her mind. But Jack, as always, seemed to know exactly what she needed.

"Emma," he said gently, his hand sliding down to rest on her shoulder, "this isn't just about what we're doing in the bedroom. This is about us. About who we are when we're not tangled in each other. I care about you. More than I ever expected."

The simplicity of his words, the rawness in his voice, made Emma's chest tighten. She had never doubted his feelings for her, not really. But hearing him say it out loud—hearing him admit it—made it feel more real, more tangible than it ever had before.

"I care about you too," she whispered, her voice a little shaky. She reached up to take his hand, her fingers lacing with his as she searched his eyes for some kind of reassurance. "But sometimes... I don't know if I can keep up with all of this."

Jack's brow furrowed in concern, and he stepped closer to her, his other hand coming to rest on her cheek. "What do you mean?"

Emma took a deep breath, trying to steady herself. "It's just... everything's moving so fast. I'm not sure if I'm losing myself in this. In you."

Jack's expression softened as he pulled her closer, his arms wrapping around her, pulling her into the safety of his embrace. She allowed herself to melt into him, her head resting against his chest as his fingers gently caressed the back of her neck, soothing the tension she hadn't even realised was there.

"I'm not asking you to lose yourself, Emma," he said softly, his lips brushing against the top of her head. "I want you to be yourself. To be everything that you are. I want us to grow together, not for you to lose what makes you, you. But I also don't want you to run from this, from us. What we have is real. And it's something I don't want to let go of."

Emma closed her eyes, allowing his words to sink in. She hadn't expected this. She had expected more distance, more hesitance, but Jack's words were unwavering, and in them, she found a quiet reassurance. He wasn't asking her to be anyone else, and he wasn't demanding more than she could give. He just wanted her.

The weight of that—of being wanted, truly wanted—was both comforting and terrifying. She had spent so many years building walls around herself, so many years of keeping parts of herself hidden away. But with Jack, those walls had come down, slowly but surely, and now, she was standing in the aftermath, unsure of who she was becoming.

"I don't know if I can be everything you want," she whispered, her voice barely audible.

Jack's hand slid beneath her chin, lifting her face to meet his gaze. "You don't have to be everything. Just be yourself. That's all I want. You."

His words were like a balm to her wounded soul, a promise that she didn't have to be perfect, didn't have to have it all figured out. She could just be.

Emma nodded, her heart swelling with emotion. "I want this too, Jack. I do. I want us."

He leaned in then, his lips pressing against hers with a tenderness that stole her breath away. The kiss deepened, growing more urgent as their bodies responded instinctively to one another. His hands roamed over her body, igniting sparks of desire with each touch, but there was something different about this moment—something slower, more deliberate, as though they were savoring the connection in a way they hadn't before.

Emma's hands moved to his chest, her fingers slipping beneath his shirt to feel the warmth of his skin, the muscles that rippled beneath the surface. Jack's breath hitched as she traced the outline of his collarbone, her fingers drawing lazy circles across his chest as the kiss deepened further.

This wasn't just passion anymore. It wasn't just desire. This was something more—something that reached deeper, into the very core of who they were.

"I need you, Jack," she whispered between kisses, her voice thick with emotion.

"I'm here," he murmured back, his voice hoarse as he kissed her again, the depth of his desire unmistakable.

They moved together, the world outside forgotten, as they rediscovered each other in a way that felt both familiar and new. There was no rush, no urgency, just the quiet exploration of one another's bodies, the heat between them simmering as they grew closer, as they allowed the intimacy to stretch into something they both needed, something they both craved.

In the silence that followed, when they finally pulled away, Emma rested her head on Jack's chest, the steady beat of his heart beneath her ear a soothing rhythm that calmed her racing thoughts. There were still so many unknowns between them, so many unspoken truths, but in that moment, she realized that they didn't have to have it all figured out.

They just had to keep going, together.

Chapter 14: Beyond the Surface

"The greatest thing you'll ever learn is just to love and be loved in return." — Eden Ahbez

The days seemed to blur into one another as Emma and Jack continued their journey together. Their connection was no longer just about the electric moments that seemed to ignite at every glance or touch. This was something deeper. More profound. They had crossed a threshold, one where emotions intertwined with physical desire, and their every interaction seemed to push the boundaries of what they had once thought possible.

But still, despite the passion that had become the foundation of their relationship, there was something unspoken between them. Something that Emma couldn't quite place. It was a weight, a tension that lingered in the background, often rising to the surface when they least expected it. It was the fantasy. The unspoken dreams they hadn't yet dared to explore. Emma could feel Jack's eyes on her, sometimes with a hunger that went beyond the simple moments of touch and pleasure they shared. He wanted more. She could sense it, feel it in the way he would brush his hand across her skin, or the way his lips would linger a little longer on hers.

She hadn't been blind to the way he looked at her when they were alone—like he was seeing more than just the woman standing in front of him. He was seeing the woman she had yet to fully discover. The woman who could surrender to every desire without fear of judgment.

And in a strange way, Emma wanted that too. She wanted to shed the layers of uncertainty that clung to her, to explore the parts of herself she had always kept hidden. But it was one thing to want it, and another to actually face it.

The night had fallen quietly, the city lights of Sydney sparkling in the distance, casting a soft glow through the windows of Jack's penthouse. The view was breathtaking, yet Emma found herself lost in her own thoughts as she stood near the edge of the balcony, the cool night air kissing her skin.

She had come here for clarity, for some semblance of peace, but she hadn't expected to be confronted with the rush of anticipation that seemed to gather within her chest. Her thoughts were consumed by Jack, by the magnetic pull that had only grown stronger since they first met.

Turning, she saw Jack leaning against the doorframe, his eyes watching her with that intensity that seemed to pierce right through her. His gaze was focused, steady, and yet there was a trace of something more—a raw desire, tempered by patience.

"Emma," he said softly, his voice rich with that familiar tone that made her heart race. "You look like you're a million miles away. What's going on in that mind of yours?"

She smiled, trying to break the tension. "Just thinking about every-thing. About us."

He stepped forward then, his presence commanding, yet gentle. "About what specifically?"

Emma paused. This was the moment, wasn't it? The moment where the walls she had built around herself would either stay intact or crumble under the weight of their desires. The walls had served her well—kept her protected, kept her safe. But they also kept her from truly living, truly feeling.

"I've been wondering what you really want from me," she said, her voice barely a whisper.

Jack's lips curled into a slow, knowing smile. He was no stranger to her doubts, her fears, but he wasn't the kind of man to back down from them. If anything, he seemed to thrive on them. He crossed the room in a few long strides, his hands sliding around her waist, pulling her close so that she could feel the heat radiating from his body.

"I want all of you," he said quietly, his breath warm against her ear. "Not just the parts you show me when it's easy. I want the parts of you that you keep hidden—the fantasies, the desires, the parts of you that are still untapped. I want to explore every inch of you, Emma. Not just physically, but emotionally, mentally. Everything."

His words were a caress, a promise of something more. His hands slid beneath her shirt, tracing the soft curve of her waist, pulling her tighter against him, urging her to feel the strength and urgency that pulsed through his veins. Emma's breath hitched, the heat building between them as the sensation of his touch sent shivers of anticipation skittering over her skin.

"But I don't know if I'm ready," she admitted, the words escaping her before she could stop them.

Jack leaned back slightly, just enough to look into her eyes, and the intensity in his gaze made her heart skip. "Then we'll take it slow. But we won't stop. Not until you're ready to let go completely."

The promise in his voice ignited something deep inside her. She had never been with a man who was so unyielding, yet so gentle at the same time. Jack's hands were both demanding and reassuring, coaxing her to relax, to trust him.

"I want to," she murmured, her voice shaky with the weight of her emotions. "But I'm afraid. I'm afraid of what I might find."

He didn't say anything at first. Instead, he kissed her. A slow, deliberate kiss that seemed to strip away every layer of doubt, every trace of hesitation. His lips moved against hers with such intensity that Emma's body responded instinctively. Her hands moved to his chest, her fingers pushing the fabric of his shirt up to feel the heat of his skin beneath.

When they finally broke the kiss, their breaths were shallow, their bodies humming with desire. Jack's lips were just above hers, his voice barely a whisper. "You don't have to be afraid. I'm not going anywhere. But you have to trust me, Emma. Trust that I won't hurt you."

"I do trust you," she said, the words slipping out, barely audible.

He smiled softly, brushing a lock of hair behind her ear before leaning down to kiss her neck. "Good," he whispered, his lips moving lower. "Then let go with me, Emma. Let go of the fear, the doubts, and just feel. Let me show you."

The heat between them intensified as Jack's hands roamed her body with growing urgency. The kiss turned deeper, more fervent, as though they were both trying to communicate everything they hadn't said aloud. Emma's pulse quickened, her body burning with desire as she yielded to the pull of his touch, the pull of him.

Every inch of her skin was on fire, every kiss igniting a spark deep inside. She wanted to give herself to him completely, to surrender in a way she never had before. And Jack was more than willing to take her there.

As the night unfolded, their bodies moved together in a rhythm that was both familiar and new. It was a dance of exploration, of desire, as Jack led her through the dark, uncharted territory of her own fantasies. His touch was both demanding and tender, each caress drawing out a part of her that she had kept hidden away for too long.

The world outside seemed to disappear as they lost themselves in each other, the only reality that mattered the one they created together. And as the hours passed, Emma realized that this was more than just sex. This was a journey. A journey of trust, of surrender, and of love that she had never truly known before.

Chapter 15: Unmasking Desire

"Desire is not what you see, but what you are blind to." — Unknown

The air was thick with a mixture of passion and uncertainty, each day spent together shifting the dynamics of Emma and Jack's connection. It was as if they were living in a world all their own—a private realm where nothing outside of their touches, whispers, and glances could breach the walls they'd created around their relationship.

Still, there were moments when the weight of their connection settled heavily between them, like the unspoken words they hadn't dared say. Emma couldn't shake the feeling that, despite the incredible intimacy they shared, there was always something just beyond reach. Something they both wanted but hadn't yet discovered. She didn't know how much longer they could dance around it before the tension would become unbearable.

But that thought was far from her mind when she woke up that morning, wrapped in the warmth of Jack's arms. His body was pressed against hers, his breathing slow and steady, his lips soft against her shoulder. She lay there for a moment, basking in the serenity of their shared space. Everything was still. Everything was safe. In this moment, she felt like she could let go of everything and just be.

But the sensation of his fingers grazing her skin shattered the stillness, and she felt her body stir with the familiar longing that had only grown stronger since they first came together.

"Good morning, beautiful," Jack's voice was low, thick with sleep and something else—a hunger that never seemed to subside. His hand slid lower, his touch moving gently over her side, sending a trail of fire through her skin. He knew how to touch her, how to make her heart race with a single caress, and he did it with such effortless ease that it always left her breathless.

"Good morning," Emma whispered, her voice still heavy with the remnants of sleep.

His fingers continued their slow exploration, moving over her body with deliberate slowness, as though he was savoring every inch of her. She let out a soft breath as his hand traced the curve of her hip, dipping beneath the sheets to find the heat of her skin.

"I can't seem to get enough of you," Jack murmured, his lips brushing against her ear. "You've got me hooked, Emma."

Her heart fluttered at the intensity in his voice, at the way he spoke as if every word he uttered was an invitation to something more—something deeper.

"Maybe it's not just me," she whispered, her hands moving to his chest, fingers grazing the hard muscles beneath the sheets. "Maybe you're just as hooked on this as I am."

Jack chuckled softly, his lips curving into a smirk. "Maybe." His hands slid higher, his touch now more urgent, as if he couldn't wait to feel her, couldn't wait to lose himself in her once again. "I think it's more than that. It's more than just the sex, Emma. It's you. All of you."

Her breath caught at his words. She wanted to say something, wanted to tell him that she felt the same, but the words seemed to slip away, lost in the intensity of the moment. Instead, she leaned in to kiss him, her lips finding his in a kiss that started slow and tender, but quickly grew more insistent as desire flared between them.

Jack responded instantly, his hands moving with a sense of urgency, his lips deepening the kiss until Emma was gasping for air, her body pressing against his, heart racing. She could feel his desire, feel it in every movement of his hands, every whisper of breath between them. There was no doubt, no hesitation. They were both consumed by it.

"Emma," he murmured against her lips, his voice rough with need. "I want you. All of you."

She felt the same. She didn't need to speak it. The way his body pressed against hers, the way his fingers traced the lines of her body—it all said more than words ever could. She wanted to give herself completely to him. To surrender. She didn't know if she was ready, but she didn't care. Not now.

Without warning, Jack flipped them over, his body hovering over hers as he kissed her with a hunger that made her knees weak. His hands moved to the back of her neck, pulling her closer, if that was even possible, before sliding down to her hips, gripping her tighter. She gasped, feeling the weight of him, the pressure of his body as he moved against her.

"Tell me what you want, Emma," he said, his voice thick, laced with desire. "Tell me how you want this to go."

It was as if a switch flipped inside her. She could feel her body respond before her mind even had a chance to catch up. She wanted him. Wanted everything about this—every touch, every kiss, every unspoken promise between them. But she also wanted to take control, to step into her own power and own her desire.

"I want you to take me, Jack," she breathed, her voice husky with anticipation. "I want you to make me feel everything."

His eyes darkened with lust at her words, and for a moment, Emma saw a flicker of something raw and primal in his gaze—a need to dominate, to claim her, that mirrored the hunger inside her. But there was tenderness there too. A promise that everything he did would be for her, that she would never lose herself in the process.

And then, just as the anticipation became almost too much to bear, he kissed her again, pulling her fully into the moment. She could feel his body moving against hers, the rhythm of their movements becoming a dance that was both urgent and languid, a mix of passion and control, of give and take.

Time seemed to stretch and bend as their bodies came together in a symphony of touches, kisses, and whispers. Jack's hands were everywhere, his lips marking her skin with a trail of fire that left her breathless. She responded eagerly, matching his rhythm, her fingers digging into his shoulders as she pulled him closer, wanting more.

With every touch, every kiss, every deep thrust, Emma felt herself letting go more and more, surrendering to the pleasure, to the intimacy, to Jack's steady presence. She was no longer just the woman standing before him. She was the woman he desired, the woman he needed. And in that moment, she felt powerful, whole, and utterly alive.

Finally, after what felt like an eternity, they collapsed together, tangled in sheets, both of them panting, covered in sweat. Jack pulled her close, his hand resting on her back as he kissed her forehead.

"I never want to stop this," he whispered, his voice soft but filled with conviction.

Emma smiled, her fingers tracing the lines of his chest as she nestled against him, her heart still racing from the intensity of what they had just shared. She didn't need to say anything. She knew that this—whatever this was—wasn't something she would easily walk away from. It wasn't just about the physical connection anymore. It was about something deeper, something they had only just begun to explore.

For the first time, Emma allowed herself to believe that maybe, just maybe, this could be everything she had been searching for. And as the night stretched on, she let herself drift into the calm of Jack's embrace, knowing that whatever came next, they would face it together.

Chapter 16: Chasing the Storm

"*Sometimes the most profound things are the ones that are never said.*" — Unknown

It had been days since their last encounter, and despite the ever-present warmth between them, Emma felt a familiar tension building once more. The kind of tension that simmered just beneath the surface, waiting to be released. Jack had been busy with work, and she had been caught up in her own thoughts—thoughts that had been swirling around in her mind like an unrelenting storm.

She hadn't meant to pull away. She hadn't intended to build walls between them. But somewhere along the way, Emma had started questioning everything. What did this really mean? Was it love, or was it something else? The moments they shared—intimate, raw, and incredibly passionate—felt like something out of a dream, but the lingering questions remained. Could she trust herself to let go fully? And more importantly, could she trust Jack?

But as much as she wanted to ignore those doubts, they kept gnawing at her. She had been down that road before, only to find herself heartbroken and alone. Could this be different? Could this truly be the connection she had been waiting for?

Her phone buzzed on the bedside table, jolting her from her thoughts. It was a message from Jack.

"I miss you. Dinner tonight? Let's make it special."

A smile tugged at the corners of her lips as she read the words. Despite everything, despite the tension, he still knew how to make her feel wanted. His messages always had that effect on her. And deep down, she knew she couldn't resist him—not now, not when she was already so tangled in the feelings he'd awakened in her.

She didn't respond right away. Instead, she stared out the window, watching the city lights of Sydney blink against the dark sky. The storm was coming. It was in the thick clouds gathering overhead, in the humid air that clung to her skin. She could feel it. The storm wasn't just in the sky—it was in her.

And as much as she feared it, she also felt the thrill of it. The need for release.

She knew what she needed. She needed to face this head-on, to stop running from the inevitable. She needed to confront the fears that had been shadowing her. And maybe, just maybe, she needed to let Jack in even more than she ever had before.

With a soft exhale, she typed back a simple response: *"Dinner sounds perfect."*

***

That evening, Emma arrived at Jack's penthouse, her mind still racing. The moment she stepped inside, she was greeted by the soft glow of candles, the smell of something delicious wafting from the kitchen, and the unmistakable presence of Jack. He stood by the window, dressed in a sharp black shirt and dark trousers, his posture casual, but his gaze sharp and knowing.

"I hope you're hungry," he said with a grin, his eyes scanning her as she stepped into the room. "I'm not much of a chef, but I thought I'd make an exception tonight."

Emma smiled, the familiar flutter in her stomach returning at the sight of him. He had that effect on her—a way of making her feel both at ease and completely unsettled at the same time. It was intoxicating.

"I'm starving," she replied, her voice betraying the nervous excitement she felt. "It smells amazing."

Jack led her to the dining table, which was set with an elegance that was unmistakably his—simple, but luxurious. The table was surrounded by soft lighting, the quiet hum of the city outside adding a layer of atmosphere to the evening. As they sat, the conversation flowed easily between them, the comfortable banter allowing Emma to forget for a moment the questions that had been plaguing her.

But as the night wore on, and they moved from dinner to the couch, the air between them shifted. The playful flirting, the teasing touches, became charged with an unspoken tension. Emma could feel it in the way Jack looked at her—like he was waiting for something, waiting for her to make the next move.

"I want to show you something," he said suddenly, his voice low, eyes filled with intent.

Before she could ask what, he stood and extended his hand to her, his fingers brushing against hers. The connection was electric, a jolt of energy that traveled up her arm and straight to her chest. Emma felt the pull, felt the heat rising between them, but there was still a hesitation in her.

"Come with me," Jack urged, his voice softer now, almost a whisper. He led her to the balcony, where the view of the city was even more breathtaking in the soft moonlight. The storm was still lingering, its promise hanging heavy in the air.

"Isn't it beautiful?" Jack asked, stepping closer to her, his hand now resting lightly on her back. "But it's nothing compared to what I feel when I'm with you."

Emma's breath caught at his words, her pulse quickening as the intimacy of the moment wrapped around her like a velvet glove. She turned to face him, feeling the undeniable pull of his gaze, the weight of his presence.

"I've been thinking a lot lately," she began, her voice a little shaky, though she tried to keep it steady. "About us. About everything."

Jack's expression softened, his hand moving to her cheek, brushing a strand of hair behind her ear. His touch was gentle, but there was a quiet intensity in his eyes. "What are you thinking?"

She hesitated, unsure of how much of her heart she was ready to reveal. "I'm thinking that maybe I've been holding back. Maybe I've been too afraid to let myself feel all of this. All of you."

He moved closer, his lips grazing the shell of her ear as he whispered, "You don't have to be afraid, Emma. I'm not going anywhere. You have all of me, and I'll take all of you. We're in this together."

His words were like a balm to her, soothing the raw edges of her fear. She turned to face him fully, her chest tight with emotion. She wanted to tell him everything, wanted to open herself up to him in a way she had never done with anyone before.

And as he kissed her then, it was different. It wasn't the hungry, urgent kiss they'd shared before—it was slow, tender, deep, as if they were both savoring the moment, letting it stretch out and breathe.

But just when Emma thought she might lose herself in the kiss, Jack pulled away slightly, his forehead resting against hers, his breath a soft whisper on her skin.

"I think it's time, Emma," he murmured, his hand slipping down to rest at her waist, his fingers tracing the curve of her hip. "Time for you to let go. Let go of the fear. Let go of the doubts. And just be with me. In every way."

Emma felt the storm inside her finally break, felt the walls she'd been holding onto crumble at the sheer intensity of his words. There was nothing left to fear. Not anymore. Not with Jack.

Her lips met his again, this time with more urgency, more need, more surrender.

Chapter 17: Breaking Boundaries

"There's a point in every relationship when the love becomes more than what you thought it could be. You can either run from it, or you can break every boundary and let it consume you." — Unknown

The morning light filtered softly through the blinds, casting delicate shadows across the room. Emma stirred in the bed, her body still humming from the night before. It had been a night of release, of vulnerability, of finally tearing down the walls she had so carefully built around her heart. And though it had left her feeling raw and exposed, there was also an undeniable sense of freedom in it.

She opened her eyes to find Jack asleep beside her, his face relaxed, his breathing steady. She studied him for a moment, his features softened in slumber, before she reached out to trace the line of his jaw with the tip of her finger. It was an intimate, quiet moment—one that felt more real than anything they'd shared so far.

Jack stirred slightly at her touch, his eyes flickering open, a small smile tugging at his lips as he looked at her. "Morning," he murmured, his voice thick with sleep.

Emma returned his smile, but there was something more in her gaze now. A deeper understanding between them. Last night had changed something. She could feel it in the way her body responded to his presence, in the way her heart raced whenever he was near. They were no longer just two people playing with fire. They were becoming something more.

"Morning," she replied softly. Her voice was low, almost hesitant, as she ran her hand over his chest. The weight of the night before was still heavy on her mind, the emotions swirling around inside her, but there was something else now too—something she couldn't quite name. But she could feel it building between them.

Jack propped himself up on one arm, his gaze intense as he studied her. "How are you feeling?" he asked, his voice laced with concern.

She hesitated, unsure of how to answer. Was she feeling overwhelmed? Confused? Or was she just terrified of how much she had given of herself to him? But deep down, she knew the truth. She wasn't afraid. Not anymore. She had given him all of her, and he had taken it willingly. The fear, the uncertainty—it was fading, replaced by something that felt even more intense: desire.

"I'm... I'm good," she said, her voice barely a whisper. "Better than good."

Jack leaned forward, his lips brushing against hers in a gentle kiss. The kind of kiss that made her heart flutter, that made her feel like she was finally giving herself permission to feel everything she had been hiding. His hands cupped her face, his touch tender, as if he was afraid to break the delicate moment between them.

"You've always been so strong, Emma," he murmured against her lips. "But I see something else in you now. Something I want to explore. I want to know all of you."

The words sent a shiver through her, a deep longing rising within her chest. She had never known someone to speak to her like that—so raw, so honest, so unguarded. He was laying himself bare before her, and it made her heart ache in the best way possible.

"I'm ready," she whispered, the words slipping out before she could stop them.

Jack's eyes darkened with desire at her admission, and he moved swiftly, his lips capturing hers again, this time with a hunger that was unmistakable. There was no hesitation, no doubt. They had crossed a line now, and there was no going back.

He pulled her into his arms, their bodies tangled in the sheets, the heat between them building once more. As their kisses deepened, Jack's hands slid down her body, caressing every inch of her, touching her like she was the most precious thing in the world. She responded eagerly, her hands moving over his skin, memorizing the feel of him beneath her fingertips.

"I want you, Emma," Jack breathed, his voice rough and full of need. "I want to take you further. Let's see just how far we can go."

The words sent a bolt of electricity through her, and without thinking, Emma lifted herself to meet him. Her hands explored his chest, tracing the ridges of his muscles, before moving lower, to where he was already hard with anticipation. Her touch was confident now, sure of what she wanted, what they both wanted. The desire was undeniable.

"Tell me you want this too," Jack's voice was low, his breath coming in short bursts as he watched her every move.

"I want this," she whispered, her voice trembling with the weight of her own desire. "I want you."

Without another word, Jack's hands slid beneath her, lifting her effortlessly and guiding her as their bodies came together in a perfect, seamless motion. The connection was intense, raw, and beautiful. It felt like nothing she had ever experienced before—no hesitation, no games, just pure passion and unrelenting desire.

***

They moved together, finding a rhythm that felt almost instinctual, the world outside the room forgotten as they lost themselves in each other. Every kiss, every touch, every whisper felt like a promise—a promise of more, of deeper connection, of an intimacy that neither of them had ever known.

Jack's hands roamed her body, exploring every curve, every part of her that he had come to crave. His lips followed the trail of his hands, leaving a trail of fire in their wake. Emma responded in kind, her hands skimming over his body, feeling the heat of his skin, the hardness of his muscles, the rawness of his need.

She was no longer just the woman he desired. She was the woman who had unlocked something inside him. And he was unlocking something in her too—something wild, something fierce, something free.

It wasn't just about the physical connection anymore. It was about trust. It was about surrendering, not only to the pleasure but to the deeper bond they were building. Each kiss, each touch, was a promise to explore, to push boundaries, to let go of the walls they had both so carefully built.

As the night stretched on, Emma found herself lost in Jack—lost in the sensation of him, the feeling of being completely consumed by him. And for the first time in a long while, she didn't fight it. She let herself fall, fall into him, into them.

The storm that had been brewing inside her broke wide open, and as they reached the peak together, it was as if everything clicked into place. Emma's body trembled beneath Jack, her heart racing, her breath ragged. She felt alive, in a way she had never felt before.

Jack held her close, his hands gentle now, stroking her hair, as they both came down from the heights they had just reached. She was breathing heavily, her body still buzzing from the intensity of their union. He kissed her forehead softly, and Emma knew, in that moment, that there was no turning back.

They had crossed a line together. And now, they would see just how far their connection could take them.

Chapter 18: A Dance of Trust

"*Trust is built in the moments when you're vulnerable, and you let someone see the parts of you that you fear the most.*" — Unknown

The morning after their night together was quiet—unsettlingly so. The soft hum of the city could be heard in the distance, the first hints of the early morning sun creeping through the blinds, casting a warm golden glow across the room. Emma lay beside Jack, her head resting on his chest, listening to the steady beat of his heart. The remnants of their passionate encounter still lingered in the air, the warmth between them undeniable, but there was something else. Something she couldn't quite name.

She had given herself completely to him, and for the first time in a long while, she wasn't sure where the line between herself and him began and ended. Was this love? Or was it something else? The intensity they shared felt so overwhelming, so consuming, that it made her wonder whether she had become addicted to him, to the passion, to the way he made her feel.

And yet, despite the uncertainty that whispered at the edges of her thoughts, she couldn't deny the satisfaction in her heart. She had been afraid of losing herself, but in Jack's arms, she felt found in a way she had never known before. He had taken every wall she had built, torn it down effortlessly, and in its place, he had woven something stronger—a connection she couldn't escape, no matter how hard she tried.

Jack's hand slid gently over her back, his touch tender, as if he could sense the shift in her mood. He pulled her closer, his lips brushing against her hair. "Are you alright?" he murmured, his voice thick with sleep but laced with concern. "You seem distant."

Emma hesitated for a moment before answering, unsure of how to express the swirl of emotions inside her. "I'm fine," she said softly, trying to keep her voice steady. "Just... thinking."

"About what?" Jack asked, his fingers gently trailing along her arm, sending shivers of awareness through her.

"I don't know," she admitted, her voice barely above a whisper. "Everything. About us. About what this is."

There was a long pause, and for a moment, Emma thought she might have said too much. But then Jack's arms tightened around her, his grip possessive yet reassuring. "You don't need to know everything right now, Emma," he said, his voice soft but firm. "You don't need to label this or figure it all out. Just let it be. Let us be."

His words settled over her like a soothing balm, and for the first time in days, Emma felt a sense of peace she hadn't realized she'd been searching for. Jack wasn't asking her to define their relationship, wasn't pushing her to make sense of what was happening between them. He was simply there, present and patient, allowing her to explore everything in her own time, on her own terms.

She leaned up, her gaze meeting his, searching for any sign of uncertainty in his eyes. But all she saw was certainty, a deep, unwavering confidence in the way he looked at her. It made her feel safe—protected in a way she hadn't felt in years.

"I don't want to lose this," she whispered, her voice trembling slightly with the vulnerability she had only just begun to understand. "What we have."

Jack smiled then, a slow, knowing smile that sent a thrill through her. He reached up to tuck a stray lock of hair behind her ear before cupping her face gently. "You won't," he said softly. "I'm not going anywhere. I want this too."

The words settled into her chest, warming her from the inside out. He wasn't just offering her his body, his passion—he was offering her something more. Something deeper. Trust.

The weight of that trust settled between them, unspoken but understood. There was no need for grand declarations. No need for promises of forever. Because what they shared now—what they were building—was enough. It was real. And it was something neither of them had ever known before.

Later that evening, Jack took Emma to one of his favorite spots in the city—a rooftop restaurant with sweeping views of Sydney's skyline. The atmosphere was intimate, soft lighting casting shadows over the tables, the quiet hum of conversation blending with the sound of clinking glasses and the occasional burst of laughter. It was elegant and understated, the perfect place for a quiet dinner—or, in their case, a place to continue their unspoken exploration of each other.

As they sat across from each other, Emma couldn't help but notice how different things felt now. Their connection had grown stronger, more complex, and with every moment that passed, she found herself falling even more deeply under Jack's spell. Not just physically, but emotionally too. He was a puzzle she was eager to piece together—every glance, every smile, every touch left her wanting more.

"You've been quiet tonight," Jack said, his voice low as he studied her, his eyes thoughtful. "Something on your mind?"

Emma hesitated, unsure of how much to say. She wasn't used to this—being so open, so vulnerable with someone. But with Jack, it felt natural. He had this way of drawing out her deepest thoughts and fears without pushing her, without rushing her.

"I'm just... trying to keep up," she said finally, her smile faint but genuine. "Everything feels like it's moving so fast, and sometimes I'm not sure if I'm ready for it. But then I look at you, and I know I am."

Jack reached across the table, his hand covering hers in a soft, reassuring gesture. "You don't need to keep up with anything, Emma. We're not racing toward an end. We're just taking this one step at a time. And as long as we're taking those steps together, it doesn't matter how fast or slow we go."

The simplicity of his words left her breathless, and she squeezed his hand in return, a surge of emotion flooding her chest. She wasn't used to this—this gentleness, this patience. It was more than she had ever hoped for.

"You make it seem so easy," she said, her voice barely above a whisper.

"That's because it is," Jack replied, his voice smooth as he leaned in slightly, his gaze unwavering. "As long as we're being honest with each other, as long as we're trusting each other, everything else falls into place. Trust is the foundation, Emma. Once we have that, nothing else matters."

The words resonated deep within her, and she realized then that Jack wasn't just speaking about their relationship. He was speaking about something much bigger—something that could change the way she viewed herself, the way she viewed the world.

And in that moment, Emma knew. She wasn't just falling in love with Jack. She was learning to trust herself again.

Back at Jack's penthouse later that night, the air between them shifted again, this time more serious, more deliberate. They had crossed many boundaries already, but there was still so much more to explore. And for Emma, the most important thing now wasn't about pushing limits or indulging in fantasies—it was about completely surrendering to the connection between them.

As Jack gently pulled her toward him, their lips meeting in a soft, lingering kiss, she felt the weight of everything—the passion, the desire, the raw, unspoken promises—wrap around her like a second skin. It wasn't just sex anymore. It was intimacy on a level she had never known before. It was trust.

And with each passing moment, she knew that their journey—together—was only just beginning.

Chapter 19: Unchartered Territory

"There's a place beyond what you've known before. It's where the unknown becomes familiar, and every step taken is a discovery of yourself and the person beside you." — Unknown

The days that followed felt like a dance—fluid, effortless, and intoxicating. Emma's life, once neatly compartmentalized, had begun to merge with Jack's in ways she hadn't expected. She no longer lived just for herself. A part of her, a deeper, more vulnerable part, now lived for the shared moments, the stolen glances, the quiet exchanges between them. It was as if Jack's presence had seeped into her life, pulling her into a world that was unfamiliar, yet thrilling.

Every day with him was another layer peeled back from the walls she'd so carefully built. He was patient, never forcing her to reveal more than she was ready to, but always giving her the space to discover things about herself she hadn't known existed. She'd always been cautious, wary of letting anyone too close, but with Jack, it felt like a natural evolution.

Still, there were moments—quiet, uncertain moments—when her past would resurface, like ghosts in the shadows. Moments when she wondered if she could truly trust this connection, if it could endure the pressures of time, of life. But whenever those doubts crept in, Jack was there, offering his unwavering support, his steady confidence, reminding her that she didn't have to have all the answers. She just had to be present.

One such evening, they found themselves in a quiet corner of Sydney, a little café tucked away on a side street, a place far removed from the high-end restaurants and glittering parties they had frequented in the past. There was something about the intimacy of this setting that made Emma feel as though they were in a world of their own. The dim lighting, the low hum of conversation, the clink of coffee cups—it all seemed to fade away when she looked at Jack. It was just the two of them, seated across from each other, the soft glow of the café light catching the angles of his face, making him look almost otherworldly.

"You've been quiet tonight," Jack said, his voice calm as he watched her over the rim of his glass. He'd become attuned to her moods, the slightest shifts in her energy. His eyes were always on her, but not in an overbearing way—rather, in a way that made her feel seen, understood.

Emma lifted her gaze to meet his, her fingers tracing the rim of her own glass absently. "I'm just thinking," she replied, her voice soft but steady. "There's a lot happening right now. I'm... still getting used to this."

Jack didn't push her, but his smile was warm and understanding. "Used to what?"

She paused, searching for the right words. There was so much she wanted to say, but the truth was, she wasn't sure how to express it all.

There was the undeniable pull she felt toward him, the overwhelming desire that had consumed her in ways she hadn't known were possible. But there was also fear—fear of losing herself in this, fear of the intensity of what they shared.

"I'm not used to feeling this much," she admitted, her voice barely above a whisper. "To having someone like you in my life, someone who…" She trailed off, unsure how to finish the sentence.

"Someone who what?" Jack asked, leaning forward slightly, his eyes full of curiosity but also something deeper—something almost protective.

"Someone who makes me feel like I'm… everything," she finished, her voice faltering as she spoke the words aloud. "Like I matter."

The vulnerability in her voice stirred something inside Jack, and he reached across the table, his fingers brushing hers in a touch that was both gentle and firm. "You do matter, Emma. More than you know."

His words sent a warmth spreading through her chest, and she found herself blinking back the unexpected tears that had suddenly welled up in her eyes. She hadn't realised how much she needed to hear that, how much she had longed for someone to tell her she mattered—truly mattered.

"You make me feel like I can be myself," she whispered, her voice trembling slightly. "Like I don't have to hide."

Jack's smile deepened, and he squeezed her hand gently, his thumb brushing over her skin in slow, comforting strokes. "That's because you can be yourself with me. Always."

The words, so simple yet profound, seemed to melt away the last remnants of Emma's doubt. She had spent so long building walls around her heart, shielding herself from the possibility of being hurt, of losing herself. But with Jack, she felt something different. She felt safe. She felt seen. She felt… loved.

As they finished their dinner and stepped out into the cool Sydney evening, the air thick with the promise of something more, Jack led Emma toward the harbour. The skyline gleamed in the distance, the city alive with lights and movement. Yet, in that moment, it felt as if the world had slowed down, just for them. The noise, the rush, all of it faded as they walked side by side, their fingers entwined, the quiet comfort of each other's presence grounding them.

Jack stopped near the water's edge, the distant sound of waves lapping against the shore filling the air. He turned to face her, his expression serious now, his eyes dark with an intensity she couldn't ignore.

"Emma," he said, his voice low and commanding. "There's something I need to ask you."

She looked up at him, her heart suddenly racing as she realised the shift in his energy. What was this? Was this the moment? The one she'd been subconsciously waiting for?

"What is it?" she asked, her voice barely above a whisper, her pulse quickening.

Jack took a step closer to her, his body now mere inches from hers, the space between them charged with tension. He cupped her face with his hands, his touch tender, almost reverent. "I want to take this further, Emma. I want to push beyond the boundaries we've set, to explore new territories with you. I want to take you places we've never been before—physically, emotionally. And I need to know if you're ready for that."

The words hung in the air, heavy with implication, and for a long moment, Emma was still, unsure how to respond. Her mind was a whirlwind, the implications of his offer stirring up both excitement and fear in equal measure.

"I don't know if I'm ready," she said honestly, her voice barely audible as the truth settled in. "But I want to be."

Jack's eyes softened, and he leaned in, his lips brushing against her forehead in a kiss that was gentle, yet full of promise. "Then let's discover it together. One step at a time."

The depth of his words left her breathless. The promise of what lay ahead was intoxicating, but the trust between them was even more powerful. She wasn't sure what they would discover in this uncharted territory, but with Jack by her side, she felt ready to explore every unknown, every unspoken desire.

And for the first time in a long while, Emma knew one thing for certain—she wasn't walking this path alone.

Chapter 20: Beneath the Surface

"*True intimacy comes not from the physical connection, but from allowing yourself to be vulnerable, raw, and completely open with someone else.*" — Unknown

The next few days were a blur of anticipation and curiosity. Emma found herself torn between the overwhelming desire to explore the new depths of her connection with Jack and the lingering fear of what that exploration might reveal. Their bond had already surpassed the boundaries of anything she had known, and now, she wasn't sure if she was ready to push further.

Jack had been patient, understanding, always giving her the space she needed, but she could feel the undercurrent of his own yearning, his own desire to delve deeper. He had spoken of taking things further—physically, emotionally—but he had not pressed her. He wanted to be sure that she was ready, that she felt safe with him.

But the more she thought about it, the more Emma realised that she didn't need to be "ready." What she needed was to let go. To trust him. To trust herself. The walls she had built around her heart had started to crumble, and with every moment that passed, she could feel herself giving more of herself to him.

One evening, Jack invited her to his penthouse again. This time, there was a sense of quiet purpose in the air. He had a way of making the simplest moments feel charged with significance. When Emma arrived, he greeted her with his usual warmth, but tonight, there was something different in his gaze—something more intense.

"I want to show you something," he said, his voice low but filled with promise. He took her hand and led her toward the balcony, where the soft sounds of the city hummed in the distance. The view from here was always breathtaking, but tonight, the city seemed almost still, as if holding its breath in anticipation.

Emma stood by his side, the cool night air brushing against her skin. She turned to him, her eyes searching his face. "What is it?"

Jack didn't answer immediately. Instead, he reached out to gently cup her cheek, his thumb brushing across her skin as if memorising the feel of her. He studied her for a long moment, as if weighing something in his mind. Finally, he spoke.

"I want you to know something about me, Emma," he began, his voice serious now. "I don't just want this... I want all of you. I want to know everything—the parts of you you've kept hidden, the fears, the desires, the things you're too afraid to say."

Emma swallowed, her heart beating faster at his words. She had always been guarded, always kept her deepest emotions and desires locked away, afraid of what would happen if someone saw too much.

"I don't know if I can give you all of that," she whispered, her voice filled with uncertainty.

Jack's smile was soft, understanding. He reached for her hand, threading his fingers through hers. "You don't have to give it all to me at once, Emma. But I want you to know that I'm here. For all of it. And when you're ready, we'll explore every part of this—together."

His words settled over her like a weight, heavy with meaning. She felt exposed, vulnerable, yet for the first time in a long while, she wasn't afraid. Jack wasn't asking for perfection. He wasn't demanding anything from her—he was simply offering a safe space for her to be herself, to let go of the past and embrace the future they could build.

For a moment, there was nothing but silence between them. The city stretched out before them, endless and full of possibility. Emma's mind raced with thoughts of what lay ahead, the uncertainty, the excitement, the promise of something deeper. She knew they had only scratched the surface, but she wasn't sure if she was ready to dive in fully. Yet, something about Jack made her feel that it would be okay—that with him, she could face whatever fears still lingered in her h eart.

Jack seemed to sense the shift in her mood. He gently tugged her toward him, his hands resting on her waist as he pulled her into his embrace. "It's okay," he murmured against her hair. "We don't have to rush. We'll take our time. But I want you to know that when you're ready, I'll be here."

The tenderness in his voice, the sincerity behind his words, stirred something deep inside Emma. She wasn't used to this kind of vulnerability, this kind of honesty. It made her feel exposed, raw, but in a way that was both liberating and terrifying. She wanted to give him all of herself, but part of her was afraid of what that would mean.

Jack pulled back slightly, just enough to look into her eyes. "You don't have to decide right now. Just know that whatever you choose, I'll be with you."

Emma nodded slowly, her heart swelling with a mixture of emotions. She didn't have all the answers, but for the first time, she wasn't afraid of the questions.

Later that night, after they had shared a quiet dinner together, Jack led her to the bedroom. There was no rush, no urgency in his movements—just a slow, deliberate connection that felt more meaningful than anything that had come before. As he undressed her, his touch was reverent, almost worshipful, as if he was savoring every inch of her skin. Each kiss, each caress, was a silent promise that he was there, that he would be patient with her as she navigated her feelings.

They moved together in a rhythm that felt both natural and electric, their bodies intertwining as if they were two pieces of a puzzle that had been waiting to be completed. The passion between them was undeniable, but it was more than just physical—it was a meeting of souls, an exploration of something deeper than either of them had known before.

Jack's hands slid over her body, mapping every curve, every soft, responsive spot that made her gasp, made her tremble. His touch was both demanding and tender, coaxing her to release the last of her inhibitions, to give herself fully to the moment. There was something powerful in the way he held her, the way he guided her movements, yet never once pushing her beyond what she was ready to give.

As their connection deepened, Emma felt herself surrendering in a way she had never done before. She had always been in control, always kept her distance, but with Jack, she felt safe enough to let go of her fears, her doubts. He was her anchor, her rock in a world that had always felt unpredictable.

When they finally came together, it wasn't a single moment—it was a symphony of moments, a collection of shared breath, shared desire, that built and crescendoed into something beyond physical pleasure.

It was an experience that left her breathless, her body trembling in the aftermath, as Jack held her close, his hand resting on her back, his lips kissing the top of her head in a gesture of quiet affection.

As they lay together, wrapped in the warmth of each other's arms, Emma realised something. This wasn't just about sex, or passion, or even love. It was about something far deeper—the kind of connection that transcends the physical and enters the realm of the spiritual. Jack had shown her that intimacy was more than just giving your body to someone. It was about giving your soul, your trust, your vulnerability.

And with him, she felt ready to explore that—fully.

Chapter 21: The Edge of New Beginning

"*We stand at the edge of the unknown, where every step we take is a leap of faith into a new world of discovery.*" — Unknown

The days seemed to blur together as Emma and Jack's relationship deepened. What had started as a tentative dance had transformed into something far more intense, a magnetic pull that neither of them seemed able—or willing—to resist. They were no longer merely exploring each other; they were uncovering new parts of themselves in the process. And as exhilarating as it was, it was also terrifying.

Jack had become her anchor, the steady force in her life, but there were moments—quiet moments—when Emma found herself questioning everything. Their connection, while undeniable, was still so new, so raw. She had always been the type to keep control, to protect her heart at all costs. But with Jack, she had begun to let go of that control, and for the first time, it felt both liberating and dangerous.

Their nights together had become something of an unspoken ritual—moments of deep connection, of physical exploration, where the world outside seemed to cease to exist. But as much as she had allowed herself to be drawn in by him, there was a growing hunger in her, a need to push past the boundaries they had set, to test just how far they could go.

One night, as the city lights glittered outside Jack's penthouse window, Emma found herself standing in front of the mirror, staring at her reflection. She was dressed in a simple silk robe, the fabric sliding over her skin like water. Her reflection seemed foreign to her—she looked different somehow. It wasn't just the way Jack made her feel; it was the way he had begun to peel back the layers of her, the way he had opened doors in her that she hadn't known existed.

She was standing on the edge, and she knew it.

A soft knock on the door broke her reverie. She turned quickly, her pulse racing, as she recognised Jack's presence on the other side. He always knew when she was lost in thought, when she was trying to sort through her emotions.

"Emma," he called softly through the door, his voice low, almost seductive. "May I come in?"

Her breath caught in her throat. She didn't have to say anything. He could feel it—the tension in the air, the charged energy that buzzed between them. The space between them had always been charged, but tonight, it felt heavier, as if something was about to shift.

"Of course," she replied, her voice soft but steady.

The door opened slowly, and Jack stepped inside, his eyes immediately locking with hers. He stood still for a moment, surveying her, as though taking in the sight of her for the first time. There was a hunger in his gaze, something primal that made her skin tingle, made her heart race.

"You look breathtaking," Jack murmured, his voice thick with desire. He stepped closer, his movements deliberate, almost predatory. "But I think it's time we take this further."

Emma felt the familiar flutter of excitement in her chest, but also a hint of apprehension. This was it—the moment they had both been edging toward. She was no longer just playing with the idea of surrendering; she was about to do it, to give herself to him in a way that went beyond anything they had shared before.

"I want you, Emma," Jack continued, his voice low and steady. "Not just in the way you think. I want all of you—the pieces of you that you've kept hidden, the ones you're afraid to share. I want to uncover every part of you, see you for everything you are. I want to see you, not just as a lover, but as a woman who is free to be her most authentic self."

His words hit her like a tidal wave, crashing over her, leaving her breathless and vulnerable. There was no room for doubt in his voice—he was speaking from a place of pure honesty, a place that made her feel both safe and exposed all at once. It wasn't just the physicality of his words; it was the emotional weight behind them. He wasn't asking her to surrender to him alone. He was asking her to surrender to herself.

Emma didn't know what to say. Her mind was racing, her heart pounding in her chest. There was a part of her that wanted to pull away, to retreat into the safety of her walls. But another part—the deeper part, the part that had grown with him, with this connection—wanted to throw herself into the unknown, to let go of the control that had defined her for so long.

Before she could respond, Jack closed the distance between them, his hands reaching for the tie of her robe. The action was slow, deliberate, each movement imbued with a sense of control that made Emma's pulse spike. He wasn't rushing her; he was simply guiding her.

As the robe fell open, revealing her bare skin beneath, Emma stood still, her breath shallow, her body tingling with anticipation. Jack's gaze dropped to her, his eyes darkening with desire, but there was something else there too—something softer, almost reverent. He took a step back, his gaze lingering on her as if committing the sight to m emory.

"Beautiful," he whispered. "You're more than I could have ever imagined."

He reached out to gently cup her face, his touch tender, his thumb brushing across her lips. Emma closed her eyes at the contact, a soft sigh escaping her. It felt as if they were standing on the precipice of something profound, something life-changing. And yet, there was no fear. Only an overwhelming sense of rightness, of inevitability.

"Jack," she breathed, her voice trembling slightly. "I don't know if I can do this..."

Jack's fingers traced the line of her jaw, his touch soothing yet filled with intent. "You don't have to do anything you're not ready for," he said softly. "I'm not asking you to be perfect. I'm just asking you to trust me. To trust yourself."

His words were a lifeline, and Emma grabbed hold of them, feeling a surge of determination rise within her. She could do this. She could step into the unknown, surrender to him, and in doing so, surrender to herself. This was not about perfection. This was about exploration. About discovering parts of herself that had long been buried beneath the surface.

Without another word, she reached for him, pulling him toward her, her lips crashing against his in a kiss that was both urgent and desperate. The world outside ceased to exist. There was only Jack. Only the two of them.

His hands roamed over her body, his touch a mixture of hunger and reverence, as though every inch of her was a treasure to be uncovered. His lips trailed down her neck, kissing and nipping at the sensitive skin there, making her gasp in response. Emma's hands slid over his chest, feeling the heat of his skin beneath her fingertips, the taut muscles that had become so familiar to her.

The air between them thickened, charged with the raw, electric tension of desire. Emma felt herself unraveling in his arms, the control she had clung to for so long slipping away. There was no holding back now—she was his, and he was hers, completely, entirely.

Jack's lips found hers again, more demanding this time, and Emma gave herself over to the kiss, to the sensation of him, to the overwhelming need to be with him, to be consumed by him. His hands slid down to her waist, pulling her closer, his body pressing against hers, the heat of him searing her skin.

The kiss deepened, more intense now, more urgent, as if they both knew that they were standing at the edge of something new, something thrilling and dangerous. And as they crossed that line, as they plunged into the unknown together, Emma realised that she wasn't afraid anymore.

With Jack, she had found the freedom to explore, to surrender, and to discover the parts of herself she had long kept hidden. And in that moment, she knew there was no turning back.

Chapter 22: Into the Fire

"*The things we desire the most are often the ones that scare us the most, and only when we embrace that fear can we truly discover what we are capable of.*" — Unknown

The days after their night together felt different, charged with an unspoken energy. Emma was no longer just anticipating what was next with Jack; she was caught in the current of it all. Every moment, every glance, seemed filled with potential—potential to push further, to go deeper into the unknown territory they had only just begun to explore.

Jack had always been a steady presence in her life, a man who made her feel safe yet alive, grounded yet ignited. But there was something in the way he held her now, the way he touched her—like he was uncovering every secret part of her, every hidden corner she had kept locked away. It was exhilarating, but it was also terrifying. She had always been a woman who guarded herself fiercely. But with Jack, she felt like she was constantly dancing on the edge of a cliff, waiting for the moment when she would either soar or fall.

And that terrified her.

But for every whisper of fear, there was a stronger pull toward him. His touch, his voice, his eyes—everything about him felt like an invitation, a challenge. And despite the fear, Emma knew she wanted to accept it. She didn't want to keep running from what they could be, what they were already becoming.

The air between them had shifted. No longer was it just a physical attraction, a meeting of bodies. This was deeper—more raw, more intense. Emma could feel the weight of it whenever they were together, the way their conversations lingered long into the night, the way their bodies fit together as if they had always been meant to be this way. But it wasn't just about their chemistry; it was about the emotional bond that had formed between them, a bond that had begun to transcend the physical.

Tonight, they were meeting at his penthouse again. There was a quiet tension in the air, an anticipation that hummed beneath the surface. Emma couldn't quite place it—there was something different about tonight, something that made her pulse race and her heart beat faster as she made her way up to his door.

When Jack opened it, his eyes immediately locked onto hers, as if he had been waiting for her, knowing she was on her way. He didn't smile right away; instead, his gaze was intense, searching her face as if reading her every thought.

"You're late," he murmured, his voice low, almost teasing.

"I'm not," she replied, her voice soft but steady, her pulse quickening under the weight of his gaze.

"Don't make me wait again, Emma," he said, his tone turning slightly more serious, the hint of control in his voice unmistakable.

There was a charge in the way he spoke—something that made her stomach flutter. Jack had always been in control, but tonight, there was something more deliberate in his actions, something more commanding in the way he moved. And Emma felt it. She felt the way her body responded to him, how her skin prickled with anticipation at the thought of what was to come.

Without a word, Jack stepped aside, letting her enter. The penthouse was bathed in soft light, the city skyline stretched out beyond the floor-to-ceiling windows, twinkling like a sea of stars. There was a sense of intimacy in the room, as though the rest of the world had faded away, leaving only the two of them.

Emma's eyes moved across the space, but her attention was quickly drawn back to Jack. He was standing just a few steps away, his gaze still fixed on her, his jaw clenched, his body tense with unspoken desire.

"You look incredible," he said softly, his voice hoarse.

Emma couldn't help but feel a rush of heat at his words, but instead of responding with words, she stepped forward, closing the distance between them. She could feel the magnetic pull of him, as if he were a force she couldn't escape, and the closer she got, the more her heart r aced.

When she reached him, she didn't hesitate. She stood on tiptoe, pressing her lips against his, a kiss that was gentle at first, as if both of them were feeling out the moment. But soon, the kiss deepened, the gentleness giving way to something hotter, something more urgent. Her hands slid up to his chest, feeling the heat of his skin beneath his shirt, the muscle of his body that she had come to know so well.

Jack responded in kind, his hands moving to her back, pulling her closer. He didn't speak, but his body language said everything—he was hungry for her, and Emma felt the same. There was no more hesitation, no more games. This was raw, this was real.

With a swift movement, Jack turned them both toward the couch, guiding her down onto the plush cushions. He knelt in front of her, his hands at the waistband of her dress, slowly pulling the fabric up and over her body. His eyes never left hers, a silent promise in his gaze: a promise that he was going to take her further than she had ever gone before.

Emma's breath hitched as the dress fell away, leaving her in nothing but lingerie, the silk straps and lace clinging to her skin. She watched him watch her, his eyes dark with desire, and something inside her shifted. For the first time, she didn't feel exposed. She felt powerful, empowered by the way he looked at her, by the way he desired her.

Jack's hands moved to her waist, his fingers grazing over her skin as if learning it all over again. His touch was slow, deliberate, each caress building the tension between them. Emma's body responded to him, every inch of her skin tingling under his touch.

"You're mine tonight, Emma," he said, his voice rough, almost primal.

She gasped at his words, her heart racing in her chest. There was something about his tone, about the command in his voice, that made her body ache with need. She had never wanted anyone this much, had never felt this kind of pull before. But with Jack, it was different. He didn't just desire her; he claimed her, every part of her, and she couldn't help but surrender to him.

With a firm yet gentle movement, Jack guided her to lie back on the couch. He positioned himself over her, his body pressing against hers, his lips trailing down her neck, planting soft kisses along her skin, each one sending waves of heat through her body.

As his hands roamed over her, Emma's mind became a blur of sensation—his touch, his lips, his heat—it all blended into one intoxicating experience. He was taking his time with her, savoring her, exploring every inch of her body as if he had all the time in the world.

But Emma knew it wasn't just about the physicality of the moment—it was about the emotional depth between them. It was about how he made her feel safe enough to let go, to give herself over to him completely. And as his hands moved lower, as his lips found their way to her breasts, she let go. She let go of every fear, every doubt, and surrendered to the pleasure he was giving her.

Jack's hands, his mouth, his body—it all felt like an invitation to something new, something dangerous. And Emma was ready to accept i t.

The world outside seemed to disappear as they came together in a storm of heat and passion, the sound of their breathing and their movement the only thing that mattered. Every touch, every kiss, every whispered word only brought them closer to the edge, and when they finally reached it, it was like nothing Emma had ever experienced before.

It wasn't just physical release—it was emotional, spiritual, a release of everything she had been holding onto for so long. With Jack, she felt free, not just in her body but in her soul.

As they lay together in the aftermath, Emma's body still trembling, she realized something—she wasn't afraid anymore. Jack had shown her that there was more to life, more to love, more to passion than she had ever allowed herself to believe. And for the first time in a long while, she was ready to embrace it.

Chapter 23: The Weight of Desire

"Desire is the difference between wanting what you have and having what you want." — Unknown

The nights with Jack had become a fevered dream, each one more intense than the last. They were no longer merely lovers; they were partners in a dance of desire, of surrender and power, of intimacy and exploration. With each passing day, Emma felt herself falling deeper into this new world Jack had opened up to her—a world where pleasure wasn't just a physical sensation, but something much deeper, something that reached into the very soul.

Yet as much as she was swept away by their connection, there were moments of uncertainty. When Jack looked at her with those smoldering eyes, when he whispered her name as though it were a secret, she wondered if she could truly keep up with the intensity of it all. She had always been a woman who kept her emotions in check, always careful, always cautious. But with Jack, it felt like the walls she had so carefully built around herself were beginning to crumble, piece by piece.

Tonight was no different. As she stood in front of her mirror, running a hand through her hair, she felt the familiar flutter of nerves in her chest. Jack had invited her to his penthouse again, and she had no idea what he had planned this time. But something told her that tonight would be different. There was a kind of energy in the air, a tension that made her skin hum with anticipation.

She had never been one to wear anything too daring, but tonight, she chose a red dress—tight, sleek, and with a plunging neckline that accentuated the curve of her breasts. It was bold, a statement, and she knew it. She knew exactly what Jack would think when he saw her, how his eyes would darken, how his hands would begin to ache to touch her.

By the time she arrived at his penthouse, the anticipation was nearly unbearable. The city lights twinkled below, and the cool night air filtered through the open windows. Jack was already there, waiting. He was standing by the window, his back to her, his posture relaxed, but Emma could sense the tension in his shoulders, the way his body seemed to hum with barely contained energy.

When he turned to face her, his eyes immediately locked onto hers, and she felt her breath catch in her throat. The look in his eyes was pure, unadulterated desire—a look that sent shivers down her spine and heat flooding between her thighs.

"You look... stunning," he said, his voice thick with need.

"Thank you," she replied, though the words barely left her lips. She felt herself caught in the gravity of his gaze, drawn to him as though he were a magnet, pulling her in, making it impossible to look away.

Without another word, Jack crossed the room and stood before her, his hands coming to rest on her waist. He didn't pull her in for a kiss right away, instead taking his time, studying her, as if he were committing every detail of her to memory. The way her dress clung to her body, the way her hair cascaded down her back in soft waves, the way her lips parted ever so slightly in anticipation.

"Every inch of you is a temptation, Emma," he murmured, his voice low and velvety. "But I want you to know—tonight, it's not just about the physical. Tonight, I'm taking you further. I'm going to show you things you've only ever dreamed about."

Her pulse quickened, and she swallowed hard. His words sent a ripple of excitement through her, but they also awakened a deeper hunger, one that she hadn't yet fully acknowledged. She wanted this—no, she *needed* this. But was she ready to go all the way? To let go of everything she had ever known and surrender to him completely?

Before she could answer, Jack's lips were on hers, silencing the thoughts racing through her mind. His kiss was demanding, hungry, but there was an edge to it, a promise that tonight would be different. His hands slid from her waist to the small of her back, pressing her flush against him. The heat between them intensified, the feeling of his body against hers making her head spin with desire.

"Take it off," he said, his voice barely above a whisper.

Emma hesitated for a fraction of a second before she reached for the zipper at the back of her dress. With a slow, deliberate motion, she let it fall to the floor, leaving her standing before him in nothing but lace lingerie. Jack's gaze darkened as he took in the sight of her, his chest rising and falling with each breath.

"You're exquisite," he murmured, his fingers tracing the edge of her lace panties. "But I want more. I want to see you, all of you."

He didn't give her time to respond. His hands were already at her hips, sliding the lingerie down her body with a tenderness that contrasted with the intensity in his eyes. Emma's breath hitched as she stood naked before him, her skin tingling under the intensity of his gaze.

Jack stepped back for a moment, as though taking in the view, his eyes drinking her in. Then, without warning, he reached for her hand and pulled her toward the center of the room. The soft glow of the city lights outside illuminated their skin, casting shadows that danced across the floor.

"Tonight," he began, his voice thick with emotion, "I want you to let go. I want you to surrender completely to me, to this moment. You're safe with me, Emma. I'll guide you."

His words stirred something deep inside her—a longing she hadn't known existed. She wasn't just letting go of her body; she was letting go of everything—her fears, her inhibitions, her past. And in that moment, she knew this was the beginning of something even more profound.

Jack moved behind her, his hands finding the curves of her body, his lips tracing the line of her neck. His touch was electrifying, each stroke sending a jolt of pleasure through her. She felt herself melting into him, her body responding to him without hesitation.

He was slow, deliberate, taking his time to explore her as though she were a precious treasure, and Emma didn't want it any other way. Her hands roamed over his chest, feeling the hardness of his muscles beneath his shirt. But she didn't want to just touch him. She wanted to feel him, to explore him the way he was exploring her.

As if reading her thoughts, Jack slowly shed his shirt, revealing the sculpted muscles of his chest. Emma couldn't help but run her hands over his body, feeling the heat of his skin, the raw power of him. He was like fire—intense, dangerous, impossible to resist.

With a low growl, Jack spun her around to face him, his hands cupping her face as he kissed her deeply. His lips were hungry, demanding, but there was a tenderness to the way he held her, a softness that made her feel cherished, wanted.

But then, with a sudden movement, Jack pulled back, his hands sliding down her body, settling on her hips. "It's time," he said, his voice rough with desire. "Are you ready?"

Emma's heart pounded in her chest. There was no going back now. She nodded, her breath catching in her throat.

Jack smiled, a dark, satisfied grin that made her pulse race even faster. And then, he moved.

Chapter 24: Bound by Desire

"Passion is energy. Feel the power that comes from focusing on what excites you." — Oprah Winfrey

The pulse of the city outside felt like a distant hum as Emma lay in Jack's arms. The night had unfolded in ways that were both intoxicating and overwhelming. She had given herself to him in ways she had never thought possible, stepping further into uncharted territory with every kiss, every touch, every moment of surrender. Jack had promised her this would be a night of exploration, and he had kept that promise, pushing her limits in ways she hadn't known she needed.

Now, as they lay together, her body pressed against his, the aftershocks of their passion still rippling through her, she found herself caught between two worlds. One was the woman she had always been—reserved, self-controlled, careful with her emotions, and hesitant to lose herself to anyone. The other was the woman Jack was drawing out of her—the woman who craved the touch, the intensity, the thrill of exploring every inch of desire without reservation.

And it wasn't just physical. No, with Jack, the connection was deeper than that. It was emotional. It was raw. It was a tangled web of trust and lust, of vulnerability and power. She wasn't just being seduced; she was being transformed.

But even as she reveled in the passion they shared, Emma knew that there was a part of her that was afraid. Afraid of losing herself entirely to this man, to this fire that burned so brightly between them. She had been down this road before, had let someone into her heart and had paid the price for it. Jack was different, yes, but still... the fear lingered.

Her thoughts were interrupted when Jack's voice broke the silence, soft but insistent. "You're quiet," he said, his hand tracing lazy circles on her back. "What's going on in that beautiful mind of yours?"

Emma swallowed, her chest tightening. She didn't want to seem distant, but her mind had begun to race with questions, doubts she wasn't sure how to voice. She shifted slightly, her fingers brushing against his skin as she turned to face him. "I... I don't know," she admitted, her voice barely above a whisper. "I'm just... trying to process everything. This is all so new, Jack. I've never let myself go like this before. I don't know how to deal with it."

Jack's expression softened, and he brushed a strand of hair from her face. His gaze was unwavering, steady. "You don't have to deal with it alone, Emma. We're in this together, remember?"

His words should have been comforting, but instead, they left a heavy weight on her chest. Together. The idea of surrendering herself completely to someone else was terrifying. She had always been in control, always been the one to manage her emotions and her life. But with Jack, all of that was slipping away, and she didn't know if she was ready to lose herself in someone else.

"I want you, Emma. In every way. But I also want you to be sure," Jack continued, his voice low and serious. "If you're not ready, I'll wait. I'll wait as long as you need. But just know, this... us... it's real. It's not some fantasy or game to me."

The sincerity in his voice made her heart skip a beat. Jack was offering her something she had never had before—true, unwavering commitment. He wasn't pushing her for more than she could give, and that made her feel safer, even as she felt herself teetering on the edge of something vast and unknown.

"I don't know if I can ever be fully ready for this," she whispered, her voice trembling. "But... I'm here, Jack. I want this. I want you. I just... I don't know what's going to happen next."

Jack leaned in, his lips brushing against her forehead. His touch was gentle, reassuring. "That's all I need to hear," he said, his tone warm. "We'll take it slow, Emma. One step at a time."

The reassurance was enough to ease some of the tension in her chest, but the hunger she felt for him was still there, an insatiable craving that gnawed at her every time he touched her. She could feel it in the way her body responded to his—how every touch, every kiss, seemed to ignite something deeper inside of her.

Jack, sensing her restlessness, smiled knowingly. "It's okay to want more, Emma. It's okay to let go and explore. To push boundaries. To feel alive in ways you never have before."

Before she could reply, Jack's lips were on hers again, silencing her thoughts with a kiss that was slow and unhurried, but no less intense. His hands roamed over her body, caressing the soft curve of her waist, the swell of her breasts, and the gentle flare of her hips. She let herself melt into his touch, feeling her body respond to him like it was a natural re flex.

She wasn't sure how long they stayed like that—caught in a swirl of sensation, of desire and anticipation, of touching and kissing—but eventually, Jack pulled back, his eyes dark with hunger.

"Come with me," he said, his voice thick with need.

Without question, Emma followed him as he led her to the sleek, black leather sofa that dominated the center of the living room. The room was bathed in dim, golden light, casting long shadows on the floor and making the space feel intimate, almost secretive. Jack sank into the cushions and patted the space next to him, inviting her to join hi m.

Emma hesitated for just a moment, but then she moved toward him, her heart racing. She could feel the heat rising between them again, the air thick with the promise of something more. As she sank onto the sofa beside him, Jack's hands immediately went to work, his fingers trailing up her inner thigh with a light touch that sent sparks of electricity through her body.

She leaned into him, her hands roaming over his chest, feeling the steady thrum of his heart beneath his skin. There was something exhilarating about being so close to him, about the way his touch made her feel both powerful and powerless at the same time. The contrast of control and surrender was addictive, and Emma couldn't get enough of it.

"Jack," she whispered, her voice trembling. "What do you want from me?"

Jack's eyes gleamed with desire, but there was something else in them—something that hinted at a depth of emotion he wasn't quite ready to reveal. He didn't answer her question right away. Instead, he simply cupped her face in his hands, bringing her lips to his for a kiss that was gentle, tender... but filled with so much longing that it left her breathless.

When they finally pulled apart, Jack's voice was husky with need. "What I want from you, Emma, is to give yourself to me completely. No reservations. No doubts. Just trust."

It was a simple request, but one that hit Emma like a wave. Trust. She had spent so long guarding her heart, guarding her body, that the thought of surrendering it all to him felt like the most thrilling and terrifying thing she could ever do.

But in that moment, as she looked into Jack's eyes—eyes that had seen so much, yet had never wavered when it came to her—she knew she was ready.

She leaned forward, kissing him deeply, her body pressing against his. She could feel his heart racing, could sense the raw desire radiating from him. They were standing at the edge, ready to take the plunge into something neither of them could turn back from.

And as their hands began to explore, as their lips met in a frenzy of passion, Emma made her choice. She was ready to give herself to him—not just physically, but emotionally, fully and completely. There was no turning back now.

The night stretched out before them, full of promise, of new experiences, and of an intimacy that was yet to be explored. Together, they would journey into the unknown, but Emma knew one thing for sure: she was no longer the woman she had been. She was his.

Chapter 25: Reckless Surrender

"The greatest risk in life is not taking one at all." — Unknown

The city outside Jack's penthouse shimmered with life, but within these walls, the world had been stripped down to nothing but raw sensation.

Emma lay sprawled across the cool sheets, her breath still ragged, her body thrumming with the aftershocks of pleasure. The night had been a slow, exquisite torture—one that had unraveled her piece by piece, until she had nothing left to give but herself. Completely.

Jack was beside her, his hand resting on her hip, the weight of his touch grounding her even as her mind spun. He had taken her to places she hadn't dared explore before, guided her past every hesitation with a knowing smile and hands that made her body sing.

And yet, as the glow of their passion settled into the quiet hush of the early hours, Emma felt the familiar pang of uncertainty creeping back in.

Because every moment with Jack felt like stepping too close to the edge—like if she let herself fall, there would be no coming back.

She shifted slightly, trying to gather her thoughts. The sheet slipped lower on her body, and Jack's fingers, warm and possessive, traced lazy circles on her bare skin.

"Where are you right now?" he murmured, his voice deep and laced with something unreadable.

Emma swallowed. "Here," she said, but they both knew it was a lie.

Jack turned onto his side, propping himself up on one elbow. His gaze, sharp and knowing, locked onto hers.

"Liar," he said, his lips curving in amusement, but his eyes were searching hers.

Emma bit her lip. "I just... I don't know what this is."

Jack's fingers slid beneath her chin, tilting her face toward him. "It's exactly what it feels like."

She exhaled slowly. "And what does it feel like to you?"

Jack's expression darkened slightly, his thumb brushing over her lower lip. "Dangerous," he admitted.

Her stomach flipped. "Dangerous?"

Jack's hand moved to cup the back of her neck, his fingers tangling in her hair. "Because I don't want to stop."

The words sent a shiver through her.

Because she didn't want to stop either.

But that was exactly what made it so terrifying.

Jack must have seen the flicker of doubt in her eyes, because he leaned in, his lips brushing against her ear. "What are you so afraid of, Emma?"

She turned away, staring at the city lights twinkling through the floor-to-ceiling windows. "I don't know," she whispered.

But she did know.

She was afraid of how he made her feel—how she could lose herself completely in his touch, how she had never felt so seen, so consumed.

Jack exhaled a soft chuckle. "You think too much," he murmured, his lips pressing a trail down the curve of her shoulder.

Emma closed her eyes, trying to fight the pull of him, but it was useless.

He knew exactly how to unravel her.

His mouth found the sensitive spot just below her collarbone, and Emma let out a soft gasp, her body betraying her. Jack smirked against her skin.

"See?" he whispered, his voice dripping with satisfaction. "You don't have to think. Just feel."

And God, did she feel.

His hands, his mouth, the way he moved against her—it was all too much, yet somehow never enough.

Emma turned into him, tangling her fingers in his hair, pulling him closer. Jack groaned low in his throat, his body pressing her into the mattress as his lips claimed hers in a kiss that was pure, unrelenting fire.

She was lost.

Completely.

And for the first time, she didn't care.

***

Hours later...

Emma woke to the first light of dawn creeping through the curtains, casting golden streaks across the bed. Jack's arm was heavy around her waist, his body warm against hers, his breath steady.

For a moment, she let herself enjoy the weight of him, the comfort of being held.

But reality was already creeping in.

What was she doing?

This was supposed to be an escape—a thrilling, passionate affair that allowed her to forget, to feel alive.

And yet, with every touch, every whispered promise in the dark, she felt herself slipping deeper into something she couldn't control.

Jack stirred beside her, his grip tightening. "You're thinking again," he murmured, his voice thick with sleep.

Emma let out a soft laugh. "Maybe."

Jack opened his eyes, studying her for a moment before he rolled onto his back, stretching. "I don't like when you think."

Emma propped herself up on one elbow, raising a brow. "You don't like intelligent women?"

Jack smirked, reaching for her wrist and pulling her on top of him in one swift movement. She let out a surprised gasp as she found herself straddling his waist, his hands gripping her thighs.

"I love intelligent women," he said, his voice dark. "But when you think too much, you get scared. And when you get scared, you pull away."

Emma swallowed. "I don't pull away."

Jack arched a brow. "You're lying again."

She opened her mouth to protest, but before she could, his hands slid up her sides, his thumbs tracing slow, teasing circles on her skin. Her breath hitched.

Jack's eyes darkened. "And the thing is, Emma..." He pulled her down so that her lips were inches from his. "I'm not going to let you run."

Her pulse pounded. "Jack..."

He kissed her before she could say another word, stealing whatever hesitation remained.

And just like that, she was his again.

Lost in the fire.

Recklessly surrendering to the man who was quickly becoming her greatest risk.

Chapter 26: Reckless Devotion

"*Love is an irresistible desire to be irresistibly desired.*" — *Robert Frost*

The glow of Sydney's city lights flickered through the glass as Emma stood by the window, her silk robe clinging to her frame. Her body was still warm, still humming from Jack's touch. The night had been an endless cycle of surrender and hunger—each encounter stripping away another layer of restraint until nothing remained between them but raw, unfiltered need.

Jack's penthouse was cast in soft shadow, the only sound the distant hum of the city below. Behind her, Jack stirred in the bed, his presence magnetic even in sleep. She exhaled, pressing a hand to her chest as if that could calm the storm raging inside her.

What was she doing?

Jack wasn't just any man. He was dangerous. Not in the physical sense, but in the way he unraveled her so effortlessly, in the way his touch could dissolve all logic, all sense of control. She was losing herself in him, and that terrified her more than anything.

"You're over-thinking again."

His voice was husky with sleep, but still laced with that edge of control that never seemed to waver. Emma turned, meeting his gaze as he propped himself up on one elbow. His dark hair was tousled, his bare chest a canvas of strength and temptation.

She swallowed. "I just needed air."

Jack arched a brow. "You didn't need air an hour ago when you were begging for more."

Heat rushed to her cheeks. "You're impossible."

He smirked, pushing back the sheets and swinging his legs over the side of the bed. In an instant, he was before her, his fingers tilting her chin up so she had no choice but to look at him.

"Tell me what's going on in that beautiful head of yours."

Emma sighed. "I don't know, Jack. This... us. It's intense."

His thumb brushed over her lower lip, his gaze darkening. "Is that a bad thing?"

"I don't know," she admitted, her voice barely a whisper.

Jack studied her for a moment before taking her hand and leading her back to bed. He pulled her down beside him, tucking a strand of hair behind her ear as he traced the curve of her jaw with his fingertips.

"I told you from the beginning, Emma. I don't do things halfway. If you're in, you're all in."

She shivered at the finality in his words. Being with Jack wasn't a casual affair. It was a full-blown reckoning, a force that would either consume her or remake her entirely.

He leaned in, his breath fanning across her lips. "So tell me, are you in?"

Her heart pounded as she stared into the depths of his gaze. There was no turning back. No halfway measures.

"I'm in," she whispered.

A slow, wicked smile spread across his face before his lips claimed hers, sealing her fate with a kiss that left no room for regret.

The morning sun streamed through the windows, casting golden hues over the penthouse. Emma stirred beneath the sheets, the remnants of the night lingering on her skin. Jack was already awake, standing by the coffee machine, dressed in nothing but his low-slung pajama pants.

She sat up, stretching. "You're up early."

Jack glanced over his shoulder, his eyes glinting with amusement. "I have meetings. Unlike some people, I do actually have to work."

She smirked, sliding out of bed and wrapping a sheet around herself. "Some people have been very busy in other ways."

He chuckled, setting his coffee down and crossing the space between them in three strides. "That they have," he murmured, fingers slipping beneath the sheet to graze her bare hip. "And I intend to keep them very busy."

Her breath hitched. "Is that so?"

Jack's lips brushed over hers, teasing. "Absolutely."

Before she could respond, his phone buzzed on the counter. He exhaled, stepping away to check the screen. His expression hardened slightly.

Emma frowned. "Work?"

"Something like that." He typed a quick reply before turning back to her. "I need to go into the office, but I want you to stay. Don't run, Emma."

Her stomach clenched at the unspoken challenge in his words. "I won't."

Jack studied her for a moment before nodding. "Good." He pressed a lingering kiss to her lips before pulling away. "I'll see you tonight."

And just like that, he was gone.

Emma stood there, the weight of his absence settling over her.

She had given herself to Jack completely last night. But as the silence wrapped around her, a single thought echoed in her mind.

Had she just given away more than she could afford to lose?

Chapter 27: Relentless Temptation

"*There is a madness in loving you, a lack of reason that makes it feel so flawless.*" — Leo Christopher

The day passed in a blur, but Emma couldn't shake the feeling that lingered in Jack's absence. The weight of his presence was still imprinted on her skin, in the sheets, in the very air she breathed. She wasn't just entangled with Jack in passion; she was drowning in him, willingly succumbing to a force she wasn't sure she could control.

By late afternoon, she found herself pacing the length of the penthouse, her bare feet sinking into the plush carpet. It was unsettling—this unspoken agreement between them. He had told her not to run, and she had promised she wouldn't. But what exactly had she promised? To stay in his bed? In his world? To surrender to whatever he wanted, whenever he wanted?

She wrapped her arms around herself as she gazed out at the city. Sydney was alive, bustling, moving forward, but she felt suspended in time, caught in a limbo between desire and uncertainty. Was this truly what she wanted?

A knock at the door startled her out of her thoughts.

She hesitated before opening it, but when she did, a familiar figure stood there, holding a sleek black box wrapped with a crimson ribbon. A delivery man dressed in all black. Jack's touch was evident even in the details of the gift.

"Miss Carter? This is for you."

Emma accepted the box, her heart hammering against her ribs. "Who sent this?"

The man simply nodded, tipping his cap. "From Mr. Kingston. He asked me to deliver it personally."

Of course, he did.

Emma shut the door, fingers trembling as she pulled the ribbon loose. Lifting the lid, she found an exquisite red dress inside, silk and lace interwoven in a way that made it both elegant and sensual. Beneath the dress was a note, written in Jack's bold, deliberate handwriting:

Wear this tonight. I expect you at eight. No excuses.

A shiver ran through her. There was no question—Jack was a man who always got what he wanted.

Emma arrived at the restaurant precisely at eight. A private rooftop venue, candlelit and secluded, the city skyline glittering around them. Jack was already there, standing at the head of a table set for two, his presence commanding as always. Dressed in a tailored black suit, he looked like he belonged in a world of power and privilege—a world she was only beginning to understand.

His gaze traveled over her, slow and deliberate, lingering on the way the dress hugged her body. A smirk touched his lips. "You look breathtaking."

Emma swallowed. "You have a habit of making demands."

Jack took a step closer, his fingers brushing along the bare skin of her arm. "Only because I know what I want. And I always get what I want."

The air between them was charged, heavy with unsaid words and electric tension. He pulled out a chair for her, and she sat, unable to look away from him as he took his seat across from her.

Dinner was an intricate dance of conversation and flirtation, each exchange laced with unspoken promises. He poured her wine, watched her lips as she sipped, and his fingers brushed over hers when he passed her a dish. Every touch was calculated, every glance a silent command.

But beneath the sensual haze, something darker stirred.

Emma placed her glass down, watching him carefully. "You said you don't do things halfway. What exactly does that mean?"

Jack leaned back, studying her. "It means when I want something, I take it. And I don't let go."

Her breath caught. "That sounds possessive."

He smirked. "It is. But you knew that the moment you said you were in."

Her pulse quickened. "And if I change my mind?"

Jack's gaze darkened, a challenge flashing in his eyes. "Are you changing your mind?"

Emma hesitated. She was in deep, deeper than she had ever intended to be. But walking away now felt impossible. Jack had consumed her, ignited something in her she hadn't known existed. Could she truly let that go?

Instead of answering, she stood abruptly. The energy between them was too much, too overwhelming. She needed air, needed space to think. But before she could take a step, Jack was there, his hands gripping her waist, pulling her against him.

"Tell me," he murmured, his lips brushing her ear. "Are you running, Emma?"

Her breath hitched as his fingers traced the line of her spine, igniting a fire that threatened to consume her. "No."

Jack turned her to face him, his hands firm yet gentle. "Then stop overthinking."

And then his mouth was on hers, demanding, intoxicating. The restaurant, the city, everything else faded away as she melted into him, surrendering once more to the force that was Jack Kingston.

They barely made it through the door of his penthouse before clothes were being discarded, hands seeking, mouths devouring. Emma's back hit the cool surface of his grand piano, a gasp leaving her lips as Jack lifted her onto it, his fingers skimming along the exposed skin of her thighs.

"You're mine," he murmured, his voice a rough whisper against her throat.

A thrill shot through her at his words. She should have protested, should have fought against the claim he was making. But instead, she arched against him, her hands tangling in his hair, pulling him closer.

She was his.

At least for tonight.

Chapter 28: Beneath The Surface

"The deeper the love, the stronger the pull." — Unknown

The next morning, Emma woke to the golden hues of the Sydney sunrise spilling through the floor-to-ceiling windows of Jack's penthouse. The sheets were tangled around her body, the silk cool against her bare skin. Beside her, Jack lay with one arm draped lazily over his head, his breathing slow and steady. He looked peaceful, a contrast to the raw intensity he exuded when awake.

Emma turned on her side, watching him, her fingers itching to trace the contours of his chiseled features. The night before had been... explosive. More than passion, more than lust—it had been a claiming. Jack had taken her with an unrelenting hunger, leaving no doubt in her mind that she was his.

But was she really?

The question lingered as she slid out of bed, wrapping herself in one of Jack's crisp white shirts. The scent of him clung to the fabric—masculine, clean, intoxicating. As she padded toward the kitchen, she barely had time to pour herself a coffee before strong arms encircled her waist from behind, pulling her against a warm, hard body.

"You're up early," Jack murmured, his lips grazing the sensitive spot behind her ear.

Emma exhaled shakily. "Couldn't sleep."

Jack turned her to face him, eyes hooded with sleep yet burning with something else. "Second thoughts?"

Emma met his gaze, searching for an answer she wasn't sure she had. "No. But..."

His grip tightened, fingers pressing possessively into her hips. "But?"

She hesitated. Jack wasn't a man who tolerated uncertainty. He thrived on control, on absolutes. But Emma was still trying to find her footing in whatever this was between them.

"I just need to be sure we're not moving too fast," she admitted, watching for his reaction.

Jack's expression darkened, but not with anger. Instead, a slow, knowing smirk played at his lips. "Sweetheart, you've already jumped. Whether or not you realize it."

Her pulse skittered. He wasn't wrong. She was already in too deep.

Later that evening, Jack had arranged something unexpected—a private yacht cruise along Sydney Harbor. As they stood on the deck, the Opera House illuminated in the distance, the sea breeze cool against Emma's flushed skin, she couldn't deny the thrill of it all. The exclusivity, the extravagance—Jack's world was as intoxicating as the man himself.

He stood behind her, hands resting on the railing on either side of her, trapping her in his space. "Tell me what you're thinking," he murmured, lips ghosting against her temple.

Emma exhaled, gripping the cool metal railing. "That this feels… unreal."

Jack turned her to face him, his hands sliding to her waist. "Does it?"

She nodded, her breath hitching as his fingers toyed with the hem of her dress, skimming the bare skin beneath. "You have a way of making reality feel like a dream."

Jack's smirk was wicked as he backed her against the railing, caging her in completely. "And what if I told you I wanted to make you forget reality altogether?"

Her stomach flipped. "Jack—"

But his lips silenced her protest, capturing her mouth in a kiss that was slow and deliberate, designed to unravel her. His hands moved with practiced ease, fingers tracing, teasing, making her forget they were in public, making her forget everything but him.

The yacht rocked gently, the world narrowing down to Jack's touch, his mouth, the way he owned every moment between them.

"I want all of you," he whispered against her lips. "No reservations. No hesitation."

Emma swallowed hard. She was already his in ways she couldn't deny. But giving him everything? That was something else entirely.

Jack sensed her hesitation, his grip tightening. "Say it, Emma."

Her heart pounded. The words trembled on the tip of her tongue, but before she could speak, the sound of approaching footsteps shattered the moment.

A crew member cleared his throat awkwardly. "Mr. Kingston, your guests have arrived."

Emma blinked. Guests?

Jack exhaled, irritation flickering across his features before he turned to the crew member. "Show them in."

Emma frowned. "Guests?"

Jack ran a hand through his hair, his intensity momentarily shifting. "Business associates."

The shift in atmosphere was immediate. Whatever moment they'd been lost in was gone, replaced by something far more controlled. Jack's world wasn't just luxury and passion—it was power, influence, strategy. And tonight, she was getting a front-row seat.

As the guests arrived, Emma schooled her expression, slipping into the role Jack needed her to play. But beneath the façade, one thing was clear—she was in deeper than she had ever anticipated.

And there was no turning back.

Chapter 29: Into The Abyss

"There is a depth to us, a desire we barely understand, but one that calls us forward into the abyss, urging us to leap." — *Unknown*

The air in the penthouse felt different the next morning. Emma couldn't place it, but something about Jack seemed distant, even as he moved with his usual confidence. The dinner with his business associates had shifted the dynamic between them, as though a part of Jack she hadn't seen before had surfaced—one she wasn't entirely sure she wanted to know.

She pulled the sheets tighter around her body, watching as he stood near the window, his phone pressed to his ear. His expression was unreadable, his voice calm, composed, but there was an edge beneath it. Whoever he was speaking to wasn't getting the warm, charming Jack she had come to know.

"I don't care what it takes," Jack said coldly. "Make it happen."

A shiver traced down Emma's spine. This was the side of Jack Kingston that made powerful men nervous, the side that commanded, that took, that played by his own rules. And yet, it was also the side of him that drew her in, ignited something deep within her.

As he ended the call, Jack turned to her, his expression softening instantly. "Good morning, beautiful."

Emma sat up slowly. "That sounded intense."

Jack moved toward her, slipping into bed, the sheets shifting as he pulled her into his lap. "Just business."

She studied him, running her fingers along his jawline. "You always say that."

He smirked. "That's because it's always true."

Before she could press further, his lips claimed hers in a kiss that was anything but gentle. It was possessive, demanding, filled with something unspoken. Emma melted into it, her body instinctively responding to the way his hands gripped her waist, pulling her against him, erasing the space between them.

Just as the moment deepened, his phone buzzed again, breaking the spell. Jack let out a low curse, grabbing the device and silencing it. Emma arched an eyebrow. "Shouldn't you get that?"

Jack exhaled sharply, tossing the phone onto the nightstand. "Right now, all I care about is you."

And then he was on her again, his mouth hot and insistent, his hands exploring, claiming, unraveling her in a way that made her forget every question lingering in the back of her mind.

Later that evening, Emma found herself standing in front of a full-length mirror, adjusting the sleek black dress Jack had laid out for her. The fabric clung to her curves, the neckline plunging just enough to be daring. Jack had insisted on taking her out tonight, somewhere special, somewhere he promised would "show her more of his world."

As she stepped into the living area, Jack was waiting, dressed in a perfectly tailored suit, his smoldering gaze raking over her. "You're breathtaking," he murmured, closing the distance between them, his fingers ghosting over her bare shoulder.

Emma smiled. "You're not so bad yourself."

He chuckled, offering his arm. "Shall we?"

The drive through Sydney was smooth, the city lights painting a mesmerizing scene against the night sky. Emma recognized the route—they were heading toward an exclusive club Jack had mentioned before. One that wasn't just about luxury and status, but indulgence, exploration.

A thrill coursed through her. She had told Jack she wanted to understand his world, to experience more, and he was giving her exactly that.

When they arrived, a valet opened the door for her, and Jack guided her inside with a firm hand on her lower back. The club was opulent, the atmosphere electric with anticipation. Crystal chandeliers cast a golden glow over the intimate booths and private lounges. Soft music hummed in the background, blending with the low murmurs of conversation and laughter.

Jack leaned in close, his breath warm against her ear. "Nervous?"

Emma lifted her chin. "Excited."

His smirk was wicked. "Good."

He led her through the crowd, past elegantly dressed guests sipping cocktails and exchanging knowing glances. They stopped at a secluded booth, where a waiter immediately appeared with two glasses of champagne. Jack took his, handing the other to Emma before clinking their glasses together. "To exploration."

Emma took a slow sip, the bubbles dancing on her tongue. "And what exactly are we exploring tonight?"

Jack studied her for a moment, then reached for her hand, bringing it to his lips. "Desire. Boundaries. Control."

Her pulse quickened. "Whose control?"

His eyes darkened. "You'll see."

Emma swallowed hard, anticipation thrumming through her. Whatever Jack had planned, she was ready. Or at least, she hoped she was.

Chapter 30: Untamed Desires

"In the depths of surrender, we find not weakness, but strength. A kind of freedom only the brave dare to embrace." — Unknown

The night was far from over. Emma had thought, briefly, that after the yacht, after the lavish dinner, they could take a breather—maybe even return to something resembling normalcy. But as she sat in the plush, velvet-lined booth of Jack's favourite private club, she knew that was a fantasy. Jack's world didn't pause. It didn't slow. It demanded all of her, and more.

She had learned that much already.

The dim lighting in the club flickered around them, casting long shadows across the leather seats. Jazz played softly in the background, the steady hum of conversation weaving in and out of the smooth saxophone melodies. But it felt like they were in their own world, disconnected from the rest. Jack sat beside her, his presence commanding, dark eyes never leaving hers, his hand never far from her body.

"Are you ready for this?" Jack's voice was a low rumble, full of promise.

Emma swallowed, feeling the heat of his gaze on her, the slow burn of anticipation that seemed to creep into her very bones. The question wasn't about the club, though—the private event Jack had arranged tonight wasn't what she expected. It wasn't some after-party or VIP affair. It was something far more intimate.

The moment he'd asked her to join him, she'd known.

"I think so," Emma answered, her voice barely above a whisper.

Jack's lips curled into that devilish smile she had come to know so well. The one that made her heart stutter, her thoughts scatter. "Don't think, sweetheart. Just follow."

And she did.

He led her through a maze of corridors, each one more private, more exclusive, until they arrived at a heavy, oak door marked with only a subtle brass plaque. The quiet murmurs of the club behind them faded into silence as Jack knocked once, then entered without waiting for a response.

Inside, a fire burned in a hearth at the far side of the room, casting flickering light on the antique furnishings. But it wasn't the décor that caught Emma's attention—it was the people. The figures seated on the plush chairs, the ones who turned their eyes toward her with silent, knowing gazes.

Jack's guests.

At least six of them—both men and women—were lounging around the room in various stages of dress, their conversations hushed, expectant. There was no mistaking the atmosphere here—it was one of quiet power, of unspoken rules, of desires too dark to speak aloud.

For a split second, Emma hesitated. She felt like an outsider, like she had stumbled into a world she couldn't fully comprehend.

Jack seemed to sense her unease. He placed a hand on the small of her back, guiding her into the room. "Don't worry," he murmured in her ear. "You're exactly where you need to be."

She couldn't tell if it was the power in his voice or the quiet intensity in his eyes that made her feel like she had no choice but to comply. Either way, she followed.

The group shifted, and one of the women—a striking blonde with piercing blue eyes—stood up. "Ah, Jack. You made it," she said, her voice smooth, practiced. She didn't stand to greet Emma, though. Instead, her gaze flicked over her, assessing, appraising.

Emma felt a twinge of discomfort. There was something cold about this woman's smile.

"Of course," Jack replied, his voice low but with an edge of authority. He turned his attention back to Emma. "This is Ella," he said, before introducing the others in the room. The names floated in and out of Emma's consciousness, but she couldn't focus on anything but the tension that hung in the air, thick with expectation.

Ella moved towards Jack, her gaze lingering a moment too long on Emma before she leaned in, pressing a kiss to his cheek. It was a friendly gesture, but one that carried weight—a promise of something more, something that Emma didn't understand yet.

"Pleasure to meet you, Emma," Ella said, her voice almost sweet, but there was an underlying edge to it.

Emma smiled politely, trying to ignore the ripple of unease that ran through her. "You too."

Jack didn't miss the flicker of hesitation in Emma's expression. He caught her eye and raised a brow, silently questioning her.

Emma steadied herself. She was here, now. And she wouldn't let herself be intimidated.

Jack's guests were an eclectic mix, but they all seemed to share one thing in common—they were used to power, used to being in control. And yet, in their presence, Emma felt oddly stripped down, vulnerable, exposed.

As the evening wore on, the conversations continued, but they felt distant. Emma could sense the subtle undercurrent running through every word. There was more going on here than what appeared on the surface.

Jack excused himself briefly to speak with someone in the corner, and Emma was left to linger on the outskirts of the group. Ella, ever the silent observer, settled beside her, offering a glass of wine.

"Would you like some?" she asked, her eyes assessing.

Emma hesitated, but took the glass, her fingers brushing against Ella's. "Thank you."

For a moment, there was silence between them. Ella sipped her drink, but Emma could feel the weight of her gaze. It was calculated, deliberate. Emma knew what Ella was doing—she was sizing her up.

"Jack's taken quite an interest in you," Ella remarked casually, her voice soft.

Emma's heart skipped a beat. "He's... kind to me."

Ella's lips quirked in a half-smile. "Kind?" She repeated the word, as though testing its meaning. Then, with an almost imperceptible flick of her gaze toward Jack, she added, "That's one way to put it."

Emma's stomach tightened. She had no idea what Ella meant, but the implication was clear—Jack wasn't a man to be easily understood.

Ella leaned in, her voice dropping low. "Just be careful, Emma. Not all games are meant to be played."

Emma's breath caught in her throat. "What are you talking about?" she whispered, her voice barely audible.

Ella shrugged, her smile as enigmatic as ever. "Nothing. Just a friendly warning."

Before Emma could respond, Jack returned, his presence immediately filling the space around them. The conversation shifted, the dynamic changing as he commanded the room's attention.

And just like that, the uncertainty Emma had felt earlier slipped away.

Jack was back, and the night had only just begun.

Later, the crowd began to thin, but Emma's pulse hadn't slowed. As the final guests departed, Jack took her hand and led her outside into the cool night air. The city lights of Sydney stretched out before them, and Jack's grip tightened around her wrist.

His expression was unreadable, his dark eyes shadowed with something Emma couldn't name. She swallowed, a shiver of anticipation running down her spine.

Jack pulled her closer, his voice a dark whisper against her ear. "You handled yourself well."

Emma tried to steady her breath. "What was all that about?"

He didn't answer immediately. Instead, he pressed a kiss to the side of her neck, the warmth of his mouth sending a wave of desire coursing through her. "The world I live in isn't like the one you're used to. It's darker. More complicated. But that's the reality of it."

"I'm not sure I understand," she confessed, her voice trembling slightly.

Jack's hand slid down to her waist, pulling her flush against him. "You don't have to understand, sweetheart. Not yet. Just trust me."

And despite everything, despite the unease gnawing at her from the edges of her mind, Emma nodded. Because when it came to Jack, she had learned that trust was the only thing she could give.

The night stretched on, and as Jack's lips met hers again, she realized—she was already falling.

And there was no turning back now.

Chapter 31: Veil of Desire

"The heart has its reasons, which reason knows nothing of." — Blaise Pascal

The evening air was thick with the heat of unspoken promises, the city's lights casting long shadows across the balcony. Jack stood beside Emma, his eyes tracing the lines of her body, lingering on the curves that had become all too familiar in the few short weeks they'd known each other. The space between them crackled with unspent energy, a tension that had been building ever since they left the private club.

Emma could feel it too. The pull between them had evolved from desire into something deeper, something more consuming. The boundaries they had once respected were blurring, dissolving with every touch, every stolen kiss.

She turned toward him, her fingers brushing against the smooth leather of his jacket. She had always loved the way he wore his power so effortlessly, how it radiated from him, making every movement seem deliberate, every word charged with an undeniable intensity. But tonight, there was something different in the air—a rawness, a hunger that hadn't been there before.

"You've been quiet," Jack observed, his voice low and smooth, like silk brushing against her skin. He leaned in, his breath warm against her ear. "What's on your mind, Emma?"

Her heart skipped a beat. She was never one to hold back, but tonight—tonight, she wasn't sure where the line between them ended. There were moments when she felt like she was on the edge of something dangerous, something thrilling, and she didn't know if she was ready to fall over that edge.

"I..." Her words faltered, but she could feel the weight of his gaze on her, pulling the answers from her as if he could read every thought in her mind. "I want more of this," she confessed, her voice trembling with the truth of it.

Jack's lips curled into that trademark smirk, the one that always made her knees weak. "More of what?"

Her eyes locked with his, and she felt the heat rise between them, the air thick with the promise of what was to come. She stepped closer, her body almost flush against his, feeling the warmth of his skin through the fabric of their clothes. "More of you," she whispered, her breath hitching as her hand slid up to rest on his chest, feeling the steady beat of his heart beneath her fingertips.

His eyes darkened with something primal, something animalistic, and he didn't hesitate. In one swift motion, he pulled her closer, his hands gripping her waist with a possessive urgency. "You've already had a taste, sweetheart," he growled. "But there's so much more I want to give you."

Emma's pulse raced, her body aching for him in ways she couldn't ignore. The way he touched her, the way he made her feel—it was a heady mix of desire and vulnerability, power and surrender. Every kiss, every caress, every moment felt like she was losing herself to him, but it wasn't frightening. It was liberating.

Jack's lips found hers in a searing kiss, hungry and demanding. She melted into him, her hands roaming over his back, tugging him closer as if she couldn't get enough. His mouth moved from her lips to her neck, his teeth grazing the delicate skin, sending shivers of pleasure down her spine.

The world outside seemed to fade away, and all that mattered was the way he made her feel—alive, desired, consumed.

"Jack," she gasped, her hands fisting in his shirt as he moved lower, his lips tracing a path along her collarbone.

His breath was ragged against her skin as he whispered, "Tell me you want me."

Emma's breath caught in her throat. She had never been one to hide what she wanted, but this was different. This was Jack. And for all the control he exuded, for all the dominance he held over every room, she knew that with him, she would surrender completely.

"I want you," she breathed, her voice low and needy.

Jack's hands slid lower, his fingers brushing against the hem of her dress, sending a rush of warmth to her core. "I'm going to make you feel things you didn't even know you craved," he promised, his voice thick with lust.

His fingers skimmed the bare skin of her thighs, and Emma gasped as he lifted her, guiding her back toward the wall of the balcony. She didn't resist—she didn't want to. She wanted him more than she could articulate.

As he pressed her against the wall, his body melding with hers, he kissed her again, this time with a deeper urgency, his hands moving to her hair, tugging her closer, as though there was nothing between them but the need that pulsed through the air.

His lips trailed down her throat, then to the curve of her shoulder, his tongue tasting, teasing. "You're perfect, Emma," he murmured between kisses, his voice rough with desire.

Emma shuddered at his words, her body instinctively pressing against his. She wanted him. Wanted all of him. And she was ready to lose herself completely.

As if reading her mind, Jack's hands moved to her waist, lifting her higher, his lips now teasing the sensitive skin of her stomach. Her fingers threaded through his hair, urging him closer, needing him to touch her where she burned for him the most.

Jack smirked as he looked up at her, his eyes dark with desire. "Patience, sweetheart," he whispered. "I'll get you there. But not yet."

Emma whimpered, the ache inside her growing unbearable. "Please..." she begged, her voice a soft, desperate plea.

"Not yet," he repeated, his hands sliding beneath the fabric of her dress, fingers grazing her skin with slow, deliberate movements. "I want to hear you beg for me, Emma. I want to hear you tell me what you need."

Her body trembled under his touch, her breath coming in shallow gasps. She had never felt this exposed, this vulnerable—but with Jack, it didn't feel like weakness. It felt like freedom.

"I need you," she whispered, the words falling from her lips with a rawness she couldn't hide. "I need you inside me, Jack. Please."

Jack's lips curled into a dark smile, and in one swift motion, he was kissing her again, hard and hungry. His hands worked quickly, pulling at the fabric of her dress, exposing her to him, to the night, to the intensity that crackled between them.

Emma's pulse pounded in her ears, every nerve alight with the promise of what was coming. She wanted him—needed him—more than she could control. And when he finally, finally entered her, she knew there would be no turning back.

Their bodies moved together, a dance of raw passion and desire, a rhythm that felt as old as time itself. Emma lost herself in the sensation of him, of the way his body fit perfectly with hers, the way his touch ignited something deep inside her that she never knew existed.

Jack groaned against her neck, his grip tightening on her as he thrust deeper, harder, pulling her into a whirlwind of pleasure that left her breathless, gasping for more.

She couldn't hold back the cry that escaped her lips as she came, her body trembling in his arms. Jack followed soon after, his release a feral, primal sound that echoed in the quiet night.

As they stood there, wrapped in each other's arms, Emma knew that this was only the beginning. There was no turning back from the abyss they had both fallen into. And somehow, she was more than ready to embrace the fall.

Chapter 32: The Essence of True Intimacy

"True intimacy is not just physical; it's a collision of souls." — Unknown

The city lights of Sydney stretched out before them as Emma sat perched on the edge of the bed, her legs crossed beneath her. The penthouse was quiet except for the soft hum of the city below and the slow, deliberate sound of her heartbeat. She could feel the tension coiling within her, an electric pull that grew stronger with every passing second.

Jack had been elusive the last few days, his mind buried in business and meetings. But she could feel the weight of his absence even when he was present, as though his presence was always tethered to something far beyond the here and now.

Tonight, however, there would be no distractions.

Emma's fingers danced along the edge of the soft silk sheets, her thoughts swirling in a haze of desire and uncertainty. It was as if Jack had taken her to the very edge of what was known, and now she stood on the precipice, her heart both pounding in anticipation and fluttering in uncertainty.

The door clicked open, and Jack's silhouette appeared in the doorway, his tall frame filling the space with undeniable presence. His eyes met hers, dark with something deeper than hunger.

"Are you ready?" he asked, his voice low, like a promise whispered in the dark.

Her lips parted, but the words didn't come. The answer, as always, was both simple and complicated. She didn't know if she was ready—but she knew she would never be more ready than she was in this moment, here with him.

Jack moved toward her with an intensity that made her pulse race. Every step he took was deliberate, the slow, steady rhythm making the air between them crackle. He stopped in front of her, his hands brushing her cheeks with tenderness that contrasted with the fire in his eyes.

"Tell me what you want, Emma," he murmured, his voice rough as if he was barely holding on. "Because I want to give you everything."

Her breath hitched, and she fought to find the words. She had never been good at verbalizing her deepest desires, but tonight, she couldn't hide behind silence. She needed him to know.

"I want you," she whispered, her voice barely audible, "in every way."

A primal growl rumbled in his chest, and before she could say another word, he was kissing her, his lips devouring hers with the same intensity that had brought them together in the first place. His hands slid down her back, gripping her waist as he pulled her flush against him, the heat of his body searing through the fabric of her dress.

Emma's hands threaded through his hair, tugging him closer as the kiss deepened, more urgent now, more consuming. Her body responded instantly to his touch, a familiar heat pooling between her thighs as his hands explored her body with a hunger that matched her own.

"Jack," she breathed, her voice trembling. "Please."

He pulled back, just enough to look into her eyes, his gaze smoldering with desire. "Tell me what you need, Emma. I want to hear you say it."

There was no hesitation this time. She needed him. She needed the release, the rawness, the connection. "I need you to make me feel everything," she confessed, her heart pounding in her chest. "I need you to take me, to make me yours."

Jack's smile was slow, seductive, and filled with promise. He knew what she needed—he had always known. And tonight, he was going to give her everything.

His hands slid to the back of her dress, undoing the zipper with practiced ease. The fabric fell away from her shoulders, exposing her skin to the cool air of the penthouse. Emma shivered at the sensation, but it was nothing compared to the fire that was ignited inside her when Jack's hands began to roam.

He ran his fingers over her collarbone, down her arms, before pulling her into another kiss—this time slower, more deliberate, as though he was savoring every moment. Every breath. Every sound she made. His lips left a trail of heat down her throat, his tongue flickering across her skin as she let out a quiet moan.

The ache inside her was almost unbearable, and she couldn't help but press herself against him, feeling the hard outline of his body beneath his shirt. Her fingers moved down his chest, unbuttoning his shirt with trembling hands, wanting to feel his bare skin, wanting to feel all of him.

Jack's lips found her ear, and he whispered, "I'm going to make you forget everything but me."

His words sent a shockwave through her, her body quivering in anticipation. She had never wanted anything more than she wanted him right now.

Before she could respond, Jack lifted her effortlessly, his strong arms cradling her as he carried her to the bed. He laid her down gently, but the intensity in his eyes told her this was no act of tenderness—this was a man who wanted control, who wanted to own the moment. And she wanted him to.

He undid his belt, his eyes never leaving hers as he slowly removed his trousers, revealing the undeniable proof of his desire. Emma's breath caught in her throat. She had always known how much he wanted her, but seeing the way his body reacted to her was a constant reminder of just how much he craved her.

When he moved over her, his body covering hers, she gasped, her pulse hammering in her chest. His lips found hers again, and this time, he took his time, savoring the kiss, as though he wanted to imprint it on her mind forever. His hand slid down her body, caressing the curves of her hips, his fingers grazing the sensitive skin of her inner thighs.

"Are you ready for me?" he asked, his voice thick with desire.

She nodded, unable to form words, the need inside her growing by the second. "Yes. Please."

Jack smiled darkly before pressing his lips to her neck. "You're mine tonight, Emma. All mine."

And with that, he took her, his body moving with a rhythmic precision that left her breathless. His hands roamed, exploring, teasing, while his lips left marks on her skin—tangible reminders of how deeply he wanted her. Every touch, every kiss, every movement was calculated to drive her wild, to make her forget everything but him.

And as the night wore on, Emma found herself losing herself completely, her body becoming a vessel for the pleasure he gave her. She let herself go, surrendering to the rawness of it all—the passion, the hunger, the need.

Chapter 33: Crossing Lines

— *Unknown*

The days that followed were a blur of passion and complexity. Jack's presence in her life was undeniable, and yet, Emma felt herself slipping into something deeper, more intoxicating than she could have imagined. It wasn't just about the heat between them anymore, the desperate desire that flared with every stolen kiss or every touch that set her on fire. No, it was something else. Something heavier. Something far more dangerous.

Jack's world was vast, a maze of business deals, power plays, and constant movement. But when he was with her, it was as though the rest of the world disappeared. His touch made her forget herself, her thoughts spiraling into a whirlpool of need and lust. But as much as she longed for him, there was a part of her that couldn't help but question whether this was all there was—just the raw, fiery connection that left her breathless, but never fully satisfied.

It was a dangerous game they were playing, and Emma wasn't sure if she was ready to dive deeper.

It was late one night when Jack surprised her again. He had been distant over the past few days, consumed by meetings, but tonight, his attention was solely on her. They were sitting in the living room, the lights dimmed to a soft glow, a bottle of wine open between them. The atmosphere was charged, crackling with the unspoken tension that had been building for days.

Emma's fingers curled around the wine glass, her thoughts distant. She couldn't help but wonder what this all meant. What did Jack want from her? What did she want from him?

Jack's gaze was fixed on her, his eyes intense, his lips slightly curved in that knowing smirk that always made her pulse quicken. "Penny for your thoughts, Emma?"

She met his gaze, the questions swirling in her mind threatening to spill out. But she didn't know how to ask the questions without sounding insecure or weak. "I was just thinking about... everything."

Jack raised an eyebrow, leaning forward as if drawn by the seriousness in her tone. "Everything?" His voice was low, a little teasing, but there was an underlying tension in it that made her heart beat faster.

"Yeah." She sighed, setting the glass of wine down on the table. "You. Me. Us. What happens next."

Jack's smile faded slightly, his expression shifting to one of guarded interest. He took a slow breath before speaking. "Is this about what you think it is?"

Emma bit her lip, unsure how to articulate the feelings that were swirling within her. "I guess I just... I don't know. I'm not sure what we're doing here, Jack. I don't know if this is just... temporary. Or if there's something more. Something real."

The silence between them was thick, charged with the weight of her words. Jack's gaze softened, and he shifted closer to her on the couch, his fingers brushing lightly over her arm, sending shivers through her. "You think this is temporary?"

Emma nodded, her throat dry. "I don't know. I mean... what do you want from me, Jack? We've been through so much together, but we've barely talked about what this is."

Jack's lips twitched into a smile, but it was tinged with something more serious. He leaned in, his voice dropping to a whisper. "What do you want from me, Emma?"

She looked at him, her heart racing. She wanted him—of course, she did. She wanted him in every way, but she also wanted to know where this was going. She didn't want to be lost in something that could vanish the moment she thought she had a hold on it.

"I want... I want to know if this is real," she admitted, her voice barely above a whisper. "Not just the sex, not just the moments. I want to know if there's more to us than that."

Jack was quiet for a moment, and Emma held her breath, waiting for his response. The air felt thick with expectation. Finally, he spoke, his voice low and steady.

"Emma, I don't just want you physically." He paused, as if weighing his words carefully. "I want you in every way. I want all of you. But I need you to trust me. Trust what we have. We don't need to define it right now. We don't need labels."

Emma stared at him, her mind racing. She wanted to believe him, but a small part of her was still unsure. Still unsure of herself. Of them.

"What happens if I can't trust you, Jack?" she whispered.

His hand cupped her cheek, his thumb grazing her skin gently. "Then we take it slow. One step at a time. But I'm not going anywhere, Emma. I'm here. And I'm not going to hurt you."

The sincerity in his voice hit her hard. She had never heard Jack speak so openly, so vulnerably. And for the first time since they had met, Emma let herself truly believe him. She closed her eyes, leaning into his touch, letting the warmth of his words sink in.

"I don't know if I can let myself trust you completely," she whispered, her voice trembling slightly. "But I want to. I really do."

Jack's lips found hers then, gently, as though he was sealing that promise between them. The kiss was slow, tender, building with each passing second. His hands slid to her waist, pulling her closer, feeling the warmth of her body against his. The kiss deepened, slow and sensual, and Emma's heart pounded as every nerve in her body came alive.

Jack broke the kiss, his forehead resting against hers. "We don't need to rush. We've got all the time in the world."

Emma opened her eyes, her chest rising and falling with the rhythm of her breath. She could feel the heat building between them once again, the desire sparking in the air. "I'm not in a hurry, Jack. But I don't want to be left wondering either."

Jack chuckled softly, his lips brushing against her temple. "I'm not going anywhere, sweetheart. You have my word."

And with that, the night stretched out before them, full of possibility and unspoken promises. For the first time, Emma felt the veil of uncertainty lift. She wasn't just in Jack's world anymore—she was in his heart. And whatever came next, she knew it was going to be intense.

But it would also be real.

Chapter 34: Unyielding Desire

"When you stop thinking about everything that could go wrong, and let yourself fall into everything that could go right, that's when you truly live." — Unknown

It was early the next morning when Emma awoke in Jack's bed, the golden light of the Sydney sunrise creeping through the blinds. The city's hum was just beginning to stir, but inside the penthouse, it felt as though time had stood still. The world outside, with its demands and obligations, felt far away, leaving just her and Jack in this small, intimate universe.

She turned on her side, watching him sleep, his features soft in repose. She had become accustomed to the heat of his body next to hers, to the magnetic pull between them that always seemed to leave her wanting more. Yet, as much as she had allowed herself to be swept up in the current of their relationship, there was a voice in her head—small, but persistent—that whispered of the risks she was taking. Was she just another conquest to him, another woman in a long line of brief affairs? Or was this something more? Something that could last beyond the boundaries of passion and desire?

Her fingers traced the lines of his jaw, brushing softly against his skin. He stirred slightly, his lips curling into a small smile without opening his eyes. "Good morning, sweetheart."

The warmth of his voice sent a thrill down her spine. "Good morning."

Jack stretched languidly, his muscles rippling beneath his skin. He rolled toward her, pulling her close, his lips finding the soft curve of her neck. "You look beautiful when you wake up," he murmured, his voice thick with sleep.

Emma closed her eyes, savoring the feel of his warmth against her. But as she breathed him in, the questions that had been swirling in her mind the night before came rushing back. She wanted more than just the heat of their encounters. She wanted something real. But was that something she could have with Jack?

She pushed the thoughts aside for the moment, letting herself be consumed by the feeling of him, the way his body seemed to fit perfectly against hers. He kissed her deeply, and for a moment, everything else faded into the background. Their connection was undeniable, and in that moment, all she wanted was to feel it, to explore it with him.

But the lingering doubt still tugged at the edges of her mind.

Later that afternoon, after a lazy breakfast and hours of quiet conversation, Jack took her to a secluded beach just outside the city. He hadn't said much about it, only that he wanted to show her something special. The sand was soft beneath her feet as they walked along the shoreline, the sound of the waves crashing against the rocks providing a soothing backdrop to the stillness between them.

Emma felt the tension between them still simmering, the pull of desire just beneath the surface. But there was something else now, something deeper—a connection that was beginning to feel more like a thread weaving its way into her very soul. She hadn't expected it, but with each passing day, Jack had begun to mean more to her than she was willing to admit.

They stopped near the water's edge, the salty breeze ruffling their hair. Jack's hand found hers, his fingers curling around hers as though he never wanted to let go. He turned to her, his expression intense, almost unreadable.

"Do you trust me, Emma?" he asked, his voice low and filled with a seriousness that made her heart race.

She met his gaze, her breath catching in her throat. "I want to."

Jack's lips curled into a small, enigmatic smile. "Then follow me."

He led her toward a small, hidden cove, the rocky cliffs towering above them like silent sentinels. The water here was calm, the shoreline protected by the natural curve of the land. The sun glinted off the surface of the water, casting a shimmering glow around them as they approached a private boat docked just beyond the rocks.

"I thought we could take a little trip," Jack said, his voice soft but laced with that familiar tension.

Emma's heart skipped a beat. She had no idea what he was planning, but the thrill of the unknown sent a shiver down her spine. "A trip?"

Jack nodded, his fingers brushing against her cheek. "A chance to escape the world for a while. Just you and me."

Her pulse quickened, the excitement of the moment making her head spin. She nodded. "Alright."

They boarded the boat, the small motor humming to life as they pulled away from the shore. The wind tousled her hair as they drifted further out to sea, the coastline shrinking behind them. Emma felt the weight of the moment settle over her, the feeling that they were embarking on something new, something exhilarating.

As they reached the center of the bay, Jack killed the engine, leaving the boat bobbing gently in the water. The silence between them was thick with anticipation. Emma could feel his eyes on her, the intensity of his gaze as he studied her, trying to gauge what she was thinking.

"Are you ready to take the next step with me?" Jack asked, his voice quiet, almost reverent.

Emma looked out at the endless horizon, her thoughts swirling. This was it. This was the moment where everything could change. She could feel the pull of him, the desire to give in to the intensity of their connection. But there was something holding her back—something she couldn't quite place. Was she ready to dive in completely? Was she ready to surrender to Jack's world entirely?

The air around them felt thick, charged with the weight of their emotions. Slowly, she turned to him, her eyes locking with his.

"I'm ready," she whispered, the words tumbling from her lips before she could stop them.

Jack's eyes darkened with something primal, something fierce. He reached for her, pulling her close, his lips claiming hers in a kiss that was nothing short of demanding. The kiss deepened, the urgency of it taking over as he pushed her back against the edge of the boat. His hands were everywhere, tracing the curves of her body, pulling her closer, as though he couldn't get enough of her.

Emma's body responded without hesitation, her hands tangled in his hair, pulling him closer, feeling the heat of him against her. She was lost in him, in the way his mouth moved against hers, in the way his hands explored her body with a confidence that made her shiver.

The world around them seemed to disappear as they fell into each other, the only sound the rush of their breathing and the steady lapping of the water against the boat. Their clothes were discarded quickly, their bodies pressing together in a frenzy of need and desire. Jack's touch was urgent, his hands claiming her as though he had every right to. And in that moment, Emma knew—she was his. Completely. Unconditionally.

The boat rocked gently beneath them as they came together, their bodies moving in sync, lost in the intensity of the moment. Emma's senses were overwhelmed—the taste of Jack on her lips, the feel of his skin against hers, the way he filled her completely. It was a collision of passion and tenderness, a push and pull that left her breathless.

When it was over, they lay there together, tangled in the sheets of the boat's small cabin, their bodies intertwined, their breaths slowly returning to normal. Jack held her close, his hand gently tracing the curve of her back.

"You're incredible," he murmured against her skin, his voice filled with awe.

Emma smiled softly, the satisfaction of their connection settling over her. She didn't know what the future held, but for the first time, she felt as though she was exactly where she was meant to be.

Chapter 35: A Desire Unraveled

"The most profound love is born not of perfection, but of an understanding that our imperfections make us whole." — Unknown

The soft sound of the ocean waves crashing against the shore outside the penthouse balcony was drowned by the pounding of Emma's heart. She stood at the window, her fingers lightly brushing against the cold glass, her thoughts racing. Everything felt like it was moving too fast. Too much desire, too many emotions, and yet, she couldn't bring herself to walk away.

Jack had always been in control. His every move, every touch, every word had been a claim on her, and with each passing day, she found herself slipping further into his world—his touch, his power, his demands.

But there was a part of her that still fought the pull, still questioned if she was ready to lose herself completely. She had come into this with a quiet, determined independence, but now she wasn't sure where it all stood anymore. Her body had surrendered to him, her heart had followed, but her mind? Her mind was still playing catch-up.

"Emma."

The deep, low voice cut through her thoughts, and she turned around to see Jack standing in the doorway, his tall, muscular frame outlined by the dim lighting. His eyes locked onto hers with an intensity that always made her pulse race, a mixture of desire and dominance swirling within them.

She exhaled shakily, forcing a smile that didn't quite reach her eyes. "What is it?"

He walked toward her, each step purposeful, his presence overpowering in the way only he could manage. He reached her in an instant, his hand lifting to gently cup her chin, tilting her face up to meet his gaze.

"You've been quiet tonight," Jack said softly, his thumb brushing across her lips, his voice low, almost coaxing. "What's on your mind?"

Emma hesitated, unsure of how to answer. She had learned quickly that Jack was a man of few words, but when he spoke, it was always to pull something deeper from her, to reveal something she had kept hidden. She swallowed hard, feeling the weight of his touch on her skin, the burn of his gaze on hers.

"I don't know if I'm ready for all of this," she whispered, barely able to hear her own words over the rush of blood in her ears. "For us. For everything you keep offering."

A dark smirk tugged at the corner of Jack's lips, his eyes gleaming with something darker, something more powerful. "Sweetheart, I think you already know. You've been ready for me from the moment we met."

Emma's breath hitched. His words were a challenge, an invitation to fall further into the depths of him. And despite her reservations, despite the part of her that still screamed for control, she found herself wanting to dive headfirst into whatever world he was offering.

"You think so?" she asked, her voice barely above a whisper, filled with a mixture of doubt and curiosity.

"I know so." Jack's hand slid from her chin, down the curve of her neck, his fingers lightly tracing the delicate skin there. "You've been mine since that first kiss. You may try to run from it, but you're not getting away."

Emma closed her eyes at the feel of his touch, the warmth of his skin against hers sending shivers through her body. Every word, every touch, was a command, an unspoken promise of what was to come. And the truth was, she didn't want to fight it anymore.

When she opened her eyes again, Jack was inches from her, his lips a mere breath away. "Tell me what you want, Emma. Tell me how badly you need me."

The words seemed to bubble up from somewhere deep within her, escaping her lips before she could stop them. "I need you, Jack. I need you more than I've ever needed anyone."

His eyes darkened, his hands coming up to grip her waist, pulling her flush against him. She could feel the heat radiating off his body, the undeniable proof of his desire for her.

"You don't have to say it, Emma," he murmured, his lips brushing against her ear, his voice sending a jolt of desire through her. "I can feel it in the way you look at me. In the way your body reacts when I touch you."

Before she could respond, Jack's lips captured hers in a kiss that was hungry, demanding. He was everywhere—his hands, his mouth, his presence overwhelming her senses as his fingers tugged at the fabric of her dress, pulling it away from her body. The urgency in his movements only intensified the heat between them, igniting something primal that Emma couldn't deny.

She had never been kissed like this before. There was no hesitation, no restraint. Jack kissed her like he was claiming her, marking her as his. And as his hands slid lower, her body responded instinctively, her hands roaming up his chest, feeling the hard muscle beneath his shirt.

"Jack," she gasped as his lips trailed down her neck, his breath hot against her skin. "Please..."

"Please what, Emma?" he asked, his voice thick with desire, his hands continuing to explore her body with a languid precision that left her breathless. "Tell me what you need. What you want."

She closed her eyes, surrendering to the sensations flooding through her. Every part of her wanted him, wanted to be consumed by him completely. But there was still a part of her that resisted, a part that feared what giving herself fully to him would mean.

But in that moment, all she could think of was the way his body felt against hers, the way his hands were tracing every inch of her skin as if he knew exactly how to drive her wild. Her thoughts scattered, her mind only able to focus on the undeniable chemistry between them.

"I want you, Jack. I want all of you," she whispered, the words feeling like an explosion of truth.

Jack's response was immediate—his lips crashing down on hers once more, more demanding this time, as if he couldn't get enough. His hands were everywhere now, pulling her closer, guiding her down onto the plush rug that had been laid out on the floor. There was no slowing down, no waiting for the moment to be perfect. It was just the two of them—two bodies intertwined in a way that left nothing but need.

As he entered her, Emma's body arched beneath him, every nerve in her body alight with the heat of their connection. There were no more doubts, no more hesitation. She was his, and she would be for as long as he wanted her.

And in that moment, Emma couldn't have imagined being anywhere else.

Chapter 36: The Art of True Surrender

"In your arms, I find my world, and in your kiss, I lose it all." — Unknown

Emma woke to the sound of waves crashing against the shore, a gentle rhythm that had become a familiar lullaby since her arrival at Jack's private villa. The light from the early morning sun filtered through the sheer curtains, casting a soft glow over the room. For a moment, everything felt normal, almost peaceful. But as she turned her head and saw Jack lying beside her, his chest rising and falling steadily with each breath, that feeling quickly faded into something far more intense.

She couldn't deny the pull he had on her. From the moment they had met, it had been nothing short of explosive—a connection that went beyond just physical attraction. But now, as she lay beside him, her heart and mind clashing with one another, she couldn't help but wonder if she was ready to fully surrender to everything he was offering.

The night before had been unforgettable. Jack had pushed her limits in ways she had never imagined—his touch, his dominance, everything about him commanding her body and mind. But even as they had explored the depths of their desire, Emma couldn't shake the nagging question: What did it all mean? Was she just another conquest, another beautiful woman who had fallen into his world of luxury, power, and passion? Or was there more?

She shifted slightly, the cool silk of the sheets brushing against her bare skin. As if sensing her movement, Jack stirred beside her, his arm snaking around her waist to pull her closer. The heat of his body against hers sent a wave of desire crashing through her, but she forced herself to push those thoughts aside.

"Good morning," Jack's voice was husky with sleep, his breath warm against her ear. "How did you sleep?"

Emma exhaled shakily, trying to find the words. "Better. You?"

Jack kissed her gently on the side of the neck, his lips lingering there for a moment. "I sleep better when you're next to me."

The words were simple, but the way he said them made Emma's heart skip a beat. His tone was soft, almost vulnerable in a way that she hadn't expected. It was rare for him to show any kind of weakness, but in that moment, she caught a glimpse of the man beneath the powerful exterior. He was just as human as she was.

Her pulse quickened as his lips trailed down her neck, his kisses growing more urgent. The attraction between them was undeniable, an almost magnetic pull that neither of them could ignore. Jack's hands moved down her body, his touch igniting every nerve, making her forget about everything else.

"Jack," she murmured, her voice breathless. "I need to talk to you."

He paused, lifting his head to look at her with an intensity that made her pulse race. His gaze darkened as he read the seriousness in her eyes. "Talk about what?"

Emma hesitated for a moment, unsure of how to put her thoughts into words. It wasn't that she didn't want him—she did, more than she could articulate—but the way he made her feel was starting to overwhelm her. She didn't know if she could keep up with the intensity of it all, and that fear was beginning to cloud her judgment.

"I don't know if I can keep doing this," she said softly, her voice trembling slightly. "It's like I'm losing myself in you, and I don't know if I'm ready for that."

Jack didn't pull away, but the weight of her words seemed to hang in the air between them. His expression softened, and for a moment, he simply stared at her, his thumb gently caressing her arm. His grip on her waist tightened ever so slightly, as if he were reassuring her that he wasn't going anywhere.

"You're not losing yourself, Emma," Jack's voice was calm, but there was a hint of something darker beneath the surface—an edge of protectiveness that she hadn't expected. "What you're feeling is normal. You're scared. But that doesn't mean you can't trust me."

Emma closed her eyes, torn between the desire to let herself fall completely into him and the need to hold on to the independence she had worked so hard to maintain. But Jack was no ordinary man, and this was no ordinary relationship. It was consuming, intense, and impossible to ignore.

"I don't know if I can just let go, Jack," she whispered. "I've always been the one in control of my life. And now, with you, I don't feel like I have any control at all."

Jack's lips curled into a knowing smile, though there was no amusement in his eyes—only understanding. "Sweetheart," he murmured, his voice dropping to a whisper, "control is an illusion. You think you're in control, but the truth is, you've already given yourself to me. Body, heart, mind—you're already mine."

His words were like a spell, wrapping around her, making her doubt everything she had believed about herself. She had always prided herself on being strong, independent, and in charge of her own destiny. But in his arms, none of that seemed to matter. She felt weak, vulnerable, and at the mercy of the overwhelming desire he stirred in her.

Emma swallowed hard, her breath coming in shallow gasps as Jack's fingers gently traced the curve of her hip, sending a thrill of warmth through her body. Her body responded to him before her mind could even catch up. She wanted him—needed him—but the fear of losing herself in the process was almost too much to bear.

Jack's lips found hers once more, his kiss slow and deliberate, coaxing her to respond. His hands slid down her body, exploring every inch of her, as if he were memorising her, committing her to memory. Emma's body reacted to his touch, every nerve firing in response. She wanted him more than she cared to admit, but the fear still lingered in the back of her mind, holding her back.

"I want to make you forget all of your doubts, Emma," Jack whispered against her lips, his voice thick with desire. "I want to make you feel things you've never even imagined."

His words were like a trigger, sparking something deep inside her. Emma could no longer hold back. She needed him. The uncertainty, the fear—they all faded into the background as her body responded to his in the most primal way.

She arched against him, her hands roaming over his chest, feeling the hardness of his muscles beneath his skin. His hands moved lower, gripping her thighs as he pulled her closer, positioning her beneath him. There was no more hesitation, no more questioning. She needed him, and she wasn't going to fight it any longer.

Jack's lips trailed down her body, leaving a trail of fire in their wake. His hands moved with purpose, teasing her, making her ache for him in ways she had never known. His touch was electrifying, igniting her senses, making everything else fade away. There was only Jack, and there was only this moment.

And then, as his body pressed against hers, she was consumed by him entirely—mind, body, soul. There was no turning back. There was no more control. There was only the wild, unrelenting desire between them.

As they moved together, every touch, every kiss, every thrust was a promise—a promise that he would never let her go, that she would never be able to escape the depths of the passion they shared. Emma gave herself to him completely, and in return, Jack showed her a world she had never known—a world where surrender was freedom, and love was all-consuming.

Chapter 37: The Depths of Love

The days that followed were a blur of passion, intrigue, and moments of intimacy that left Emma reeling. Each new encounter with Jack felt like a step deeper into a world she was both terrified and exhilarated to be part of. He had warned her, in a way, that once she crossed the line, there would be no going back. And with every touch, every kiss, every gasp and shiver he drew from her, Emma found herself questioning whether she truly wanted to return to the life she had known.

But every time Jack's eyes found hers, filled with such intensity, she knew she couldn't escape. Not if she tried.

That evening, they had returned to his penthouse after a long day spent navigating the high-profile world Jack dominated with ease. Emma had accompanied him to several meetings, her presence by his side acting as both a shield and a statement. She couldn't deny that she enjoyed the attention—the power and control that oozed from him, making everyone around them bow to his will. There was something intoxicating about being his, about knowing she had a place in his world, a place that felt more permanent with each passing day.

As the sun dipped below the horizon, casting a fiery glow over the Sydney skyline, Emma and Jack settled on the balcony. The city lights twinkled like stars below them, but Emma's attention was completely consumed by Jack, who stood just a little too close for comfort.

He was always close—physically, emotionally—and it was starting to unsettle her in the most thrilling way. She had always prided herself on being in control, but with Jack, the lines blurred in a way that left her breathless.

"You look lost in thought," Jack's voice broke through her musings, and Emma blinked, suddenly aware of the space between them. He was looking at her with that intense gaze of his, his lips curling into a small smile, though it was hard to discern whether it was amusement or something darker behind it.

"I was just thinking," Emma replied, her voice slightly breathless. "About how much my life has changed since I met you."

Jack's smirk deepened, but there was no humor in it. "How much has it changed, exactly?"

She met his gaze, her heart pounding in her chest as she fought to keep her composure. "Everything," she whispered. "You've turned everything upside down."

Jack took a slow step toward her, his hands sliding into his pockets as he moved with a purposeful grace. The air around them thickened, charged with the electricity that always sparked between them.

"You're mine now, Emma," he said, his voice low, almost growling. "You've given yourself to me, and there's no going back."

The words hit her like a wave, crashing over her senses and stealing her breath. She swallowed hard, trying to hold on to some semblance of control. She wanted to argue, to say something that would put some distance between them, but the truth was that her body was already betraying her. The moment Jack spoke, her pulse quickened, her legs felt weak beneath her, and her heart hammered in her chest.

Emma took a step back, retreating instinctively, but Jack followed her in an instant, his movements too fast for her to keep up. In a fluid motion, he reached out and cupped her face, tilting it so that she had no choice but to look into his eyes.

"Don't run from me, Emma," he whispered, his thumb stroking her lower lip. "You're mine. And I'm not letting you go."

There was no malice in his words, no anger, but the force of them, the certainty in his voice, left Emma feeling as if she had no control at all. And part of her—most of her—wanted it that way.

Without another word, Jack lowered his head, capturing her mouth in a kiss that was deep, hungry, and possessive. His lips moved against hers with a desperation that left Emma breathless, her mind spinning with the sensations he was stirring inside her. She melted into him, her body instinctively responding to his touch. His hands slid down her sides, finding the curve of her hips, pulling her closer, pressing her against the heat of his body.

Emma's hands found their way to his chest, fingers curling into the fabric of his shirt as she struggled to keep her balance under the onslaught of desire he was unleashing in her. But Jack wasn't content with simply kissing her. His hands began to roam, sliding under the hem of her dress, fingers brushing the soft skin of her thighs. The warmth of his touch made her shiver, the tingling sensation radiating out to every part of her body.

"Jack," she gasped, her voice shaky as his lips moved down her neck, leaving a trail of fire in their wake. "We can't... people could see us."

Jack didn't stop. His mouth found her pulse point, kissing and sucking gently, sending waves of pleasure crashing through her body. "I don't care who sees us," he muttered, his voice thick with desire. "I want everyone to know you're mine."

His words sent a thrill through Emma, her body reacting against her will. The idea of being claimed so openly, so completely, stirred something deep inside her—something dark and primal.

Jack's hands slid higher, pulling her dress up until it bunched around her waist. His fingers grazed the lace of her underwear, and Emma's breath hitched. "I want you, Emma," he said, his voice low and demanding. "Right now."

Her pulse raced, her body already betraying her as her legs parted slightly to give him more access. She didn't want to give in—not like this, not so easily—but the need for him was overwhelming, overpowering.

Jack slid her underwear down, the cool air hitting her skin, and his fingers moved to tease her, brushing against her most sensitive areas, making her body tremble with anticipation. Emma let out a soft moan, her hands moving to his back, digging into the muscles there as she pulled him closer.

"I'm not stopping until I've had all of you," Jack growled, his lips trailing down her chest as his hands expertly guided her toward the edge of the balcony, the sensation of the cold railing against her back heightening her arousal.

Emma gasped as Jack's mouth found its way between her legs, his tongue teasing her in ways she hadn't known were possible. Every touch, every stroke, pushed her closer to the edge, and she knew she wouldn't be able to hold out for much longer. Jack knew exactly what she needed, and he was determined to give it to her.

His hands gripped her thighs, holding her steady as he worked his magic, his tongue swirling in slow, deliberate motions that had Emma's mind spinning. She could feel the tension building in her body, the pressure mounting as the waves of pleasure grew stronger.

"I want you to come for me," Jack murmured against her, his voice thick with lust. "Let go. Give me everything."

Emma's body tensed, and with a sharp gasp, she was undone. The orgasm hit her like a wave, crashing over her, leaving her breathless and trembling in Jack's arms. He didn't stop, though—his mouth never left her as he continued to push her higher, drawing out every last bit of pleasure.

When she finally collapsed against him, gasping for air, Jack stood, pulling her into his arms. His lips brushed against her forehead as he whispered, "You're mine, Emma. Always."

She melted into his embrace, the heat between them still palpable as she closed her eyes, the lingering traces of pleasure pulsing through her. She had given herself to him in ways she never thought possible, and despite the uncertainty that still lurked in the back of her mind, part of her knew she would never be able to walk away. Not from him. Not from this.

Chapter 38: Unspoken Promises

"In your arms, I found everything I never knew I was looking for." — Unknown

The night had fallen over Sydney, and Jack's penthouse was alive with the soft hum of city lights filtering through the grand windows. Emma stood at the large window, gazing out at the horizon. The skyline stretched before her, a canvas of lights, movement, and life—everything that was out of her reach and yet, somehow, within her grasp now.

The warmth of the apartment contrasted with the cool night air outside. She had grown accustomed to the luxury surrounding her, to the opulence and grandeur that Jack had brought into her life. But it wasn't just the physical indulgence that made this life intoxicating—it was him.

Jack.

He was a force. A man whose touch could command her body with the slightest brush of his fingers. His lips could steal her breath away, and his words had the power to make her lose herself, to forget who she was before he came into her life.

Emma had known that giving herself to him would change her, but what she didn't expect was the depth of her surrender. The more she was with him, the more she became entangled in his world, in his mind, and in his desires. He wasn't just a man; he was a universe she was slowly losing herself in, and, at times, it terrified her.

But tonight, she had no room for fear.

Jack had invited her to a private event. The type of event where the city's elite mingled—rubbing elbows with the movers and shakers who controlled the future of Sydney. The guests were already arriving, their laughter and chatter faintly reaching Emma from the living room where she stood alone, lost in her thoughts.

She heard the sound of footsteps approaching from behind, followed by a warm breath against her neck. Jack's presence was always a magnetic pull, a force she couldn't resist.

"Are you ready for tonight?" His voice was low, with that huskiness she loved, the kind that sent shivers through her body before he even touched her.

Emma turned to face him, her heart skipping a beat as she took in his appearance. Dressed in a tailored black suit, his dark hair tousled just so, and his eyes gleaming with something dangerous and exciting, Jack was the embodiment of power and allure.

"You look stunning," he murmured, reaching for her hand, lifting it to his lips for a soft kiss.

Emma's lips parted as she gazed up at him. The moment they shared, so quiet and intimate amidst the rush of preparations for the event, made her pulse quicken. It was the little moments like this—the ones where they were alone, where it was just the two of them—that left her wanting more, even when she didn't know how much more she could give.

"I'm not sure I'm ready for all these people," Emma confessed, her voice wavering slightly as the weight of the evening's expectations pressed on her.

Jack's gaze softened for just a moment, and he cupped her cheek, guiding her back toward him. "You don't need to worry about anyone else. Tonight is about us. I've made it clear you're mine, and nothing else matters."

Emma's heart skipped a beat at his words. The possessiveness in his voice was like a spark to her insides. She had never been one to enjoy being controlled—never imagined she would be drawn to someone who wanted to possess her so completely—but Jack wasn't just any-one. He was something different, something she couldn't deny, even as the edges of her old self fought to remain in control.

"Jack, I..." She didn't know how to finish the sentence. Her thoughts scattered every time he was near. His presence, his touch, his words—they all had the same effect. They unraveled her, made her forget the world outside and focus only on him.

Jack didn't wait for her to finish. Instead, he leaned in, capturing her lips in a kiss that started off gentle but quickly deepened. His hands slid to her back, pulling her close, pressing their bodies together. The heat of his touch, the warmth of his body—it was overwhelming, making Emma feel as though the floor beneath her was about to give way.

Her breath hitched as his hands roamed down her sides, grazing her hips before slipping beneath the fabric of her dress. His fingers brushed the bare skin of her thighs, sending a jolt of desire through her body. She couldn't help but gasp against his mouth.

"You are so beautiful," Jack murmured, his lips trailing down her neck as his hands continued to explore. "Every inch of you is mine."

The possessive nature of his words made Emma's head spin. She wanted to argue, to remind him that she was not just some possession, but every part of her wanted to give in. She was already his in every sense that mattered. She had given herself to him, body and soul, in ways she never thought possible.

As his lips moved lower, Emma let herself be lost in the sensations he was creating, her body responding to his every touch with a need that couldn't be ignored. Jack was a master of anticipation, always pushing her to the edge without letting her fall, and every time he did, she thought she might break.

His lips found the curve of her collarbone, and Emma couldn't suppress the soft moan that escaped her. His hands moved to the back of her dress, unzipping it slowly, teasingly, until the fabric fell away, leaving her exposed to his hungry gaze. She stood there, her body vulnerable and exposed to him, but there was no fear—only desire.

Jack's gaze flickered to hers, the raw intensity in his eyes making her heart race. "You're perfect," he said, his voice thick with desire. "I want all of you, Emma. Every part of you."

Before she could respond, Jack's lips found hers again, and this time, the kiss was anything but gentle. It was urgent, hungry, filled with a need that matched her own. His hands moved with purpose, cupping her breasts, teasing the sensitive tips through the thin fabric of her bra, making her gasp into his mouth.

Emma felt herself falling, the edges of her thoughts blurring into the intensity of the moment. She had never wanted anything—or anyone—this much. Jack was a drug, and she was hopelessly addicted.

"Jack," she whispered, pulling away for just a moment, her breath coming in short gasps. "We... we can't. We have to go downstairs."

Jack's eyes darkened, his gaze flicking to the door before returning to hers. "No. Not yet. I need you, Emma. I won't be able to focus on anything tonight until I've had you, completely."

His words sent a shiver down her spine. There was something both thrilling and terrifying about the raw need in his voice. She had known Jack was a man who took what he wanted, but hearing him say it so plainly made her weak with desire.

And in that moment, she knew there was no escaping this—no walking away from what they had. She was already too deep, too lost in the world he had pulled her into.

"I need you too," she confessed, her voice trembling as she let go of any remaining reservations. "Take me, Jack. I'm yours."

With those words, Jack pulled her into his arms, lifting her effortlessly and carrying her toward the bed, where he laid her down gently, as though she were something precious, something he would protect with his life.

He stripped away the last barriers between them, leaving her naked and exposed to him in every sense. The sight of her beneath him, vulnerable and willing, pushed him to the edge of control. He kissed her again, this time with a desperation that matched the fire between them, and then, without hesitation, he moved inside her.

The world disappeared as they moved together, their bodies in perfect sync, lost in the heat of each other. Every thrust, every touch, every kiss was an exploration, a discovery of the depths they could reach together. Emma's body responded to him like it never had to anyone else, and Jack's touch was a balm, soothing and igniting every nerve in her.

When they finally reached the peak together, the world exploded around them. Emma cried out his name, her body shaking with the force of her release, and Jack followed right after her, his own pleasure crashing through him in waves.

They lay there, tangled in each other's arms, both breathless, both lost in the moment. Jack pressed a soft kiss to her forehead, his lips lingering as he whispered, "You're mine, Emma. Forever."

Chapter 39: Shifting Currents

The sun had set, but the city was still alive with energy. Sydney's lights twinkled below, casting a romantic glow across the harbor. Emma stood at the balcony of Jack's penthouse, her hands gripping the cold metal of the railing. She was lost in thought, her gaze sweeping over the horizon as her mind churned with the events of the past few days.

She had given herself to him—completely. Not just physically, but emotionally, spiritually. Jack had become more than just a lover to her; he had become an obsession, a need that she couldn't escape. Every touch, every kiss, every shared glance left her breathless, craving more.

But the intensity of their relationship, the way it consumed her, left her with a sense of unease. Emma had always been independent, always had a life outside of her relationships. But Jack—he was all-encompassing. His world, his presence, his demands—they had become her world too. And it terrified her.

She heard footsteps behind her, the sound of them soft on the marble floors before Jack's warm, steady presence enveloped her. She didn't need to turn around to know it was him—she could feel him. The magnetic pull that always seemed to exist between them was unmistakable.

He stood just behind her, his body close enough that she could feel the heat radiating from him, yet he didn't touch her. He never did when she was lost in thought.

"Penny for your thoughts?" Jack's voice was low, filled with a mixture of curiosity and something else—something darker, more possessive.

Emma swallowed hard, not sure how to answer. How could she put into words the way he made her feel? How could she explain the chaos swirling inside her, the conflict between desire and fear, passion and uncertainty? She didn't know if there was a way to make him understand, or if he even would.

She turned to face him, her eyes locking with his, and for a moment, it was like the rest of the world disappeared. It was just the two of them, alone in this space, with nothing but the unspoken tension between t hem.

"I don't know, Jack," she said softly, her voice trembling ever so slightly. "I just... I don't know."

Jack studied her for a long moment, his gaze unwavering, before he stepped forward, closing the distance between them. His hands found her waist, pulling her close, his body a familiar warmth against hers.

"Tell me," he urged, his breath warm against her lips. "What's going on in that beautiful mind of yours?"

She closed her eyes for a brief second, gathering her thoughts. "I've never felt like this before," she whispered, her voice barely above a breath. "It's like... I'm losing myself in you. I'm not sure who I am anymore."

Jack's hands tightened slightly on her waist, but he didn't speak. He let her continue, let the words spill out, unsure if she could even stop herself.

"Every time we're together, it's like I forget everything else," she continued, her voice fragile, as if she were confessing a sin. "And I want it. God, I want it more than anything. But at the same time, I'm scared. Scared of losing myself completely."

Jack's thumb brushed against her skin, sending a shiver of desire down her spine. His gaze softened, and for the first time, she saw something in his eyes that wasn't just about control. It was understanding, something that made her feel less alone in her confusion.

"I don't want to control you, Emma," he said, his voice almost gentle, though there was an undercurrent of something darker beneath it. "I want to be everything to you, but I never want you to lose yourself. I need you to be you."

Emma looked up at him, surprised by his words. He'd always been so assertive, so possessive. Hearing him say that—hearing him speak with such care—was unexpected, but it made something inside her ease.

"Jack," she murmured, her heart aching. "I'm not sure I know how to navigate this. You... you make me feel things I never knew existed. But what if I can't keep up with what you need? What if I can't be the woman you want me to be?"

Jack's expression darkened for a moment, a flicker of something possessive flashing in his eyes, but then he pulled her closer, his hand cupping her cheek as he leaned in to press a kiss to her forehead.

"You don't have to be anything but yourself, Emma," he whispered. "That's all I've ever wanted. All I will ever want."

His words settled over her, like a warm blanket, and Emma found herself leaning into his embrace, letting him hold her. In his arms, she could forget the outside world, forget the worries that had been clouding her mind. She let herself be vulnerable, let herself be his.

"I'm not going anywhere," Jack murmured, his lips grazing the top of her head. "I'm here for the long haul. But if you need time, if you need space, you just need to tell me. I'll give you everything you need."

Emma closed her eyes, feeling the weight of his words. She didn't know what the future held, but for the first time in a long while, she felt like maybe, just maybe, she didn't need to have all the answers right away.

The warmth of his embrace was grounding, comforting. It was a safe space, a place where the world faded away, and it was just the two of them.

"I'm not going anywhere either," she whispered, her voice thick with emotion. "I need you, Jack. More than I ever thought possible."

Jack's hand slid down her back, pulling her flush against him. She could feel the heat of his body, the strength in his arms as he held her close. It was a silent promise—one that he would never let her go, no matter what.

"I've wanted you from the moment I laid eyes on you," Jack said, his voice low and intimate. "I'm not letting you slip away now."

Emma's breath hitched at the intensity of his words. She had never experienced anything like this before—this deep connection, this sense of being wanted, needed. It was overwhelming, exhilarating, and terrifying all at once.

And yet, in that moment, she knew one thing for certain: she wasn't ready to let go of him either.

As if reading her thoughts, Jack's lips found hers, soft and tentative at first, as though he was waiting for her to pull away. But Emma didn't pull away. She kissed him back, her hands threading into his hair as she deepened the kiss, her body aching with desire. The passion between them flared once again, as natural as breathing.

Jack's hands roamed over her body, caressing her skin as if he were marking her, reminding her that she was his. And she let him. She let him take her in every way, body and soul.

They moved to the bedroom, their clothes discarded haphazardly along the way. Emma's heart raced with anticipation as Jack guided her onto the bed, his gaze never leaving hers. There was no hesitation, no second-guessing this time. They had reached a point where nothing else mattered but the connection between them.

As Jack lowered himself over her, his body warm and powerful, Emma's breath caught in her throat. She was his—completely, undeniably. And in that moment, she realized she didn't need to know what the future held. All she needed was to be here, with him, in this moment.

And when Jack entered her, the world exploded into a blaze of sensation. The kiss, the touch, the heat—it was everything, and more. It was no longer just about the physical. It was about the way they fit together, the way they completed each other in a way Emma had never known before.

She met his gaze as he moved inside her, her body arching to meet his, her hands clutching at his back as though she were afraid he might slip away. But he didn't. He was always there, always present, his every movement a declaration of ownership, of love.

The pleasure between them was mind-blowing, overwhelming, but it wasn't just the physical connection that left Emma breathless. It was the intimacy, the closeness, the sense of being utterly seen, of being cherished.

As they reached the peak together, Emma cried out his name, her body trembling with the force of her release. Jack's grip on her tightened, his own release following soon after, his body collapsing over hers as they rode the wave of pleasure together.

And as they lay there, tangled in each other's arms, Emma realized that, for the first time in a long time, she was exactly where she was meant to be.

Chapter 40: Boundless Temptation

"In you, I've found my home. In your touch, I've found my salvation." — Unknown

The city lights were blurred behind the glass as Emma sat at the edge of the large kitchen island, her fingers tracing the rim of her wine glass absentmindedly. She had been in Jack's penthouse for over a week now, and yet, the reality of what they were becoming still felt surreal.

Her life had always been simple in comparison to the world Jack lived in. His world was luxury, power, and expectation. Her world had been more modest, grounded. But being with him—being in his world—felt both intoxicating and suffocating at times.

She sipped her wine, lost in thought, as she waited for Jack. It had been a day of complications, of meetings and business dealings, of moving parts she didn't understand. And it all left her feeling out of place, uncertain. But the deeper she got, the more she knew that she couldn't back out now. Jack was a force of nature, and she was swept up in it, whether she liked it or not.

Her phone buzzed, pulling her from her thoughts. It was a message from him.

Jack: "Come to the balcony. We need to talk."

A shiver of unease ran through her, but she set her glass down, her legs carrying her across the penthouse before she could think twice. As she stepped out onto the balcony, the cool night air kissed her skin, and the twinkling lights of the harbour seemed to shimmer more brightly.

Jack stood with his back to her, staring out over the city. He had changed into a black shirt and trousers, his usual commanding presence amplified by the sharp silhouette of his form against the glittering skyline.

"Jack?" Emma called softly, stepping closer. Her pulse quickened, unsure of what this conversation was going to bring.

He turned, his eyes dark with something unreadable. "Come here," he murmured, his voice low.

Emma approached him slowly, her heart racing in her chest. There was something in his expression that both intrigued and terrified her.

"I don't like keeping secrets from you, Emma," Jack began, his voice steady, but there was an edge to it. "But I think it's time you know the full extent of what you've gotten yourself into."

The air between them seemed to thicken. Her heart skipped a beat. "What do you mean?"

Jack took a step closer, his gaze intense, locking with hers. "You're not just some woman I'm casually seeing. You're mine, Emma. And I need you to understand what that means. You belong in this world. My world."

Emma swallowed hard, her throat tightening. "I know that. But I—" She was cut off by the sudden intensity of his presence. He reached for her, his hand resting on her arm, fingers curling gently.

"Don't say anything more," he murmured, his voice hushed but commanding. "Just listen."

His lips brushed across her forehead, then traced a slow path to her temple. She closed her eyes, letting herself lean into him, drawn to the warmth of his touch. But there was an unease gnawing at her gut, a question she hadn't been able to shake.

"I've been waiting for someone like you, Emma," Jack whispered, his voice dipping with an intimacy that sent a thrill through her body. "I've been waiting for the one who could keep up with me. The one who could handle the pressure. Who could handle this life."

She nodded, though she wasn't entirely sure she understood what he meant. She had thought she was handling it all. She was here, wasn't she? With him, in his world. But there was something more, something she wasn't seeing, something darker that lay beneath the surface.

Jack's grip tightened on her, his hand sliding to the back of her neck as he pulled her closer. "I'm not a man who does things halfway, Emma. And I need you to understand that. When I take something, I take it completely. And I want all of you. No holding back."

His words hit her like a wave. She'd known from the start that he wasn't a man to be trifled with, but hearing him speak so bluntly about what he expected from her... It made her feel small, vulnerable, and yet, there was an undeniable pull in his voice, a magnetism that made her body ache for him.

"I'm not sure I can give you all of me, Jack," she said softly, her words laced with hesitation. "I don't know what that even looks like."

Jack's lips curled into a dark smile. "You will. You're already mine, Emma. You're more mine than you realize. Everything you've given me, it's been enough to prove that. The question is, what will you do when you've given me all of you? When you've let me have everything?"

The words lingered in the air, thick with tension. Emma's body shivered, and for a moment, all she could do was stare at him, wondering if she was ready for this kind of total surrender.

Before she could respond, Jack's lips captured hers, silencing the thoughts in her mind. His kiss was all-consuming, deep and hungry, as if he were claiming her all over again. His hands slid down her back, pulling her into him until there was no space between them.

Emma's breath caught, and she responded instinctively, her hands threading into his hair as she pressed herself closer, feeling the heat of him radiating through the thin fabric of her dress. His touch was a steady force, a reminder of just how much control he had over every moment between them.

He broke the kiss and pulled away just slightly, his lips brushing against her ear. "You've already begun, Emma," he whispered, his voice a dark temptation. "You've already given yourself to me in ways you can't undo."

She swallowed, her pulse racing. "I don't want to undo anything," she murmured, the words escaping before she had a chance to stop them.

Jack's eyes darkened with approval, a smile curling at the corners of his lips. He leaned in again, his kiss more fervent this time, as though he couldn't wait another second to possess her again. His hands roamed, and Emma's body responded, the heat between them growing with each second.

This time, there was no hesitation. There was only need, only the raw hunger that had always existed between them, only the mutual desire that had been slowly consuming them both.

Jack's lips trailed down her neck, his fingers teasing the hem of her dress, pushing it higher, inch by inch, until it pooled around her waist. The cold night air brushed against her exposed skin, but all she could focus on was the warmth of his hands, the way he touched her with such urgency, as if he were marking her, staking his claim.

She could feel him against her, the undeniable hardness of his arousal pressing into her as he guided her back towards the bedroom. There was nothing gentle about his movements now—there was no room for doubt or uncertainty. Jack wanted her. And she wanted him just as badly.

As they reached the bed, Jack pushed her onto the soft sheets, his body hovering over hers. He didn't waste any time; his lips crashed down on hers once more, and Emma melted into him, her body already anticipating the intensity of what was to come.

There was no question anymore. She wasn't just his physically. She had already surrendered to him in every way that mattered.

Chapter 41: Unveiling Desires

"You can't control the wind, but you can adjust your sails." — Unknown

The night was heavy with anticipation as Emma stood before the grand floor-to-ceiling windows in Jack's penthouse, the city lights of Sydney twinkling below like scattered stars. Her reflection in the glass seemed distant, a woman caught between two worlds. The one she had known, and the one she was rapidly being swept into. Jack's world—his power, his sensuality, his dominance—had consumed her in ways she hadn't expected. And now, as she gazed out over the city, she wondered if she was losing herself to him, or if she had simply found a version of herself she didn't know she could be.

Behind her, the soft padding of bare feet across polished hardwood floors brought her back to the present. She didn't need to turn around to know who it was. The heat of his presence filled the room before he even spoke. Jack.

"Do you know what I want, Emma?" His voice was low, predatory, yet with that familiar undercurrent of tenderness that never failed to make her pulse quicken.

She finally turned, her eyes locking with his, searching for the truth in them. The truth she hadn't yet been able to fully decipher. There was always something more with Jack, something hidden just beneath the surface, something that called to her, that beckoned her closer.

"I'm not sure," she said softly, though she could guess. His desires were as relentless as his touch, but there was always that part of her that wanted to challenge him. To test the limits of what they could be, what they could do.

Jack took a step toward her, his gaze never leaving hers. "I want all of you, Emma. No hesitation. No boundaries."

Her breath caught in her throat. This wasn't the first time he'd said something like this. But there was something in the way he said it now—an intensity that bordered on desperation.

"You already have all of me," she whispered, her hands gripping the back of the chair behind her for support. But even as the words left her lips, she knew they didn't fully express the complexity of what she felt. She wasn't sure if she was ready to give him every part of herself—the part that would be his, completely and irrevocably—or if she was still holding something back. A piece of her heart. Her soul.

Jack was standing in front of her now, his hand sliding along her arm, the touch light at first but quickly becoming more insistent, more demanding. "Then let me have it all, Emma. Let go of whatever it is that's holding you back."

She shuddered as his hand traced the curve of her collarbone, and for a moment, she felt as though she might crumble under the weight of his gaze, under the force of the emotions swirling between them.

"I'm scared," she admitted, the words slipping from her lips before she could stop them. It wasn't something she was used to saying, especially not to him. But there it was—the truth she'd been running from. The fear that had been simmering beneath the surface for so long.

Jack's fingers stilled, his expression softening for just a moment. "What are you afraid of?"

"Losing myself," she confessed, her voice barely above a whisper. "In you. In all of this. I don't want to lose who I am."

The vulnerability in her words hung in the air like a fragile thread, and for a heartbeat, neither of them moved. Jack, always so composed, seemed to be at a loss for once. His eyes searched hers, as though looking for an answer he wasn't sure he would find.

"Emma..." His voice was rough now, almost tender, as he cupped her face in his hands. "You won't lose yourself. I won't let you. But I need you to trust me."

The warmth of his touch seemed to melt away some of the tension in her chest, but it didn't erase the knot of uncertainty that still lingered in the pit of her stomach. Trust. It was the one thing she'd given him freely from the start, and yet, here she was, questioning if it was enough.

"I trust you," she said, and it was the truth, even if she wasn't sure it would be enough to overcome the doubts swirling in her mind. "But I need more from you, Jack."

He stepped closer, their bodies nearly touching now, the heat between them palpable. His hands slid down her back, drawing her closer, pressing his lips to her forehead in a kiss that was soft, lingering.

"You already have more from me than anyone ever has, Emma," he murmured against her skin. "But I'll give you everything. Every part of me. All of it."

A shiver ran through her as his words sank in. She wanted to believe him. To let herself believe that this—whatever it was between them—could be enough. That he could be enough.

And then, without another word, Jack's lips found hers. The kiss was slow at first, almost tentative, as though testing the waters of something deeper. But as soon as Emma parted her lips, inviting him in, the kiss deepened. It became more urgent, more demanding, as their bodies pressed together, the tension between them finally snapping.

She could feel the power of his desire, the raw hunger that always simmered just beneath the surface. And for once, she allowed herself to give in to it completely. She let him guide her, let him take control, her body responding to his with a mind of its own. His hands slid beneath her clothes, the heat of his touch searing her skin as he traced the curve of her hips, the soft swell of her breast. He knew every inch of her body now, knew what made her gasp, what made her moan, what made her feel as though she were flying.

And still, he didn't stop. His touch was everywhere, exploring, teasing, coaxing her into surrender. His lips traveled down her neck, kissing the sensitive spots that made her pulse race. She arched into him, her breath coming in short gasps as he made her forget everything but the feel of his hands, his mouth, his body pressed against hers.

He lifted her effortlessly, carrying her to the bed as though she weighed nothing, his lips never leaving her skin. As he laid her down, he hovered over her, his eyes dark with desire.

"Tell me you're mine," he whispered, his voice a low growl that sent a wave of heat coursing through her.

"I'm yours," she breathed, her hands gripping the sheets as he moved over her, taking her in a way that left her breathless. "I'm yours, Jack."

And in that moment, as their bodies came together, as they explored each other in ways that only they could, Emma finally understood what it meant to be truly free. To be truly his.

Chapter 42: Unspoken Desires

"In your arms, I found everything I never knew I was looking for."
— Unknown

The morning after their passion-fueled night together, Emma woke to the sound of soft waves crashing against the shore. The penthouse was quiet, save for the occasional hum of the city outside, but inside, the air between her and Jack crackled with something more—something powerful, undeniable.

She lay there for a moment, eyes closed, relishing the feeling of his warmth beside her. Jack's body was an intoxicating presence—every inch of him a force that consumed her, yet somehow, he made her feel like she could breathe freely. And as her gaze wandered to the window, where the first light of dawn was beginning to bathe the city in hues of gold and pink, she realised she had never felt more alive.

But despite the overwhelming connection she felt to him, there was a part of her that remained cautious. A part of her that feared getting lost in him, losing herself completely.

Her thoughts were interrupted as Jack stirred beside her. His hand reached out instinctively, seeking her body in the darkness, his fingers brushing across her bare skin as though he couldn't stand the distance, even in sleep.

"Good morning," he murmured, his voice husky with the remnants of sleep, his lips brushing against her shoulder as he pressed his body closer to hers.

"Good morning," Emma replied softly, her pulse quickening at the proximity of his body.

He slid his arm around her waist, pulling her closer, his lips trailing kisses along her neck, his breath warm against her skin. "Last night was incredible," he whispered, his voice thick with desire.

Emma let out a shaky breath, her heart hammering in her chest. "It was," she agreed, unable to hide the way his touch affected her, the way it always seemed to unravel her in the best possible way.

Jack's lips found the sensitive spot behind her ear, his teeth grazing her skin lightly. "Tell me what you need, Emma," he whispered, his hand sliding lower along her body, leaving a trail of heat in its wake.

She could feel the power of his desire, the way he seemed to anticipate her every move, every breath. And though a small part of her still hesitated, she couldn't ignore the pull of him—the undeniable magnetism that drew her in every time. She wanted him. She wanted all of him.

"I need you," she breathed, turning her head to meet his lips with a searing kiss.

And that was it. The moment everything else faded. The outside world disappeared. All that existed was the two of them, caught in the grip of their desire, their bodies moving together in perfect synchrony. The kiss deepened, becoming more frantic as their need for each other grew, a slow burn that ignited into a blazing fire.

Jack rolled on top of her, his weight comforting, yet commanding. His hands slid beneath the covers, caressing her skin with expert precision, each touch driving her further into a state of mindless need. He kissed her with a hunger that mirrored her own, his tongue tracing her lips, claiming her with a possessiveness that made her heart race.

"Tell me again," Jack growled against her mouth, his voice low and filled with a tension that made her pulse race. "Tell me you're mine."

"I'm yours," she breathed, her hands clutching at his shoulders, pulling him closer. "All of me, Jack. I'm yours."

A growl of satisfaction escaped him, and in that moment, she knew he was completely hers too. There were no boundaries left between them, no walls to hold them apart. They were two souls, tangled together, exploring every inch of each other, every need and desire.

Jack's hands slid lower, caressing the curve of her hips, his fingers tracing the line of her body as if committing it to memory. "You drive me crazy, Emma," he muttered against her neck, his lips moving along her skin, tasting her.

Her hands roamed across his chest, fingers trailing down the firm muscles of his abdomen. "I don't think you're the only one," she whispered, her voice husky with desire.

A smirk tugged at the corner of his lips. "No, I'm definitely not the only one," he agreed, his hands moving to her thighs, spreading them apart as he settled between them.

Emma gasped as she felt the intensity of his touch, the way his body seemed to press into hers with a force that left her breathless. She closed her eyes for a moment, losing herself in the sensations—the heat of his skin, the way he filled her completely.

She arched into him, her body instinctively responding to his every touch. "Jack..." she whispered, her voice trembling with need.

"Shh," he murmured, kissing her lips softly. "Let go. Let me take you to the edge."

And just like that, he did. He took her to the edge of everything. The edge of her emotions, her desires, her very sense of self. And when she finally tumbled over, she didn't just fall—she soared.

They moved together in perfect harmony, their bodies entwined, their hearts racing. It was a dance they had danced before, and one they would continue to dance for as long as they were bound together. Their passion was a constant ebb and flow, never once losing its intensity, its power.

Afterward, as they lay together, their bodies still intertwined, Emma felt a sense of peace she hadn't expected. She wasn't sure if it was the aftermath of their physical connection or the feeling of being completely and utterly connected to him on every level. But it was real, and it was something she hadn't felt in years.

Jack kissed the top of her head, his fingers idly tracing circles on her back. "I want this, Emma," he murmured, his voice soft yet firm. "I want you. All of you. No more hesitation. No more fear."

Emma's heart skipped a beat at his words. The uncertainty that had lingered within her for so long began to fade away, replaced by something else—a sense of belonging, of purpose. For the first time in what felt like forever, she wasn't afraid of what this was between them. She didn't want to hold back any longer.

"I'm not scared anymore," she whispered, her voice steady with the truth of her words.

Jack's lips curled into a satisfied smile. "Good. Because I'm not letting you go."

And in that moment, as the world outside continued on without them, Emma realized she didn't want to go anywhere. She was exactly where she was meant to be—by Jack's side.

Chapter 43: Surrendering to Desire

"*Sometimes the greatest adventure is simply being in the moment with someone who truly sees you.*" — *Unknown*

The morning sun poured through the expansive windows of Jack's penthouse, casting a warm golden glow over the room. Emma awoke to find herself tangled in the soft sheets, her body pressed intimately against Jack's. His steady breathing stirred her senses as she ran her fingers across his chest, her gaze tracing the contours of his muscular frame. Despite the fierce intensity of their physical connection, she'd never felt so at peace, so safe.

The night before had been... a blur of passion, emotions running wild, bodies entwined. But beneath the heat of it all, something deeper had begun to form—a connection that went beyond desire. Emma had given herself to Jack in ways she hadn't expected, but each moment had felt right, as if she was meant to be here with him.

Jack stirred beside her, his hand reaching out instinctively to pull her closer. His lips found the back of her neck, pressing soft kisses against her skin. Emma smiled softly, allowing herself to indulge in the warmth of his embrace.

"Morning," he murmured, his voice rough with sleep, but laced with a sensual undertone that sent a jolt of desire through her.

"Morning," she replied, her voice quiet, almost shy. She wasn't sure if it was the lingering effects of their passion or the vulnerability she felt in his arms, but something inside her stirred.

His lips traced along her jawline, and Emma closed her eyes, tilting her head slightly to give him better access. "Last night..." Jack's voice trailed off as he pressed a lingering kiss to her lips. "You were incredible."

Emma's heart raced at his words, the raw sincerity in them making her feel things she hadn't allowed herself to feel in a long time. His praise meant something—something more than just the physical pleasure they'd shared.

"You're not so bad yourself," she teased, the words escaping her lips before she could stop them.

Jack chuckled low in his throat, a sound that sent warmth flooding through her. "I like it when you tease me," he murmured, his lips brushing against her earlobe.

"Maybe I like it, too," she admitted, a soft shiver running down her spine.

There was a silence between them, filled only with the sound of their breathing and the hum of the city below. Jack's fingers trailed down her arm, leaving a trail of warmth in their wake. Emma let her eyes flutter closed as the weight of his touch settled over her like a comforting blanket.

"I've been thinking," Jack began, his voice soft, yet filled with intent.

Emma turned her head to look at him, curiosity piqued. "About?"

He paused for a moment, his fingers drawing lazy circles on her skin as he met her gaze. "About us. Where we're headed. What this is, Emma."

Her pulse quickened, and her heart skipped a beat. This was the conversation she had been dreading, the one she hadn't been sure she was ready for. But there was no avoiding it—not anymore.

"I don't know what it is," she admitted, her voice barely above a whisper. "But I know I don't want it to end. I don't want to pull away."

Jack's eyes softened, and his hand cupped her cheek gently, his thumb tracing the curve of her jaw. "Neither do I," he said, his voice filled with sincerity. "I'm not looking for a casual fling, Emma. I want you. I want all of you."

The words lingered in the air between them, heavy with meaning. Emma felt her heart race as the realization hit her. This wasn't just about sex, about desire. It was about something deeper. Something far more vulnerable.

Jack continued, his voice lower now, more serious. "I know I've pushed you. But I'm not going anywhere. I want to explore everything with you. The good. The bad. All of it."

Emma's breath hitched, and for a moment, she couldn't find her voice. The weight of his confession—the intensity of it—was overwhelming. And yet, something inside her stirred, a spark of hope that maybe this could be something real.

"Jack..." she breathed, her voice shaky, uncertain.

He leaned forward, brushing his lips against her forehead in a tender kiss. "I'm not asking for answers right now," he murmured. "But

I'm not going to hide what I feel. I care about you, Emma. More than you know."

Her chest tightened at his words, a mixture of fear and longing stirring inside her. She wanted to believe him. She wanted to let herself fall, let herself trust him completely. But a small part of her still hesitated, afraid of what it meant to give herself fully to him.

"Jack..." she started again, but he silenced her with a soft kiss, a gentle press of his lips against hers.

"Don't worry about the future right now," he said softly. "We'll take it one step at a time. I'm not rushing anything. I just want you to know how I feel."

Emma exhaled shakily, her fingers weaving into his hair as she pulled him closer. "I'm here. I'm with you," she whispered, her voice thick with emotion.

Jack smiled against her lips, the smile of a man who knew he had her—body and soul.

Hours later, they found themselves walking along the beach, the salty air of the ocean tangling in their hair. The sun had begun to set, casting a vibrant orange glow over the horizon. Emma felt a sense of peace in Jack's presence, as though the world outside didn't matter when they were together.

Jack had always been a man who moved with purpose, who took charge in every situation. But today, as they walked side by side, he seemed different—more relaxed, more present. And Emma couldn't help but wonder if that was because of her.

"Tell me about your world," she said suddenly, breaking the comfortable silence between them. "What's it like to live in your world?"

Jack glanced at her, his expression thoughtful as they continued walking. "It's fast. It's intense. But it's not everything. Sometimes I get caught up in it all—the business, the power. But you... you make me want something different. Something real."

Her heart fluttered in her chest. "And what is that?"

"A life where I'm not just the man with the power," Jack said, his voice soft yet firm. "But the man who can give you everything you deserve."

Her breath caught in her throat. There was so much he wasn't saying, so much emotion that lingered in his words. But she didn't need him to say anything more. She understood.

The sound of waves crashing against the shore filled the space between them, but the silence that passed between them was one of understanding. They didn't need words anymore. Not when everything they felt was already written in the way their hands clasped together, the way their bodies fit against each other.

As the sun sank below the horizon, Emma felt a deep sense of peace. She didn't know what the future held, but for the first time, she wasn't afraid of it.

For now, she was exactly where she was supposed to be.

Chapter 44: The Edge of Transformation

"The greatest thing you'll ever learn is just to love and be loved in return." — Eden Ahbez

The evening air was cool as Emma sat by the window of Jack's penthouse, looking out at the glowing skyline of Sydney. The city had come alive with lights, the streets bustling, the hum of life outside echoing into the apartment. But inside, there was an almost eerie quiet, the stillness broken only by the soft clinking of glass as Jack poured them both another drink.

Her mind raced as she watched the world outside, the flickering lights almost hypnotic. Things had changed between her and Jack, but she wasn't sure if she was ready to accept it. The weight of the last few days was heavy, pressing down on her with a force that felt both comforting and suffocating. Jack's presence in her life had become undeniable, but the question of whether she was ready to let him fully into her heart still lingered.

Jack's voice broke through her thoughts, low and steady. "Penny for your thoughts?"

Emma turned to find him standing just behind her, a glass of amber whiskey in his hand. His expression was unreadable, but his eyes—those dark, intense eyes—held a knowing glimmer. He could always read her, even when she tried to hide her feelings.

"You know me too well," she said, offering him a half-smile as she turned toward him. "I was just thinking."

He raised an eyebrow, a slight smirk pulling at the corner of his lips. "About?"

Her gaze drifted to the city below, unwilling to meet his eyes. "About how much has changed. How much we've both changed."

Jack took a slow step forward, setting his drink on the nearby table before leaning in close. "Change isn't always a bad thing, Emma. Sometimes it's exactly what we need."

His presence loomed large, both comforting and overwhelming, and she felt the familiar pull toward him. His closeness made her heart beat faster, the intoxicating mix of desire and confusion swirling within her. She didn't know how to reconcile the emotions she felt—one minute, she was completely immersed in him, and the next, doubt crept in, making her question if this was real, or if she was just caught up in the whirlwind of it all.

Jack's hand gently cupped her chin, lifting her face until their eyes locked. "Tell me what you're really thinking," he urged softly.

Her breath hitched as his thumb traced the outline of her lips. There was something about his touch, something about the way he made her feel like she was the only person in the world that mattered. But there was also the nagging voice in her head, telling her to be careful.

"I'm just trying to figure out what this is," she confessed, her voice barely above a whisper. "What we are."

Jack's eyes softened as he took a step back, giving her space to breathe. "You don't need to have all the answers right now. We've only just begun to scratch the surface. But whatever it is, I'm in. I'm here for you. For this."

His words settled in her chest, and for a brief moment, Emma felt a flicker of hope. Maybe this wasn't just a fleeting connection. Maybe it was something more.

But as much as she wanted to believe him, there was a part of her that still couldn't shake the fear. The fear of losing herself in him, of becoming something she wasn't sure she could control.

Jack seemed to sense her hesitation, and without a word, he closed the distance between them once again. His hands slid gently to her waist, pulling her closer until their bodies were nearly touching. She could feel the heat radiating off him, the strength in his frame, and it was both exhilarating and terrifying.

"I'm not asking for your trust," Jack murmured, his lips brushing against her ear. "I'm asking for a chance. A chance to show you that we can have everything we want. Together."

His words wrapped around her like a slow, seductive promise, and despite the lingering doubt in her mind, she felt herself giving in to the pull of him. Her breath became shallow as she tilted her head back, allowing him to nuzzle her neck, his lips pressing soft kisses to her skin.

Emma's fingers found their way to the collar of his shirt, tugging him closer until their lips finally met. The kiss was slow at first, a gentle exploration, but the intensity quickly built as Jack's hands slid beneath her shirt, tracing the curve of her back with possessive tenderness.

She let out a soft sigh, her body reacting to the heat of his touch, the way he made her feel alive in ways she hadn't felt in a long time. Her hands roamed to his chest, feeling the rapid beat of his heart beneath his clothes. He was so much more than just the man she saw on the surface—the powerful businessman, the charismatic figure. Beneath it all was a man who wanted her. Who craved her.

As Jack deepened the kiss, his tongue sweeping into her mouth, Emma couldn't help but surrender to the moment. She had given herself to him before, in body, but now, with every touch, every kiss, she was slowly giving him pieces of her heart.

His hands moved to her waist, pulling her even closer as his lips trailed down her neck, leaving a hot, wet trail that made her skin tingle. Emma gasped, her hands gripping his shirt as she tilted her head back to give him more access. The sensation of his mouth against her skin, his body pressed against hers, sent shivers through her.

"I want you," Jack whispered between kisses, his voice rough with desire. "I want to make you forget everything but me."

The rawness of his words, the need in his voice, made her pulse race. She wanted to let go, to let him take her the way he wanted, but there was still a part of her that hesitated. Still a part of her that feared what might happen if she let herself fall too deeply.

But Jack wasn't giving her the option to pull away. His hands moved down her body, sliding over her hips, his fingers brushing the skin of her thighs. The contact was electric, and Emma's body responded instinctively, pressing closer to him as she felt the heat between them intensify.

Jack's lips found hers again, this time with more urgency, more desperation. The kiss deepened, his hands slipping beneath her shirt, brushing against the softness of her skin. His touch was possessive, demanding, and Emma found herself losing herself in it.

Before she knew it, her shirt was on the floor, her body bare before him. She stood there, breathless, vulnerable, and yet, in his gaze, she felt empowered. Jack's eyes swept over her, a look of admiration and desire flickering in his gaze before he closed the distance between them once more.

"You're beautiful," he murmured, his hands sliding down her body with reverence. "And you're mine."

The words sent a thrill through Emma, and she could feel herself melting beneath his touch. She wasn't sure if it was the alcohol from earlier or the intensity of the moment, but everything about Jack—his touch, his words—was making her feel like she was floating. She had no idea where this would lead, but in that moment, all she could do was give herself over to the feeling, to the desire that burned between th em.

Jack's lips found hers again, and this time, the kiss was wild, frantic, as though they were both trying to consume each other. Emma's hands roamed over his chest, her fingers brushing over his muscles, tracing the lines of his body as she pressed herself against him.

"I need you, Emma," Jack growled, his voice thick with desire. "Now."

The urgency in his voice was all the encouragement Emma needed, and without another word, they moved together, their bodies colliding in a rush of heat and passion. The world outside, the fears and doubts that had plagued her, faded into nothingness as she lost herself in him.

For the first time, she was willing to be vulnerable—to let go completely and give herself to him, body and soul.

Chapter 45: Into the Unknown

"We loved with a love that was more than love." — Edgar Allan Poe

The following morning, the soft light of dawn streamed through the curtains of Jack's penthouse, casting a warm glow over the room. Emma stirred beneath the covers, her body still aching in the most delicious way. Her head rested on Jack's chest, the steady rise and fall of his breathing a comforting rhythm. The sheets were tangled around their bodies, a mess of silk and skin, and the air was thick with the remnants of the night's passion.

As she woke, Emma felt a strange sense of calm mixed with uncertainty. It was as if the physical connection they had shared had somehow bridged the emotional distance she had kept between them. She wasn't sure if it was love or just an overwhelming desire, but whatever it was, it felt undeniable.

Jack's hand was resting on her waist, his thumb brushing gently against her skin as he began to stir. He shifted slightly, his lips grazing the top of her head in a tender kiss. "Good morning," he murmured, his voice rough with sleep.

"Good morning," Emma replied softly, her voice still thick with the remnants of their shared intimacy. She lifted her head to meet his gaze, his dark eyes full of that familiar intensity.

He didn't say anything at first. Instead, he traced the line of her jaw with his fingertips, his touch light and slow, as if savoring the sensation of her skin beneath his. There was a quiet moment between them, an unspoken understanding that felt like a promise—one they had both made without fully acknowledging it.

Jack's lips curled into a smile, but it was different this time. There was something softer in it, a trace of vulnerability that he didn't often show. "You're still here," he said, his voice barely above a whisper, as though he couldn't quite believe it himself.

Emma's heart fluttered in her chest, and for the first time in what felt like forever, she allowed herself to truly feel the weight of his words. "Of course I'm still here," she replied, her voice steady despite the rush of emotions swirling inside her. "Where else would I go?"

He chuckled softly, a sound that was both teasing and genuine. "I don't know," he said, his hand sliding up to cup her cheek. "I didn't think I'd be able to keep you."

There was a flicker of something in his eyes then—a hint of doubt, perhaps, or maybe just the realization that this wasn't just another fleeting encounter. This was something deeper, something that both of them were grappling with in their own ways.

Emma shifted in his arms, her fingers tracing the lines of his chest as she sought to ground herself in the moment. "You don't have to keep me, Jack," she said, her voice softer now, filled with honesty. "I'm here because I want to be. I'm here because I want *this*." She gestured between them, encompassing everything that had transpired—the connection, the passion, the uncertainty.

Jack's eyes darkened slightly, his hand slipping to the back of her neck as he pulled her closer. "I want you, Emma. In ways I never thought I would want anyone. But sometimes, it scares the hell out of me."

The honesty in his words sent a wave of warmth through her. She understood that fear, because she felt it too. She had spent so long building walls around her heart, convincing herself that she could control her emotions. But with Jack, everything was different. She couldn't control the way her body reacted to him, nor the way her heart seemed to beat only for him.

"I'm not afraid of you, Jack," she said, her voice steady, despite the storm of emotions swirling inside her. "But I am afraid of what happens if I let go completely. If I let myself fall too far."

He didn't reply immediately. Instead, he pressed a kiss to her forehead, his lips lingering there for a moment as if trying to convey everything he couldn't say. When he pulled back, his gaze was steady, filled with determination. "You don't have to be afraid, Emma. I'll never push you into something you're not ready for. But I want you to know, I'm in this. I'm all in."

Emma swallowed hard, the vulnerability in his words leaving her speechless. She had been afraid of losing herself in him, of becoming someone she didn't recognise, but the truth was, she was already lost. Lost in the way he made her feel, in the way he held her, in the way he consumed every part of her. And maybe that wasn't such a bad thing.

Jack's lips found hers again, this time gentle, almost reverent, as if he was trying to communicate all the things he couldn't put into words. The kiss was slow and tender, a quiet promise that spoke volumes.

Emma responded in kind, her hands sliding up to tangle in his hair as she deepened the kiss.

As they pulled apart, their breaths mingling in the small space between them, Jack's gaze never wavered. "I'm not asking you to give me everything all at once," he murmured. "But I want you to trust me. To trust that I'll never hurt you. That I'll always be here."

Emma closed her eyes, feeling the weight of his words sink in. For so long, she had kept her distance, afraid of losing herself, afraid of trusting someone again. But with Jack, something had shifted. Something had broken free inside her, and now she was beginning to see that maybe, just maybe, it was worth the risk.

She opened her eyes and met his gaze, her voice barely above a whisper. "I trust you, Jack. I trust you more than I've trusted anyone in a long time."

A slow, satisfied smile spread across his face, and for the first time, Emma saw the real Jack—vulnerable, open, and entirely hers.

"I'll never let you go," he promised, his voice thick with emotion. "No matter what."

Chapter 46: New Beginnings

"Sometimes, you have to let go of the life you planned to make room for the life that's waiting for you." —Joseph Campbell

Emma stood by the window, her reflection faintly visible in the glass as the city lights below twinkled like stars. Sydney, in its quiet splendor, stretched out before her, but her focus remained entirely on the man behind her. She could feel him there without needing to look. Jack had an undeniable presence—unmistakable, magnetic, and intoxicating.

It had been weeks since she'd let herself drift this far into the whirlpool of emotions that had taken root in her heart. She'd allowed herself to become tangled in the complexities of her relationship with Jack, knowing all too well that it was a journey without a clear end. What began as an exploration of desire had turned into something deeper, something more dangerous. The boundaries she had once set were now mere suggestions, and with every day that passed, she found herself falling further under his spell.

Her heart pounded in her chest, a slow but steady rhythm that seemed to echo the uncertainty swirling inside her. There was a storm inside of her, one that Jack had begun to stoke with every kiss, every touch, and every whispered word. But she wasn't sure if it was the kind of storm that would destroy everything in its wake—or if it would finally bring her the release she so desperately sought.

Emma turned slowly, meeting his gaze. Jack was standing near the door, his posture relaxed yet somehow poised with an unmistakable intensity. His dark eyes fixed on her, unreadable at first, but there was something in the way his lips curled, something that sent a flutter of anticipation through her body.

"You're quiet tonight," he remarked, his voice a velvet purr that seemed to wrap around her, pulling her closer to him with every syllable. It was as though the world had stilled, leaving only the two of them in this moment, in this space where nothing else mattered.

"I'm thinking," she replied, her voice sounding foreign in her own ears. The words felt heavy, like she was trying to move through water.

Jack's gaze softened for a moment, but only for a fraction of a second. Then, as if on cue, he took a step toward her, closing the gap between them with an ease that made her heart race. He didn't need to ask for her permission; he knew she was already lost to him.

The space between them seemed charged, like a live wire about to snap. Emma's breath hitched as he reached out, his fingers grazing the back of her neck, sending a ripple of warmth through her body. His touch was deliberate, slow, and as it lingered, her body responded instinctively, leaning into his touch, wanting more.

"You've been thinking about me, haven't you?" he asked, his voice low and teasing, but there was an edge to it, a challenge that made Emma's pulse quicken.

Her throat tightened as she nodded, unsure if she could trust her voice to speak the words. But in truth, she had been thinking about him nonstop—the way he made her feel, the way his presence consumed her, how every moment with him was a delicate balance between thrill and fear.

"Tell me," he continued, his thumb brushing the sensitive skin of her neck. "What have you been thinking about, Emma?"

Her eyes flickered to his lips before returning to his gaze. She wanted to speak, to put into words the turmoil that had been swirling in her heart for weeks, but the words felt too inadequate, too simple for the complexity of what she was feeling. Instead, she took a step forward, her hand reaching up to touch his chest. The warmth of his skin beneath his shirt was comforting, yet it sent a spark of heat through her fingertips.

"I've been thinking about how much I want you," she whispered, the honesty of her admission both exhilarating and terrifying. "How I can't stop wanting you."

Jack's eyes darkened, the intensity of his gaze sharpening. He didn't say anything at first, but there was a change in the air—an electric charge that seemed to hum between them, filling the space with an undeniable tension.

He leaned in slowly, his lips brushing against her ear. "And what will you do about it?" His words were soft, almost a challenge, but the heat in his breath, the weight of his presence, made it feel like something far more than just a question.

Emma's body responded before her mind could catch up. She tilted her head, offering her neck to him, an invitation that she wasn't sure she was ready to give but couldn't resist. His lips brushed against her skin, and she gasped as a shiver ran down her spine. His kiss was soft at first, teasing, as if he was gauging her reaction, waiting to see if she would pull away. But when she didn't, when she tilted her head further, giving herself over to him completely, his kiss deepened.

The sensation of his lips on her skin sent waves of desire crashing through her. It was as if he could touch every hidden part of her soul, unearthing emotions she didn't even know existed. Emma's hands found their way to his shoulders, then slid down to his chest, feeling the solid strength of his body, the heat that radiated from him. Her breath came quicker as she pressed herself closer to him, needing to feel more of him, to lose herself in the intensity of the moment.

Jack pulled back just enough to look her in the eyes, his gaze piercing, yet filled with a depth of understanding that unsettled her. He was still smiling, but it was no longer the playful, teasing smile that he so often wore. Now it was something darker, something that made her heart skip a beat.

"Tell me you want this, Emma," he said softly. "Tell me you want me as much as I want you."

The words hung in the air between them, a question, a demand, and yet an invitation all at once. Emma swallowed hard, her mind racing. She had wanted this for so long—wanted him in a way that was consuming, all-encompassing. But it wasn't just the physical attraction that pulled her in. It was the way he made her feel—alive, seen, heard. He made her feel like she was worthy of something more than just the ordinary life she had always known.

"I do," she whispered, her voice thick with emotion. "I want you. More than I've ever wanted anything."

Jack's lips curled into a smile, the satisfaction in his eyes sending a thrill through her. Without another word, he kissed her again, this time with a ferocity that stole her breath. The kiss was hungry, urgent, as if he were claiming her, marking her as his own. And Emma let him.

She let him take control, let him guide her into the depths of the desire she had tried to deny for so long.

His hands moved with purpose, unfastening the buttons of her blouse, his fingers brushing against the soft skin beneath. Each touch, each movement was deliberate, calculated, and yet filled with a rawness that made Emma's body ache with need. She couldn't remember the last time she had felt so completely consumed by another person—by Jack.

When the fabric of her blouse finally fell away, leaving her skin bare to his touch, Emma couldn't help but gasp. The cold air in the room contrasted sharply with the heat between them, making her skin break out in goosebumps. But Jack's hands were warm, his touch burning, and she leaned into him, allowing him to explore the delicate curves of her body. She could feel his heart pounding against hers, each beat syncing with the rhythm of her own. They were moving in tandem, as if they were two halves of a whole.

"God, you're so beautiful," Jack murmured, his lips brushing against her neck. The words were a soft caress, a reverent adoration that made her feel both vulnerable and powerful all at once.

Her hands found their way to the back of his shirt, tugging it off, desperate to feel more of him against her. He allowed her the freedom to explore, to touch, as if he were giving her the reins, but only because he knew she would never truly take them. She was already his, in body, mind, and soul.

The kiss deepened once more, their bodies pressing closer, moving as one. Emma could feel the heat between them, could feel the hunger that had been building for weeks. It was no longer just about the physical, though that was undeniably powerful. It was about something more—a connection that went beyond the surface, beyond the touch of skin. It was about two souls colliding, about the edge of something that neither of them had been brave enough to cross until now.

And as the night stretched on, as they lost themselves in each other, Emma knew one thing for certain: they had crossed that line. And there was no going back.

Chapter 47: The Depths of Trust

"Trust is built with consistency." — Lincoln Chafee

The morning after was always the hardest.

Emma lay beside Jack, her head resting against his chest, listening to the steady rhythm of his heartbeat. The soft morning light filtered through the blinds, casting shadows across the room. The air was still, quiet, save for the occasional whisper of wind that tugged at the curtains. The world outside was waking up, but in this moment, in this space, it felt as though time itself had suspended, holding them in a fragile cocoon of intimacy and rawness.

She hadn't expected to feel this way—this mixture of contentment and unease. With Jack, it was never simple. Every encounter left her both exhilarated and unsettled, a perfect balance of surrender and defiance. She knew she was teetering on the edge of something that could change everything, and yet, she couldn't bring herself to pull away. She wasn't sure she even wanted to.

But in the quiet of the morning, as the lingering heat of their passion slowly faded into the coolness of the sheets, Emma's mind began to wander. Where was this leading? What did it mean for them, for her?

She couldn't ignore the growing ache inside her—the fear that the more she gave to Jack, the more she might lose of herself. She had never been the type to lose control, to let someone else dictate her emotions, her desires. But with Jack, it was different. He made her feel things she hadn't known she was capable of feeling—things she wasn't sure she could contain.

Jack shifted beside her, pulling her closer. His lips brushed the top of her head, his arm wrapping around her waist as though he were trying to anchor her in place. "You're thinking too much," he murmured, his voice still thick with sleep, but there was an underlying certainty in his tone that made Emma pause.

"I don't know how not to think, Jack," she replied softly, her fingers tracing the lines of his chest as if they could anchor her to him, to this moment. "Everything is so... complicated."

He chuckled, the sound low and warm, vibrating through her. "That's just how we are, Emma. Complicated. And maybe that's why we fit so well together."

Emma lifted her head to look at him, her gaze searching his face. Jack's eyes were half-lidded, a soft smile playing at the corners of his lips. He looked so relaxed, so at ease, and for a brief moment, she envied his ability to be so unaffected by the complexities of their connection.

"But what does this mean?" she asked, her voice barely a whisper. "I mean, where are we going with this?"

The question hung in the air, unresolved, unspoken for so long. She could feel the weight of it between them, a question that neither of them had dared to ask before now.

Jack's expression shifted, becoming more serious. He lifted his hand to her cheek, his thumb grazing the curve of her jaw. "It means whatever we want it to mean, Emma. This is ours to define. Not anyone else's. Not the world's. Ours."

His words, though reassuring, only deepened the storm brewing inside her. She wanted to believe him, to embrace this uncertainty and allow herself to be carried along by it. But she couldn't deny the part of her that craved more—craved something concrete, something that felt like it could stand the test of time.

"I don't know if I can just... live in the moment forever," she admitted, her voice faltering. "I need to know if this... if *we* have a future."

Jack's hand faltered for just a second, his fingers pausing over her skin as if considering her words. He let out a slow breath, his chest rising and falling beneath her, and for a moment, Emma thought he might pull away, might retreat back into the distance that always seemed to linger just beyond the reach of their connection.

But then, as if the decision had already been made for him, Jack leaned forward, capturing her lips in a kiss that was gentle but filled with purpose. It was a kiss that spoke volumes—of reassurance, of a promise he wasn't yet ready to voice, but one that was unmistakable in its intensity.

When he finally pulled away, his eyes locked onto hers, and Emma could see the unspoken resolve there, the certainty that he had made up his mind. "I'm not going anywhere, Emma," he said quietly. "I'm here. For as long as you'll have me."

Her heart stuttered, a mixture of relief and fear swirling inside her. She wanted to believe him, wanted to surrender to the feeling of being anchored by him, of knowing that someone was as invested in this as she was. But there was still so much she didn't understand. So many unanswered questions.

But for now, in this moment, she chose to take him at his word. She chose to trust that this—whatever this was—was enough.

"I'm scared, Jack," she whispered, the vulnerability in her voice raw and honest. "Scared of losing myself. Scared of getting hurt."

Jack's hand tightened around her, pulling her even closer. "I know, Emma. But I'm not going to hurt you. I won't. Not unless you let me."

His words, soft yet firm, settled around her like a blanket, offering warmth and safety, but also stirring something deeper inside of her. She couldn't explain it, but there was something about Jack that made her want to believe him. Maybe it was the way he looked at her, as though he could see into the deepest parts of her soul, or maybe it was the way he held her—always steady, always certain.

She closed her eyes, resting her head against his chest once more, allowing herself to be enveloped by the comfort of his embrace. For now, that was enough. She would let the rest unfold in its own time, trusting that whatever happened next would happen because it was meant to.

They stayed like that for a while, simply existing together in the stillness of the morning. But as the minutes stretched on, Emma knew that things couldn't stay this simple for long. Their connection was too intense, too consuming to remain in this delicate equilibrium. She could feel the tension building again, the pull between them growing stronger, but now there was something else—a new layer to their bond, a promise of more to come.

Eventually, Jack broke the silence, his voice thoughtful. "We need to talk about the trip," he said, his tone shifting from intimate to business-like.

Emma's heart skipped a beat. She had almost forgotten about it, the trip they had planned, the one that had seemed so distant and abstract just a few weeks ago. But now, it loomed over them, its significance taking on new meaning.

"Right," she replied, her voice still thick with the remnants of their shared warmth. "The trip."

"We're leaving tomorrow," he reminded her, his fingers gently running through her hair. "We'll have some time to think things through. To... figure out what comes next."

Emma nodded, though her mind raced with a thousand questions. A part of her was eager to escape the confines of her own doubts and fears, to lose herself in the unfamiliarity of a new place. But another part of her felt a rising tide of anxiety, unsure of what this trip would bring, what it would mean for her relationship with Jack.

She had never been one to back down from uncertainty, but this—this was different. This was a step into the unknown.

But maybe, she thought, as Jack pressed a kiss to her forehead, maybe it was the step she needed to take.

Chapter 48: The Heat of The Moment

"Love is an endless act of forgiveness. Forgiveness is the key to action and freedom." — Maya Angelou

The flight to Bali was longer than Emma had expected. She had always imagined jetting off on an adventure, but as the hours passed and the hum of the plane's engines blended with the soft murmur of the passengers, she found herself lost in thought, her mind adrift on the sea of uncertainty that had been growing inside her for weeks.

Sitting beside Jack, she couldn't help but feel both a sense of relief and trepidation. The prospect of escaping Sydney, of stepping away from everything familiar, was a welcome change. Bali represented freedom, adventure, and a temporary reprieve from the heavy weight of the questions that had been haunting her. But even as the plane soared through the sky, her mind kept returning to the same thought: what did this mean for them?

She glanced over at Jack, who was leaning back in his seat with his eyes closed, his face relaxed, but there was a subtle tension in the way his hand rested on the armrest between them. He was always so composed, so in control, and Emma found herself wondering if this trip was as much a journey for him as it was for her.

Jack had been relatively quiet since their conversation that morning, but Emma could sense the shift in him. He was distant in a way that made her uneasy. It wasn't anything she could put into words—it was a feeling more than anything else—but she couldn't ignore it. The trip had been his idea, and while she had agreed to go, a small part of her felt like it was more about him than about them. He needed this escape more than she did, and she couldn't help but wonder why.

As the flight progressed, Emma found herself drawn into her own thoughts. The weeks that had passed since their night together in his apartment had been a blur of emotions—passion, fear, exhilaration. They had fallen into an unspoken rhythm, one that existed mostly in the physical space between them. But she needed more than that. She needed to know if this was real, if Jack's words from that morning—about staying with her, about defining their future—were as sincere as they sounded.

What did Jack want from her?

She knew she wasn't the only one with doubts. She could sense it in the quiet moments between them, the way he sometimes looked at her, as though he were waiting for something. Emma had spent so much of her life protecting herself from getting too close to anyone. And now, with Jack, she was learning just how much of herself she was willing to give.

The gentle jolt of the plane landing brought Emma back to the present, her thoughts scattering like leaves in the wind. She glanced out of the window, her gaze catching the lush, tropical landscape of

Bali as the plane descended. A deep sense of excitement stirred inside her, followed by a tinge of nervousness. This was the beginning of something, but what exactly?

Jack turned his head toward her as the plane taxied to the gate, his eyes meeting hers. His smile was warm, yet there was a trace of something more—something unreadable.

"We're here," he said softly, his voice a little more guarded than it had been back home.

Emma nodded, forcing a smile. She knew the trip was a chance for them to reconnect, to get away from the pressures of daily life, but she also sensed that it was more than that. She could feel the tension between them, thickening like a storm cloud just on the horizon.

When the seatbelt sign turned off, Emma stood, her legs stiff from the long flight. She grabbed her bag from the overhead compartment, trying to shake off the growing knot in her stomach. Jack was already standing, gathering his things with a quiet efficiency.

As they made their way off the plane and into the terminal, Emma was struck by the vibrant energy of the airport. The air was thick with humidity, the smells of incense and spices swirling around her, reminding her that she wasn't in Sydney anymore. Bali was alive, full of promise and excitement, a stark contrast to the quiet tension that had followed them from the moment they'd boarded the flight.

The drive to their hotel was just as captivating, the streets of Bali bustling with activity, motorcycles weaving between cars, vendors calling out their wares, and the colorful sights of the island greeting them at every turn. Emma felt a rush of excitement, but the knot in her stomach remained. She glanced at Jack, who was watching the scenery outside with a quiet intensity. His jaw was set, his expression unreadable, and for a moment, she wondered if he had been just as lost in his thoughts as she had been.

When they arrived at the hotel, a beautiful boutique resort nestled against the edge of a cliff, the tension between them only deepened. The place was stunning, an oasis of tranquility and luxury. White sand stretched out before them, the turquoise waters of the Indian Ocean crashing against the shore below. It was the perfect setting for relaxation, a place to unwind and escape the world. But Emma couldn't shake the feeling that they were standing at the edge of something far more complex.

The receptionist greeted them with a warm smile and a cold drink, handing them the keys to their villa. As they walked down the path toward their accommodation, Emma tried to shake off her unease. Bali was supposed to be a fresh start, a place where they could forget the world and focus on each other. But the deeper she thought about it, the more she realized that there was no escaping the reality of their relationship. No matter how far they went, no matter how beautiful the setting, the complexities of their connection would follow them.

Inside the villa, the cool air greeted them as the door swung open. The space was just as magnificent as she had imagined—open-plan living areas with high ceilings, large windows that framed the stunning views of the ocean, and a private pool that seemed to stretch out into the horizon. But even in this paradise, there was an undercurrent of tension between them.

Emma dropped her bag on the bed, her eyes flickering over the room. The villa was a dream, but in the back of her mind, she knew that the real challenge lay ahead. What was this trip truly about? Was it a way for them to reconnect? Or was it a test, a chance for Jack to prove something to himself—or to her?

Jack's voice broke through her thoughts. "You okay?" he asked, his eyes watching her carefully.

Emma turned to face him, her gaze searching his face for some sign of what he was thinking. "I'm fine," she replied, though the words didn't feel entirely true. "Just... a lot on my mind."

He nodded, taking a step toward her. "Let's make tonight about forgetting everything else. No pressures. Just you and me."

She met his gaze, the sincerity in his eyes unmistakable. For the first time in what felt like forever, Emma allowed herself to relax, to let the walls she'd built between them crumble, even if just for a moment. Maybe this was the fresh start they both needed.

"Okay," she said softly, her voice a mix of hope and uncertainty.

Jack's lips curved into a smile, and he took her hand in his, guiding her toward the outdoor terrace. The night was warm, the sounds of the ocean echoing in the distance. They didn't say much as they sat by the edge of the pool, watching the stars appear overhead like diamonds scattered across the dark sky.

In that moment, as Emma leaned against Jack, her thoughts drifting to the future, she felt something shift—something that had been building ever since they met. The air around them was charged with possibility, and though the road ahead was uncertain, Emma knew one thing for sure: this was the beginning of something new. Whether it was a journey toward love, healing, or self-discovery, she was ready to find out what it would be.

Chapter 49: Echoes of the Past

The days in Bali seemed to blur together, each one more beautiful than the last, and yet, each one carrying with it a weight Emma couldn't ignore. The island, with its intoxicating blend of vibrant colors and soothing rhythms, was meant to be a refuge. Yet, despite the beauty surrounding them, there was an undercurrent of tension that lingered between her and Jack, something unspoken but always present, a pull she couldn't quite understand.

They had spent the first few days of their stay in relative peace—exploring the beaches, indulging in spa treatments, and wandering through the streets of Ubud, where the dense jungle and the scent of frangipani filled the air. They were still learning each other, still in that phase of tentative connection, where passion and uncertainty danced around them in equal measure.

But now, as the days wore on, Emma could feel something shifting between them, something more profound than the physical chemistry that had drawn them together in Sydney. It was as if they were standing on the edge of something—something far more vulnerable and fragile than either of them had anticipated.

Tonight, the villa was quiet, save for the distant sound of the ocean waves crashing below. The air was thick with heat, the humidity pressing in on her skin as Emma stood by the open balcony, gazing out at the endless expanse of water. The view was breathtaking, but it couldn't distract her from the growing restlessness inside her.

Jack was in the other room, finishing up a call with his business partner, his voice low and measured as he discussed the latest developments with their project back in Sydney. It wasn't the first time he'd retreated into work mode since they arrived. In fact, Emma had come to realize that while Jack was always present physically, there were times when his mind seemed to be elsewhere, caught up in the demands of his life beyond her.

She couldn't help but wonder if it was a defense mechanism, a way for him to keep some distance between them. The thought unsettled her, and for the first time since arriving in Bali, she couldn't shake the feeling that maybe they were running out of time—or worse, running out of chances.

The sound of Jack's footsteps approaching brought her back to the present. She turned to find him standing in the doorway, his eyes scanning her face with that familiar intensity. He was dressed casually in a loose shirt and shorts, but there was something different about the way he held himself tonight—a tension in his posture that mirrored her own.

"Everything okay?" he asked, his voice soft but with an edge of concern.

Emma hesitated, weighing the words she was about to speak. She could feel the pull between them, a magnetic force that was drawing her in, but it was more than just physical. It was deeper, and she needed to understand what it meant before it consumed her.

"I don't know," she admitted, her voice quieter than she intended. "I just feel like... like we're not really here, Jack. Not really *together*."

The words hung in the air, heavy with the weight of truth. She saw his expression shift slightly, a flicker of surprise crossing his features before he masked it with that practiced composure.

"We're together," he said carefully, stepping closer to her. "I'm here with you, Emma. I'm not going anywhere."

"But you're not really *here*, Jack," she said, her frustration seeping through. "Physically, yes, but you're distant. And I don't know how to bridge that gap."

Jack's jaw tightened, his gaze locking onto hers. For a moment, Emma wondered if he would pull back, if he would retreat into himself as he often did when faced with her vulnerability. But instead, he reached out, his hand resting gently on her shoulder, his thumb brushing over her skin in slow, deliberate movements.

"I'm sorry," he said, his voice low, almost as though the words were difficult for him to say. "I didn't realize I was being distant. I guess I've been... preoccupied with work. But that's no excuse."

She turned slightly to face him, her heart pounding in her chest. "It's not just the work, Jack. It's everything. We came here to escape, to reconnect. But now I'm wondering if we're just running away from the real conversation we need to have."

Jack's eyes softened, the hardness in them fading as he looked at her, and for a brief moment, Emma could see the vulnerability in him, the same vulnerability she'd seen in herself. She had always known there was more to him, more beneath the surface, and she had been waiting for him to let her in, to share that with her.

"I know what you mean," he said quietly. "And you're right. I've been holding back. Not just from you, but from myself, too."

Emma's breath caught at his admission. She had suspected it, but hearing him say it aloud made everything feel more real, more palpable. He had been holding back—not just from her, but from the connection they shared, the one that threatened to unravel everything they thought they knew about themselves.

"What are you afraid of, Jack?" she asked, her voice steady despite the swirling emotions inside her. "What's stopping you from fully being here with me?"

Jack's eyes searched hers, as though weighing the answer. "I'm afraid of losing control," he confessed. "Of losing myself in something that I can't fix, that I can't control. I've spent so long building a life where everything has its place, where everything is managed. But with you, Emma, I feel like I'm being pulled into something I can't predict, something I can't plan for. And that terrifies me."

Her heart ached as she listened to him, her hand instinctively reaching for his. "But that's what this is, Jack. Life isn't about control. It's about the unknown, about the risks we take, the things that scare us the most. And right now, you're letting fear keep you from embracing what could be the best thing in both our lives."

Jack's gaze softened, his hand finding hers, their fingers entwining in a simple but powerful gesture. For a long moment, neither of them spoke, but the silence was no longer uncomfortable. It was understanding, a shared space where both of them could just be—no walls, no barriers.

Finally, Jack broke the silence. "So, what now?" he asked, his voice quiet but full of a new resolve. "Where do we go from here?"

Emma smiled softly, her thumb gently tracing the back of his hand. "We take it one step at a time. No more running. No more pretending. Just... us. And wherever that leads us, we'll figure it out together."

Jack nodded, his expression more open than she had ever seen it. He leaned forward, brushing his lips against hers in a kiss that was tender, but filled with an unspoken promise—one that held both the weight of their shared history and the possibility of everything that was still to come.

When he pulled away, his forehead resting against hers, Emma couldn't help but feel a sense of peace settle over her. For the first time in a long while, she felt like she was exactly where she needed to be.

Together, with Jack, everything was uncertain, but it was also full of possibility.

And for the first time in her life, that uncertainty didn't scare her.

Chapter 50: Unraveling Threads

"*S ometimes, the hardest part of healing is accepting that the person who hurt you is also the person who helped you survive.*" — *Unknown*

The days in Bali had become an ethereal blur, each one folding into the next like an endless tide. Emma and Jack had found a rhythm here—one that was quieter, more intimate, but laden with the tension of unspoken words. It was clear that they were no longer merely two people sharing a moment of passion or excitement. No, something much deeper was stirring between them. The first layers of their relationship had been peeled away, revealing raw, unrefined parts of themselves—parts they hadn't known how to share with anyone before.

Emma sat by the edge of the infinity pool, her feet submerged in the cool water, watching the way the waves crashed against the rocks below. The sun had dipped beneath the horizon, and the sky was now painted in shades of deep purple and fiery orange. Everything here felt more alive—more intense—than it ever had in the fast-paced life she'd left behind in Sydney. Yet, as beautiful as it all was, there was a heaviness in her chest, a quiet uncertainty that she couldn't shake.

Jack had been different ever since their conversation on the terrace two nights ago. Since then, they'd drifted into something more comfortable, but it wasn't the ease of affection that came from long-term intimacy. It was something more fragile—two people standing at the edge of an abyss, testing the waters before plunging in. Emma wasn't sure if they were both ready to leap, or if they were just standing still, waiting for the other to make the first move.

A soft sound behind her alerted Emma that Jack was approaching. His footsteps were light but purposeful, his presence always intense—never overwhelming, just quietly commanding. She turned to find him standing a few feet away, his eyes studying her, his lips curved in that small, knowing smile that always made her heart skip a beat.

"You've been quiet tonight," he said, his voice low and warm as he moved closer to her, stepping lightly around the edge of the pool. "What's on your mind?"

Emma didn't immediately respond. Instead, she let her gaze travel across the landscape again, taking in the soft glow of the moon reflected on the water. There was so much she wanted to say, but the words were tangled in her throat. She had always been a careful person, never one to leap into the unknown without a plan, without certainty. But with Jack, the plan had become irrelevant. What was left was the moment—this moment—and the space they both occupied in it.

"I'm thinking about how everything has changed since we arrived here," she said, her voice quieter than usual. "I think we've both been... running from something, haven't we?"

Jack didn't answer right away. Instead, he lowered himself to sit beside her, his eyes never leaving her face. The air between them felt thick with anticipation, with something neither of them was quite ready to address directly. It had been this way for days now—this slow unraveling of all the walls they'd built around their emotions, around their pasts.

"I don't know if I would call it running," Jack said, his tone thoughtful, as though he were carefully choosing his words. "Maybe we've both been trying to figure out who we are in all of this. Who we are with each other."

Emma nodded, her gaze drifting back to the water below. There was something in his words that resonated with her—a truth she hadn't wanted to acknowledge before. She'd spent so much of her life protecting herself, building walls around her heart, but Jack had found a way to dismantle them, piece by piece. And now, here she was, standing on the precipice, uncertain about whether she could truly let herself fall into this.

"You said something the other night," she began, her voice steady but filled with an emotion she couldn't quite control. "You said you were afraid of losing control. But I think we're both afraid of the same thing: losing ourselves in this."

Jack's eyes softened as he listened to her, his expression unreadable but full of something deeper. "I don't want to lose myself, Emma. I just... I don't know how to let go. Everything I've built in my life, everything I've worked for, it's been about control. About knowing where I stand, about being able to fix things when they go wrong."

"I get that," Emma said, her voice quieter now. "But sometimes, control isn't enough. Sometimes, you have to let go and trust that the fall will be worth it."

She felt his gaze on her, steady and searching, as if trying to read the depths of her soul. Jack had always been good at that—figuring people out, understanding the complexities beneath their surfaces. But what

Emma hadn't expected, what she hadn't anticipated, was that Jack himself would be a puzzle she couldn't quite solve.

"Do you think you can trust me?" Jack asked, his voice quiet but serious. "Do you think you can trust us?"

The question hung in the air, and for a long moment, Emma didn't know how to answer. Could she trust him? Could she trust herself?

The truth was, she wasn't sure. But there was something in the way he was looking at her, something in the way he held himself that made her believe he wasn't just saying the words for the sake of it. Jack was standing here, vulnerable in his own way, offering her something she hadn't known how to ask for. His trust.

"I want to," she said finally, her voice trembling just a little. "I want to trust you. I want to trust us."

Jack leaned forward, his hand finding hers, his fingers curling around hers in a gesture that was both intimate and full of resolve. He wasn't pushing, wasn't demanding anything from her. He was simply there, offering her the space to figure it out, to choose him—or choose herself—at her own pace.

"We'll take it slow," he said, his voice gentle but firm. "No expectations, no pressure. Just... us."

Emma nodded, feeling a wave of emotion rush over her, threatening to overwhelm her. She could feel the pull of him, the draw of his energy, the depth of his emotions, and in that moment, she realized just how much she wanted him in her life. Not as a fleeting experience, not as something temporary, but as someone who had come into her world and turned it upside down. Someone she couldn't imagine living without.

The silence between them stretched out, comfortable and warm, as if they were both content just being in each other's presence. The world outside—everything she had known before—faded into the background. All that mattered was this moment, this connection.

Finally, Jack spoke again, his voice soft but full of promise. "You know, I think we're both still figuring this out. But I'm willing to try, Emma. For you. For us."

For the first time in a long time, Emma felt a sense of peace settle over her. It wasn't the certainty she had always craved, the kind of assurance that came with having everything planned out. It was a different kind of peace—the kind that came from knowing she wasn't alone in this anymore.

She squeezed his hand, feeling the steady beat of his pulse beneath her fingertips. "I'm ready to try, too."

The moment felt fragile, but beautiful—like a delicate flower beginning to bloom, unsure of what it would look like in the end but knowing it had to grow. And for the first time, Emma felt like she was ready to embrace whatever came next.

Chapter 51: Torn Between Worlds

"The strength of a woman is not measured by the impact that all her hardships have had on her, but by the courage with which she has suffered them." — Unknown

The night had descended on Bali like a velvet curtain, quiet and full of promise. The air around them had softened, wrapping itself around Emma and Jack as they stood together, just a few feet away from the pool, the flickering light of the candles casting dancing shadows on the walls. Everything about this moment felt weightless—unreal, almost—as if time had slowed down just for them, allowing them to savor the closeness they had worked so hard to cultivate.

It wasn't just the allure of the tropical paradise that made this moment so intoxicating. It was the way the air hummed between them, filled with a delicate tension. They had spent days exploring their connection—both physical and emotional—but tonight felt different. Something had shifted between them. There was an understanding now, a shared awareness that they had crossed a line, and there would be no going back.

Jack's gaze rested on Emma, his eyes intense, searching, as if trying to read the unspoken emotions swirling in her eyes. The softness of his expression gave way to something deeper—a yearning, a hunger that had been growing quietly since the very first night they had come to Bali. It was no longer about testing limits, about holding back for fear of getting hurt. It was about surrendering to what was happening between them, trusting in it, and allowing it to unfold.

Emma had always been cautious, always in control of her emotions and her desires, but tonight... tonight she felt different. She felt brave. She felt ready.

Her heart raced, and her pulse quickened as Jack took a step toward her, his movements slow, deliberate. Every step he took seemed to draw him closer, yet he kept his distance, as if asking her permission, waiting for her to make the next move.

"You're quiet," Jack murmured, his voice low and velvety, a gentle question. "What's on your mind?"

Emma took a deep breath, steadying herself. She had so many thoughts swirling through her head—thoughts of trust, of vulnerability, of the walls she had spent years building and the pieces she had allowed him to see. What had begun as something impulsive, something driven by desire, had grown into something far more intricate. This wasn't just about passion anymore; it was about discovering something much deeper, something that might change them both forever.

"I'm thinking about how far we've come," she said quietly, her voice barely above a whisper. "How much we've shared. And how much is still left to discover."

Jack didn't say anything for a moment, his eyes scanning her face with the quiet intensity that always seemed to set her on edge. She felt her body temperature rise as he stepped closer, the heat of his presence sending shivers down her spine. He reached out, his hand brushing lightly over her arm, sending a surge of warmth through her.

"I know," he said softly, his fingers tracing the line of her jaw, the touch almost reverent. "But that's what makes this... so damn beautiful. It's the unknown. The space between us. The things we still have to explore."

His words hung in the air, heavy with the weight of truth. Emma could feel her heart racing, the tension building as he leaned in closer, the space between them growing smaller, more charged with each passing second. She could smell the faint trace of his cologne, feel the heat of his breath on her skin. The world outside them had faded away, leaving only the two of them in this small corner of paradise.

"I want this," she said, the words tumbling from her lips before she had a chance to second-guess them. "I want to explore this with you."

Jack's eyes darkened with desire, his hands moving to her waist, pulling her closer until their bodies were just inches apart. He could feel the rapid beat of her heart, the way she trembled slightly under his touch, and it stirred something deep inside of him. He had known this moment would come—knew it the second they had both dared to let go of their fears, of the walls they had built around themselves. This was the culmination of everything they had been moving toward, and Jack knew, without a shadow of a doubt, that he wanted it just as much as she did.

"I've wanted you, Emma," Jack murmured, his voice rough, filled with the raw edge of longing. "I've wanted you from the moment I met you. And I've been fighting it. But now, I don't want to fight it anymore."

Emma's breath caught in her throat as Jack's lips brushed against hers in the most tender of kisses. It wasn't a kiss of urgency, but one of understanding, one that seemed to say everything they had both been afraid to say aloud. He tasted of sweetness and salt, of the memories they had already begun to build together, and the promise of everything yet to come.

She responded to him, her hands finding the back of his neck, her fingers threading through his hair as she pulled him closer. The kiss deepened, growing hotter, more insistent. Emma's body pressed against his, her senses overwhelmed by the feel of him—by the way he made her feel alive, as if every nerve was firing at once, igniting something within her she hadn't known was there.

As the kiss broke, Emma's chest rose and fell with quick breaths, her mind racing as Jack's hands moved lower, skimming the curve of her hips, his touch possessive and yet gentle. She let him guide her backward, her back meeting the soft cushions of the nearby lounge. Her body followed his lead without hesitation, drawn to him as if they were two forces of nature, unable to resist the pull of gravity.

Jack lowered himself beside her, his lips trailing along the line of her jaw, down her neck, leaving a trail of heat in their wake. Emma's body arched toward him instinctively, her hands moving to his shirt, tugging at it urgently, the fabric sliding off his shoulders to reveal the sculpted muscles beneath. Every inch of him was intoxicating, every touch igniting a fire inside her that she hadn't known she was capable of.

"Emma..." Jack's voice was strained now, his breath hot against her skin. "Are you sure?"

She nodded, her fingers tracing the lines of his chest, memorizing the feel of him. She was sure. She had never been more certain of anything in her life.

"I'm sure," she breathed, her voice steady despite the whirlwind of emotions crashing through her.

And with that, they let go of everything—the doubts, the fears, the hesitation. There was no more waiting. There was no more holding back.

What followed was a slow, deliberate exploration, each movement an act of trust, of surrender. They moved together as if they were a single entity, two souls entwined in the heat of the moment. Every touch, every kiss was a conversation in itself—an unspoken dialogue that revealed more about them than words ever could.

Time seemed to stretch, to bend, as the two of them lost themselves in each other, in the raw intimacy they had built and now embraced fully. There were no more games, no more uncertainties—just two people finally allowing themselves to be vulnerable, to be real.

And in the quiet aftermath, as they lay together, bodies intertwined and hearts racing, Emma realized that the trust she had feared was no longer something to be scared of. It was something that had grown between them, something that had been forged in every kiss, every touch, every shared moment.

She didn't need to know what came next. For the first time in a long time, she felt that she was exactly where she was meant to be.

Chapter 52: The Weight of Secrets

"Secrets are like scars. They don't disappear, no matter how hard you try to hide them." — Unknown

The night after their intimate connection in the villa, Emma and Jack lay under the soft covers, their bodies close, but the silence between them thick with unspoken thoughts. The moon hung low in the sky, casting its pale light through the open windows, bathing the room in a soft glow. It was peaceful, almost serene, but Emma couldn't shake the feeling that something was lurking beneath the surface of their perfect moment—something she hadn't yet fully confronted.

She lay on her back, staring at the ceiling, her fingers tracing the delicate pattern of the quilt beneath her. Jack had fallen asleep beside her, his breathing slow and steady, but Emma's mind was wide awake. Her thoughts spiraled back to the past—her past—things she had tucked away for so long.

She had never truly allowed herself to examine the scars that had shaped her. Her divorce, the betrayals, the broken dreams, all the things she had hidden behind her perfect life and successful career. Even with Jack, there was a part of her that kept a distance, a protective wall that she hadn't yet fully lowered. She could feel herself unraveling in ways she wasn't ready to confront, but she knew that the time was coming to face it.

As she turned her head to glance at Jack, she saw the way the moonlight caught his features—his strong jawline, the curve of his lips that had so often whispered promises and secrets to her. He seemed so perfect, so effortless in his presence, and yet Emma knew that Jack, too, had his own demons. There was a darkness in him, something he had never fully shared with her.

In the stillness of the night, Emma's thoughts drifted to her childhood—the years of emotional neglect from her father, the weight of expectations her mother had placed on her, pushing her to be perfect, to be the best at everything. Her relationship with her mother had always been strained, and after her father left, there had been a deep sense of abandonment. That abandonment had followed her into her marriage, leaving her unable to trust anyone, even herself.

Jack had pulled her into this world of passion, of freedom, but now she had to ask herself: Could she trust him with all of her? Could she let him in, really let him in, or would she push him away like everyone else she had ever loved?

The quiet room suddenly felt too small, the weight of her thoughts pressing down on her. She slid out of bed as quietly as she could, careful not to wake Jack. She needed air—needed to clear her mind. The soft sound of the ocean waves crashing on the shore outside beckoned her, and she moved toward the open balcony, stepping out into the cool night air.

The ocean breeze was refreshing against her skin, and as she leaned on the railing, she let the salty air fill her lungs. It was a small moment of peace, a fleeting escape from the turmoil inside her. Yet, no matter how much she tried to push it away, the question lingered: Could she truly let go?

As she stood there, lost in her thoughts, she heard a sound from behind her. A voice. "Emma?"

Jack's voice, low and rough with sleep, broke the silence. She turned to find him standing in the doorway, his expression a mixture of concern and curiosity. His hair was disheveled, his shirt still unbuttoned from earlier, and in that moment, he looked every bit as vulnerable as she felt.

"I couldn't sleep," she admitted, a faint smile tugging at her lips, though it didn't quite reach her eyes. "Needed some air."

Jack's gaze softened, and without a word, he stepped toward her, his bare feet silent against the stone floor. He didn't ask her what was on her mind, didn't pressure her to open up. Instead, he simply stood beside her, letting the moment stretch between them. The stillness felt comfortable, familiar even, as if they both understood that some things didn't need to be said.

After a long pause, Jack spoke, his voice barely above a whisper. "I know you're holding something back, Emma. You don't have to tell me everything. But if you need to... I'm here."

His words hit her like a wave, knocking her breathless. The sincerity in his voice, the honesty, was more than she had expected. She had thought he would push her, demand more of her, but instead, he was offering her the space to be vulnerable without judgment.

"I don't know if I can trust you," she confessed, the words slipping out before she could stop them. "I don't know if I can trust anyone with all of this. With me."

Jack didn't flinch. He didn't pull away. Instead, he gently reached for her hand, holding it in his with a quiet strength. "I won't ask you to trust me all at once. But I'll show you that you can. One step at a time."

The simplicity of his words, the clarity, settled something inside of her. She wasn't ready to let go completely, but she was willing to try. For him. For them.

As the night stretched on, the air between them grew warmer, the tension lifting bit by bit. They didn't need to speak anymore. The connection between them was undeniable, and as they stood side by side, looking out over the moonlit ocean, Emma realized that this was the beginning of something new.

***

The next morning, the villa buzzed with the energy of a new day. The sun had risen high, casting golden light over the expansive grounds. Emma and Jack had spent the night talking—about their pasts, about the things they had both kept hidden for so long. It had been a breakthrough, a moment of clarity, but as much as they had shared, there was still much to be understood.

Emma was in the kitchen, preparing breakfast, when she felt Jack's presence behind her. She turned to find him leaning against the doorway, watching her with an unreadable expression.

"You've been quiet this morning," he remarked, his voice a little too casual.

Emma smiled, though it was a touch strained. "Just thinking."

Jack took a step closer, his gaze flickering to her face. "What about?"

"Everything," she replied, her tone steady. "Our pasts, our fears, our future… I'm not sure what it looks like yet."

Jack nodded slowly, as though processing her words. Then, without warning, he stepped forward and took her hand, his fingers warm against her skin. "Maybe we don't have to figure it all out right now. Maybe we can just take it one day at a time."

There was an honesty in his eyes, a sincerity that Emma had never quite seen before. She met his gaze, her heart pounding in her chest. For the first time in a long time, she felt like she could believe in something more than just herself.

And then, just as quickly, the peaceful moment shattered.

The sound of a phone ringing echoed through the villa.

Emma's stomach tightened. She recognized the number.

It was her ex-husband, Ben.

Chapter 53: Shadows of the Past

he past is never where you think you left it." — *Katherine Anne Porter*

The phone continued to ring, its harsh sound slicing through the silence that had settled between Emma and Jack. Emma hesitated for a moment, her fingers frozen midair as she reached for the phone. She could feel Jack's gaze on her, heavy with expectation, as if the air itself had thickened with the weight of her decision.

Ben's name flashed on the screen again, and Emma's stomach churned. It had been years since she'd heard from him, and though her heart had healed from the wounds he had left, a part of her still recoiled at the thought of reopening old scars.

"What do you think?" she asked Jack quietly, not taking her eyes off the phone.

Jack's expression was unreadable, though there was a flicker of concern in his eyes. "It's your call," he replied simply, but there was something in his voice that made her pause. "But if you're not ready, you don't have to answer."

Emma took a deep breath, her mind racing. She had made peace with the end of her marriage to Ben—at least, she thought she had. But the truth was, there were unresolved pieces of that chapter of her life. Pieces that Ben might want to bring back into her world, whether she was ready for it or not.

The phone stopped ringing. For a moment, she thought it was over, but then, to her surprise, a message notification popped up.

Ben: We need to talk. It's important. Call me when you can.

Her heart rate quickened. The words felt too casual, too insistent all at once. It wasn't just a friendly check-in—it was a demand.

"Is it about..." Jack started, but he trailed off, clearly sensing the shift in Emma's mood.

Emma nodded, her throat dry. "It's Ben. He wants to talk."

"Are you going to call him?" Jack asked, the question loaded with unspoken tension. His eyes held a mix of curiosity and concern, but there was also something deeper—an unvoiced fear that this call might threaten what they had built together.

She didn't know. She wasn't sure she was ready to face him, to step back into the mess that had been their marriage. But at the same time, she couldn't deny the sense of unresolved closure that lingered in her chest.

Before she could make a decision, the doorbell rang, startling both of them. Jack raised an eyebrow, as if questioning the timing of everything. "Who could that be?"

Emma quickly glanced at her phone again, but Ben's message still glowed on the screen. "I have no idea," she said, her voice tight. "I wasn't expecting anyone."

Jack moved toward the door, and Emma stood still, torn between the unresolved message from her past and the unexpected interruption at her door. She could feel a knot forming in her stomach, a gnawing sense of anxiety that refused to let go.

When Jack opened the door, the figure standing in the doorway made Emma's breath catch in her throat.

"Olivia?"

It was her best friend, Olivia, standing there in the doorway, a duffel bag slung over her shoulder. Her face was flushed, her eyes wide with an unreadable expression, as if something had driven her to seek refuge here.

"What are you doing here?" Emma's voice was a mix of shock and confusion, her pulse quickening. Olivia had been living in Melbourne, far from Sydney, and Emma hadn't expected her to drop by, especially without any warning.

Olivia looked past Emma to Jack, her face softening into a faint smile. "I need your help," she said simply, her voice trembling just slightly.

"Of course," Emma said, stepping aside to let her in. "What's going on? What happened?"

Jack gave Emma a questioning glance, his eyes flickering with curiosity and concern, but he stayed silent, giving them space.

Olivia stepped inside, her presence filling the room like a storm. She seemed exhausted, her usual spark dimmed by something she hadn't shared yet. "Can we talk in private?" she asked, her gaze flickering briefly to Jack before returning to Emma.

"Sure," Emma said, her heart pounding in her chest. She led Olivia to the kitchen, her mind racing with questions.

Once they were seated, Emma couldn't hold back any longer. "Olivia, what's going on? You look... you look like you've been through hell."

Olivia's eyes clouded over, a distant sadness taking over her features. She hesitated for a moment, then spoke in a voice that barely broke above a whisper.

"I—I'm pregnant, Emma." Her voice shook, and Emma's stomach lurched.

Emma stared at her friend, disbelief written all over her face. "What? Olivia, are you sure?"

Olivia nodded, her hand instinctively going to her stomach. "I found out last week. And I don't know what to do. I don't know who the father is. It could be either one of two men." She looked up, her eyes desperate. "I'm so scared, Em. I don't know what to do."

The words hit Emma like a punch to the gut. Olivia was her rock, the person who had always been there for her through everything. And now, her best friend was facing a crisis of her own, one that Emma hadn't seen coming. It was too much, too soon.

"I don't know what to tell you," Emma said softly, her voice filled with uncertainty. "I'm not sure how to help."

Olivia's expression softened, and she reached out, grasping Emma's hand tightly. "You don't have to have all the answers, Em. I just... I need someone to talk to. I need you right now."

The weight of Olivia's words hit Emma hard. She could feel the pressure mounting—her own unresolved issues with Ben, the uncertainty surrounding her relationship with Jack, and now this. She had always prided herself on being in control, but in this moment, everything felt like it was slipping through her fingers.

Jack entered the kitchen, his eyes lingering on the two of them. He'd clearly overheard some of the conversation, his brow furrowed with concern. He didn't speak, but the question in his eyes was clear: *What's going on?*

Emma exhaled, her voice shaking as she turned toward him. "Olivia's pregnant. She doesn't know what to do, and I... I don't know how to help her."

Jack's eyes softened, and he took a step toward them, his presence reassuring. "I think we need to get to the bottom of this. You're not alone in this, Emma. We'll figure it out."

His words, so simple and kind, took some of the weight off Emma's shoulders. But the storm was far from over. What Olivia was going through had opened a door Emma hadn't expected—and it was one that would change everything.

Chapter 54: The Breaking Point

"Sometimes the hardest thing and the right thing are the same."
— The Fray

The morning after Olivia's arrival was a blur for Emma. She had hardly slept, her mind racing with worry for her best friend and the weight of the situation she found herself in. Olivia had asked for help, but Emma had no idea what to do. She wasn't even sure if she could help herself, let alone another person.

After a tense breakfast, Olivia had excused herself to take a nap, overwhelmed by the emotional strain of her revelation. Emma, meanwhile, found herself caught between two worlds—the world she had built with Jack, the world of passion, hope, and connection, and the world of her past, filled with unresolved issues, fears, and long-forgotten wounds. Her thoughts constantly drifted back to the message Ben had sent her. She hadn't called him back, but the pull was there, the undeniable temptation to seek closure or, perhaps, to face the unresolved tension between them once and for all.

The day had barely begun, but Emma was already exhausted. She stood at the kitchen counter, staring at the freshly brewed coffee in front of her, but her mind was a thousand miles away. The soft clink of the coffee cup as she picked it up sounded louder than usual, echoing in the empty space.

Jack entered the kitchen, his presence as steady as ever. He had showered and dressed, and there was something about the way he moved that exuded confidence, but Emma could sense the undercurrent of worry beneath his calm exterior. He had heard enough of the conversation with Olivia to know the gravity of the situation, and his concern for Emma was palpable.

"Are you okay?" Jack's voice was soft, but the question carried a weight that was hard to ignore. He stood a few feet away from her, his posture open and inviting, as though offering her the space to talk if she needed to.

Emma took a deep breath, trying to calm the swirling chaos in her chest. "I'm fine. Just... thinking."

Jack nodded, but she could see the skepticism in his eyes. "I don't believe you."

She smiled faintly, trying to mask the tension that still lingered. "I'll be okay. It's just... a lot to process."

He stepped closer, his eyes never leaving hers. "You don't have to go through this alone, Emma. Whatever it is, you can share it with me."

Emma's chest tightened at his words. He was offering her everything, everything she had wanted, yet she couldn't shake the feeling that there was something she hadn't told him. Something that, if revealed, might pull them apart instead of bringing them closer. Her fears, her insecurities—they were still too fresh, too raw to expose to someone like Jack, someone who seemed so sure of himself, so comfortable in his own skin.

"I'm just not sure I'm ready for all of this," she confessed, her voice barely above a whisper. She gestured between them, her hand trembling slightly. "I've spent so long building walls around myself... I don't know how to let them down."

Jack's gaze softened, and he reached for her hand, gently lifting it in his. "You don't have to let them all down at once. We can take it slow, Emma. I'm not going anywhere."

The sincerity in his voice hit her like a wave, and for the first time in what felt like forever, Emma allowed herself to lean into the comfort of his touch. She had been running for so long—running from the pain, from the hurt, from the fear that she might lose control if she let someone in. But Jack wasn't asking for her to fix everything. He was simply asking her to trust him. And maybe, just maybe, she could.

Before she could respond, there was a knock on the door, pulling them both out of the moment. Emma blinked, startled, her heart pounding in her chest. Who could it be now? Olivia had gone to lie down, and Emma hadn't expected any other visitors.

Jack moved toward the door, opening it without hesitation, his brow furrowing as he found the visitor standing on the other side.

"Ben," Jack's voice was flat, but the tension in his posture was palpable.

Emma's heart skipped a beat as she stepped forward, her pulse racing. Ben stood at the doorway, his familiar face a mask of unreadable emotion. His once youthful features were now tinged with the signs of age—lines around his eyes, the weight of stress and worry. But his presence still sent a jolt of recognition through her, a feeling she hadn't fully anticipated.

"I need to talk to Emma," Ben said, his voice tight. His eyes flickered over to Jack, sizing him up, but there was something guarded in his expression, something that hinted at the distance that had grown between them over the years.

Emma's stomach churned. She hadn't expected him to show up here, not like this. Not so suddenly. Not after all this time.

Jack's jaw tightened, but he didn't speak, simply stepping aside to let Ben in. Emma could feel the tension between them, the unspoken questions hanging heavy in the air. She knew Ben well enough to understand that whatever he had to say wasn't going to be easy, and it certainly wasn't going to be simple.

"I'll be in the other room," Jack said, his voice low and steady. He gave Emma one last look, his eyes filled with understanding, before turning and walking away.

Emma swallowed hard, her eyes still on Ben as he stepped inside. She could feel the familiar ache in her chest, the pull of the past that she had worked so hard to escape. She had always imagined that when she finally saw him again, she'd have the upper hand, that she'd be strong enough to face him with the confidence she now had with Jack. But seeing him now, in the flesh, after all this time, it was as if no amount of healing could erase the years of hurt.

"What do you want, Ben?" she asked, her voice shaking slightly despite her efforts to remain composed.

Ben didn't immediately respond. He seemed to be searching for the right words, his gaze flickering to the floor before meeting her eyes again. "I... I don't know how to say this, but I've been trying to reach you for months now. I've been going through something, and I need your help."

Emma's heart sank. "Help with what?"

Ben hesitated again before speaking, his voice strained. "I'm not sure how to explain it, but... I've gotten myself into some trouble, Emma. And I need someone I can trust. Someone who knows me, who understands me."

The words hung in the air, and Emma felt a cold wave of realization wash over her. He wasn't here to apologize. He wasn't here to make amends for the past. No, Ben was here because he needed something from her—something that would force her to confront everything she had tried to forget.

Emma stood tall, her posture rigid. "You need someone to fix your mistakes, Ben. But I'm not that person anymore."

The sharpness of her words stung, but it was the truth. She wasn't going to be pulled back into the vortex of his chaos, not when she had fought so hard to build something better for herself.

Ben's face darkened, and for a moment, it seemed as though he might say something more. But instead, he simply nodded, his jaw clenched. "I thought you might say that."

He turned and walked toward the door, leaving Emma standing there, the room suddenly feeling too small. She hadn't expected it to be this hard. She hadn't expected him to still have the power to hurt her, to pull her back into his orbit.

But as Ben left, Emma felt something shift inside her—a quiet sense of closure. She wasn't the same woman who had married him. She wasn't the same woman who had been betrayed, who had felt abandoned. She had grown. She had built a new life, one that was stronger than she had ever imagined.

And with that, she turned back toward the kitchen, where Jack was waiting, his presence a steady anchor in the chaos. She didn't have all the answers yet, but in that moment, she knew one thing for certain: She was ready to face whatever came next—together.

Chapter 55: Unraveling The Truth

"There are two ways to live: you can live as if nothing is a miracle; you can live as if everything is." — Albert Einstein

The quiet of the house was deafening in the hours after Ben's visit. Emma found herself walking around the rooms, unable to sit still. She had tried to lose herself in the mundane—organising a few things, tidying up—but the weight of the conversation, the weight of Ben's words, lingered in her mind like a fog she couldn't escape. She knew he hadn't come to make peace. He hadn't come to apologise. He had come because he needed something. And that need—whatever it was—felt like a shadow over her life, casting doubts on everything she had worked so hard to rebuild.

But Jack had been there, standing by her side, unwavering in his support. His presence had been a balm to her wounds, even if unspoken. After Ben had left, Emma had found herself retreating into his arms, the comfort of his warmth grounding her. Jack hadn't asked for details. He hadn't pried into her emotions. He simply held her, as if to remind her that, no matter the weight of her past, she didn't have to carry it alone anymore.

The clock on the wall ticked relentlessly, dragging time forward as Emma mulled over her thoughts. It was late afternoon when Jack finally emerged from the office, where he had been working most of the day. He appeared, as always, composed and put-together, but Emma knew him too well now. She could see the subtle tension in his shoulders, the way he rubbed the back of his neck—a telltale sign that he was just as affected by the events of the past day as she was.

"Are you okay?" Jack asked, his voice low but concerned. He had that steady, reassuring tone that always managed to bring her a sense of calm.

Emma nodded, but the gesture was automatic. She wasn't okay—not entirely. There were so many layers to her feelings, too many tangled threads that were difficult to pull apart. "I don't know, Jack. I'm not sure what to think anymore."

He moved closer, his hand brushing against hers in a small but comforting gesture. "You don't have to figure it out right away, you know."

She looked up at him, her eyes searching his face for something—reassurance, perhaps, or even the strength she had come to rely on. But what she found in his eyes was different. There was something in the way he was looking at her—an intensity that made her heart race, made her wonder if he was hiding something, too. The thought made her hesitate.

"What's wrong?" she asked softly, her voice barely a whisper.

Jack's lips pressed together for a moment, as if he were carefully choosing his words. "There's something I haven't told you. Something about my past. Something I didn't think was important until now."

The confession hung between them like a fragile thread, one that could snap at any moment. Emma could feel her pulse quicken as the weight of his words sank in. She had always known that Jack was a man with his own demons, but she had never pushed him to open up about them. His walls were strong, and she respected that. But now, it seemed as though those walls were starting to crumble, revealing cracks she hadn't expected.

"I know this sounds cryptic," Jack continued, his voice low, "but there's a reason I've been so careful about not getting too close to you. It's not because I didn't want to—I did. I just didn't want to bring my baggage into this, into us."

Emma's mind raced. What could he possibly be hiding? She had always felt that there was more to Jack's past than he let on, but she had never pressed him. It had always seemed like an unspoken rule between them: no questions about the past, just focus on the present. But now, that rule seemed to be unraveling, and Emma wasn't sure if she was ready to confront whatever lay beneath the surface.

"You don't have to tell me everything, Jack," she said gently, her voice steady despite the storm swirling inside her. "But if you're keeping something from me, I need to know. I can't keep guessing."

Jack let out a breath, his gaze steady as he met her eyes. "I wasn't sure if I ever wanted to share this with anyone, but I guess it's time. You deserve to know the truth."

He paused, as if gathering his thoughts. Emma waited, her heart pounding in her chest. She could feel the tension between them, the weight of their shared silence. When he finally spoke again, his words were quiet but filled with an emotion that made her stomach churn.

"I was married before," Jack admitted. "A long time ago. It was a relationship I thought I could fix. But I was wrong. We both were. She was... different, Emma. Not like you."

The words hit Emma like a punch to the gut. She had suspected, of course—she had known that Jack had a history, just as she did. But hearing him say it out loud, hearing him speak about his ex-wife in such an intimate way, made her feel something she hadn't expected. Was she jealous? No, not exactly. But it stirred something inside her, a mix of insecurity and fear.

"I didn't know that about you," she replied, her voice barely above a whisper.

"I never wanted you to know," Jack said, his voice tinged with regret. "I thought if I kept it buried deep enough, it wouldn't affect what we had. But I see now that it's impossible to keep it hidden forever. And the last thing I want is for you to feel like I'm hiding things from you."

Emma nodded, taking in his words. She understood, she truly did. Everyone had a past, and Jack's was no less significant than her own. But hearing about his ex-wife, about a relationship that had obviously left scars, made her feel vulnerable in a way she hadn't anticipated.

"I appreciate you telling me, Jack," she said, her voice soft but steady. "I really do. But I think... I think we both need time to process everything. To figure out where we go from here."

Jack's eyes darkened, and for a moment, Emma could see the pain flicker behind his gaze. "I don't want to lose you, Emma. I don't want to lose what we have."

She reached for his hand, squeezing it gently. "You won't lose me. But we both need to be honest with each other. And we need to figure out how to heal from our pasts—together."

Jack smiled faintly, a mix of relief and sadness in his eyes. "Together," he echoed, his grip on her hand tightening. "I can do that. As long as you're with me."

Emma nodded, her heart filled with a quiet hope. She didn't have all the answers, and she wasn't sure what the future would hold. But for the first time in a long while, she felt like she was ready to face it—ready to face whatever was lurking in the shadows, as long as they faced it together.

Chapter 56: The Road Ahead

"There are no guarantees, only choices. And the choices we make define us." — Unknown

The night was still. The quiet hum of the city outside the apartment only accentuated the silence inside. Emma sat on the edge of their bed, her thoughts heavy and restless. She hadn't been able to sleep much the past few nights, not since Jack had shared the secret about his previous marriage. Her mind was a whirlwind of conflicting emotions: a deep sympathy for his pain, a creeping sense of insecurity, and a gnawing question that refused to be ignored.

Had she really been the only one who had been hiding parts of herself?

There had always been a part of Emma's past she had kept locked away, a part that had shaped her but remained carefully hidden from the people who had come to care for her. But in the wake of Jack's revelation, she began to wonder if it was time to finally confront it.

Could she continue this relationship knowing that her own history had the potential to shake everything? Or would it be better to face it head-on and risk losing what she had fought so hard to build?

She glanced at Jack, who was asleep beside her. His features, usually so composed, were relaxed in slumber, and for a moment, Emma allowed herself to simply look at him. He had been a constant in her life for months now, steadfast in his support, offering her an unwavering hand even when her past had threatened to pull her under. But the truth was, Emma wasn't sure what Jack would think of the truth she carried with her. The truth of her own failed marriage. The truth of what had really driven her to leave Ben.

She had always tried to push those memories to the back of her mind, to pretend they didn't shape her decisions, but now, sitting here in the quiet darkness, she realised how much they still defined her.

Her phone buzzed on the bedside table, pulling her from her thoughts. She reached for it absently, her mind still swirling with uncertainty, but when she saw the name on the screen, her heart skipped a beat.

It was Ben.

Her ex-husband.

The message was brief, but the words hit her with a force that made her stomach churn.

We need to talk. It's about Jack.

Emma's fingers hovered over the phone screen. She hadn't heard from Ben in weeks, and certainly hadn't expected this. Part of her wanted to ignore it, to delete the message and move on. But another part of her, a part she didn't fully understand, was desperate for answers.

She sat there, staring at the phone for what felt like an eternity. Finally, she hit the reply button.

What do you want to say?

The response came almost immediately.

Meet me. Tomorrow at the old café. 10 AM.

The old café. The place where they used to go when their marriage was still new and filled with possibility. The place where they had shared dreams and promises, before everything had slowly started to fall apart.

Emma's heart raced in her chest. Part of her wanted to tell Ben to go to hell, to refuse to meet him and to leave the past where it belonged. But another part, the part that still carried the unresolved pain of their marriage, knew that there was something Ben wanted to tell her. Something important.

She knew Jack would never understand. He had always been clear about his boundaries, about not wanting to revisit the past. He had trusted her with his secrets, but this was something different. This wasn't about Jack's past—this was about Emma's. And she couldn't help but feel a sense of dread about what would happen if the two worlds collided.

The next morning, she found herself at the café, standing in front of the familiar entrance, her stomach twisting with nerves. The small café, with its mismatched chairs and the scent of freshly baked croissants, was unchanged. But everything about it felt different now. The warm memories she had once associated with the place had been replaced by an overwhelming sense of unease.

When she stepped inside, her eyes scanned the room, finally landing on the figure sitting at the far corner. Ben.

He was older, more worn than she remembered, but the sharpness in his eyes was unchanged. He looked up when she approached, a faint, almost predatory smile curling on his lips.

"Emma," he said, his voice like gravel, low and heavy. "I knew you'd come."

She sat down across from him, her fingers tightly gripping the edge of the table. "What do you want, Ben? Why now?"

Ben took a slow sip of his coffee before responding, his eyes never leaving hers. "You know why. There are things you don't know. Things you never knew about me. About Jack."

Emma's blood ran cold. "What do you mean?"

Ben leaned forward, his eyes narrowing. "I've been keeping an eye on him, Emma. I've been watching. I know what he's been hiding from you, and I know why."

A chill ran down Emma's spine. She had always known Ben was manipulative, that he had a way of twisting the truth to suit his needs, but this? This felt different. "Stop playing games, Ben. What are you talking about?"

He smirked, clearly enjoying the tension he had created. "You really don't know, do you? Jack's not who you think he is. He's been lying to you, Emma. And I can prove it."

Emma's mind raced. She had trusted Jack. She had given him a part of herself that she hadn't shared with anyone in years. And now, here was Ben—her ex-husband, the one person she had tried so hard to forget—throwing doubt into everything.

"I don't know what you're trying to do, Ben," she said, her voice shaking with a mixture of fear and anger, "but whatever it is, you need to stop. I don't care about your games. You've done enough damage."

Ben's expression darkened, and for a moment, Emma saw the man he used to be—the man who had once made her feel like she was never enough. "I'm not playing games, Emma. I'm trying to help you see the truth."

Emma stood up abruptly, her chair scraping against the floor. "I don't want to hear it. You've already hurt me enough. If you really cared, you wouldn't be doing this."

But Ben's words followed her, lingering like a poison in the air. "You think you know him, Emma. You think you've found someone who's different. But in the end, they're all the same."

With those final words, he turned and walked out of the café, leaving Emma standing there, her heart pounding in her chest.

Her mind was a blur as she walked back to the apartment, her thoughts swirling like a storm. What had Ben meant? What was he trying to say about Jack? Was this just another one of his manipulative tactics, or was there some truth to his words?

When she walked through the door, Jack was there, waiting for her, his expression concerned but calm. He could always sense when something was wrong, and today was no different. He moved toward her, but she held up her hand, stopping him.

"Jack... I need to talk to you. I need you to tell me everything."

Jack frowned, his brow furrowing with concern. "What's going on, Emma? What happened?"

She hesitated, the weight of the truth pressing on her chest, but this time, she couldn't keep it to herself any longer. "Ben came to see me. He said some things about you, things I don't understand. And I need to know if they're true."

Jack's face went pale, his eyes narrowing as he looked at her, trying to gauge whether she was serious or just caught up in the whirlwind of emotions. But the look in her eyes told him everything he needed to know.

"Emma, listen to me," Jack said, his voice firm but gentle. "There's nothing you need to worry about. I've been honest with you. I don't know what Ben is trying to pull, but you have to trust me."

But Emma wasn't sure she could. Not anymore.

Chapter 57: Into The Unknown

"We are all the sum of the choices we make. The good, the bad, and the ones we never saw coming." — Unknown

Emma sat on the edge of the bed, her mind spinning with thoughts of Ben and what he had said. The conversation at the café, his cryptic warnings about Jack—it all weighed heavily on her chest. She had spent hours replaying the words in her mind, dissecting every syllable, trying to understand what they meant.

Jack had been patient when she returned home, but Emma hadn't been able to tell him everything. Not yet. She couldn't bring herself to repeat Ben's accusations—to ask Jack to explain something so deeply personal, something that had remained buried for years. The thought of confronting him, of questioning his past, left her feeling raw and vulnerable.

She had trusted Jack with so much already. She had let him in, let him see the parts of her that no one else had ever known. But now, a shadow of doubt hung between them, threatening to unravel everything they had worked for.

Jack had always been a pillar of strength in her life, and now she found herself questioning whether he was hiding something that could tear them apart. Her heart felt torn in two, caught between the love she had for him and the fear that his past would eventually consume them both.

She ran her fingers through her hair, trying to steady her breath. She needed answers—she needed to know the truth, no matter how painful it might be. But the thought of confronting Jack, of asking him about the things Ben had said, terrified her. Could she face the possibility that the man she had come to love wasn't who she thought he was?

Jack stepped into the room, breaking her from her thoughts. His expression softened when he saw her sitting there, her gaze distant. He moved closer, his footsteps quiet, and gently placed a hand on her shoulder.

"Emma," he said softly, "what's going on? You've been so distant lately. I can feel it."

She didn't answer right away, her emotions a tangled mess of confusion, hurt, and fear. Finally, she looked up at him, her eyes searching his face for any sign of deception. "Ben came to see me today."

The words felt heavy on her tongue, like a confession she hadn't been prepared to make. Jack's eyes darkened, and she saw the subtle shift in his posture, the way his muscles tensed.

"I figured he would," Jack said, his voice low. "What did he say?"

Emma swallowed hard, trying to steady her nerves. "He said... he said some things about you. About your past. Things that I don't understand."

Jack's jaw tightened, and for a moment, the room was thick with tension. Emma could feel the weight of his silence pressing down on her, making it harder to breathe.

"What did he say, Emma?" Jack's voice was firm now, his tone controlled but with an edge of something Emma couldn't place.

"He said that you've been lying to me," she replied quietly. "He said there are things about your past that you haven't told me. Things that could change everything."

Jack's eyes darkened further, and Emma saw the flicker of something—something fierce and protective—flash in his gaze. He stepped back, running a hand through his hair, as if trying to compose himself.

"Jack..." she started, her voice shaky. "I need to know if it's true. I can't keep living in this uncertainty. You've been so open with me about your past, but I—" she paused, trying to steady her emotions, "—I need to know everything. I need to understand."

Jack turned away from her, his back to her as he stared out the window. The silence between them stretched on, and Emma felt as if the walls were closing in around her. She could feel the weight of his internal battle, the conflict he was trying to suppress.

Finally, after what felt like an eternity, Jack spoke. His voice was softer now, tinged with regret.

"Ben is playing games, Emma. You know that. He always has."

"I know," she whispered, though the doubt still lingered. "But what did he mean? What is it that you haven't told me?"

Jack took a deep breath, and when he spoke again, his voice was laced with something deeper, something that carried the weight of a lifetime of pain. "I never wanted to tell you about her. I never wanted to bring my past into this."

"Her?" Emma asked, the word catching in her throat. She had never heard Jack refer to someone in such a way. "Who are you talking about?"

Jack turned to face her, his eyes darker now, his expression shadowed by something she couldn't quite read. "My ex-wife. The one Ben keeps mentioning."

Emma felt a chill crawl up her spine. "You've been married before?" The question felt foreign to her, even though it shouldn't have. It seemed impossible that she had never known this. They had shared so much—how had this part of his life remained hidden for so long?

Jack nodded, his gaze falling to the floor. "Yes. I was married for five years. It was a disaster from the start. I made mistakes. She made mistakes. We both thought we could fix it, but we couldn't."

Emma's heart ached as she watched him, his face drawn with a quiet sorrow. She had always suspected that Jack carried pain, but hearing the depth of it now, hearing the rawness in his voice, made her realise just how much he had buried.

"Why didn't you tell me?" she asked, her voice barely above a whisper. "Why keep it from me?"

"I didn't want to bring it into our relationship," Jack said, his voice thick with emotion. "I didn't want you to see me as someone broken, someone damaged by his past. I wanted to be the man you deserved, Emma, not the man who had failed at love before."

Emma reached out for him, her hand gently touching his arm. She understood now. She understood the fear that had kept him from opening up to her fully. He had been protecting himself, just as she had been protecting her own heart. The truth was, they both carried scars that were far from healed. But somehow, they had found each other—broken, imperfect, but willing to try again.

"I don't care about the mistakes, Jack," Emma said, her voice steady now. "I care about what we have. I care about you."

He looked up at her then, his eyes filled with gratitude and pain. "But Ben... he's still out there. He'll always be there, Emma. And I don't want him to keep hurting you."

Emma shook her head, her mind finally clearing. "He can't hurt me anymore. I'm not the same person I was when I was with him. And I'm not going to let him control my life, or yours, anymore."

Jack stepped closer, his hands cupping her face, his thumb brushing away the stray tear that had escaped her eye. "Then we fight this together, Emma. We face whatever's coming, together."

Her heart raced as she leaned into his touch, feeling the warmth of his presence, the sincerity of his words. For the first time in what felt like forever, she felt like they could overcome anything. Together.

Chapter 58: The Choice

"*Sometimes the hardest part isn't letting go but learning to start over.*" — Nicole Sobon

The morning sunlight streamed through the blinds, casting a soft glow over the room. Emma stood by the window, her gaze lost in the view of Sydney's sprawling skyline, but her mind was far from the serenity outside. It had been a sleepless night for both her and Jack, filled with the tension of unspoken words, lingering doubts, and the weight of revelations that could change everything.

Jack had spent most of the night in the guest room, giving Emma space to process everything they had discussed. She understood why he had pulled away; it wasn't just the revelation about his previous marriage. It was the emotional burden that came with sharing parts of oneself that had been buried for so long. He had trusted her with the raw truth, and now, Emma had to decide whether she could do the same. Whether she could let go of her own fears and face the man standing just beyond the door.

The truth had always been something she feared. Not because she couldn't handle it, but because the weight of it often felt unbearable. She had learned long ago that hiding behind a wall of silence was easier than confronting the messiness of her own heart. But with Jack, it felt different. With him, she wanted to try.

She heard the door creak open behind her, and then the soft padding of footsteps across the room. Jack was there, standing in the doorway, his figure framed by the light from the hallway. For a moment, neither of them spoke. They simply stood there, looking at each other, as if trying to gauge the right moment to break the silence.

"Emma," Jack's voice was hoarse, raw, as if he had been wrestling with his own thoughts, "I know last night was... a lot. I know I've kept things from you, and I'm sorry. But I want you to understand something. It's not because I don't trust you. It's because I didn't want to burden you with a past that I couldn't change."

Emma turned to face him, her heart aching at the vulnerability in his words. He looked so different in this moment—stripped of the confident, sometimes guarded man she had fallen for. Right now, he was just a man, a man with scars, just like her.

"I know, Jack," she said softly, her voice trembling slightly. "But you've never burdened me. You've always made me feel safe, like I could trust you. I didn't want to find out about your past from Ben. I needed to hear it from you."

He nodded, his eyes locking onto hers. "I never wanted you to find out like this. I wanted to be the one to tell you. But every time I thought about it, I just couldn't bring myself to—" He broke off, running a hand through his hair, frustration evident in his movements. "I don't know why it's so hard. Maybe it's because I don't want to lose you. Or maybe because telling you means finally facing it myself."

Emma's heart ached at the rawness in his words. She crossed the room and stood before him, her hand reaching out to gently grasp his. "I need you to understand something, too. I'm not afraid of your past, Jack. I'm afraid of what's happening right now, with us. I don't want to lose you, either."

For a long moment, they stood in silence, the weight of their shared vulnerability hanging in the air between them. And in that silence, something shifted. It was like the last wall that had been standing between them crumbled, leaving only the bare truth—two people, broken in their own ways, but still reaching for each other.

"I've been married before, Emma," Jack said again, his voice steady this time, "and it wasn't pretty. But I've learned from it. And I've done a lot of things wrong, but leaving her was the right thing. I didn't just leave her because we were unhappy. I left because I knew I couldn't be the man I needed to be for her. And I certainly couldn't be the man I wanted to be for someone else."

Emma squeezed his hand, her heart swelling with empathy. "What happened, Jack?"

He inhaled deeply, as though preparing to open a wound he had kept tightly sealed for far too long. "Her name was Olivia. We met when I was younger—too young, really. We both had big dreams, but we had no idea what it would take to build a life together. I was caught up in my career, in my ambition, and she was... well, she was beautiful, and I thought that was enough. But the truth is, we were never really compatible. And the more I tried to fix it, the more we drifted apart."

Jack paused, his gaze distant, as though lost in the memory. "I'm not proud of how I treated her. I was selfish, I was cold, and I put my own needs ahead of hers. But there was something else. Something I didn't see until it was too late."

Emma felt her chest tighten, and she took a step closer to him. "What do you mean?"

Jack turned to face her fully, his hands now clasped in front of him, as if trying to hold himself together. "I wasn't the only one with demons, Emma. Olivia had her own. She had... an addiction. A secret that she kept from me for months. I didn't know the extent of it until it was almost too late. By then, we were both trapped in a cycle of dysfunction."

His voice faltered, and Emma could see the shame etched into his features. "I couldn't save her. I couldn't fix what was broken between us, and I couldn't fix her. So I left."

The words hung in the air between them, heavy with the weight of truth. Emma could feel the sorrow in his voice, the guilt he carried for a love that had never been what it seemed. She reached out to him, her touch gentle on his arm.

"You don't have to carry that guilt, Jack," she said softly. "Not anymore. You didn't cause any of that. You made a choice to leave because you knew it wasn't healthy. That's the right thing."

Jack looked at her, his eyes filled with a mixture of gratitude and sadness. "I never thought I'd find someone like you, Emma. Someone who would understand, who wouldn't judge me for my past."

Emma smiled faintly, her heart swelling with affection for him. "I don't judge you, Jack. We all have our scars. We all have our pasts. But it's what we do with them that matters."

There was a pause, and Emma could feel the tension between them begin to dissipate, replaced by a fragile sense of connection. The past was something they both carried with them, but it no longer had to define their future. They could choose to leave it behind.

"I know this isn't easy, Emma," Jack said quietly, his gaze softening. "But I'm not hiding anything from you anymore. The past is the past, and I'm here, with you, in the present."

Emma nodded, her heart finally at peace. "We'll face whatever comes next, Jack. Together."

She stepped closer, her hand finding his again, and they stood there, in the quiet stillness of the room, knowing that the journey ahead would be far from easy. But for the first time in a long while, Emma felt a glimmer of hope. The truth had been painful, yes, but it had also been freeing. And now, as she stood beside the man she had come to love, she knew that the future was theirs to shape.

Chapter 59: Breaking Points

"*When you love someone, you're supposed to believe in them. But what happens when that belief is shaken, when trust becomes a fragile thread?*" — Unknown

The weeks that followed were a delicate dance of closeness and distance. Emma and Jack had navigated the aftermath of the revelations, each learning how to process the weight of the past while trying to rebuild a future together. They spent hours talking, more than they ever had before, but there were still moments where silence felt heavier than words.

Emma had come to understand that Jack's past, though painful, was a part of him—just as her own scars were a part of her. But even as they navigated the delicate balance of trust and vulnerability, a new challenge loomed on the horizon. One that neither of them had anticipated.

Jack had thrown himself into his work, as he always did when things became overwhelming. He would disappear into the office, his mind consumed by the intricacies of his projects, leaving Emma to face her own thoughts. At first, it had been a comfort—his focus meant he wasn't avoiding their relationship. But as the days wore on, she began to feel the distance creep in again. It wasn't just physical. It was emotional, too.

Emma sat at the kitchen table, the sunlight filtering through the window, casting long shadows across the room. She had been reading through a contract for her latest project, but the words blurred together as her mind kept drifting back to Jack. He hadn't been home for dinner again. It had become a pattern—a pattern she had learned to ignore, to rationalise. But something inside her was starting to crack. She could feel it in the pit of her stomach, an unsettling sense that things weren't as they seemed.

Her phone buzzed, pulling her from her thoughts. She glanced at the screen, seeing a message from Ben.

I need to talk to you. It's important.

Emma hesitated, her finger hovering over the reply button. The last time she had heard from Ben, it had been a warning about Jack, about things Emma didn't fully understand. She had told herself that she wouldn't let Ben's words affect her anymore, but the truth was, a part of her still listened. That same part that couldn't ignore the nagging feeling that something wasn't right.

She tapped out a quick reply. *What's going on?*

It's about Jack. You need to know something. It's time.

Emma's heart skipped a beat. There it was again. The shadow of doubt. She quickly typed a response: *I don't know what you're talking about, Ben. Stop playing games.*

But before she could send the message, a knock at the door interrupted her thoughts. She jumped, her heart racing, and quickly set the phone aside. As she approached the door, she could see the outline of a figure through the frosted glass. She opened the door, her breath catching in her throat as she saw who it was.

Standing there was a woman, tall, with long, dark hair and piercing green eyes that seemed to stare right through her. She wore a business suit, sharp and professional, but there was something about the way she held herself—an air of authority—that immediately made Emma uneasy.

"Can I help you?" Emma asked, trying to keep her voice steady, despite the sudden rush of unease that flooded her chest.

The woman's lips curved into a tight smile. "I'm Grace Parker. I work with Jack."

Emma's heart dropped. Grace Parker. She knew the name. Jack had mentioned her before—only in passing, but still. Grace was one of the senior partners at Jack's firm, someone he trusted. She had never imagined the day would come when Grace would show up at her doorstep, especially not after the tensions that had arisen between her and Jack in recent weeks.

"Is Jack here?" Emma asked, her voice a little shakier than she intended.

Grace's smile faltered for a fraction of a second. "No, he's not. But I need to speak with you. It's important."

Emma hesitated, her instincts telling her to shut the door, to turn away from whatever this woman wanted. But there was a strange look in Grace's eyes, something urgent, and for reasons Emma couldn't explain, she felt compelled to listen.

"Okay," Emma said finally, stepping back to allow Grace to enter. "Come in."

Grace walked into the apartment with a fluid grace, her heels clicking against the hardwood floor. Emma closed the door behind her, the sense of foreboding growing with every step Grace took.

"I won't beat around the bush, Emma," Grace said, turning to face her once they were both seated. "I know about your relationship with Jack, and I think it's important that you know the full truth about him."

Emma's stomach churned. There it was again—truth. The one thing she had been searching for, but the one thing that seemed so elusive, slipping just beyond her grasp.

"What do you mean?" Emma asked cautiously.

Grace's gaze flickered to the side, and for a moment, Emma thought she saw a flash of something like regret. But it was gone as quickly as it appeared, replaced by the calm, controlled exterior that Grace was projecting.

"I'm not here to cause trouble," Grace continued, her voice low. "But I think you need to hear the full story about Jack's past. There are things he hasn't told you. And frankly, I think it's time you knew. Not just for your own peace of mind, but for your safety."

Emma's pulse quickened. Safety? What was she talking about? She felt her breath catch in her throat, the air suddenly thick with tension.

"Jack's not who you think he is," Grace said, leaning in slightly, her eyes locked on Emma's. "There are things in his past that have been kept under wraps, things that could ruin everything. I'm not just talking about his ex-wife, either. There's something else, something darker. Something that could destroy him—and anyone close to him."

Emma's head spun. She didn't know what to believe. Grace's words were like a hammer to her chest, breaking apart the fragile trust she had tried so hard to rebuild. She had to know more. She needed to hear the full story.

"What is it?" she asked, her voice barely above a whisper.

Grace took a deep breath, her gaze unwavering. "Jack's been hiding something from you, something that goes back years. I'm not going to pretend I know all the details, but what I do know is this: Jack isn't the man he's led you to believe he is. And if you're not careful, he could drag you down with him."

Emma's mind raced as she tried to process Grace's words. What was Jack hiding? What could be so terrible that it could tear them apart?

Before she could speak, Grace stood up, her expression hardening. "I've said what I needed to say. Do with it what you will. But be careful, Emma. The man you love might not be the man you think he is."

With that, Grace turned and walked out, leaving Emma standing in the middle of the room, her heart pounding, her world once again shaken to its core.

Chapter 60: Unraveling Desires

"There's a fine line between love and obsession. And when you fall, it's easy to forget where one ends and the other begins." — Unknown

Emma stood by the window, the night stretching out before her, its darkness mirroring the uncertainty that had taken root in her heart. Grace's visit had left her shaken, her mind racing with questions she wasn't sure she wanted the answers to. What could Jack be hiding? How deep did the shadows of his past run, and what could this mean for them, for their future?

She replayed Grace's words over and over in her mind: *"Jack's not the man he seems to be. There are things he's hiding, things that could destroy everything."* The chill of fear settled in her chest, tightening like a vice. She had trusted Jack with her heart, with her vulnerabilities, and now she was left wondering if everything she knew about him was a lie.

The knock on the door startled her from her thoughts, and her heart skipped a beat. She had half-expected it to be Jack, returning from wherever he had been, but when she opened the door, it wasn't him. It was Ben. His face was grim, his usual easygoing demeanor replaced by something darker.

"Ben, what are you doing here?" Emma asked, a mix of relief and apprehension flooding her chest. She hadn't spoken to him in days, but now, seeing him standing before her, she felt like the universe had delivered him to her for a reason.

"I need to talk to you," Ben said, his voice low and urgent. "It's about Jack. And Grace."

Emma's heart pounded in her chest as she stepped back, allowing him to enter. She could feel the tension between them, but it was more than just the heavy air of unfinished business. This conversation—whatever it was—would shift the course of everything.

"I'm listening," Emma said, her voice steady despite the storm brewing inside her.

Ben shut the door behind him and moved further into the apartment, his eyes darting around nervously. "I've been working with Grace on a project at the firm, but I had no idea just how much trouble Jack's in. I didn't want to be the one to tell you this, but you need to hear it from someone who's not involved."

Emma's breath caught. "What are you talking about?"

Ben ran a hand through his hair, visibly uncomfortable, but his resolve remained firm. "Jack's involved in something bigger than you realize. He's made some decisions over the years that put him on a dangerous path. And Grace... she's scared. Scared of what will happen when everything finally comes to light."

Emma's stomach twisted. She had always known there were parts of Jack's life he kept private, but this—this was something different.

She didn't know whether she was being paranoid or if Ben was telling the truth, but the fear in his eyes told her that he wasn't just trying to make drama out of nothing.

"I don't understand," Emma said, her voice faltering for the first time in their conversation. "What's he done, Ben?"

Ben hesitated before answering, his eyes flickering with uncertainty. "Jack... he's been involved in some financial dealings that are highly questionable. I'm talking about serious money, Emma. Investments, illegal transactions, the kind of things that can ruin a person if they're ever discovered. And he's been hiding it all, pretending like everything is fine. But it's not."

Emma felt a cold wave of disbelief wash over her. This couldn't be true. Jack, the man she had come to love and trust, wasn't just keeping secrets—he was involved in something that could destroy him. Her mind raced, trying to reconcile the man she thought she knew with the one Ben was describing.

"Are you sure?" Emma whispered, almost afraid to hear the answer. "Jack has been... hiding illegal activities from me?"

Ben nodded, his expression serious. "I don't know all the details, Emma. But I've seen enough to know that this is bad. Really bad."

A thousand thoughts flooded her mind, each one more confusing than the last. Could she trust Jack? Could she trust anyone anymore? The man she had let into her heart, the man who had shared his past with her, was now wrapped up in something so much darker than she had ever imagined. The truth was, she didn't know where to go from here.

"Why are you telling me this, Ben?" Emma asked, her voice low. "What do you want me to do with this information?"

Ben seemed to struggle with the answer, but finally, he spoke. "I'm not asking you to do anything, Emma. I'm just telling you what you need to know. I don't want you to be blindsided if things get worse. Grace thinks this is all going to blow up, and when it does, it's going to destroy Jack. And maybe you, too."

Tears welled in Emma's eyes as she processed his words. She had trusted Jack—trusted him with everything. But now, everything she knew felt like it was slipping through her fingers. How could she even look at him the same way again? And yet, a part of her didn't want to believe it. She didn't want to believe that the man she loved was capable of something so catastrophic.

"Ben..." Her voice broke as she reached out for him, needing comfort, needing to understand. "What do I do? I don't know how to handle this."

Ben stepped closer, offering her a sympathetic look. "I don't know what to tell you, Emma. All I know is that you deserve the truth, the whole truth. Jack might never tell you. He's too proud, too afraid of what it'll mean if you find out. But you deserve to make your own choice."

Before Emma could respond, she heard the soft click of the front door opening. Jack had returned.

Her heart leapt in her chest as she turned toward the sound, her stomach twisting into knots. She had to face him now. She had to confront him and ask him the questions that had been tormenting her for hours. She couldn't keep living in the shadows of his secrets.

Ben, sensing the tension, gave her a nod. "I'm going to leave. But think about what I said, Emma. Please. Don't let him drag you down with him."

With that, Ben was gone, leaving Emma standing in the quiet of the apartment, her world upended. She had to make a choice now. Could she confront Jack about what she had learned? Could she believe in him, despite everything? Or was this the end of the road for them?

As Jack stepped into the living room, his eyes immediately locked with hers, and for a moment, the weight of everything between them hung in the air. Neither of them spoke. But in that silence, Emma knew one thing for sure: things would never be the same again.

"Emma," Jack said softly, his voice filled with a quiet unease. "We need to talk."

And for the first time in a long time, Emma wasn't sure she wanted to hear what he had to say.

Chapter 61: The Weight of Secrets

"Some truths are better left hidden, but the ones that matter always come to light." — Unknown

The silence between them was thick, suffocating. Jack stood just a few feet away, his gaze locked onto Emma, his face a mix of concern and something darker—guilt, perhaps, or fear. Emma could feel her pulse racing in her chest, the weight of the moment pressing down on her like a heavy burden. She hadn't expected him to walk through that door, not like this, not after everything she had just learned. The space between them felt wider now, more fragile than ever before.

He hadn't even taken off his coat yet, still standing in the doorway as if unsure of how to enter her world again. His eyes searched hers, but he seemed unable—or unwilling—to speak. The tension between them was palpable, the questions hanging in the air like a storm ready to break.

Emma's voice trembled as she finally broke the silence. "Jack, what's going on? What's the truth?"

His face hardened for a brief moment, and Emma could see a flicker of something—perhaps defensiveness, or the remnants of a lie he hadn't yet committed to. But then, as if realizing the gravity of the situation, he softened. He stepped into the room slowly, his every movement deliberate.

"I think you know," Jack said quietly, his voice low but heavy with meaning.

Emma's heart pounded in her chest, and every nerve in her body was on edge. "No, Jack. I don't know. Not anymore. I don't know what's real. I don't know what you've been hiding from me." Her voice wavered as the anger and hurt she'd been holding back began to rise. "What's going on? Why didn't you tell me the truth?"

Jack's eyes fell, guilt flickering across his face. He ran a hand through his hair, his frustration evident. "I didn't want to drag you into it, Emma. You deserve better than this."

"Better than this?" she repeated, her voice rising with the sting of betrayal. "I deserve honesty. I deserve trust. I deserve to know who I'm with, not some... shadow version of the person you've built for me."

He closed his eyes briefly, as though the words were cutting him more than they cut her. But when he opened them again, the walls that had been built around him for so long seemed to crack, just a little.

"Okay," Jack said, his voice hoarse. "You're right. You deserve to know the truth. But it's not what you think. It's not as simple as some illegal dealings or bad investments. It's complicated, Emma. So much more complicated than that."

Emma swallowed hard, her chest tight with anticipation and fear. "Then tell me. Please. I can't keep living in this limbo, not knowing if I can trust you."

Jack seemed to hesitate, his gaze dropping to the floor. He walked further into the room, his movements slow and deliberate, and took a seat on the couch. Emma remained standing, unable to bring herself to sit. The space between them felt insurmountable, like an ocean that neither of them could cross.

"The truth is..." Jack began, his voice low and pained. "I got involved with people I shouldn't have, years ago. It started innocently enough—business deals, investments. But then it became something more. Something dangerous." He paused, his hands clenched into fists as if bracing himself. "I tried to leave it behind when I moved to Sydney, when I met you. I told myself I could start fresh. But the past has a way of coming back, Emma. It always does."

Emma's stomach churned, but she forced herself to remain calm. "How? How did it come back?"

Jack sighed, rubbing his face as though the weight of his confession was crushing him. "I thought I could cut ties completely. But they... they found me. People I owed, people who never forget. And now they're threatening everything, Emma. My career, my life, and yours. I didn't want to involve you, not like this."

Emma's mind spun with the weight of his words. The life she thought she was building, the trust she thought they had—was it all a lie? Her heart broke as she felt the distance grow even more. "So what now? What are we supposed to do, Jack?"

"I don't know," Jack admitted, his voice raw. "I don't know what the right thing is. But I need to protect you. And I need to fix this, before it's too late."

"Protect me?" she asked, incredulous. "How can you protect me when you've been keeping this from me? When you've been hiding this entire side of your life? I don't know who you are anymore, Jack."

Her voice cracked, and the tears she had been holding back finally spilled down her cheeks. The dam had broken, and there was no turning back now.

Jack reached out to her, but she stepped back, shaking her head. "I can't just pretend like this doesn't matter, like this is some small mistake. You've been lying to me. You've been hiding who you really are from me. And I don't know if I can keep living like this."

The silence stretched between them again, both of them caught in the gravity of the moment. Jack's eyes were full of regret, but it was too late. The damage had been done, and Emma could feel it in every fiber of her being.

"I'm sorry, Emma," Jack said quietly, his voice breaking as he looked up at her. "I didn't mean to hurt you. I never wanted to."

"I know you didn't," Emma whispered, her chest tightening with pain. "But you did. And now I need time to figure out what I'm supposed to do with all of this."

Jack nodded slowly, as though he knew there was nothing more he could say. "I'll give you the time you need. But whatever you decide, I'll be here. I'm not going anywhere."

The finality of his words settled in her chest like a stone. She felt numb, as though everything she had believed in had been ripped away. For the first time in what felt like forever, she didn't know who to trust—not even herself.

She turned away, unable to look at him anymore, unable to face the consequences of everything that had been set into motion.

"I need some air," she murmured, her voice barely a whisper.

Jack didn't move, but she could feel his gaze on her back as she walked toward the door. He didn't stop her. He didn't ask her to stay.

And as she stepped out into the cool night air, the weight of her choices crashed down on her. She didn't know what the future held—didn't know if she could forgive Jack, or if the love they had shared was enough to overcome the shadows of his past.

But one thing was certain: her world had shifted, and she had no idea where it was going next.

Chapter 62: Fractured Truths

"The things that haunt us are the things we never said, the words we never spoke." — Unknown

The cool night air bit at Emma's skin as she stood on the balcony, her hands gripping the railing. The city stretched out before her, the lights of Sydney sparkling in the distance, but they felt far away now—like a life she could no longer touch. The weight of Jack's confession hung over her, heavy and suffocating, threatening to crush everything she had built with him.

Her mind was a storm of conflicting thoughts. She had trusted him, loved him, let him into her life and her heart. But now? Now she didn't know what to believe. Was he the man she thought he was? Or was this just another mask he had worn, hiding the truth from her all along?

Emma had always prided herself on being strong, on facing challenges head-on. But this—this was different. The man she loved had lied to her, and now his lies were unraveling everything. She didn't know if she could keep going down this path, not without knowing the full truth, not without understanding the extent of the mess he had created.

A soft knock at the door startled her, and she turned toward the sound. She had hoped, at first, it was Jack—coming to talk, to try and explain, to fix things. But when she opened the door, it wasn't him. It was Grace.

"Emma," Grace said, her voice heavy with something Emma couldn't quite place. "We need to talk."

Emma stepped aside to let her in, her heart pounding in her chest. Grace had always been an enigma to her, someone who had complicated her life from the very beginning. She hadn't expected her to show up now, not after everything that had happened with Jack. But there she was, standing in front of her with a look of urgency on her face.

"Grace, what's going on?" Emma asked, her voice hoarse, as though speaking was a struggle. She hadn't realized how much of her strength had been drained away until now, standing here in front of Grace, trying to figure out what came next.

Grace closed the door behind her, her face serious. "I know you're hurting right now, Emma. But I need to be honest with you, just like I was with Jack. There's something you don't know. Something you need to understand."

Emma's heart raced. She had already been through so much, and the last thing she wanted to hear was more secrets. But she couldn't stop herself from asking. "What is it, Grace? What do I need to know?"

Grace sighed, her eyes flickering with regret. "It's about Jack. And about me."

Emma's brow furrowed, her mind scrambling to keep up. "What about you?"

"I was involved in more than just a 'project' at the firm," Grace said, her voice quiet but intense. "I wasn't just trying to warn you out of concern for Jack. I have my own reasons. And I think you deserve to know the full truth."

Emma crossed her arms over her chest, her emotions a jumbled mess. "What do you mean?"

Grace's gaze shifted, her lips pressed together in a tight line. "I've been in love with Jack for years. Long before you came into the picture."

The words hit Emma like a punch to the stomach. She staggered back slightly, trying to process what Grace had just confessed. It wasn't jealousy that Emma felt—not exactly—but a deep, overwhelming sense of betrayal. Grace had been there, in Jack's life, in his world, long before Emma ever had a chance.

"I don't understand," Emma whispered, her voice shaky. "You... you've been in love with him?"

Grace nodded, her expression unreadable. "Yes. I never told him, though. I couldn't. But I've watched him, Emma. Watched him with you. And I know how much he loves you."

A bitter laugh escaped Emma's lips. "If he loves me, then why hasn't he been honest with me? Why did he keep all of this from me?"

"Because he's scared, Emma. Scared of losing you. Scared that the truth would drive you away."

Emma's chest tightened, her heart torn between the love she still felt for Jack and the painful reality of what was unfolding. "I don't know what to believe anymore."

Grace stepped closer, her voice softer now. "You need to understand something, Emma. Jack isn't just protecting himself. He's trying to protect you. He made mistakes, big ones, but he's not the same person

he was back then. He's trying to fix things. He's trying to be better, for yo
u."

"Why didn't he just tell me?" Emma whispered, her voice breaking. "Why didn't he trust me enough to let me in?"

Grace's eyes softened with empathy. "Because the truth is messy, and sometimes it's easier to keep things hidden. But Emma, Jack loves you. I can see it. I know it."

Emma's breath hitched as her emotions swirled. She had so many questions, so many doubts. But in this moment, standing before Grace, she realized something—she had been so focused on Jack's lies that she hadn't stopped to think about her own feelings, her own truths. What did she want? What did she need?

"I don't know if I can keep going like this, Grace," Emma admitted, her voice barely above a whisper. "I don't know if I can keep pretending that everything's okay, that I can forgive him for keeping this from me. I don't even know if I can trust him anymore."

Grace reached out, placing a hand on Emma's shoulder. "I get it, Emma. Believe me, I do. But you're going to have to make a choice. You can either walk away, let the past tear you apart, or you can fight for what you have. For what you could have. But you can't keep running away from the truth. You need to decide what's more important to you: the man you love, or the man you thought you knew."

Emma closed her eyes, letting her words sink in. She hadn't asked for any of this, hadn't expected her life to be turned upside down. But here she was, standing at a crossroads, with no easy answers. Jack's secrets, Grace's confession, and the storm that was brewing in her own heart—they all collided in that moment.

"Thank you, Grace," Emma said, her voice hoarse. "I don't know what I'm going to do, but I needed to hear this. I needed to know the truth."

Grace nodded, her expression softening. "Take your time. But whatever you decide, just remember that you're not alone in this. You have people who care about you. And sometimes, that's enough to start over."

As Grace left, Emma stood alone in the apartment once more, her heart a mess of emotions. She couldn't pretend that she wasn't torn. She couldn't pretend that her love for Jack was the same, not after everything that had happened. But she also couldn't ignore the love that still flickered inside her, the hope that somehow, they could find a way through this darkness together.

But was it too late?

The night was still young, but Emma knew her decisions, her choices, would echo far beyond this moment. She wasn't sure if she was ready for what came next, but she knew one thing: she couldn't keep running. She had to face her fears, her doubts, and the man who had both shattered and saved her heart.

Chapter 63: Between The Lines

The hours after Grace's departure felt like they moved in slow motion. Emma had barely been able to sleep, tossing and turning in her bed, her mind replaying everything. Jack's secrets, his past, Grace's confession—it all swirled together in a haze of confusion, guilt, and desire.

Emma had always thought that when love was tested, it was the external forces—the circumstances—that were the hardest to navigate. But now, in the silence of her apartment, she realized the hardest battle was within herself. The emotions she felt for Jack weren't just love; they were a deep, uncontrollable longing that stirred something darker within her. Something primal.

She could still feel the way his lips had tasted against hers, the way his body had molded to hers in the heat of their passion. There had been moments when everything had felt so real, so unbreakable. But now? Now it felt like everything was slipping through her fingers, like sand in an hourglass that had already run dry.

Her phone buzzed on the nightstand, breaking the heavy silence. Her heart jumped, but when she saw the caller ID, her stomach twisted. Jack.

For a moment, she debated letting it go to voicemail, but then the desire for answers—the need to understand—pushed her to pick up.

"Emma," Jack's voice crackled through the speaker, a rawness to it that made her stomach tighten. "Can we talk?"

Her pulse quickened, but she didn't want to be weak, not anymore. "I don't know if I'm ready for that, Jack."

"I need to see you," he pressed, his voice thick with something she couldn't quite place—regret, perhaps, or longing. "Please, Emma. I don't know what's happening between us, but I don't want to lose you. Not like this."

She bit her lip, standing by the window as the city lights flickered in the distance. The very air seemed charged, crackling with tension. A part of her wanted to say no, wanted to protect herself from more heartbreak. But another part—one that she couldn't ignore—yearned for him. Yearned for the man who had consumed her in ways she hadn't even fully understood.

"I'll meet you," she said, her voice barely above a whisper. "But don't think you can fix this with just words."

Jack exhaled sharply, relief and guilt mingling in his breath. "I won't try to. Just... please let me explain."

As the line went dead, Emma's mind swirled with conflicting emotions. She wanted to hear him out, wanted to understand the depth of his pain, but she also knew that each second she spent near him was a second she couldn't take back. The trust between them had shattered, and the shards of it seemed to pierce her heart with every thought.

But what was it about Jack that had such a hold on her? What was it about their chemistry, their intimacy, that made it so impossible to walk away from him?

The answer lingered just beyond her reach as she grabbed her jacket and headed out the door.

Jack's apartment was just as she remembered it—sleek, minimalist, with an air of controlled chaos. He was sitting on the couch when she entered, his eyes darkened with something deeper than the usual cool detachment. There was an edge to him now, a rawness that spoke of the guilt he had been carrying, the fear of losing her.

Emma stood just inside the door, her arms crossed over her chest. "You wanted to talk."

Jack's gaze never left her as he stood slowly, his movements careful, deliberate, as though every step was weighed down by the burden of his confession. "I need you to understand that everything I did, I did to protect you. And to protect myself. The people I'm dealing with... they're not like the people you're used to."

Her eyes narrowed. "And you thought keeping this from me would protect me?"

"No," Jack said, stepping closer, his voice soft but insistent. "I thought it would give you a chance to not be dragged into all of this. To live a normal life, free of my mistakes."

Emma shook her head, frustration boiling within her. "But it's too late for that, Jack. You brought me into this the moment you lied to me. The moment you made me believe that everything was perfect. That we were perfect."

"I never meant to hurt you." His voice cracked, and Emma saw something in his eyes—a vulnerability that made her breath hitch. "I just... I just wanted you to be happy. To love me without the baggage. Without the weight of my past."

Before she could respond, he was in front of her, his chest rising and falling with the intensity of his emotions. His hands found her waist, pulling her close, and despite herself, Emma didn't pull away. She could feel the heat radiating off him, the familiar presence of his body that still made her ache.

"Jack..." she murmured, her voice trembling.

"I'm sorry," he whispered, his forehead resting against hers. "I'm so fucking sorry, Emma. I don't deserve you. I don't deserve your love, but God... I need you. I can't lose you."

Her heart raced as his lips brushed against hers—gentle, tentative, as if he was testing the waters, unsure if she would pull back or let him in. She hadn't expected this—hadn't expected the tenderness mixed with desperation. She hadn't expected to feel the same heat pulse between them, the same hunger that had once consumed her.

But it was still there, undeniable, pulling her under like a rip tide.

Without thinking, she responded, her lips pressing against his with more urgency this time. The kiss deepened, the tenderness dissolving into something more intense, more urgent. His hands slid to her back, pulling her closer, and she could feel the tension in his body, the way he was trembling beneath her touch.

His fingers found the zipper of her jacket, tugging it down slowly, and she didn't stop him. Instead, she arched into him, needing him, wanting him in a way that didn't feel like a mistake, but a necessity. Every moment without him felt like a part of her was missing, a part she didn't know how to live without.

When the jacket fell to the floor, Jack's hands skimmed over her skin, sending shivers of anticipation through her. His lips left hers for a moment, trailing down her neck, the roughness of his stubble scraping against her sensitive skin. She moaned softly, tilting her head back to give him better access, the heat between them building to a fever pitch.

"Emma..." Jack breathed, his voice thick with desire. "Tell me what you need."

She could barely think, the overwhelming need to feel him, to erase the distance that had grown between them, clouding her judgment. "I need you," she whispered, her hands tugging at his shirt. "I need you to show me... show me that we can still have this. That we can still have something real."

Jack's hands moved with more urgency now, his lips crashing back into hers, as if trying to communicate everything he couldn't put into words. The kiss was frantic, hungry, as they both gave in to the intensity of the desire that had been building between them for so long.

In that moment, the world outside ceased to exist. There was no past, no secrets, no betrayals. There was only the two of them, tangled in the heat of their connection, seeking something in each other that they couldn't find anywhere else.

But as their bodies pressed closer, their hearts still weighed with the knowledge that this was only a temporary reprieve, a brief escape from the truths that would inevitably tear them apart again.

Chapter 64: The Edge of Everything

"We loved with a love that was more than love." — Edgar Allan Poe

The aftermath of their passionate reunion left Emma in a whirlwind of emotions. Jack's touch still lingered on her skin, his scent on her clothes, but as the reality of the situation settled over her, the weight of the past few days began to take hold. The tension that had been bubbling between them hadn't disappeared. If anything, it had only grown stronger, more complex.

As she lay in Jack's arms, his chest rising and falling beneath her head, Emma closed her eyes, letting herself rest in the silence between them. But no matter how much she tried to drown out the noise in her mind, it persisted—those haunting questions, those unresolved feelings. The things that Jack had said, the way he had looked at her... Was this truly the beginning of a new chapter for them, or was it just another fleeting moment, a desperate grasp at something that could never be?

Jack shifted slightly, his fingers lightly grazing her back, sending a shiver through her. She could feel his gaze on her, even without looking up, the weight of it heavier than the tension in the air. She wanted to believe in the connection they had, in the bond they'd shared, but she couldn't ignore the deep sense of unease that gnawed at her.

"Emma," Jack murmured, his voice low and steady. "I'm not going to let this go. I can't. I can't lose you again. Not after everything."

His words were both a promise and a plea, a delicate balance between hope and desperation. Emma lifted her head, meeting his eyes, searching for something—an answer, a glimpse of truth—but all she saw was the same intensity that had always been there.

"Jack..." she started, her voice faltering. She hated that it felt so hard to speak the words that had been on the tip of her tongue for days. But she had to say them. She couldn't keep running from the truth, even if it scared her. "We need to talk about what happened. All of it. The lies, the secrets, the way you've kept me in the dark. I can't... I can't pretend everything is fine when I'm drowning in confusion."

Jack's expression shifted, the confidence he'd once worn like armour faltering. He pushed himself up on his elbows, gazing down at her, and Emma noticed the way his jaw tightened, the tension in his eyes. For a moment, she thought he might pull away, retreat back into his guarded shell. But instead, he sighed, his hand reaching out to gently brush a lock of hair from her face.

"I know I've hurt you," he said, his voice thick with remorse. "I never meant to. But I didn't know how to tell you the truth without losing you. The people I'm involved with... they're dangerous.

I've made enemies, Emma. People who wouldn't hesitate to use you against me."

Emma felt a chill sweep over her at his words. The reality of what he was saying—what he had been hiding from her—was sinking in. She had always known there was more to Jack than he had let on, but this... this was different. This was a world she had never imagined, a world she didn't want to be part of.

"Dangerous?" she repeated, her voice barely a whisper. "What are you mixed up in, Jack?"

His gaze darkened, the flicker of something unreadable crossing his face. "Things I should have never gotten involved in. But once I did, it was too late. And now..." His voice trailed off, the weight of his unspoken words hanging heavy between them.

The silence stretched out, thick with unspoken fears and unresolved questions. Emma wanted to push him for more, to demand the full truth, but a part of her was afraid of what she might hear. Could she live with the reality of Jack's dangerous world? Could she handle the truth of everything he had been keeping from her?

But another part of her—one that had always believed in their connection, in the raw intensity between them—wanted to trust him. Wanted to believe that they could make it through whatever storm was coming.

"I don't know what to say," she whispered, her voice trembling. "I don't know if I can live in a world like that, Jack. I don't know if I can live with knowing that you've been keeping me in the dark, pretending everything was normal."

"I never wanted you to feel like you were a part of that world," Jack replied, his voice soft but urgent. "I never wanted you to feel like you had to be involved in the mess I've made. But I'm not asking you to understand everything right now. I just… I need you to trust me. I need you to believe that I'm trying to protect you."

Emma swallowed hard, fighting the tears that threatened to well up in her eyes. The emotions were overwhelming, and for the first time since their tumultuous journey began, she didn't know if she could continue down this path. Could she trust Jack with her heart, knowing that his life was so far removed from hers? Was it worth it?

She turned away, her back to him, and closed her eyes. The distance between them felt insurmountable, even though he was still close enough to feel the heat of his body. There was so much she didn't know, so much she couldn't comprehend. The truth was a jagged pill, one that she wasn't sure she was ready to swallow.

Jack reached for her, his hand gently resting on her shoulder. "Emma…"

"Please, don't," she said softly, her voice muffled by the pillow beneath her head. "I need time to think. I need to figure out what this all means. What you mean to me. What I mean to you."

He didn't answer immediately. The silence stretched, and Emma could feel him weighing his words carefully, choosing his next move with caution. She wasn't sure if it was the right decision—asking for space, for time—but it was the only thing she could do to gather herself. She had to regain control of the situation, even if that meant stepping back from the whirlwind that Jack had pulled her into.

"Okay," he finally said, his voice low. "I'll give you space. But I won't give up on us, Emma. I won't."

And with that, Emma felt the air between them shift, the tension dissipating slightly, though the unresolved feelings remained. She wanted to believe him, wanted to trust in the love they had shared. But for the first time, she wasn't sure if love was enough.

As she lay there in the quiet of the room, her mind racing with a thousand thoughts, one truth became clear: whatever decision she made, it would change everything.

Chapter 65: A Web of Lies

"The truth will set you free, but first, it will make you miserable."
—James A. Garfield

Emma had spent the entire day in a haze of confusion. Every corner of her mind seemed to lead her to a different conclusion, and the weight of her uncertainty pressed heavily on her chest. The space between her and Jack felt palpable, like an invisible wall that neither of them had the courage to dismantle.

She hadn't heard from him since their conversation earlier. There had been no calls, no texts, nothing but silence. Emma wasn't sure what to make of it. Was it his way of giving her space, or was it a sign of something deeper? Perhaps he needed time to process his own thoughts, too.

But despite her determination to keep her distance, her mind kept drifting back to him—the way he had looked at her with those dark, unreadable eyes, the way his touch had ignited a fire inside her. Jack was a puzzle, a mystery she had been trying to solve ever since they first crossed paths. And now, she was more lost than ever.

It wasn't just the secrets, the lies, or the dangerous world he was tangled in. No, there was something more profound at play. It was the fear of being hurt again, of being left behind in the chaos of his world. The idea of walking away from him, of shutting him out completely, was terrifying. But staying... staying meant risking everything.

Her phone buzzed suddenly, pulling her from her thoughts. She stared at the screen, her heart skipping a beat as she saw Jack's name.

She hesitated for only a second before answering, her thumb hovering over the green button. She took a deep breath, trying to steady her racing heart.

"Emma," his voice came through the phone, rough and tentative. "Can we talk?"

Her stomach twisted at the sound of his voice, and despite her inner turmoil, she couldn't deny the pull she felt toward him. "Of course," she replied softly, keeping her tone neutral, as if she were speaking to someone she didn't know intimately.

"I'm coming over," Jack said, his voice laced with urgency. "Please, just... let me explain everything. I know I've fucked up, but I need you to understand. I can't lose you."

Before she could respond, he hung up. Emma stared at the screen for a long moment, her mind a swirl of emotions. Was she ready for this conversation? Could she face the truth of everything Jack had hidden from her? Could she allow herself to trust him again, knowing how deeply he had deceived her?

She didn't know. But one thing was certain—she wasn't going to be able to move forward until they both confronted the truth.

Within an hour, there was a knock on her door. Emma's heart pounded in her chest as she opened it, her gaze meeting Jack's. He stood there, his posture rigid, his eyes searching hers with a vulnerability she hadn't seen before. It was raw, almost desperate, and it made her heart ache.

"I know I've hurt you," he said immediately, stepping inside when she motioned for him to. His voice was thick with regret, and his eyes seemed to search for any sign that she might still care. "But I'm here now, and I want to fix things. I want us, Emma. I've been a coward. I kept you at arm's length because I was afraid of losing you. But I can't do this anymore. I can't pretend I don't feel everything I feel for you."

Emma swallowed hard, her heart racing. His words sent a mixture of warmth and fear through her. She didn't know if she was ready to dive back into this, to open herself up to the possibility of being hurt again.

But as she looked at him—his dark, penetrating gaze, the vulnerability in his posture, the raw honesty in his voice—she knew deep down that this wasn't just about the lies. This wasn't about the secrets. This was about something more profound: a connection that refused to die, no matter how much they tried to bury it.

"You've been hiding things from me, Jack," Emma said, her voice shaky but determined. "You've kept me in the dark about everything, and I can't keep pretending it doesn't matter. I need to know what's going on. I need the truth, or we can't keep doing this."

Jack exhaled sharply, his shoulders sagging. "I know. And I want to give it to you, Emma. I want to tell you everything. But there's so much at stake. You have to understand that."

She stepped closer to him, her eyes narrowing with a mixture of concern and anger. "I don't care about the stakes anymore. I care about you, and I care about us. But I can't be a part of your world if it's filled with lies and deceit."

Jack ran a hand through his hair, frustration and helplessness flashing in his eyes. "You don't get it," he muttered under his breath. "I've made promises to people that I can't break. And if I tell you everything, it could destroy everything we have. I don't want that, Emma. I can't lose you."

The emotion in his voice was palpable, but Emma was tired of living in the shadows of his secrets. She was tired of being left to wonder, to guess, to feel like a stranger in her own life.

"Then let me decide, Jack," she said, her voice firm, but with an edge of vulnerability. "Let me be a part of this. Let me decide if I want to stay, if I want to risk everything for you. But I can't do that without knowing the truth."

There was a long silence between them, the air thick with the weight of her words. Jack's eyes softened as he stepped closer, his hand reaching for hers. The touch was tentative, as if he was afraid she might pull away. But Emma didn't move. She let him hold her hand, their fingers intertwining in a simple yet intimate gesture that spoke volumes.

"I'll tell you everything," he whispered. "But you need to trust me. You need to believe that I'm doing this because I love you, and I can't live without you. You're my reason, Emma. The only reason."

Tears welled in Emma's eyes at his words. She had never heard him speak with such raw emotion, such sincerity. She could feel the truth in his touch, in the depth of his gaze. And for a moment, she allowed herself to believe him—to believe that they could work through this, that they could build something solid out of the ashes of their fractured past.

She nodded slowly, her voice barely audible. "I trust you."

Jack's face broke into a small, relieved smile, and for the first time in what felt like forever, Emma allowed herself to lean into him, to let the warmth of his embrace surround her. The fear was still there, lurking in the back of her mind, but in that moment, it didn't matter. What mattered was the truth between them, the chance to rebuild and redefine their love.

And as their lips met in a slow, lingering kiss, Emma knew that this was only the beginning. Whatever lay ahead, they would face it together.

Chapter 66: The Fire Within

"P assion is energy. Feel the power that comes from focusing on what excites you." — Oprah Winfrey

The days that followed were a blur for Emma. Jack's words lingered in her mind, echoing in the quiet moments when she was left alone with her thoughts. He had promised to tell her everything, to open up in ways he had never done before, but part of her feared that the more she learned, the more she might wish she hadn't asked. The weight of his secrets was still fresh, a shadow that hung over them both.

Despite the lingering tension, the quiet moments they shared began to build a fragile peace between them. They spent more time together—dinner dates, walks by the harbor, nights spent in the comfort of each other's arms. It was as if they were trying to rebuild something that had been broken, piece by delicate piece. But even the intimacy between them felt tinged with hesitation. Every kiss, every touch, was underscored by the knowledge that there were still things unsaid.

One evening, as the sun dipped below the horizon, painting the Sydney skyline in shades of purple and gold, Emma found herself sitting beside Jack on the balcony of his apartment. The soft hum of the city was a distant murmur, drowned out by the quiet stillness of their shared space. He hadn't said much since he arrived that evening, and Emma wasn't sure if she should bring up the conversation they had been avoiding. She knew they couldn't keep running from it—there was too much at stake.

"Jack," she said softly, breaking the silence, her voice tentative but firm. "You promised me the truth. I need to know what's really going on."

He didn't respond immediately. Instead, he stared out at the city, his face unreadable in the dimming light. Emma waited, her fingers absently tracing the edge of her wine glass as she watched him, the weight of her unspoken words pressing on her chest.

"I know," he replied finally, his voice low. "I've been trying to find the right way to tell you. But the truth... it's not something I can just say without it changing everything. You don't know what you're asking for, Emma."

Emma felt a chill at his words, the fear and uncertainty creeping back into her veins. "Then maybe I should know," she said quietly, her gaze meeting his. "Maybe I need to understand what you've been hiding. Maybe we're not meant to be in the dark anymore."

Jack turned to face her, his eyes darker than she had ever seen them. The weight of his stare felt like a physical thing, pressing her back into her seat. "I'm not trying to protect you from the truth because I don't trust you," he said, his voice tight with emotion. "I'm doing it because I'm afraid you won't be able to handle it. This life... the people I've dealt with... it's dangerous, Emma. And it's a life I didn't want you to be a part of. Not when you didn't ask for it."

She felt a pang in her chest. The fear in his eyes, the raw vulnerability, stirred something deep inside her. He had always kept his distance from her, never truly letting her in. But now, she realized, it wasn't just his desire to protect her from harm—it was his own fear of losing her, of showing her a side of him that could push her away forever.

"I've already seen glimpses of it, Jack," Emma replied softly, her fingers reaching for his. "I've seen the way you pull away, the things you've been hiding. I'm not stupid. I know there's more to this than you're telling me. And I can't keep pretending like I'm okay with that. I can't keep living in the shadows."

Jack closed his eyes for a moment, exhaling a deep breath. When he opened them again, his gaze softened, but the tension in his jaw remained. "You're right. I owe you more than this. But you have to understand, the world I've been caught in isn't a simple one. There's more at play than just me and you. And I... I've made enemies, Emma. Powerful ones."

His words sent a shiver down her spine. Enemies. Powerful ones. The pieces of the puzzle were beginning to fall into place, but they only made the picture more complex, more frightening.

"I'm not afraid of your enemies, Jack," she said, her voice steady despite the fear rising in her chest. "I'm afraid of what this is doing to us. I'm afraid of losing you to a life I don't understand. I'm afraid of not being able to trust you anymore."

Jack reached for her hand, his grip gentle but firm. "I won't let you lose me, Emma. Not like this. I've been keeping my distance because I thought it was easier for you to live without knowing everything. But I was wrong. I can't keep lying to you. Not anymore."

He stood up and began to pace, his steps slow, deliberate. Emma watched him, her heart aching as she saw the internal struggle written on his face. He was caught between the man he wanted to be and the one he had become. The walls he had built around himself were beginning to crumble, piece by piece.

"Who are they, Jack?" she asked softly, her voice breaking through the silence. "Who are these people that are making you so afraid?"

Jack stopped pacing and turned to face her, his eyes dark with a mixture of regret and fear. "It's not just one person, Emma. It's a network of people. Criminals, politicians, people with power who don't care who they hurt to get what they want. I've done things I regret, things I never thought I'd be a part of, and now... now I'm in too deep. And the only way out is to either destroy them or get destroyed."

Emma's heart thudded in her chest, the enormity of his words settling over her like a heavy fog. "And you think you can protect me from all of this?" she whispered, her voice barely audible.

Jack stepped closer, his hands reaching for her. "I don't know. But I'll do whatever it takes to keep you safe. I swear."

He pulled her into his arms, and Emma closed her eyes, letting herself lean into the comfort of his embrace. The love she felt for him was still there, as strong and undeniable as it had ever been. But now, the reality of their situation was impossible to ignore. They were standing on the edge of something dangerous, something that could pull them both under.

"I don't want to lose you," she whispered, her fingers tightening around his shirt. "But I can't live in a world like this. I can't live in fear of everything falling apart."

"We'll figure it out," Jack murmured against her hair. "We'll find a way."

But Emma knew that the path ahead wouldn't be easy. The road they were walking was fraught with danger, with lies and betrayal lurking around every corner. And no matter how much they loved each other, she couldn't shake the feeling that the more they uncovered, the more they would both lose.

Chapter 67: In the Depths of Desire

"There is no remedy for love but to love more." — *Henry David Thoreau*

The night had stretched long, the city lights below casting a cool glow over the balcony where Emma and Jack sat in silence. The conversation they had started earlier was far from over, but it felt like they had both run out of words for the moment. The weight of the truth hung between them like an unspoken promise, one that neither of them was ready to face entirely. Jack was lost in thought, his fingers absentmindedly tracing the edge of his glass, his expression unreadable in the soft light of the room.

Emma watched him, feeling a knot twist in her stomach. There was so much more she wanted to say, to understand, but she couldn't shake the feeling that every answer would only lead to more questions. She had always thought of their love as something unbreakable, something they could navigate through any storm, but now... now the storm felt closer than ever. She had seen the cracks, felt them deep in her bones. And she couldn't ignore them anymore.

"Jack," she said, her voice breaking the silence. "Do you ever regret it? Regret everything that's happened, the choices you've made?"

He didn't answer at first. His jaw tightened, his eyes distant as though he was reliving moments from a past that was better left forgotten. Emma reached out, her hand brushing against his, seeking some kind of connection—some kind of answer that would give her the peace she so desperately needed.

"I do," he said finally, his voice rough, the weight of his admission heavy. "I regret it every damn day. I never thought I'd end up here, in this mess, with everything on the line. But the choices I made—those were my choices, Emma. And I can't take them back."

Emma squeezed his hand, her heart aching for him. She knew the guilt that haunted him, the burden of decisions made in a world he couldn't escape. But she also knew that they couldn't continue like this, walking in the shadow of the past without ever stepping into the light of the future.

"Then what are we doing, Jack?" she whispered, the question hanging in the air like a fragile thread. "What are we really doing if we're not being honest with each other?"

His eyes met hers, and for a moment, everything else seemed to disappear—the city, the world outside, the tension between them. It was just the two of them, alone in this fragile moment, bound by the love they had shared and the weight of the secrets they had yet to fully confront.

"I'm trying," Jack said softly, his voice filled with emotion. "I'm trying to make things right. But this... it's not just about us anymore. It's about everything I've built, everything I've destroyed. And I'm scared, Emma. I'm scared that no matter what I do, it won't be enough."

Emma stood up then, her legs shaking slightly as she walked to the railing of the balcony. The wind was gentle against her skin, carrying with it the smell of salt from the harbor below. She closed her eyes, letting the cool air soothe the heat of the moment, trying to make sense of everything she had learned, everything she had yet to understand. She could feel Jack's presence behind her, his energy just a few feet away, but there was a chasm between them now. A chasm she wasn't sure how to cross.

"You don't have to do this alone," she said, her voice stronger now, the certainty rising in her chest. "We can figure it out together. Whatever it is, Jack, we can face it together. But you have to trust me. You have to stop pushing me away."

Jack didn't answer immediately, but when he did, there was a shift in his voice. "I want to believe that, Emma. I really do. But I've seen how this ends before. I've seen how people get hurt, how everything falls apart when you're not careful. And I won't let that happen to you. Not if I can stop it."

Emma turned to face him, her eyes locked onto his with a quiet intensity. "I don't want you to protect me, Jack. I want you to trust me. I want us to be honest with each other. And if you can't give me that, then I don't know what we have left."

For a long moment, neither of them spoke. The tension in the air was thick, almost suffocating. But then, slowly, Jack took a step forward, his hand reaching for hers. "I'm sorry," he murmured, his voice raw with regret. "I've been selfish, Emma. I've been trying to protect you from the worst parts of myself, but in doing so, I've kept you in the dark. I've kept you at arm's length. And I can't do that anymore. I'll tell you everything, but you need to know that it won't be easy. And it won't be safe. Not for either of us."

Emma nodded, her heart pounding in her chest as she held his gaze. "I'm ready," she said quietly, though a part of her feared that she wasn't. "I need to know, Jack. I need to know if we can make it through this. If we can survive what's coming."

Jack's grip on her hand tightened. "We can survive," he said with more conviction than Emma felt. "But it's not just about surviving anymore. It's about living, together. We owe it to each other to try.'

And then, just as the words hung in the air, there was a shift in the atmosphere. The hum of the city seemed to fade into the background, and Emma felt a chill sweep through her as the sound of a car engine revving in the distance grew louder. The tension in the air became palpable, an unseen warning that something was about to change.

Jack's eyes narrowed, his jaw setting as he looked toward the street below. Emma felt a sudden unease coil in her stomach. She had seen that look on Jack's face before—when danger was near, when things were about to spiral out of control.

"Stay here," Jack said quietly, his voice hardening with the familiar edge of authority. "I'll be right back."

Before Emma could protest, he was already gone, disappearing into the night with a speed and purpose that left her breathless.

Chapter 68: Inescapable Tides

"We are most alive when we're in the depths of love." — Anonymous

The night had fallen, casting a dark veil over the city that stretched endlessly before them. The once gentle hum of Sydney's bustling streets now felt like a distant murmur, drowned by the stillness between Emma and Jack. They had come so far, fought so hard for this moment of connection, but now, the shadows that hung between them seemed to stretch longer than ever. Jack had left in a hurry, his footsteps disappearing into the night like a ghost slipping away. Emma stood on the balcony, the cool breeze pulling at her hair, as she tried to make sense of everything that had been said, everything that had been left unsaid.

The truth was a heavy thing. Jack's admission, his fear of losing her, had shaken her to her core. She had always known there were parts of him that he kept hidden, but hearing him speak so openly about his regrets, his fear of dragging her into his dark world, made everything feel so much more real. He had been protecting her—no, shielding her—from the truth, but she had always known that there was more. And now that the veil had been lifted, Emma found herself questioning everything she thought she knew.

What if she wasn't strong enough to handle the truth? What if the weight of it all would break them apart instead of bringing them closer?

As the minutes stretched into hours, Emma's thoughts began to spiral. She couldn't shake the image of Jack disappearing into the night, the urgency in his steps a clear sign that something wasn't right. She knew he wasn't telling her everything. She knew he was still hiding something, keeping her at arm's length even as he promised to open up. It wasn't just about the danger he had faced or the enemies he had made—it was about something deeper, something more personal. And she wasn't sure if she was ready to hear it.

Her phone buzzed in her pocket, snapping her out of her thoughts. She pulled it out quickly, her heart racing as she saw the name on the screen.

It was Jack.

For a moment, she hesitated, unsure of what he would say. Her pulse quickened as she swiped to answer, holding the phone to her ear. "Jack?" she said, her voice quiet, unsure.

"Emma," his voice came through, strained, yet steady. "I need you to listen to me. I—there's something you need to know, and it can't wait."

Her heart skipped a beat. The urgency in his tone sent a wave of anxiety through her chest, and she quickly moved away from the balcony, pacing back into the apartment. "What's going on?" she asked, her voice tight. "What happened? Why did you leave so suddenly?"

"I'm sorry," he said, his voice carrying a note of regret. "I didn't want to drag you into this, but I think it's time you know. I... I don't have much time. There's someone I need to meet. Someone who's been watching us."

Emma froze, her breath catching in her throat. "Who? Who's been watching us?"

Jack's voice lowered, the tension palpable even through the phone. "Someone from my past. Someone I thought I'd left behind. But they're back, and they're not going to stop until they get what they want."

Emma's mind raced, her heart pounding in her chest. This was it—the moment she had been dreading. The truth was no longer a distant threat. It was here, in the form of someone who had been lurking in the shadows all along. "What do they want, Jack?" she whispered, her voice barely audible.

"I don't know," he admitted, his voice filled with frustration. "But I won't let them hurt you. I'll make sure of it. But you need to stay away from this, Emma. Please. I can't lose you to this world I've been a part of."

Her hands trembled as she gripped the phone, the weight of his words settling over her like a crushing burden. "I'm not afraid of your past, Jack," she said, her voice gaining strength. "I'm not afraid of you. I'm afraid of losing you, of never really knowing who you are. Of you shutting me out."

There was a long pause on the other end of the line. For a moment, Emma thought he might have hung up, but then he spoke again, his voice softer now. "You deserve the truth, Emma. And I promise, when all this is over, I'll tell you everything. But I need you to trust me. Please."

"Trust you?" Emma echoed, her voice trembling with emotion. "How can I trust you when you keep pushing me away? How can I trust you when you don't even trust me enough to tell me the whole truth?"

"I'm doing this for you," Jack replied, his voice laced with frustration. "Because I don't want you to get hurt. I don't want to pull you deeper into this world of lies and deception."

Emma's heart ached. She wanted to believe him. She wanted to believe that everything he did, every decision he made, was in her best interest. But the more he pushed her away, the more she realized that she couldn't keep living in the dark. She couldn't keep pretending that everything would be okay if she just waited for him to come back to her with all the answers. She needed the truth now, and she needed it from him.

"Jack," she said, her voice steady, "I love you. But I can't keep living like this. I can't keep pretending that I'm okay with not knowing who you really are. If you want me to trust you, then you have to trust me. You have to let me in, completely."

Another silence stretched between them, thick with unsaid words. Finally, Jack spoke, his voice a mixture of resolve and vulnerability. "You're right. You deserve more than this. I'll come back to you. But I need to finish what I started first. I'll be back as soon as I can. Just... stay safe. Please."

"I will," Emma promised, though she couldn't shake the nagging feeling in the pit of her stomach. As much as she wanted to believe him, she knew that nothing would be the same after tonight. The truth was out there, waiting for them both, and she wasn't sure if she was ready to face it.

Jack didn't return that night. The hours ticked by in a haze of restless anticipation, leaving Emma unable to sleep, unable to think of anything but the threat Jack had mentioned—the person from his past who was now hunting them both. Her mind whirled with possibilities, each darker and more dangerous than the last. She tried to tell herself that Jack would come back, that he would keep his promise to tell her everything, but the more she thought about it, the more she realized that the life Jack had kept hidden from her was not one she could simply ignore. It was all-consuming, suffocating, and the longer she stayed in the dark, the more it would destroy them both.

As the night bled into early morning, Emma found herself pacing, waiting for the sound of Jack's footsteps to return to her apartment. But it never came. The only sound was the rhythmic ticking of the clock, counting down the seconds of her uncertainty.

The phone rang just after sunrise.

Chapter 69: Fractured Realities

The city outside had long since settled into the stillness of the early hours. Emma stood in the dimly lit apartment, the glow from the kitchen window casting long shadows across the room. Her body was alive with anticipation, her senses heightened from the events of the night before. Jack's absence left her with a sense of emptiness, but it was more than just the physical absence of his presence. It was the emotional void that lingered—a hole she hadn't even known existed until now.

She had always known Jack was hiding something from her. She had always sensed there was a darkness to him, something that pulled at him from deep within. But what had happened last night, when he had left her standing there, uncertain of what he was truly facing, had shaken her. It wasn't just the secrets he kept from her—it was the way he made her feel. The way he pushed her away, only to pull her back in with an intensity that left her breathless.

She couldn't deny it anymore. The way he affected her—the way he made her ache for him, to the core of her very being—was unlike anything she'd ever experienced. And in his absence, that longing had only grown stronger. The touch of his hand, the heat of his breath against her skin, the way his body moved against hers—it had all left an indelible mark on her.

Emma moved to the balcony, gazing out over the city. The night sky was clouded, but the faintest glimmer of stars shone through, just enough to make her feel connected to something bigger than herself. She wanted to be close to him again. To feel the weight of his body against hers. To lose herself in the flames that always seemed to burn between them.

Her phone buzzed in her pocket, startling her. She pulled it out, the screen illuminating her face as she saw the name.

It was Jack.

She didn't hesitate this time. Her thumb pressed against the screen, answering the call almost instinctively. "Jack," she breathed, her voice trembling despite her best efforts to remain calm.

"Emma," Jack's voice came through, raw, urgent. "I'm coming back. I need to see you. I can't stand being away from you any longer. But there's something you need to understand. I don't just want you, Emma. I need you. In ways I never thought possible."

Her heart skipped a beat. She closed her eyes for a moment, the ache in her chest intensifying. "Jack, you don't have to say that," she whispered. "I already know how you feel. But what you're hiding... What's going on? Why can't you let me in?"

He exhaled slowly, his breath shaky. "It's not that simple. There's a part of me that's darker than you could ever understand. But I won't let that part of me tear us apart. Not now, not ever."

Emma's heart was racing, her body alive with anticipation as she moved back to the couch, her legs shaky beneath her. "Then come back," she urged, her voice barely above a whisper. "Come back to me. Let me in. Let me feel you. Let me help you carry whatever it is you're burdened with."

She could hear the hesitation in his breath, the vulnerability that he so rarely allowed her to witness. "Emma," he said softly. "I've been fighting this. Fighting you. Fighting the way you make me feel. But it's useless. I want you. I need you. And I need you to know the truth. All of it."

Her pulse quickened, her breath shallow as the words hung between them like a promise, a dare, a challenge. "Then tell me. Please. No more secrets."

There was a long silence on the other end of the line. She could almost hear him wrestling with himself, trying to find the courage to be completely vulnerable. "I'm coming," he finally said, his voice low and thick with desire. "And when I do, I won't leave until you understand every part of me. The good, the bad, the dark."

"I'm ready," she breathed, the fire inside of her igniting again. She had wanted him for so long, had needed him in a way that transcended mere physicality. She wanted him—the whole of him. His darkness, his light, every part of him that he had kept hidden from her. It was time for them to be raw together.

"I'll be there soon," Jack's voice was rough, filled with longing. "Hold on, Emma. Just hold on."

She closed the phone, setting it gently on the table, her body humming with excitement. The need for him was almost unbearable, a constant ache that she couldn't ignore. She moved to the bedroom, slipping out of her clothes slowly, savoring the moment of anticipation. She wanted to look her best for him, wanted to make him see her—see the depth of her longing, the way her body ached for him in ways that she had never known before.

As she slipped under the sheets, the cool fabric against her bare skin only heightened the heat of her desire. The minutes ticked by, each one stretching longer than the last. She closed her eyes, imagining his touch, the feel of his hands on her body, the way he kissed her with such urgency, as though he couldn't bear to wait any longer.

When the door finally opened, Emma's breath caught in her throat. Jack stood in the doorway, his eyes burning with an intensity that took her breath away. His gaze swept over her, lingering on the curves of her body, the softness of her skin, the flush of desire painting her cheeks. He didn't speak at first, just stood there, taking her in like a man starved.

She swallowed hard, her body trembling with anticipation. "Jack," she whispered, her voice barely audible. "Come to me."

Without another word, Jack closed the door behind him, his movements purposeful, predatory. He crossed the room in two strides, his body an irresistible force as he stood beside the bed. His eyes never left hers as he reached for the hem of his shirt, pulling it over his head in one smooth motion.

Emma's breath caught in her throat as the sight of him—his broad chest, the definition of his muscles, the tattoos that traced the lines of his skin—washed over her. He was the embodiment of desire, a vision of strength and sensuality that made her heart race even faster. He was everything she wanted and more.

She reached for him, her fingers trembling as she ran them down his chest, feeling the warmth of his skin, the heat radiating off of him. He was a living flame, and she was desperate to get closer, to feel the fire of him against her own.

Jack groaned as her fingers traced the line of his abs, his hands gripping the edge of the bed. "Emma," he murmured, his voice rough. "I can't wait anymore. I need to feel you. Now."

Her heart pounded in her chest as she pulled him down onto the bed with her, her body arching into his, urging him closer. She wanted to taste him, to feel every inch of him, to lose herself completely in the heat between them.

Their lips met in a fiery kiss, their mouths hungry, demanding. The kiss deepened, became more urgent as their hands roamed over each other's bodies, pulling, pushing, exploring. Every touch, every caress, set off a spark inside her, a fire that burned hotter with every second they were together.

Jack's hands were everywhere, exploring the curves of her body, the softness of her skin, the places only he knew how to touch to make her feel alive. She responded in kind, her hands tracing the lines of his body, the muscles that tensed under her touch, the hardness of him that she could feel even through his jeans.

Her body surged with need, and she could feel Jack's pulse racing, matching her own. The tension between them was a living thing, palpable, suffocating. They both knew they couldn't hold back any longer.

With a low growl, Jack moved, flipping her onto her back, his body pressing down against hers. He hovered over her for a moment, his face inches from hers, his breath hot on her skin. "I need you, Emma," he whispered, his voice raw with desire.

"I'm yours," she breathed, her hands tugging at his jeans, pulling them down as she kissed him with all the urgency of her need.

And in that moment, there were no more walls, no more secrets. Just the heat, the passion, and the undeniable truth that they belonged to each other.

Chapter 70: Drenched in Desire

"When you love someone, it's not about owning them. It's about seeing them as they truly are, and still wanting them with all your soul." — Unknown

The morning light filtered softly through the curtains, casting a warm, golden hue over the room. The air was thick with the aftermath of the night—a haze of passion, urgency, and longing that had yet to dissipate. Emma lay in Jack's arms, her head resting on his chest, feeling the steady rhythm of his heartbeat beneath her ear. His fingers played with the strands of her hair, each movement slow and deliberate, as though savoring the moment before reality fully took hold.

She had never felt this way before. So connected, so utterly consumed by someone else. Jack's presence in her life had become a storm, both thrilling and terrifying, and now, lying here with him, she felt as though her entire world had shifted. It was no longer just about the physical connection—the intensity of their desire—it was something deeper, more profound. Something that pulled at her heart in ways she couldn't yet understand.

For the first time in her life, Emma was forced to confront her own vulnerability. With Jack, she didn't need to hide her desires, her fears, or her passions. They had stripped away the walls she had spent years building around herself, leaving her bare and open to the rawness of her own emotions.

And she wanted it. All of it. She wanted to know him completely, to understand every part of him—the dark, the light, the pain, and the pleasure. Because, somehow, she had come to realize that in loving him, she would also find the deepest parts of herself.

Jack shifted slightly, his lips grazing her forehead in the softest of kisses. "Good morning," he whispered, his voice rough from the night before.

Emma smiled softly, lifting her head to meet his gaze. His eyes were dark, still heavy with sleep, but there was a tenderness in them that melted her heart. "Good morning," she replied, her voice thick with the remnants of their passion.

For a long moment, they simply stared at each other, the silence between them comfortable and intimate. Emma could feel the pull between them once again, a magnetic force that drew her in closer. Her fingers traced the outline of his jaw, feeling the stubble beneath her touch, the familiar warmth of his skin.

Jack's gaze never left hers, his hand cupping her face with a gentleness that made her heart race. "Emma," he murmured, his voice barely audible. "Last night... it was everything. You're everything."

Her breath hitched, her pulse quickening at his words. She had always known that their connection was intense, but hearing him say it out loud, feeling the weight of his sincerity, made her heart flutter with something more. Something deeper.

"I've never felt this way before," she confessed, her voice a mix of wonder and vulnerability. "About anyone. About you."

Jack's thumb traced her bottom lip slowly, his expression a mixture of longing and uncertainty. "I know," he said softly, his voice filled with a quiet intensity. "It scares me, Emma. I've spent so long hiding from this—hiding from you. But I can't anymore."

Her heart pounded in her chest, the truth of his words sinking deep within her. "Jack," she whispered, her hand moving to his chest, feeling the rise and fall of his breath. "I'm not going anywhere. Not now. Not ever."

The words hung between them, heavy with the promise of something profound. Something neither of them could fully grasp yet, but both of them were willing to explore.

Before she could speak again, Jack leaned down, capturing her lips in a kiss that was slow, languid, and full of unspoken desire. His hands roamed over her body, tracing the curves of her waist, the softness of her skin, as if committing every inch of her to memory. The kiss deepened, and Emma responded in kind, her body coming alive under his touch.

The fire that had burned between them last night reignited, the intensity of their connection flaring back to life as their lips moved together in perfect harmony. She could feel the heat building once again, the desire pooling deep within her, a hunger that would not be denied.

Jack pulled back for a moment, his eyes dark and smoldering with want. "You're mine, Emma. You have to know that. I can't lose you."

Her heart swelled at his words, but a flicker of doubt crossed her mind. She could see the conflict in his eyes, the shadows of his past still looming over him, even in this intimate moment. She reached up, cupping his face in her hands, willing him to see the truth in her eyes.

"I'm not going anywhere," she repeated, her voice firm, filled with conviction. "I'm here. With you. Whatever it takes."

He exhaled sharply, as though the weight of her words had finally settled into him. "I want to believe you," he whispered, his voice tight with emotion. "But I've pushed you away before. I've hurt you before."

Emma shook her head gently, her thumb tracing his lower lip. "You didn't push me away. You were protecting yourself. I get that, Jack. But I'm not going anywhere. I'm not afraid of your darkness. I'm not afraid of what's inside you."

His eyes flickered with something—surprise, gratitude, or perhaps relief—but it was fleeting. Before she could register it fully, Jack's lips were on hers again, kissing her deeply, his hands pulling her closer, as though he couldn't get enough of her.

And for a moment, the rest of the world ceased to exist. There was only the two of them—lost in each other, consumed by the need that burned between them. Emma's body ached for him once again, her hands tugging at the waistband of his shorts, her nails grazing his skin as she pulled him closer. She could feel the tension between them growing, the anticipation mounting as his body responded to hers.

Jack's lips trailed down her neck, his breath hot against her skin as he kissed her, his hands exploring every inch of her body. He was desperate, hungry, but there was something else in the way he touched her—something tender, as though he wanted to savor every moment, every sensation.

"Jack..." she gasped, her voice trembling as his hands slid lower, teasing her, sending waves of pleasure coursing through her. She arched into him, urging him to take her, to give her everything she needed.

"I can't wait any longer," he growled, his voice thick with desire. His lips captured hers again, and this time, there was no holding back. Their bodies collided, pressing together as if they couldn't get close enough, as if they were two halves of the same whole.

And as they came together, their passion reaching a crescendo, Emma realized something. She wasn't just craving him physically—she needed him emotionally, mentally, in every way imaginable. And for the first time in her life, she was willing to let herself completely, utterly, fall.

The fire between them blazed brighter than ever.

Chapter 71: Turning the Page

"*Love isn't a feeling; it's a choice. A choice to fight for someone, even when the fight seems impossible.*" — *Unknown*

The sun had set, casting an orange glow across the horizon. The world outside the window was quiet, almost eerily still, but inside Jack's penthouse, the air was thick with unspoken words. Emma sat on the edge of the couch, her fingers idly tracing the rim of her glass, but her mind was far away. Her thoughts were consumed by Jack, by the weight of everything they had shared in the last few days. Their connection was undeniable, but so were the questions that lingered in th e air.

Jack had gone quiet after their passionate exchange earlier. His usual confidence seemed to have evaporated, replaced by a brooding intensity. She had noticed it in his eyes, the way his jaw tightened whenever their gazes locked. It wasn't that he was pushing her away, but there was a distance—one that she couldn't quite bridge.

Emma had always prided herself on being able to read people, to understand what they weren't saying, but with Jack, it felt different. He was a mystery, layers upon layers of complexity that she was only beginning to peel back. And each time she thought she understood him, he surprised her in ways that made her crave him more.

She could feel the tension building, an unspoken current that swirled around them, binding them together even as it pushed them apart. Her heart raced with both desire and fear—fear of the unknown, fear of where this was all heading.

She couldn't deny that she wanted him, wanted everything about him, but there was something else gnawing at her, something she couldn't name. It was like being caught in a tide, pulled deeper with every passing moment, unable to escape, yet unwilling to fight it.

"Jack?" she said softly, her voice tentative, almost unsure. She hadn't spoken his name like that in a long time—not since they had first crossed that invisible line between friendship and something more.

Jack didn't respond immediately, his gaze fixed on the city lights outside. When he did finally turn to face her, his expression was unreadable, but there was a flicker of vulnerability in his eyes, something raw and exposed.

"What's on your mind?" His voice was low, heavy with the weight of his own thoughts. He took a step toward her, closing the distance between them with deliberate slowness.

Emma hesitated, unsure how to begin. She had always been honest with him, but there was something different now—something deeper. "I... I feel like there's something you're not telling me."

He let out a quiet sigh, running a hand through his hair, as if he were struggling to find the right words. "Emma, it's not that simple."

She felt her pulse quicken. "Then make it simple. I can't keep guessing what's going on in that head of yours."

His gaze softened, and he stepped closer, his body heat radiating against hers. "It's not about you," he said, his voice barely above a whisper. "It's about me. About things I've never let myself face. Things I'm scared to face."

The raw honesty in his voice sent a shiver down her spine. She reached out, her hand brushing lightly against his chest, feeling the steady beat of his heart beneath her fingertips. "Jack, you don't have to do this alone," she said, her voice tender but firm. "Whatever it is, I'm here. I'm not going anywhere."

He swallowed hard, his throat working as if he were fighting against emotions too big to contain. "You don't know what you're asking, Emma."

She stepped closer, their bodies now nearly touching. Her heart was pounding in her chest as she looked up at him, searching his eyes for the truth. "I know exactly what I'm asking. I'm asking for you. All of you. The parts that scare you. The parts you've hidden. Because I want to know everything about you, Jack."

For a long moment, neither of them moved. The tension between them was palpable, electric, and for a heartbeat, it felt as though the world had stopped. And then, finally, Jack exhaled, his shoulders slumping as if the weight of his secrets had grown too much to bear.

"I didn't think I could let anyone in," he confessed, his voice raw, breaking in ways she had never heard before. "I've always kept people at arm's length. It's easier that way. I've spent years building walls around myself, pushing away anyone who tried to get too close."

Emma's hand slid up to his cheek, her thumb grazing the roughness of his stubble. "And what if you don't have to push me away?" she whispered, her words like a plea, her heart reaching for him.

He closed his eyes at her touch, his jaw tightening, and then he did something that shocked her—he kissed her, but it wasn't the hungry, desperate kiss they had shared earlier. No, this one was different. This kiss was slow, reverent, as though he were savoring every second of it, as though he were memorizing the way she felt against him. It was a kiss of surrender, of trust, and when he finally pulled away, his eyes were darker than she had ever seen them.

"I've never felt like this before," he admitted, his voice hoarse, his breath shallow. "You've broken through my walls, Emma. And it terrifies me."

Her heart ached at the vulnerability in his words. "Good," she said softly. "Because I want to break them down, Jack. All of them. I want to be the one to pull you out of that darkness, to show you that you don't have to hide anymore."

For a moment, he didn't say anything, just watched her as though he were weighing her words. And then, without warning, he pulled her to him, crashing his lips to hers with a force that stole her breath away. His hands moved over her body, possessive and urgent, as though he couldn't get enough of her.

Emma's body responded instantly, her desire flaring up once more, but beneath it all, there was something deeper, something more intimate. Their connection wasn't just physical anymore; it was emotional, spiritual, and she could feel it in the way their bodies moved together, in the way he held her, in the way their hearts beat in sync.

She wrapped her arms around him, pulling him closer, needing him like she had never needed anyone before. She could feel the tension in his muscles, the tightness in his grip, and she knew that he was struggling to let go, to fully surrender to what they had.

And then, as if a dam had finally broken, Jack let out a low groan, his hands moving over her skin with a newfound desperation. The kiss deepened, became more urgent, more wild, as though they were both drowning in the depth of their desire.

When they finally broke apart, both breathless and flushed, Emma could see the change in Jack. There was a softness in his gaze now, a vulnerability that hadn't been there before. For the first time, he looked at her not as a temptation or a distraction, but as something more—a partner, a confidante.

"I'm not afraid anymore," he whispered, his voice thick with emotion.

Emma smiled, her hand resting on his chest. "Good. Because I'm not going anywhere."

And as they stood there, tangled in each other's embrace, Emma knew that this was only the beginning. They had crossed a threshold together, one that would lead them into uncharted territory—territory where love, passion, and vulnerability would intertwine in ways they couldn't yet understand. But they would face it together.

Chapter 72: Turning the Page

"Every ending is just the beginning of something new." — Unknown

The morning after their emotional conversation was filled with a charged silence, the kind that lingered between them like a fog. Emma could feel the weight of it pressing down on her, the unspoken words that had not been fully said hanging in the air like a heavy cloud. She lay in Jack's bed, tangled in the sheets, her body still humming from the night before, but her mind was racing.

Jack had pulled her closer than ever before, but she knew that their intimacy was more than just physical. They had crossed into a territory where emotions bled together—where nothing was simple, nothing was easy. And despite the passion that had simmered between them, there was a lingering question that gnawed at her. Could they really make it work? Could they navigate the darkness that haunted Jack, and the vulnerability that now wrapped itself around both of them?

The soft sound of Jack's breathing beside her drew her out of her thoughts. She glanced over at him, his face still relaxed in sleep, but there was something different about him. Something more open, more exposed. She knew that what they had was fragile, but she also knew that it was real.

Her fingers traced the edge of his jaw, the rough stubble catching against her skin, and for a moment, she let herself just be. She allowed herself to feel the weight of his presence beside her, the connection they shared that transcended their physical attraction.

Jack stirred, his eyes slowly opening, and when he met her gaze, a small smile played on his lips. "Morning," he said, his voice still thick with sleep, but there was a warmth in it that made her heart flutter.

"Morning," she replied softly, her fingers still lightly brushing against his skin.

For a long moment, neither of them said anything. There was no need. The silence between them wasn't uncomfortable—it was comfortable in its own way. But Emma couldn't shake the feeling that something was shifting between them. There was a change, something that was yet to be understood, but it was there.

"Are you okay?" she asked, her voice a little hesitant.

Jack nodded slowly, his gaze never leaving hers. "Yeah," he said quietly. "I think I'm starting to be."

She smiled, relieved to hear him say that. "Starting to be?" she repeated.

He chuckled, a low sound that made her stomach flutter. "Well, it's a process, right? But I feel like I'm finally letting myself—letting us—be real. And that's terrifying. But it's also... freeing." His words resonated deep within her, a sense of both relief and uncertainty washing over her. She had wanted him to open up, to let her in, and now that he had, she realized just how much she wanted to be a part of this process—this journey of vulnerability and healing.

Jack shifted, turning to face her fully, his arm draping around her waist as he pulled her closer. "I'm not good with this whole... being vulnerable thing," he confessed, his voice raw. "I've spent so long keeping everything bottled up, keeping people at a distance. But with you..." His eyes softened, his fingers gently caressing her skin. "It's like I'm learning how to breathe again."

Emma's heart swelled at his words, the weight of them heavy with truth. She had never felt more connected to him than she did in that moment. "You don't have to do it alone," she said, her voice thick with emotion. "You never have to do it alone."

There was a long pause as Jack searched her eyes, a silent exchange between them, a moment of understanding. Then, slowly, he leaned in, his lips brushing against hers in a tender kiss. It was soft at first, a gentle exploration, but the intensity of their emotions soon made it deeper, more urgent.

As the kiss deepened, their bodies pressed together, the heat of their desire rising again. Emma could feel the pull of him, the way his hands roamed over her, seeking to draw her closer. She responded in kind, her own hands moving over his chest, feeling the strength of his muscles beneath her touch. There was something raw and passionate in the way they touched, something that spoke to the depth of their connection, a connection that had only just begun to unfold.

Jack's lips moved from her mouth to her neck, his breath warm against her skin. She gasped softly, her fingers tangling in his hair as he kissed her with a new intensity, his hands roaming over her body with a familiar possessiveness that made her pulse race.

But just as the passion between them was about to erupt, Jack pulled away slightly, his forehead resting against hers. His breathing was shallow, his chest rising and falling rapidly.

"Emma," he whispered, his voice hoarse, "I don't know if I can give you everything you deserve."

Her heart tightened at his words, the vulnerability in them cutting through her like a knife. But she refused to let fear take root. She cupped his face, her fingers tracing the outline of his jaw, and she kissed him gently, reassuring him without words.

"You already have, Jack," she murmured. "You already have."

Chapter 73: Tangled Hearts

"We are shaped by our thoughts; we become what we think."
— Buddha

The air between Emma and Jack had shifted in the days that followed their intimate conversation. What had begun as a tentative step toward vulnerability had blossomed into something far deeper, far more intense. Every moment together was laced with tension—emotional and physical—and Emma could feel it between them like an invisible thread pulling them closer. But with that closeness came uncertainty, a sense of unease that neither of them could fully shake off.

Emma had always been the type to wear her heart on her sleeve, to love freely and openly. But Jack... Jack was a man who guarded his heart fiercely, and though he was slowly letting her in, there were times when she felt the walls rising again—times when the depth of his past would resurface and the weight of his fears would press down on him, keeping him at arm's length.

It was frustrating, but Emma was determined. She wasn't going to give up on them, not when the connection they shared was so strong. She wanted to be the one to help him tear down the walls he had built around his heart, to be the one who could make him believe in love again.

That night, they sat on the balcony of Jack's penthouse, the city lights twinkling below them, casting a soft glow over the two of them. The night air was warm, with a slight breeze rustling the leaves of the plants on the balcony. The distant hum of traffic and the occasional sound of laughter from the streets below drifted up to them, but all Emma could focus on was Jack—his profile against the skyline, the way the light caught his features, making him look almost other-worldly.

Her heart ached at the sight of him, at the rawness she saw in him when he let his guard down. But the hesitation was still there—he was still holding back, still unsure of what it all meant. Emma had felt it ever since their last conversation, and she knew she had to do something about it. She couldn't wait any longer for him to make the first move. She had to take charge, to show him that they could have something real, something lasting.

She turned toward him, her heart pounding in her chest. Their eyes met, and for a moment, the world seemed to stop. There was no more noise, no more distractions—just the two of them, tangled in the unspoken connection that had been building between them for so l ong.

"Jack," she whispered, her voice low and husky, "I don't want to be afraid anymore."

His eyes flickered with uncertainty, but he didn't pull away. Instead, he leaned closer, his face inches from hers, his breath warm against her lips. The space between them was electric, charged with an intensity that neither of them had been willing to acknowledge before now.

"I don't know if I can give you everything you need," Jack murmured, his voice barely audible. "I've never been good at this. At letting people in."

"I don't need everything," Emma whispered back. "I just need you. I need us. What we have."

She could see the struggle in his eyes, the battle between wanting to give in and being terrified of it. But she wasn't about to let him retreat again, not this time. She reached out, her hand brushing against his jaw, feeling the rough stubble beneath her fingertips.

"Jack, I'm not asking you to be perfect. I'm asking you to be real. To let me in."

His eyes softened, and for the first time, Emma saw the walls begin to crumble. Slowly, as though he was testing the waters, he leaned in, his lips brushing against hers. It was a gentle kiss at first, a soft meeting of mouths, but the moment their lips touched, something inside both of them shifted. The kiss deepened, becoming more urgent, more desperate, as if they were both trying to consume each other, to bridge the gap that had been between them for so long.

Emma's hands slid up his chest, feeling the hard muscles beneath his shirt, and then lower, to the waistband of his jeans. She could feel his heartbeat racing beneath her touch, the heat of his body growing more intense with every second. His hands roamed over her back, pulling her closer, his fingers splaying across her skin as if he couldn't get enough of her.

The kiss became more heated, more passionate, their bodies moving in sync as if they had always known how to fit together. Emma's heart raced, her pulse quickening as she responded to him, her lips parting to allow him deeper access. Her body arched into his, pressing against him, and she could feel the hardness of him against her, reminding her of just how much she desired him.

Jack's hands slid down her sides, resting on her hips before slowly pulling her against him, his touch possessive, urgent. She moaned softly into his mouth, her body responding to him instinctively, wanting him in a way she had never wanted anyone before.

But as the heat between them intensified, Jack pulled away just slightly, his forehead resting against hers. His breath was shallow, his chest rising and falling rapidly as he tried to regain control of himself.

"Emma," he breathed, his voice strained. "I need to be sure... that you know what this is. What I am."

Her heart skipped a beat. "I know exactly what this is," she whispered, her fingers tracing the lines of his jaw, trying to ground him, to remind him of the connection they shared. "This is real. This is us."

She kissed him again, but this time, there was something different in it—something deeper, something that spoke of trust, of surrender. Emma could feel Jack's resistance melting away, could feel the walls he had spent so long building crumble beneath her touch.

When they finally pulled away again, both of them breathless and flushed, Jack's hands gently cupped her face, his thumb brushing over her lips. He looked at her with such intensity, such raw emotion, that Emma's heart swelled in her chest.

"I want to give this to you, Emma," he said softly, his voice thick with emotion. "I want to give you everything. But I need to know you're not going to walk away when it gets hard."

She smiled, her fingers brushing through his hair as she gazed up at him. "I'm not going anywhere, Jack. Not ever."

And with that, they both knew that they had crossed into something new—something fragile, but real. The connection they shared was no longer just a fleeting moment, but something they were both willing to fight for. Together.

Chapter 74: Secrets Unveiled

"Sometimes, the only way to know if something is meant to be, is to let it go." — Unknown

The night had fallen into a peaceful hush, but inside Jack's penthouse, the air was thick with anticipation. The kiss they had shared earlier was still alive in Emma's mind, an electric current that thrummed through her body. She could still feel the imprint of his lips on hers, the way his hands had roamed over her skin, igniting every nerve, every desire that had been buried for so long. She had wanted him—no, needed him—more than she'd ever been willing to admit to herself. But tonight, things felt different. The passion they shared wasn't just physical; it was deeper, richer, more profound. It was the beginning of something neither of them could easily put into words.

Emma had always been the type to hold her emotions close to her chest. She was independent, self-sufficient, used to standing on her own two feet. But with Jack, it was different. She didn't want to stand apart anymore. She wanted to be with him, to share every part of herself, even the darkest corners she'd been too afraid to open up. And in that moment, as they lay together, entwined beneath the sheets, Emma made a promise to herself: she would fight for this—whatever this was—no matter what it took.

Jack was lying beside her, his arm draped around her waist, his chest rising and falling steadily as he drifted into a peaceful sleep. Emma could hear the soft rhythm of his breathing, the sound of his heartbeat in the silence of the room. The city outside continued to pulse with life, the hum of traffic and the distant laughter of people below creating a strange contrast to the quiet intimacy that enveloped them.

She turned her head slightly, her gaze settling on Jack's sleeping form. His face was relaxed, his expression softened in sleep, and for the first time in a long time, Emma allowed herself to truly take him in. She had seen glimpses of the man he was—the vulnerable, conflicted, passionate man—but now, in the quiet of the night, she was seeing him with new eyes.

There was something about him that had always drawn her in. His strength, his quiet intensity, the way he carried himself as though he had been through hell and back and emerged stronger for it. But now, as she lay there next to him, Emma realized just how much she longed to know more about him—the parts of him he kept hidden, the fears he had yet to face. She had her own demons to confront, but Jack's were just as present, just as raw. She had seen the way he had pulled away from her in moments of doubt, seen the way he wrestled with his own emotions, but she was determined to help him face them.

Turning on her side, Emma propped herself up on her elbow, her fingers lightly tracing the contours of Jack's chest, the warmth of his skin beneath her touch sending a shiver through her. He stirred slightly, his hand resting on her waist, but didn't wake. She couldn't help but smile at how peaceful he looked, so vulnerable in his sleep, as though the weight of the world had been lifted, even if only for a moment.

Her thoughts were interrupted by the sudden buzz of her phone, vibrating softly on the nightstand beside the bed. Emma hesitated for a moment, torn between the quiet intimacy of the moment and the need to check who was calling. With a sigh, she reached for the phone, careful not to disturb Jack.

The message was from Laura, one of Emma's closest friends. It read: *"Hey, I know things are a bit crazy right now, but I wanted to check in. You okay? We need to catch up soon."*

Emma smiled softly, appreciating her friend's concern. Laura had been her rock through so many ups and downs, always there to offer a listening ear, a shoulder to cry on, or a laugh when everything felt like it was falling apart. But now, with everything that was happening between her and Jack, Emma wasn't sure how to navigate the shift in her relationships.

She hesitated before typing a quick response: *"I'm good. Just... taking things one day at a time."*

After sending the message, Emma set the phone back on the nightstand and gazed at Jack again, her mind racing with thoughts she wasn't quite ready to confront. She had always been good at compartmentalizing her feelings, but now, with Jack so close, she realized she could no longer do that. Her emotions, her desires, her fears—they were all tangled together, creating a knot she didn't know how to untangle.

Jack shifted in his sleep, pulling her closer, his arm wrapping around her waist in a protective gesture. Emma let herself melt into him, allowing the warmth of his body to soothe the tension that had built in her chest. She had never felt so at ease, so safe, yet so vulnerable at the same time. There was a part of her that longed for more—more of him, more of them—but another part of her was terrified of the uncertainty.

As if sensing her inner turmoil, Jack's voice broke through the quiet. His voice was husky, still heavy with sleep, but there was something tender in it that made Emma's heart skip a beat.

"Emma," he murmured, his fingers lightly brushing the curve of her hip. "Are you okay?"

The simple question caught her off guard, and for a moment, she didn't know how to answer. She had wanted this, wanted him, for so long, but now that it was here, she was unsure of how to navigate the next step. There were so many unanswered questions—about their relationship, about their future, about everything.

"I'm fine," she replied, her voice soft, though the uncertainty lingered beneath her words. "Just... thinking."

Jack's hand traced her back slowly, his touch gentle, almost soothing. "About what?"

Emma sighed, feeling the weight of the question settle on her shoulders. She didn't want to bring up all the complexities of what they were, what they could be—not yet. Not when she wasn't sure where she stood herself.

"About us," she admitted quietly. "What this is... and what it means."

For a moment, there was silence. Emma could feel Jack's gaze on her, his piercing eyes reading her in a way she hadn't expected. She wondered if he was feeling the same unease, the same need for clarity.

Jack shifted, pulling away just enough to look into her eyes, his gaze soft but intense. "I know," he said quietly. "I've been thinking about

that too. But I don't want to rush this, Emma. I don't want to mess it u
p."

Her heart clenched at his words, and for a moment, all the walls she had been building around herself started to crumble. She wasn't sure where this was going, but in that moment, all she knew was that she wanted to keep moving forward. Slowly, cautiously, but together.

"Neither do I," she whispered, her hand resting against his chest. "But I don't want to be afraid anymore. I want to see where this goes."

Jack's lips curved into a faint smile, and he leaned in, pressing a soft kiss to her forehead. "Then let's take it one step at a time. Together."

And for the first time in a long time, Emma felt like she had found the answer. She didn't need to have all the pieces in place. She just needed to keep moving forward, trusting in the connection they shared.

The night stretched on, the silence between them comfortable, filled with the quiet certainty that they had both chosen to fight for something real. And in that moment, Emma knew that whatever happened, whatever the future held, she wasn't facing it alone.

Chapter 75: Facing the Truth

"The truth may hurt for a little while, but a lie hurts forever." — Unknown

The morning light filtered softly through the curtains, casting a warm, golden glow over the room. Emma stirred beneath the sheets, the coolness of Jack's absence already settling into the space beside her. She had woken up alone, but it wasn't the kind of loneliness she'd once feared. The emptiness was different this time—faint, fleeting, almost welcoming. It was the quiet that followed the storm of emotions, the calm before the next wave.

For a moment, Emma closed her eyes again, letting the peacefulness of the room wash over her. There was a strange comfort in knowing that, even in the stillness, she wasn't truly alone. Jack was just on the other side of the apartment, probably in his office, finishing some work before their day began. She could hear the faint sound of his voice as he spoke on the phone, but it wasn't just the ordinary hum of daily life. There was something about it—something about how he had integrated into her world so seamlessly, like an anchor she hadn't known she needed until it was there.

She turned to look at the empty space next to her, the memory of the night before still fresh in her mind. The soft whispers, the shared breath, the gentle pressure of Jack's hands on her body as he held her close. There had been a certain weight to it, a gravity pulling them together, binding them in a way that felt as though it had always been inevitable.

And yet, as much as Emma wanted to embrace the connection they shared, a part of her still struggled to release the hesitations she had carried for so long. She had given herself to Jack in a way that was raw, exposed, and utterly transformative, but the remnants of her doubts still lingered at the edges of her mind.

She sighed, running a hand through her tangled hair as she sat up, letting her feet dangle off the edge of the bed. The sunlight was warm on her skin, and the morning air smelled faintly of coffee brewing from the kitchen. She knew she should get up, get dressed, and begin the day, but she couldn't shake the feeling that something had shifted within her overnight. There was an energy in the air, an unspoken promise of change, and she wasn't sure if she was ready for it.

Her phone buzzed on the nightstand, snapping her out of her thoughts. She picked it up, seeing a message from Laura.

"Hey, are you free today? I need to talk to you about something. Let me know when you have a minute."

Emma's fingers hovered over the screen, her mind racing. Laura had always been a trusted friend, someone who knew her better than anyone else. She had been there for every major turning point in Emma's life, from the end of her marriage to the moment she first met Jack. But now, things felt different. She wasn't sure if she was ready to explain the complexities of what was happening between her and Jack, or if she even knew how to put it into words.

Still, she couldn't ignore the pull to reach out to her friend. She typed a quick reply.

"Yeah, I'm free this afternoon. Let's talk then."

After sending the message, Emma tossed her phone back onto the bed and stood up, stretching as she went. The room felt a little too quiet now, too still. She was used to the noise of the city outside, the constant hum of life happening just beyond the walls of Jack's penthouse. But today, the quiet seemed almost suffocating. She needed to fill the space with something—anything—that would help her break free from the uncertainty clouding her thoughts.

She walked toward the window, pulling back the heavy curtains to reveal the view. The skyline of Sydney stretched before her, the sparkling waters of the harbour glistening in the morning sun. It was a sight she had grown accustomed to over the past few weeks, but today it felt different. There was a clarity to it now, a sense of possibility in the way the light hit the buildings, in the way the city seemed to be calling her forward.

It was strange how a single person could change the way you saw the world. Jack had done that for her—had made her look at everything with new eyes, as though the blinders she'd worn for so long had finally fallen away. She wasn't the same woman she had been before she met him. And that scared her more than she was willing to admit.

Emma walked over to the bathroom, splashing some cold water on her face to shake off the remnants of sleep. She caught a glimpse of herself in the mirror, studying her reflection with a critical eye. She had always been hard on herself, always looking for flaws that others couldn't see. But today, as she studied the woman in the mirror, she saw something different. There was a quiet strength in her eyes now, a certain fire that hadn't been there before.

After a few moments of contemplation, she turned away from the mirror and walked back into the bedroom to get dressed. She couldn't hide from what was happening between her and Jack. She had to confront it, face it head-on, and figure out what it meant for both of them.

When she walked into the kitchen, Jack was standing at the counter, a cup of coffee in his hand. He was dressed casually in a grey t-shirt and dark jeans, his hair still damp from a quick shower. He looked up as she entered, his eyes meeting hers with a warmth that sent a flutter through her chest.

"Good morning," he said, his voice low and full of that same intoxicating warmth she had come to crave.

Emma smiled, though there was a touch of hesitation in her gaze. "Good morning. I didn't realize you were up already."

Jack leaned against the counter, his expression softening. "I've been up for a while. I had a few things to take care of. But I was just waiting for you."

Emma's heart skipped a beat at his words. There was something in the way he said it, in the way he looked at her, that made her feel like she was the center of his world. She wasn't used to being anyone's priority—not in the way Jack seemed to make her feel. And yet, here he was, putting her first in a way that felt both comforting and overwhelming.

"I was just thinking," Emma said, her voice quieter now. "About us, and where we go from here."

Jack set his coffee down on the counter, his eyes never leaving hers. "I've been thinking about that too. And whatever happens, I want you to know that I'm here. For you. For us."

Emma swallowed the lump that had formed in her throat, her heart swelling with emotions she hadn't been ready to process. "I don't know what this is, Jack. I don't know what the future holds. But I want to try. I want to see where we can go from here."

Jack's smile widened, and he stepped closer to her, his hand brushing against her cheek. "Then we'll take it one day at a time. Together."

Emma nodded, the weight of his words sinking in. For the first time in a long time, she felt like she was ready to embrace the unknown. She didn't need to have all the answers. All she needed was the courage to keep moving forward, with Jack by her side.

The future might be uncertain, but for the first time, Emma was willing to face it head-on.

Chapter 76: Broken Bonds

"*Sometimes the one who loves you is the one who hurts you the most.*" *— Unknown*

The tension in the air was palpable as Emma sat across from Jack at the café. Her hands wrapped around her coffee cup, seeking comfort from the warmth of it, though it did little to soothe the storm brewing inside her. She had barely slept the night before, her thoughts a whirlwind of questions and doubts that refused to settle. The conversation with Laura had left her feeling unsettled, like she was being forced to face something she wasn't ready for.

"Are you okay?" Jack's voice broke through her thoughts, a soft concern in his tone. He had been watching her closely, his eyes searching hers with a tenderness that made her heart ache.

She offered him a half-smile, but it didn't reach her eyes. "Yeah, just tired," she said, her voice quieter than usual.

He studied her for a moment, his gaze lingering. "You've been distant since this morning. Something's on your mind."

Emma hesitated. She wanted to tell him what had been troubling her, to pour out all the emotions she had kept bottled up. But something held her back. She wasn't sure if it was fear of vulnerability, or the nagging sense that she still wasn't ready to fully expose herself to him.

"Nothing that can't wait," she said, though her words sounded more like an excuse than a reassurance.

Jack didn't push, but she could see the flicker of frustration in his eyes. He leaned back in his chair, his fingers tapping absently against the edge of his cup. "If you say so, but I can't help but feel like there's more to it than that. You're not the same, Emma. And I'm not the only one who's noticed."

Emma's breath caught at his words. She had thought she could hide it, bury the discomfort she was feeling beneath the surface, but Jack always seemed to see right through her. He had this uncanny ability to read her, to know when something wasn't right—even when she herself wasn't sure what was wrong.

She exhaled slowly, gathering her thoughts. "It's just... I don't know, Jack. I feel like everything's moving so fast. I didn't expect any of this, and I'm not sure I'm ready to dive in so deep. There's still a part of me that's unsure, that wants to hold back."

Jack's expression softened, and he reached out, his hand covering hers on the table. The simple gesture grounded her, even if just for a moment. "I understand that, Emma. I really do. But I want you to know that I'm not going anywhere. I'm here, no matter how slow or fast you want to take things. This is about us, and I want you to feel comfortable with the pace."

She met his eyes, searching for any hint of hesitation, any sign that he was just saying the right thing to calm her down. But there was nothing. He was being honest, as he always had been with her. And for the first time in days, Emma allowed herself to believe him.

But there was still a lingering doubt—something in the pit of her stomach that told her she couldn't trust everything. Not yet.

Jack squeezed her hand gently, pulling her from her thoughts. "You're allowed to take your time, Emma. You don't have to have all the answers right now. But if something is on your mind, I want you to tell me. I'm not going to pressure you, but I don't want you to carry this alone."

A lump formed in Emma's throat as she looked at him, her heart swelling with conflicting emotions. She had always been the one to carry her burdens alone. She'd gotten used to managing her life, her heart, and her desires without leaning on anyone. But Jack... Jack was different. He made her want to let go, to trust him, even when it terrified her.

"Laura and I talked yesterday," she finally admitted, her voice barely above a whisper. "She asked me something that made me think... maybe I'm not ready for all of this. Maybe I'm not ready for you."

Jack's grip on her hand tightened, but he didn't interrupt. He let her speak, allowing her to express the turmoil that had been eating at her. "What did she ask you?"

"She... she asked if I was truly ready to give myself completely to someone else. If I was really ready to be vulnerable, to trust again." Emma swallowed hard, trying to steady her breathing. "And I don't know. I'm scared. I'm scared of losing myself in someone else, of letting go so completely."

Jack sat quietly for a moment, taking in her words. His gaze never wavered, his expression unreadable. But when he finally spoke, it was with the kind of understanding that made her heart ache.

"Emma, I don't want you to lose yourself. Not for me. Not for anyone. I want you to be the woman you are, the one I fell for—strong, independent, with all your flaws and quirks. I don't want to change that. But I also don't want you to hide from what we could have together, just because of fear."

"I don't know if I can do this," she admitted softly. "I don't know if I'm strong enough to give you all of me, to open myself up like that. It feels too risky, too dangerous."

Jack leaned forward, his thumb gently brushing across her knuckles. "Life is risky, Emma. Everything we do carries some risk. But the real danger is never taking that leap—never letting yourself experience the kind of love, the kind of life, that could make everything else worthwhile."

Emma looked down at their joined hands, the warmth of his touch spreading through her. She could feel the truth of his words deep inside her, but it didn't make the decision any easier. Letting someone in was never easy for her. She had built walls around herself for so long, afraid of being hurt, of being vulnerable.

"Do you want this?" she asked quietly, lifting her gaze to meet his. "Do you want me, even with all the baggage I carry?"

Jack smiled softly, a slow, genuine smile that made her heart skip a beat. "I want you, Emma. All of you. I've always wanted you, from the moment I met you. I know there's a lot of history between us, and I know there's still work to be done. But I'm willing to do whatever it takes. For us."

The sincerity in his voice reached deep into her chest, and for the first time in what felt like forever, Emma allowed herself to feel hope.

She wasn't sure where this journey would lead, or if she would ever be ready to give Jack everything he wanted. But she wasn't alone anymore. And maybe that was enough for now.

She gave him a soft smile, her heart lighter than it had been in days. "Okay," she said, the word barely more than a breath. "I'll try. I'll try to let go. And maybe—just maybe—I can trust that you won't let me fall."

Jack's smile deepened, and he leaned forward, brushing his lips against her forehead in a gentle kiss. "I won't let you fall, Emma. I promise."

And for the first time in a long while, Emma believed him.

Chapter 77: New Beginnings

"It's not about how you start, but how you finish." — Unknown

The afternoon sun hung low in the sky, casting long shadows over the bustling streets of Sydney. The café where Emma and Jack had met earlier that morning was a small oasis amid the chaos of the city—a place where they had spent hours talking, laughing, and baring parts of themselves they had kept hidden for so long. Yet, as the sun began to set, Emma found herself feeling a strange sense of unease creeping back into her thoughts.

She and Jack had made progress, she could feel it. But there was something still unsaid, something lingering beneath the surface. She wasn't ready to push it out into the open, but it was there, quietly building inside her, demanding her attention. It had been too long since she had allowed herself to truly consider the consequences of giving her heart away.

As she walked down the narrow street toward her apartment, the familiar weight of the city on her shoulders, Emma's phone buzzed in her pocket. She pulled it out, her heart skipping a beat when she saw the name on the screen: Laura.

"Hey," she said as she answered, trying to sound casual despite the knot forming in her stomach.

"Emma," Laura's voice was urgent, with a hint of worry, "I need you to meet me. It's important. Can you come to my place right now?"

Emma frowned. Laura wasn't the type to ask for her company unless it was something serious. "What's going on? Is everything okay?"

There was a pause on the other end of the line. "Just come. Please. It's about Jack."

Her heart immediately started to race, her thoughts spinning out of control. "What about Jack? Is he okay?"

"I can't explain over the phone. Just get here as soon as you can."

Emma hesitated, the unsettling feeling from earlier now merging with a sense of dread. She had no idea what this was about, but the mention of Jack made her stomach churn. She had promised him she would trust him, but now... now there was a voice in the back of her mind whispering that perhaps she should have trusted Laura's instincts a little more.

"I'll be there in fifteen minutes," Emma said, her voice tight with worry.

"See you soon," Laura replied, her tone heavy with something Emma couldn't quite place.

She clicked off the phone and stood still for a moment, gathering her thoughts. The walk to Laura's apartment was short, but the distance felt like miles as she tried to piece together what might be going on. Jack had been so open with her today. He had made it clear that he was in this for the long haul, that he wasn't going anywhere. So why did she feel like something was slipping through her fingers? Why did she feel like the ground beneath her feet was crumbling, despite all the progress they had made?

As she arrived at Laura's building and made her way up to the apartment, Emma couldn't shake the feeling that she was about to uncover something she wasn't prepared for. When she knocked on the door, it was Laura herself who opened it, her face pale and drawn.

"Come in," Laura said softly, stepping aside to let Emma pass.

Emma followed her into the apartment, noting the tense atmosphere that hung in the air. Laura led her to the living room, where she motioned for Emma to sit. She took a deep breath before sitting down, her hands wringing together in her lap.

"What's going on, Laura? What's this about Jack?"

Laura bit her lip, looking like she was trying to decide whether or not to speak. Finally, she met Emma's eyes. "I've been thinking a lot about everything lately. About you and Jack. And I think you need to know something—something I should have told you a long time ago."

Emma's stomach tightened. "What do you mean?"

Laura hesitated for a moment, before she spoke again. "Jack isn't exactly who he says he is."

Emma blinked, feeling as though the ground had shifted beneath her. "What are you talking about?" she asked, her voice barely above a whisper.

"I didn't want to say anything before, but now... now I think you deserve to know." Laura's eyes darkened with a mix of concern and regret. "Jack has a past. A past that's tangled up in things he's not been honest about."

Emma's pulse quickened. She leaned forward, trying to make sense of Laura's words. "What kind of past? What are you saying, Laura?"

"I'm saying he's been hiding things from you. Big things." Laura's voice was tight, as if the words were physically painful for her to say. "He's been lying, Emma. Lying about his past, his family, and some of the people he's involved with. And I think you need to hear this before you get in too deep."

Emma felt a cold shiver run down her spine. "What do you mean, lying? How do you know all of this?"

Laura's gaze softened, but the tension in her body remained. "I know because I've seen things, Emma. I've seen how Jack can be when things aren't going his way. He's been involved in things—business dealings, money, people that you would never expect. And I don't think you realize just how dangerous it could all be."

Emma felt the words wash over her like ice water. Everything Jack had said about wanting a fresh start, about wanting to be with her... Was it all just a façade? Had he been playing her, using her to escape his past? She couldn't breathe, her chest tightening as her mind raced through a thousand questions she couldn't answer.

"Laura, I..." she started, but her voice faltered. The shock of it all was too much. She had trusted Jack, let herself believe that this was real. But now she wasn't sure what to believe anymore.

"I know you care about him, Emma," Laura said, her voice softer now, though still heavy with concern. "But I'm telling you this because I don't want you to get hurt. I don't want you to walk into something you're not prepared for."

Emma closed her eyes for a moment, trying to process what Laura was saying. She didn't want to believe it, but a part of her—deep down—knew there was a truth in Laura's words that she couldn't ignore. Jack had always been a bit elusive, a little too careful with the details of his life. Could it be that he had been hiding more than just his emotions?

"What do I do, Laura?" Emma whispered, her voice raw. "What am I supposed to do with all of this?"

"You need to talk to him," Laura replied gently. "You deserve the truth, no matter how difficult it is."

Emma sat in silence for a long moment, the weight of the situation settling heavily on her shoulders. She wanted to believe Jack, wanted to trust that everything he had said about his intentions with her was true. But now, she wasn't so sure.

She had to know the truth.

Chapter 78: Building Bridges

"Sometimes the hardest part isn't letting go, but learning to start over." — Nicole Sobon

The air was thick with uncertainty as Emma stepped out of Laura's apartment, the weight of her friend's words echoing in her mind. Her thoughts spiraled, tangled in a web of doubts, fears, and questions. Jack. Could he really be hiding something so significant from her? Was everything they had shared, every moment, every whispered confession, just a lie?

She wrapped her arms around herself, as if to shield herself from the cold that seemed to seep deeper into her bones. The sky had darkened since she'd entered Laura's apartment, and the city now felt more oppressive than ever. It was as though every corner, every street, held a new secret she wasn't ready to uncover.

Emma pulled out her phone and stared at it for a long moment, torn between calling Jack and confronting him immediately or waiting, processing, and trying to make sense of the chaos in her mind. But there was no escaping it now. She had to face him.

Her fingers hovered over the screen, her mind racing with all the things she wanted to say. Was she even ready to hear the truth? What if it shattered everything? What if he'd been lying all along?

Before she could send the message, a familiar name flashed across the screen. It was Jack.

Her heart skipped a beat as she answered the call, her pulse quickening.

"Emma," Jack's voice was low, soft, yet there was an underlying tension in it that she hadn't heard before. "Are you okay? I've been trying to reach you."

"I'm fine," Emma replied, her voice steadier than she felt. "I just left Laura's place. She... told me something."

A pause on the other end. Emma could practically hear Jack's breath catch, as if he knew exactly where this conversation was heading.

"What did she tell you?" His tone was cautious now, careful.

Emma didn't hesitate. "She told me that you've been lying to me. That you're involved in things—business dealings, money, people—that I don't know about. Is it true, Jack?"

Silence. The kind of silence that told Emma everything she needed to know. It wasn't the silence of shock, or confusion, but the silence of someone trying to find the right words, the right way to navigate a storm that was about to break.

Emma's heart thudded in her chest as she waited for his response. She could almost hear the wheels turning in his mind as he chose his words.

"Emma," he finally said, his voice tight, "I wasn't lying to you. I just... didn't tell you everything. I wanted to keep you safe from all of this. From the mess I've been a part of."

"Safe from what?" she demanded, her voice rising with a mix of frustration and hurt. "What mess? Why didn't you tell me, Jack? Why keep me in the dark?"

He sighed, the sound heavy with regret. "Because I didn't want you to see me the way I really am. I didn't want you to be part of this... this world I've been trying to escape."

"Escape?" Emma's voice faltered. "From what?"

Another pause. She could hear him shifting, the weight of whatever he was about to say pressing heavily on him.

"I've done things I'm not proud of, Emma," Jack admitted, his voice low. "Things that I thought I could bury. I've been involved with people who—" he stopped, collecting his thoughts. "People who deal with things that you don't want to get involved with. I was tangled up in it before we met, and I thought I could leave it all behind. But sometimes, the past doesn't let you go as easily as you think."

Emma's throat tightened, the fear of what he was saying settling deep inside her. This wasn't just a misunderstanding, wasn't just about a few secrets he'd kept from her. This was something darker, something that had the potential to tear everything apart.

"You're telling me you've been running from your past?" she asked, her voice trembling. "Running from what, Jack? What kind of things are we talking about?"

"Business dealings that got complicated," Jack explained, his voice tinged with guilt. "And people I thought I could trust, but they... they're not who I thought they were. It's messy. It's dangerous. I wanted to protect you from it. But I realize now, I've only made it worse by hiding the truth."

Emma's heart shattered as the realization hit her. She had fallen in love with a man who had so many hidden layers, so many secrets that she couldn't even begin to comprehend. He wasn't just a man with a past—he was someone whose very life was entangled in a web of danger and deceit.

"I should have told you," Jack continued, his voice quieter now. "I should have been honest with you from the start. But I didn't want to lose you, Emma. And now I'm scared that it's too late to fix this."

Emma closed her eyes, trying to process everything he had just said. She had known Jack wasn't perfect, but this... this was more than she could have ever imagined. The man she had been falling for was not the man she thought he was. He had been hiding from something—something that threatened to consume him, and her along with him.

But despite the fear swirling in her chest, despite the betrayal that gnawed at her, she couldn't walk away. She loved him. And in a way, she could understand why he had done what he did. He was trying to protect her. Even if it meant lying to her.

"I don't know what to think, Jack," Emma said, her voice soft but firm. "This is... a lot. I need time to think. I need space to process all of this."

"I understand," he said quietly. "But whatever you decide, Emma, know that I never wanted to hurt you. I just... I wanted to keep you safe. And I still want that. But I can't do it alone anymore. I need you, Emma. I need you to trust me again."

Emma felt a lump form in her throat. She wanted to believe him. She wanted to be the person who could see past the darkness, who could help him heal. But she wasn't sure she was strong enough for that. The weight of it all felt like too much to bear.

"I don't know if I can trust you, Jack," she whispered. "Not yet. But I'm willing to try. I need to figure out what this all means."

She could hear the hope in his voice as he replied, "Take all the time you need. I'll be here, waiting for you."

As Emma hung up the phone, the finality of the conversation left her reeling. The world she had built with Jack—the trust, the connection, the intimacy—had been built on a foundation of secrets. Could they survive the weight of those secrets? Or was this the beginning of the end?

Chapter 79: Embracing the Unknown

"*Every step you take is a step into the unknown. Don't fear the journey—embrace it.*" — *Unknown*

The city lights blurred into streaks of gold and white as Emma sat at the edge of her bed, her fingers nervously tracing the rim of the glass of wine in front of her. She hadn't touched it, but the bottle was still open, the promise of something to drown her thoughts sitting right there, taunting her.

Her phone sat on the nightstand, a constant reminder of Jack. His words, soft and pleading, kept ringing in her ears. She knew he needed her. She knew he wanted her to trust him again, but how could she? How could she ever trust him after everything he'd kept from her?

The past few days had been a blur of confusion and emotion. She had tried to get some distance, to think about what Jack had said, but it only made the storm in her head worse. She wanted to believe he was a man who had made mistakes, that he truly wanted to protect her. But the truth was, she couldn't ignore the fact that he'd lied. He'd lied about things that mattered. Things that could have jeopardized not just their relationship, but her safety as well.

She sighed and set the glass down, feeling the coolness of the ceramic against her skin. The silence in her apartment was suffocating. The truth was, she felt lost. She didn't know what was worse—the idea of never seeing Jack again or the fear of letting him back in, only for him to betray her once more.

Her thoughts were interrupted by a sudden knock at the door.

Emma's pulse quickened, and she stood from the bed instinctively, her heart skipping as she approached the door. She had no idea who it could be at this hour. The only person who had been on her mind, the only person who had been absent, was Jack. Was he here? Had he come to force her to confront the truth, to make her face the situation head-on?

She opened the door slowly, her breath caught in her chest.

Standing there, drenched from the rain, was Jack. His face was unreadable, but the tension in his jaw and the dark circles under his eyes told her everything she needed to know. He looked like a man who had been carrying the weight of the world on his shoulders. A man who had been unraveling, but who hadn't given up just yet.

"Jack..." Emma's voice broke as she stepped back to let him in.

He didn't speak right away. Instead, he entered the apartment and closed the door behind him, his movements slow, deliberate. His eyes never left hers, as though searching for some sign of what she was thinking, what she was feeling.

"Emma," he began, his voice hoarse from the weight of unspoken words, "I didn't know where else to go. I couldn't stand the thought of you shutting me out."

"I haven't shut you out yet," Emma whispered, though she wasn't sure if she believed her own words. "But I'm not sure what to believe anymore. I don't know if I can trust you."

Jack's expression faltered for a moment, but then he stepped closer, his eyes intense and full of regret. He reached out, but she took a step back, needing space, needing to breathe.

"I know I've made mistakes," he said, his voice trembling slightly. "And I know I've hurt you. But I've never been more sure of anything in my life than I am about this—about us. I'll do whatever it takes to make it right. I'll tell you everything, all of it. The good, the bad, the ugly. I'll do whatever it takes to show you that I'm not that man anymore."

Emma stared at him, her chest tightening. She could feel her walls crumbling, bit by bit, with every word he spoke. Her mind told her to stay strong, to hold onto the pain so she wouldn't get lost in him again. But her heart—the one that had fallen for him so deeply, so passionately—was fighting against her logic.

"Why didn't you tell me, Jack?" Her voice cracked. "Why did you hide everything from me? Why didn't you trust me enough to tell me the truth?"

Jack winced at her words, as if they cut deeper than anything she could say. "I thought I could protect you by keeping you in the dark. I thought if I shielded you from this world, you'd never have to face the danger, the mess I created. But I realize now that keeping you in the dark was the biggest mistake of all."

Emma swallowed hard, her throat dry as she struggled to keep her emotions in check. She wanted to scream, to rail at him for everything he had done. But she couldn't. She could see the pain in his eyes, and for some reason, that made everything more complicated.

"I'm not some innocent little girl, Jack," she said quietly. "I can handle the truth. But this... I don't know if I can handle you keeping things from me. I don't know if I can handle being part of a life I didn't choose."

"I know," Jack replied softly. "I should have trusted you. I should have told you everything from the beginning. But I was scared—scared that you'd walk away, scared that I'd lose you. I should have never let that fear control me."

A heavy silence stretched between them, the air thick with unspoken emotions. Emma closed her eyes, trying to make sense of everything that was swirling inside her. She wanted to forgive him. She wanted to believe that their love was strong enough to withstand the damage that had been done. But the fear lingered, the doubt, the uncertainty.

"You're right," she said finally, her voice steady but full of emotion. "You should have trusted me. But you didn't. And now I'm the one who has to figure out if I can trust you again."

Jack's face fell, and for a moment, Emma saw a flash of vulnerability, a side of him he rarely allowed to show.

"I'm not asking you to trust me right now," he said, his voice low. "But I'm asking for the chance to prove to you that I can be the man you deserve. The man you thought I was. If you'll give me that chance."

Emma took a deep breath, her chest tightening with the weight of the decision she was about to make. Could she give him that chance? Could she risk her heart again after everything that had happened?

"I don't know if I can," she admitted, her voice barely a whisper. "But I'm willing to try. For us. For what we had. I'm not promising anything, Jack. But I will listen to you. I will hear you out."

Jack reached for her hand, his fingers trembling as they brushed against hers. The contact was electric, sending a shock through her veins. He didn't say anything; he just held her hand in his, as though the simple act of touching her was enough to convey everything he couldn't put into words.

"Thank you," he whispered, his voice hoarse with emotion. "I won't let you down again."

Emma met his gaze, her heart torn between fear and hope. She didn't know what the future held. She didn't know if they could ever fully repair the damage done. But in that moment, as Jack held her hand and their eyes locked, she knew one thing for certain—she wasn't ready to let go just yet.

Chapter 80: The Edge of Desire

"In the heat of passion, we find the courage to reveal our truest selves." — Unknown

Emma's mind raced as she sat across from Jack, the café's ambient noise around them fading into nothingness. The weight of the conversation they had begun yesterday hung over them both, but there was a strange comfort in the way they had begun to rebuild. A slow, delicate dance of words and emotions, each step feeling like a leap of faith.

Jack's fingers drummed nervously on the edge of his coffee cup, and he stole glances at Emma every now and then. His eyes were full of remorse, but they also held a quiet hope—hope that maybe, just maybe, they could move forward together.

"I've been thinking," Emma began, breaking the silence that had settled between them. Her voice was steady, but her eyes betrayed the turmoil within. "We can't just pretend like nothing happened. We can't pretend like I'm not still hurt, or that I don't have questions. But I also can't ignore what we've built together. I can't ignore what's still there between us."

Jack leaned in slightly, his expression softening as he listened intently. "I never meant to hurt you, Emma. And I know words can only do so much. But I need you to know that I'm committed to doing whatever it takes to prove myself to you, to earn back your trust."

Emma nodded slowly, feeling a mix of emotions swirling inside her. She hadn't been ready to forgive him entirely, but she was willing to take the first steps toward understanding, toward something better. The past was never going to fade entirely, but perhaps there was room for something new to grow.

"Do you ever wonder..." she trailed off, unsure of how to ask the question that had been gnawing at her for days. "Do you ever wonder what we would have been if everything had been different? If there hadn't been so many secrets?"

Jack exhaled deeply, his eyes searching hers as if trying to gauge the depth of her question. "All the time," he admitted quietly. "I wish things had been different. I wish I hadn't kept so much from you, but I can't go back and change that. All I can do is move forward, and I hope you'll move forward with me."

Emma felt a pang of sadness in her chest. It wasn't just the secrets, it was everything—the lies, the betrayals, the fears that had kept them both locked in their own worlds. But there was something in Jack's eyes now, a sincerity she hadn't seen before. He wasn't asking her to forget, but he was asking for a chance to move past it.

"I don't want to live in the past anymore," she said softly, meeting his gaze. "But I need time, Jack. Time to process everything, time to rebuild the trust that was broken."

Jack's hand reached across the table, his fingers brushing against hers. It was a simple touch, but it spoke volumes. He wasn't rushing her, he wasn't pushing her. He was offering her space, but he was also offering his heart, wide open, raw and vulnerable.

"I can give you that time," he said, his voice barely above a whisper. "And I'll wait. I'll wait for as long as it takes. But I'll never stop trying to show you that I'm worth it."

A soft smile tugged at the corners of Emma's lips. There was a tenderness between them now, a quiet understanding that hadn't been there before. She could feel the walls she had built around her heart beginning to crack, not because she was ready to give everything back to him, but because she was starting to believe that there might be a future for them. A future that was different. A future that didn't have to repeat the past.

Jack squeezed her hand gently, his thumb caressing the back of her fingers. His touch was comforting, grounding her in the moment. She took a deep breath, trying to calm the butterflies that had taken flight in her stomach. This wasn't easy—none of this was—but she was willing to try. For him. For herself. For them.

"I want to move forward, Jack," she said, her voice steady but filled with emotion. "But I need you to understand something. I can't forget what happened. I can't just forgive and forget. But I want to give us a chance. I want to see if we can find a way to make this work."

Jack's face softened, and he leaned closer, his forehead almost touching hers. "We will, Emma. We'll find a way. I promise."

The moment hung between them, charged with emotion and the unspoken promise of a fresh start. It wasn't going to be easy, and there would be challenges ahead. But for the first time in a long time, Emma felt a glimmer of hope that they could make it. They could rebuild, piece by piece, and maybe, just maybe, they could find something beautiful in the wreckage of their past.

Later that evening, as Emma walked through the streets of the city, the cool air brushing against her skin, she felt a sense of calm that had eluded her for so long. She had always believed in the power of second chances, but she had never imagined one would be given to her in this way. It wasn't the fairy tale she had once envisioned, but it was something real. Something worth fighting for.

Her phone buzzed in her pocket, interrupting her thoughts. She pulled it out and saw a message from Jack.

Jack: *"Thinking of you. I know things won't be easy, but I'm ready to fight for us. Every step of the way. Always."*

Her heart fluttered as she read his words, a small smile playing on her lips. She hadn't asked for this. She hadn't asked for any of this. But there was something undeniable about the way Jack made her feel. He made her feel alive in a way no one else ever had.

Emma typed a quick response, her fingers moving instinctively.

Emma: *"I'm ready too. Let's take it one step at a time."*

She hit send, then looked up at the skyline, feeling the weight of the world lighten just a little. The future was uncertain, but for the first time, it didn't seem so daunting.

Chapter 81: The Weight of Desire

"Desire is the most intense form of wanting, but it is also the most fragile." — Unknown

The night was alive with the soft hum of the city, its lights casting long shadows on the streets below. Emma stood at her apartment window, her eyes tracing the path of the cars below as they zipped by, unaware of the storm that had passed through her heart in the last few days. There had been moments of doubt—moments where she questioned everything she and Jack had gone through—but tonight, she felt something different. A shift. A lightness.

Jack had been patient, more patient than she ever expected him to be. He had given her the space she needed, but he had also remained ever present, offering comfort and tenderness in a way she couldn't ignore. She had spent the last few days reflecting on what she wanted—on what she was ready for—and one thing was clear: she was tired of being afraid.

Afraid of opening her heart again. Afraid of the pain she knew could come. But maybe that was the price for love—the risk of falling only to rise again, stronger and wiser. And maybe, just maybe, she could trust Jack with that part of her heart that had remained hidden for so long.

Her phone buzzed, a soft vibration against the marble countertop. She glanced over and saw Jack's name on the screen. A smile tugged at her lips before she could stop it.

Jack: *"I'm outside. Ready when you are."*

Her heart skipped a beat. She hadn't expected him to show up tonight, but she should have known he wouldn't back down. It was a side of him she had always admired—his determination, his unwavering commitment to her, no matter how many times she tried to push him away.

Emma typed back quickly.

Emma: *"I'll be right down."*

The anticipation was almost unbearable as she grabbed her coat and rushed downstairs, her mind racing with thoughts of what Jack had in store for them tonight. She wasn't sure if they were ready to take the next step, but there was something in the air between them, an electricity that hadn't been there before. It felt like they were on the brink of something, and she was willing to take the plunge.

When she reached the street, she spotted Jack standing by his car, leaning casually against it. He was dressed in a black jacket and jeans, looking effortlessly handsome, as always. But tonight, there was something different in his posture—a vulnerability that hadn't been there before. It was as if he, too, was unsure about what the future held, but he was ready to face it with her by his side.

"Hey," she said softly as she approached him, her voice betraying the rush of emotions swirling inside her. She had always thought she would be the one to hold back, the one to resist, but tonight, she felt different. Stronger.

Jack looked up, his eyes softening as they met hers. He smiled that smile—the one that always made her heart race—and for the first time in weeks, Emma allowed herself to relax into it. She wasn't just surviving anymore. She was living.

"Hey," Jack replied, his voice low and warm. He opened the passenger door for her, and as she slid inside, she caught the faint scent of his cologne—a familiar, comforting fragrance that seemed to wrap itself around her like a warm embrace.

The drive was quiet, the kind of quiet that spoke volumes. They didn't need words right now. They just needed to be together. Emma stole a glance at Jack as they drove, watching the way his jaw tensed every so often as he focused on the road, but his eyes were soft, vulnerable, a mirror of her own emotions.

Finally, after what felt like an eternity, Jack pulled into a secluded spot near the edge of a cliff overlooking the ocean. The sound of the waves crashing against the rocks below filled the air, and the vast expanse of the sea stretched out before them, its dark waters shimmering under the pale moonlight. It was a scene straight out of a dream, a perfect backdrop for the moment that was about to unfold.

Jack turned off the engine and faced Emma, his eyes searching hers for any sign of hesitation. But she wasn't hesitating. Not anymore.

"I wanted to bring you here," he said quietly, his voice thick with emotion. "Because this place...it's where I come when I need to clear my head. And it's where I come when I'm ready to face the hard truths. I've been thinking about everything we've been through, and I've realized something."

Emma raised an eyebrow, intrigued. "What's that?"

Jack took a deep breath, his gaze unwavering as he looked directly into her eyes. "I don't want to just be the man who fixes things when they're broken. I don't want to be the man who tries to make up for the past. I want to be the man who builds something with you—something real, something lasting."

Emma felt her chest tighten at his words. It wasn't what she expected him to say, but it was exactly what she needed to hear. This wasn't just about apologies and forgiveness. It was about a future. It was about moving forward, hand in hand.

"You already are that man, Jack," she said softly, her voice thick with emotion. "You've been that man for me. But I need you to know that I'm not perfect either. I have my flaws, my doubts, and sometimes, I don't know if I can fully let go of the past. But I'm willing to try."

A smile tugged at Jack's lips as he reached over and took her hand in his, his thumb brushing over her knuckles. "We don't have to be perfect, Emma. We just have to be willing to try. To fight for each other. To fight for this."

There was a silence between them, but it wasn't the awkward kind. It was the kind of silence that spoke volumes, the kind where two people could simply exist in the moment, knowing that the next step was theirs to take together.

Without another word, Jack opened his door and stepped out, extending his hand toward her. Emma hesitated for a moment but then placed her hand in his, allowing him to pull her into the cool night air. Together, they walked to the edge of the cliff, their fingers intertwined, the wind rustling through their hair.

"Look at this," Jack said, motioning toward the horizon. "It's beautiful. And it's endless. Just like us."

Emma nodded, her heart swelling with a mix of emotions. "Endless," she repeated softly, her eyes tracing the path of the waves below.

She didn't know what the future held, but for the first time, it didn't scare her. She didn't need to have all the answers. She just needed to take the next step.

And with Jack by her side, she was ready.

Chapter 82: Beneath the Surface

"The deepest rivers flow with the least sound." — Quintus Curtius Rufus

The days seemed to stretch into weeks as Emma and Jack navigated the delicate, unpredictable path they were forging together. What had started as tentative glances and cautious conversations had blossomed into something deeper. Something raw. Their bond was no longer defined by the mistakes of the past or the lingering shadows of distrust; it was being built in the present, with every touch, every whispered word, every moment shared between them.

Emma had always been the one to control the narrative. She had mastered the art of self-preservation, of keeping her heart locked away behind layers of defence. But Jack, with his persistence, his gentle patience, had begun to chip away at the walls she had spent years constructing. She wasn't sure when it had happened—when she had started to believe that maybe, just maybe, she could love him again—but it felt as though it had always been inevitable.

Tonight, the air was different. They had come to a quiet understanding, but the weight of what lay ahead still hung over them. There was an intensity in the way Jack looked at her now, something that went beyond the surface—a depth that spoke of secrets yet to be revealed and promises yet to be made. It wasn't enough for either of them to simply exist in the moment. They wanted more.

It was a cool evening, the kind where the air clung to your skin like a gentle caress. The city, with all its noise and chaos, seemed to fade into the background as they walked through the quiet streets. They were alone in their bubble of silence, their footsteps in sync as they made their way down a narrow path that led to the water. Emma could feel the tension in the air, but it wasn't uncomfortable. It was anticipation.

Jack's hand brushed against hers, and the simple touch sent a shiver through her body. She turned her head, meeting his gaze, and saw that same intensity in his eyes. He was about to say something, she could feel it in the air, but he didn't speak. Instead, he took her hand in his, lacing their fingers together.

"Do you ever wonder what would have happened if we hadn't met?" he asked, his voice quiet, thoughtful. "If we had never crossed paths?"

Emma blinked in surprise at the question. It wasn't something she had considered before, but now that Jack had brought it up, it lingered in her mind, a curiosity that gnawed at the edges of her thoughts.

"I used to," she replied, her voice almost a whisper. "I used to think about how different my life would have been without you. But then I realised... I wouldn't be who I am now without everything we've been through. And I wouldn't be ready for what's ahead."

Jack squeezed her hand gently, his thumb tracing the back of her fingers. "I used to think the same thing. But now... I just know that I want to see what we can build. I want to take the leap, even if it means stepping into the unknown."

The weight of his words sank deep into Emma's chest. She had always been afraid of the unknown, afraid of what could happen if she allowed herself to truly let go. But with Jack, something was different. She didn't have to be afraid anymore. Maybe that was the real lesson—learning how to trust not just him, but herself.

"You're right," she said, her voice steady. "I don't want to be afraid anymore. Not when it comes to us."

The words hung between them like a promise, unspoken but understood. They stopped walking at the water's edge, where the moonlight reflected off the rippling surface of the ocean. The sound of the waves crashing against the rocks was a soothing backdrop to the intensity of the moment. Emma turned to face Jack, her heart pounding in her chest.

"You've never asked me what I want," she said suddenly, her voice low and serious. "What I really want. Not just in this moment, but in the future. Have you ever wondered?"

Jack's gaze softened, and he stepped closer to her, the space between them shrinking until they were inches apart. "I've wondered, every day since I met you," he confessed, his voice hushed. "But I'm not asking you for answers, Emma. I just want you to know that I'm here, and I'm willing to fight for whatever comes next. With you."

There was no hesitation in his eyes, no doubts clouding the certainty of his words. He wanted her. Not just for the moment, but for the long haul. Emma felt a lump form in her throat as the weight of his declaration settled over her.

"I've always wanted more than I was willing to admit," she whispered, her voice trembling slightly. "I just... I didn't know if I could have it. If I deserved it."

Jack reached out, his fingers brushing along her jawline, lifting her chin so their eyes met. "You deserve everything, Emma. Everything. And I want to give you that. I want us to have it all, if you'll let me."

The vulnerability in his voice was so raw, so sincere, that Emma felt her heart swell with emotion. This wasn't just about passion, or chemistry, or anything fleeting. This was about two people who had faced the darkest parts of themselves and each other, and had somehow come out on the other side stronger.

A soft breeze ruffled her hair as she stepped closer, closing the gap between them. She could feel the heat radiating from his body, the tension that had been building all evening finally coming to a head.

Without thinking, she reached up, her hands cupping his face, and pulled him toward her. Their lips met in a kiss that was slow at first, exploratory, as if they were both trying to gauge the weight of this new chapter. But it didn't take long for the kiss to deepen, to turn into something more urgent, more desperate.

Jack's arms wrapped around her, pulling her close, his fingers threading through her hair as the kiss grew more passionate. Emma's breath caught in her throat as she felt the intensity of his desire, matched by her own. She had always prided herself on being in control, but with Jack, she found herself giving in, surrendering to the chemistry that had always simmered between them.

When they finally pulled apart, breathless and disheveled, Emma rested her forehead against his, her heart still racing.

"This," she said softly, her fingers tracing the line of his jaw, "this is what I want. I want to feel like this with you. I want us to make something real out of this, something lasting. I want to build a life with you, Jack."

A smile spread across Jack's face, and he kissed her once more, gently this time, as if sealing the promise they had just made. He pulled back slowly, his eyes filled with warmth.

"I don't know what the future holds, but I know one thing for sure," he said, his voice low and confident. "I want to build that future with you, Emma. One step at a time. No more hiding. No more pretending."

Emma nodded, her heart swelling with love for the man in front of her. For the first time in a long time, she felt truly seen, truly understood. And in that moment, as they stood together, the waves crashing against the rocks and the moon casting its soft glow over them, she knew that they were ready to face whatever came next—together.

Chapter 83: Ghosts of the Past

"The greatest moments in life are the ones you can't put into words." — Kobi Yamada

The quiet after their kiss felt like an eternity. Emma could feel her pulse racing, her body still thrumming with the aftermath of their connection. They had crossed a line, a line that neither of them could take back. But the look in Jack's eyes told her that there was no going back, not now. And she didn't want to.

"Tell me what you need, Emma," Jack whispered, his voice rough and low. He had stepped away just enough to look at her, but the heat in his gaze never faltered. It was a question, but also an invitation—an open door, and Emma had never been one to shy away from what she wanted.

She closed her eyes, breathing in the cool air, gathering her thoughts. For so long, she had kept herself contained, afraid to truly surrender to the pull of desire, to give in to the raw, overwhelming passion that Jack stirred within her. But now, standing before him, all of those old walls felt fragile, like they were crumbling around her, leaving nothing but the truth of what she longed for.

"I need to feel everything," Emma murmured, her voice barely audible. "I need to feel you. Every part of you."

Jack's breath hitched at her words, but he didn't hesitate. His hands moved to her waist, pulling her closer, until the heat of his body enveloped her, making the air around them feel charged with electricity. Emma let out a soft gasp as his lips brushed against her ear, his breath hot against her skin.

"You have me, Emma," he whispered, his voice thick with desire. "All of me. Every part. And I'm going to show you just how much you mean to me."

The intensity in his words matched the fire burning in her chest. Emma's hands moved to the hem of his shirt, fingers trembling slightly as she lifted it over his head. The sight of his bare skin, the way his muscles flexed as he moved, made her pulse quicken. She traced the lines of his chest with her fingers, feeling the warmth of his body, the soft beat of his heart beneath her touch.

"You're perfect," she breathed, her voice full of wonder as she studied him. "I've never known anyone like you."

Jack's hand cupped her face, lifting her chin so their eyes met. His gaze was filled with something deeper than just desire—it was reverence, admiration. "You're perfect, Emma. And I'm going to make sure you feel that."

Without another word, Jack leaned down, his lips finding hers in a kiss that was all urgency, all need. The world around them seemed to fade, the only thing that mattered was the way they fit together, the way their bodies responded to each other. Emma's hands tangled in his hair, pulling him closer, as if she couldn't get enough of him.

She felt the heat building between them, a fire that threatened to consume them both, and she couldn't stop herself from leaning into it. She wanted this. She wanted him.

Jack's hands were everywhere—sliding over her back, pulling her closer, pressing her against him. His lips trailed down her neck, and Emma shivered at the soft kisses he planted along her skin, his breath warm against her. She tilted her head back, giving him more access, as the sensations built to an almost unbearable intensity.

"Jack..." She gasped his name, her voice raw, almost a plea. The hunger in her was growing, and she wanted him to see it. To feel it.

"I'm here, Emma," he murmured, his lips brushing over her collarbone, his breath hot on her skin. "I'm right here. And I'm not going anywhere."

Her heart fluttered at his words, the sincerity in them reaching deep inside her. She had always feared being vulnerable, afraid that letting go would lead to heartache. But with Jack, she felt safe. Safe enough to surrender, safe enough to give herself completely to him.

As if sensing her hesitation, Jack pulled back just slightly, his eyes searching hers. "You're not alone in this, Emma. You never will be again."

The vulnerability in his voice, the tenderness in his gaze, sent a rush of emotion through her. For the first time, Emma truly believed that she wasn't alone. That they were in this together, no matter what.

With a breathless laugh, she reached for him, her hands moving to the waistband of his jeans. She pulled him toward her again, kissing him with a fierceness that mirrored the passion between them. This was no longer just about the physical—the need to touch, to kiss—it was about something much deeper. Something that Emma couldn't quite name yet, but she knew it was there, growing stronger with each moment they shared.

Jack groaned against her lips as her hands explored, her touch igniting a fire within him. His hands were at her waist again, pulling her shirt over her head, and Emma let him, the fabric sliding off her body with a sensual grace. The night air was cool against her exposed skin, but Jack's touch was like fire—burning, searing. His mouth found hers again, hungry and possessive, and Emma melted into him, losing herself in the heat of their kiss.

They moved together like two bodies in perfect sync, each touch, each kiss, driving them closer to the edge. Emma's breath was ragged as she tugged at Jack's jeans, desperate to feel him fully, to be as close to him as possible. And when the last barrier between them was gone, when they were skin to skin, the world seemed to stop.

Jack's hands moved over her body, every caress, every touch, making her feel as though she were on fire. "You're so beautiful," he murmured, his voice low and full of awe. "So damn beautiful, Emma."

The words sent a shiver through her. She had always felt self-conscious about her body, but with Jack, she felt like she could finally be herself—vulnerable, open, and free. He was making her see herself in a way she never had before.

Their movements were slow at first, exploring, savoring the sensation of being together. But as the intensity between them grew, so did the urgency. The rhythm of their bodies matched the beating of their hearts, quick and frantic, as if they were both desperate to feel the other. Emma's body arched toward Jack, and he groaned in response, his hands gripping her hips as he moved with her, his touch possessive, like he couldn't get enough. Everything blurred—time, space, the world around them. All that mattered was the connection between them, the way their bodies came together in a perfect symphony of heat and need.

"Emma," Jack whispered, his voice hoarse as he leaned down to kiss her neck. "I need you. Need to feel you."

She nodded, her breath catching in her throat as she reached for him, pulling him closer, wanting nothing more than to be lost in him. To lose herself completely in this moment, in the heat of their passion.

With a final, powerful movement, the world seemed to explode around them. Emma cried out, her fingers digging into Jack's back as the pleasure coursed through her. Jack's name escaped her lips in a breathless whisper, and Jack followed her, his body tensing as the wave of ecstasy washed over them both.

They collapsed together in a tangle of limbs, breathless and spent, but the connection between them remained—stronger than ever. As they lay there, tangled in the sheets, Jack pulled her close, his arms wrapping around her as if he couldn't bear to let go.

"I'm not going anywhere, Emma," he murmured, his voice full of warmth and promise. "This is just the beginning."

Emma smiled softly, her heart full, and snuggled into him, knowing that he meant every word. And in that moment, she finally understood what it meant to be truly seen—truly loved.

Chapter 84: The Storm Within

"Jealousy is a poison, but sometimes, it tastes so sweet." — Unknown

The morning sun filtered softly through the sheer curtains, casting a warm, golden hue across the bedroom. Emma stirred beneath the crisp white sheets, her body instinctively seeking the comforting presence beside her. As her eyes fluttered open, she found herself nestled against Jack, their limbs entwined in the intimate aftermath of the night before.

She lay still for a moment, savoring the rhythmic rise and fall of his chest, the steady heartbeat beneath her palm. The events of the previous evening replayed in her mind—a tapestry of whispered confessions, lingering touches, and the unspoken promises that had woven them closer together. A smile tugged at the corners of her lips as she traced delicate circles on his skin, marveling at the ease with which they had connected.

Jack's breathing shifted, a subtle change that signaled his ascent from slumber. His arm tightened around her, pulling her closer as his eyes slowly opened. A lazy, contented smile spread across his face as he met her gaze.

"Good morning," he murmured, his voice husky with sleep.

"Morning," Emma replied, her voice soft, almost hesitant. She searched his eyes, seeking reassurance, wondering if he felt the same profound shift that she did.

Jack brushed a stray strand of hair from her face, his fingers lingering against her cheek. "Penny for your thoughts?" he asked, his tone gentle.

Emma hesitated, biting her lower lip. "Last night was... unexpected," she admitted. "But in the best possible way."

He chuckled softly, the sound vibrating through his chest. "I couldn't agree more."

A comfortable silence enveloped them, each lost in their own reflections. Emma's mind raced with questions and uncertainties. She had always been cautious, guarded with her heart. Yet, with Jack, those walls seemed to crumble effortlessly.

"Jack," she began tentatively, "do you ever wonder if we're moving too fast?"

He propped himself up on one elbow, his expression thoughtful. "Perhaps," he conceded. "But sometimes, when something feels right, it's worth embracing, even if it defies logic."

Emma nodded slowly, absorbing his words. "It's just... I've always been independent, focused on my career and personal goals. I'm afraid of losing myself in this."

Jack's gaze softened, and he reached out to cup her face, his thumb tracing gentle patterns along her jawline. "Emma, being with someone doesn't mean losing yourself. It means finding a part of you that you didn't know was missing."

His words resonated deep within her, easing some of the apprehension that had taken root. She leaned into his touch, allowing herself to be vulnerable in a way she hadn't before.

"You're right," she whispered. "I just need to learn to let go and trust."

Jack smiled, pressing a tender kiss to her forehead. "We'll navigate this together, one step at a time."

The day unfolded with a newfound sense of intimacy. They moved through the hours seamlessly, sharing stories, laughter, and stolen glances that spoke volumes. The connection between them deepened, each moment solidifying the bond that had formed so unexpectedly.

As evening descended, they found themselves curled up on the couch, a bottle of wine between them and the soft glow of the fireplace casting flickering shadows across the room. The atmosphere was thick with unspoken emotions, a palpable tension that neither could ignore.

Jack poured them each a glass of wine, handing one to Emma with a playful smile. "To unexpected beginnings," he toasted, his eyes twinkling with warmth.

"To new chapters," Emma echoed, clinking her glass against his.

They sipped their wine in comfortable silence, the crackling of the fire providing a soothing backdrop. Emma leaned her head against Jack's shoulder, feeling the steady rhythm of his breathing. The simplicity of the moment was both comforting and exhilarating.

"Jack," she began softly, "do you ever think about where this is heading?"

He turned to face her, his expression serious yet tender. "I do," he admitted. "And while I don't have all the answers, I know that being with you feels right. I want to explore this, wherever it may lead."

Emma's heart swelled at his honesty. "I feel the same," she confessed. "But I can't help but wonder if we're setting ourselves up for heartbreak."

Jack reached for her hand, intertwining their fingers. "There's always a risk," he acknowledged. "But sometimes, the greatest rewards come from taking chances."

She gazed into his eyes, finding solace in their depth. "You're worth the risk," she murmured.

A slow smile spread across Jack's face, and he leaned in, capturing her lips in a tender, lingering kiss. The world around them faded, leaving only the two of them suspended in a moment of pure connection.

As the night wore on, they remained entwined, sharing whispered dreams and silent promises. The weight of desire hung heavy in the air, a delicate balance of passion and vulnerability. In each other's arms, they found a sanctuary—a place where fears were quelled, and the future, though uncertain, seemed a little less daunting.

Chapter 85: Shadows of Doubt

"*The past is never where you think you left it.*" — *Katherine Anne Porter*

The morning sun had long since risen, casting its golden rays across the city, but Emma and Jack remained ensconced in the cocoon of their shared sanctuary. The previous night's confessions and intimacies had woven a new tapestry between them, one rich with unspoken promises and burgeoning emotions.

Emma sat cross-legged on the bed, her gaze fixed on the steaming cup of coffee cradled in her hands. The aroma was comforting, grounding her amidst the whirlwind of thoughts that swirled in her mind. Jack emerged from the bathroom, a towel draped around his neck, droplets of water tracing paths down his bare chest.

"You're quiet this morning," he observed, seating himself beside her.

She offered a small smile, her eyes meeting his. "Just... processing," she admitted. "Everything feels like it's moving so fast."

Jack nodded, understanding evident in his expression. "I feel it too," he confessed. "But sometimes, the best things happen when we least expect them."

Emma took a sip of her coffee, the warmth spreading through her. "I don't want to overthink this," she said softly. "I want to embrace it. Us."

He reached out, his fingers gently brushing against hers. "Then let's take it one step at a time," he suggested. "No pressure, no expectations. Just us."

The simplicity of his words eased the tension in her shoulders. She nodded, a genuine smile breaking across her face. "I'd like that."

The day unfolded with a sense of newfound ease. They ventured out into the bustling city, exploring hidden bookstores and quaint cafes, each moment adding layers to their growing connection. Laughter came easily, and the weight of their individual pasts seemed lighter in each other's company.

As evening approached, they found themselves walking along the riverbank, the city's skyline reflecting off the water's surface. The air was crisp, carrying the scent of autumn and the distant hum of city life.

Jack paused, turning to face Emma. "There's something I want to show you," he said, a hint of excitement in his voice.

Curiosity piqued, Emma followed as he led her through a series of winding streets, eventually arriving at a nondescript building. Jack produced a key, unlocking the door and gesturing for her to enter.

The space was vast, illuminated by the soft glow of string lights draped across exposed beams. Canvases of various sizes lined the walls, each depicting scenes that seemed to pulse with emotion and depth.

Emma's breath caught as she took in the artwork. "Jack, did you paint these?" she asked, awe evident in her voice.

He nodded, a touch of vulnerability flickering in his eyes. "It's been a while since I've shared this part of myself with anyone," he admitted.

She approached a canvas that depicted a stormy sea, the waves crashing with a ferocity that was almost tangible. "They're incredible," she murmured. "Each one tells a story."

Jack moved to stand beside her. "Painting has always been my way of processing," he explained. "Emotions, experiences... it's how I make sense of the world."

Emma turned to face him, her heart swelling with admiration. "Thank you for sharing this with me," she said sincerely. "It means a lot."

He reached out, tucking a strand of hair behind her ear. "You mean a lot," he replied, his voice barely above a whisper.

The space between them seemed to shrink as they stood amidst the echoes of Jack's soul laid bare on canvas. The air was thick with unspoken words, the gravity of the moment pulling them closer.

Emma broke the silence, her voice tinged with curiosity. "Is there a story behind this one?" she asked, gesturing to a painting of a lone figure standing at the edge of a cliff, gazing into the abyss below.

Jack's gaze softened as he regarded the piece. "It's about standing on the precipice of change," he explained. "The fear, the anticipation, the unknown. But also the courage to take the leap."

She nodded, the metaphor resonating deeply within her. "I feel like that's where I am right now," she admitted. "On the edge, ready to jump but terrified of the fall."

Jack turned to her, his eyes searching hers. "Maybe we can take the leap together," he suggested, his hand reaching for hers.

Emma felt the warmth of his touch, the steadiness of his presence grounding her amidst the uncertainty. "I'd like that," she whispered.

They spent hours in the studio, Emma learning more about Jack through his art than words could ever convey. Each painting was a window into his soul, revealing facets of his being that deepened her affection for him.

As night settled over the city, they found themselves seated on the floor, a bottle of wine between them and a blanket draped over their shoulders. The conversation flowed effortlessly, weaving between lighthearted anecdotes and profound revelations.

"Do you ever wonder about destiny?" Emma mused, her head resting against Jack's shoulder.

He considered her question, his fingers tracing idle patterns on her arm. "I think we create our own destiny," he replied. "But sometimes, the universe gives us a nudge in the right direction."

She smiled, finding comfort in his perspective. "Meeting you feels like one of those nudges," she confessed.

Jack pressed a kiss to the top of her head. "I'm glad the universe brought us together," he murmured.

The studio's ambiance, with its art and intimate lighting, created a cocoon where time seemed to stand still. They shared dreams and fears, each revelation weaving them closer together.

As the night deepened, Jack stood, extending a hand to Emma. "Dance with me," he invited.

She laughed softly. "There's no music," she pointed out.

He grinned, undeterred. "We'll make our own."

Emma allowed herself to be pulled to her feet, her arms encircling his neck as his hands found her waist. They swayed gently, the rhythm of their hearts setting the tempo. The world outside faded away, leaving only the two of them moving in harmony amidst the canvases that bore witness to their unfolding story.

In that moment, beneath the soft glow of the studio lights and surrounded by the essence of Jack's soul, Emma realized that the leap she feared was not into the unknown, but into the depths of a connection that felt as inevitable as it was profound.

As their dance slowed, Jack leaned in, his lips capturing hers in a kiss that spoke of promises unspoken and desires unveiled. Emma responded in kind, her fears melting away in the heat of their embrace.

The night stretched on, a tapestry of whispered confessions, tender touches, and the silent understanding that some connections are written not by destiny, but by the choices we dare to make.

Chapter 86: The Weight of Secrets

"Three things cannot be long hidden: the sun, the moon, and the truth." — Buddha

The city hummed softly outside, the distant waves crashing against the shore as Emma lay sprawled across the bed, her body still humming from the night before. The scent of him lingered on her skin—a blend of salt, musk, and the intoxicating essence of him. She stretched languidly, the silk sheets sliding over her bare skin, a delicious reminder of how thoroughly Jack had unraveled her in the late hours of the night.

Jack stirred beside her, his fingers lazily tracing along the curve of her hip. "Morning, beautiful."

She turned to face him, a slow smile spreading across her lips. "Morning."

His gaze roamed over her, hunger flickering in his dark eyes. "I should let you rest... but I don't want to."

Emma's pulse quickened. "Then don't."

He rolled her beneath him in one swift motion, capturing her lips in a slow, languorous kiss that sent fire curling in her belly. The way he kissed her—thorough, possessive, intoxicating—made her forget every coherent thought. His hands skimmed over her body, mapping every dip and curve with deliberate, reverent strokes.

Just as their passion threatened to consume them once more, a sharp knock at the door shattered the moment.

Emma groaned, burying her face in Jack's chest. "Ignore it."

Jack sighed, pressing a lingering kiss to her forehead before reluctantly untangling himself from her. "Stay right there."

She watched as he slipped on a pair of low-hanging pajama bottoms and strode to the door, running a hand through his tousled hair before pulling it open.

"Jack."

The sound of that voice made Emma's stomach twist. She sat up, clutching the sheet to her chest as a tall, elegant blonde woman stood in the doorway, arms crossed. A smirk played at the corners of her lips, though her eyes flickered with something unreadable.

Jack stiffened. "Victoria. What the hell are you doing here?"

Victoria arched an eyebrow, letting her gaze drift past Jack, straight to Emma. "I see you've moved on quickly."

Emma swallowed hard, her mind racing. She had imagined this moment before—meeting the infamous Victoria. But not like this. Not when she was still tangled in Jack's sheets, still feeling the echoes of his touch on her skin.

Jack's jaw tightened. "What do you want, Victoria?"

"Relax, Jack. I'm not here to cause trouble," she said smoothly. "I just need to talk to you. Alone."

Emma felt a pang of unease at the way Victoria's eyes lingered on Jack, the subtle challenge in her tone.

Jack hesitated, glancing back at Emma. "Give me a minute?"

Emma forced a nod, though her stomach twisted painfully. She wasn't naive. Victoria wasn't here for idle conversation.

Jack stepped into the hallway, closing the door behind him.

Emma exhaled slowly, running a hand through her tangled hair. She had trusted Jack implicitly, but something about Victoria's sudden arrival unsettled her. There was history there, deep and tangled, and she wasn't foolish enough to think that history could be erased overnight.

Minutes passed. Then more. The distant murmur of voices reached her through the thick walls, but she couldn't make out the words.

Doubt gnawed at her.

Finally, the door opened, and Jack stepped back in, his expression unreadable.

Emma sat up straighter. "What did she want?"

Jack ran a hand through his hair, exhaling slowly. "She wants to talk. About the past."

Emma searched his face, reading the tension in his shoulders. "Are you okay?"

He sat beside her, brushing his fingers over her cheek. "Yeah. I just... I wasn't expecting to see her."

Emma hesitated, then asked the question burning in her mind. "Do you still have feelings for her?"

Jack's eyes snapped to hers, dark and intense. "No. That part of my life is over. You are my present, Emma. My future."

She held his gaze, wanting to believe him. But the ghost of Victoria lingered in the air between them, a silent threat neither of them knew how to exorcise just yet.

Jack sighed, pulling her into his arms. "I won't let her come between us."

Emma pressed her cheek against his chest, her heart hammering. She wanted to believe him. But something told her Victoria wasn't leaving without a fight.

The tension between them lingered long after Victoria had left. The rest of the morning passed in a haze, the shadows of Jack's past threatening to intrude on their present.

Emma couldn't shake the feeling that Victoria wasn't just here to reminisce.

By midday, Jack had gone silent, his mind clearly elsewhere. The easy intimacy they had shared earlier felt distant, replaced by something unspoken. Emma decided to break the silence.

"You never really told me much about her," she said, watching him from across the room as he poured himself a drink.

Jack exhaled, running a hand over his jaw. "There wasn't much to say. She was part of my life for a long time. We had history, but it ended badly."

Emma waited, sensing there was more. "And now? What does she want now?"

He turned to her, his eyes shadowed. "Closure, she says. But I don't believe that's all. Victoria never does anything without a reason."

A chill ran down Emma's spine. "So what do we do?"

Jack's lips quirked, though there was little humor in it. "We wait. And we don't let her get in our heads."

Emma nodded, but she wasn't convinced. Something about the way Victoria had looked at her, the way she had spoken, made her certain—this wasn't over.

Chapter 87: Beneath The Surface

"The only way to truly know someone is to see them in their rawest, most vulnerable form." – Unknown

Emma sat on the plush couch in the living area of Jack's penthouse, staring out at the Sydney skyline. The morning sun was golden and crisp, yet a storm of emotions brewed inside her. Victoria's sudden reappearance had sent her mind spiraling. Even though Jack had reassured her, the unease coiled tightly in her chest like a snake ready to strike.

She tapped her fingers restlessly against her thigh, unable to shake the lingering sensation of Victoria's presence. There had been something calculated about the way she had looked at Jack, something possessive that made Emma's skin prickle.

The sound of the shower turning off signaled Jack's return. Moments later, he stepped into the room, a towel slung low on his hips, droplets of water gliding down his sculpted chest. His presence alone was enough to set her body alight, but for once, desire was shadowed by doubt.

"Penny for your thoughts?" Jack asked, his voice rich and knowing. He grabbed a second towel and ran it through his damp hair, watching her carefully.

Emma forced a small smile. "Just... thinking."

He sat beside her, close enough for her to feel his body heat. "Thinking about Victoria?"

Emma hesitated before nodding. "She's still in love with you."

Jack exhaled, his jaw tightening. "It doesn't matter what she feels, Emma. I'm not in love with her."

"I know that." She turned to face him fully, searching his eyes. "But she's not the type to give up easily, is she?"

Jack's expression darkened slightly, his fingers trailing along the bare skin of her arm in a soothing motion. "No, she's not."

Emma's stomach twisted. "What if she's here to cause trouble?"

Jack cupped her face, his touch gentle yet firm. "Then let her try. She doesn't get to control what we have, Emma. Only we do."

She exhaled slowly, wanting to believe him. "I just don't trust her."

"Neither do I," he admitted. "But I do trust us."

Emma swallowed hard, nodding. Jack kissed her softly, a slow and deliberate reminder of everything they shared. The tension in her body eased slightly under the warmth of his touch, but the unease remained, a ghost lingering just beneath the surface.

Later that afternoon, Emma found herself alone in the penthouse, Jack having left for an important meeting. She was still wrapped in one of his shirts, her legs curled beneath her on the couch when her phone buzzed.

Unknown Number.

Frowning, she hesitated before answering. "Hello?"

Silence, then a familiar, velvety voice. "I was hoping we could have a little chat."

Emma's breath hitched. "Victoria."

A low chuckle drifted through the line. "So he's mentioned me."

Emma's grip on the phone tightened. "What do you want?"

"I think we should meet."

Emma scoffed. "I don't see why."

"Because, darling, there are things you should know about Jack. Things he might not have told you."

Emma's pulse pounded. "I know enough."

Victoria hummed, almost sympathetically. "Do you?"

There was something chilling about her tone, something that sent warning signals flashing in Emma's mind. Every instinct told her not to engage, not to play into whatever game Victoria was spinning.

And yet, a part of her—a dark, curious part—needed to know.

"Fine," Emma said after a beat. "Where?"

Emma arrived at a sleek, upscale bar in the city, her nerves thrumming beneath her calm exterior. Victoria was already seated in a dimly lit booth, her long fingers wrapped around a glass of deep red wine. She looked every bit the femme fatale—effortlessly poised, exuding confidence and danger in equal measure.

"Emma," Victoria greeted smoothly, gesturing to the seat across from her. "I'm so glad you came."

Emma slid into the seat, keeping her expression neutral. "You have five minutes."

Victoria chuckled, swirling her wine. "Straight to the point. I like that."

Emma waited, her patience thinning by the second.

Victoria leaned forward slightly, her blue eyes sharp. "Tell me, Emma, how much do you really know about Jack's past?"

Emma's fingers curled into her lap. "Enough."

Victoria tilted her head, a ghost of a smile playing on her lips. "Did he ever tell you how we ended?"

Emma hesitated, her heartbeat spiking. "He said it was bad."

Victoria's lips curled into something resembling amusement. "Oh, it was more than bad, sweetheart. It was explosive."

Emma exhaled sharply. "I'm not here for games. If you have something to say, say it."

Victoria studied her for a moment before setting her glass down. "Jack and I were together for years. We had passion, intensity... and destruction. We were toxic for each other, but we couldn't let go."

Emma's stomach tightened. "And?"

"And I wasn't the one who ended things," Victoria said, a flicker of something dangerous in her eyes. "He left me. He walked away, just like that. One day, I was his world, and the next, I was nothing."

Emma swallowed hard, but remained silent.

Victoria's smile sharpened. "Tell me, Emma, do you really think Jack is capable of giving you something permanent? Because he wasn't capable of giving it to me."

A flicker of doubt crept in, unbidden and unwanted. "People change," Emma said firmly.

"Perhaps." Victoria's gaze was unwavering. "But some habits die hard."

Emma forced herself to meet her stare. "I'm not you."

Victoria smirked. "No, you're not. But that doesn't mean history won't repeat itself."

Emma stood abruptly, her pulse racing. "We're done here."

Victoria merely sipped her wine, a knowing glint in her eyes. "For now."

Emma turned and walked away, but the words clung to her, wrapping around her mind like an unwanted caress.

She needed to talk to Jack.

Chapter 88: The Unspoken Truth

"*The truth may be uncomfortable, but it will set you free.*" — Unknown

Emma's pulse raced as she left the bar, Victoria's words echoing in her mind. The city's cool night air did little to calm the firestorm raging inside her. Was she being naïve to believe in Jack so fully? She wanted to dismiss Victoria's venom as the ramblings of a bitter ex, but the way she spoke—so confident, so knowing—made Emma uneasy.

Her heels clicked against the pavement as she hailed a taxi back to Jack's penthouse. By the time she arrived, she felt no more settled than when she had left. The tension coiled inside her was suffocating.

Jack was standing near the floor-to-ceiling windows, dressed in a crisp white shirt, sleeves rolled up to reveal his forearms. He turned at the sound of the door, his expression instantly shifting from neutral to concern. "Emma."

She dropped her purse on the counter and crossed her arms. "I met with Victoria."

Jack's jaw tightened. "I figured as much."

"Did you?" She tilted her head. "Then why didn't you stop me?"

Jack exhaled and walked towards her. "Because I knew nothing I said would change your mind."

Emma let out a dry chuckle. "So, what, you just let me go and get a lecture from your ex about how you'll eventually toss me aside like you did her?"

His brows furrowed. "That's what she told you?"

Emma met his gaze, searching for cracks, signs of guilt. "She said you left her. That you made her believe she was your world and then one day, it was over. Just like that."

Jack ran a hand through his hair, his usual composed demeanor slipping just slightly. "It wasn't 'just like that,' Emma. It was toxic. It was unhealthy. And I didn't want to keep hurting her or myself."

Emma swallowed, willing herself to stay steady. "So, what makes me different?"

Jack stepped closer, his hands sliding to cup her face. "Everything."

The conviction in his voice, in his touch, sent a shiver through her. She wanted to believe him—God, she did—but a part of her was still unsettled.

"I don't want to be left in the dark," she whispered. "If there's anything you're not telling me—"

"There's nothing," Jack interrupted firmly. "I promise you, Emma, there is nothing about my past that changes what we have now."

His lips found hers, hot and insistent, but she could sense the urgency in his touch, the silent plea to trust him. And for now, she d id.

The next day, Emma tried to shake off the lingering tension by throwing herself into work. She met with clients, reviewed designs, and poured herself into projects. But her mind kept drifting back to Victoria's words.

By late afternoon, she was in her office, going over some final sketches, when an unexpected visitor walked in.

"Emma Carter?"

She looked up, startled to see a tall man in a tailored navy suit. His salt-and-pepper hair was neatly styled, his sharp eyes assessing her carefully.

"Yes?"

He extended a hand. "Richard Holloway. I'm an investigator."

Emma's stomach flipped. "Excuse me?"

"I understand you're involved with Jack Sullivan," Richard said, his tone unreadable.

Emma's pulse pounded. "What is this about?"

Richard exhaled. "Jack's past isn't as clean as he might want you to believe."

Emma's breath caught. "I don't know what you're insinuating—"

"I have files, Emma," Richard said, setting a folder on her desk. "Documents. Evidence. Things you might want to see before you decide how deep you really want to go with him."

Emma's hands shook as she hesitated, staring at the folder like it might explode. Every instinct screamed at her not to look, not to let doubt take hold.

But curiosity, that dangerous, treacherous thing, won out.

Slowly, she reached for the folder, her heart hammering.

The pages inside the folder were neatly stacked, bound together with a simple black clip. Emma's fingers trembled as she pulled them free, her breath hitching at the first photograph she saw.

Jack, younger, sitting at a candlelit dinner with a woman Emma didn't recognize. A loving, intimate gaze passed between them. The caption beneath it made her stomach lurch. *Jack Sullivan and mystery woman, private engagement dinner.*

Her mind raced. Engagement? Jack had never mentioned being engaged before.

She flipped through more pages—financial records, company transactions, a report detailing Jack's involvement in a questionable offshore deal years ago. Nothing explicitly illegal, but enough to raise red flags.

Emma clenched her jaw. She had known Jack wasn't perfect. He had a past, a complicated history. But had he deliberately hidden this from her?

Richard watched her closely. "I'm not here to tell you what to do, Ms. Carter. I'm here to make sure you know what you're getting into." Emma met his gaze. "Why do you care?"

Richard hesitated before responding. "Let's just say I have a vested interest in making sure Jack Sullivan doesn't destroy another life."

A cold shiver ran down her spine.

Her fingers curled tightly around the edges of the papers. She wanted to march straight to Jack and demand answers, but a voice in her head whispered caution. What if confronting him now made things worse? What if there was more she hadn't yet uncovered?

One thing was certain—Jack had secrets. And if she wanted to find the truth, she needed to be smart about how she uncovered them.

With a deep breath, Emma carefully closed the folder and placed it in her bag.

She wasn't going to run. Not yet.

But she also wasn't going to walk blindly anymore.

Chapter 89: Breaking Boundaries

"You never know how strong you are until being strong is your only choice." — Bob Marley

Emma's fingers hovered over the folder's worn edges, her pulse hammering in her ears. She wasn't sure if she wanted to know what was inside. A part of her screamed to shove it back toward Richard Holloway and walk away—to trust Jack, to ignore the shadows of doubt creeping in. But another part, the one burned by past betrayals and heartbreak, demanded answers.

She swallowed hard and slowly flipped the folder open.

Inside, a series of documents, photographs, and reports were neatly arranged. Her eyes darted across the pages, scanning dates, names, and events she didn't recognize. But one phrase caught her attention immediately— **Sullivan Enterprises Fraud Investigation.**

Emma's breath hitched. Fraud? That was impossible. Jack was brilliant, calculated, and meticulous. There was no way he would be involved in anything remotely illegal.

Her gaze snapped to Richard. "What is this?"

Richard studied her reaction carefully. "It's documentation of a case that was quietly buried years ago. Jack Sullivan was implicated in a financial scheme that nearly cost investors millions."

Emma's grip on the papers tightened. "Implicated doesn't mean guilty."

Richard nodded. "No, it doesn't. But it means there were enough questions that someone was looking for answers. And then—just like that—the case vanished."

She shook her head. "Jack would never—"

"You think you know him." Richard's voice was steady, patient. "But do you? Completely?"

Emma wanted to say yes. She wanted to scream it. But instead, silence wrapped around her, thick and suffocating.

Richard exhaled. "Look, I have no stake in this. But I've seen people get in too deep before realizing they're in over their heads. I just think you should be careful."

Emma closed the folder, her hands trembling. "I need to talk to Jack."

Richard didn't argue. He simply gave a small nod and walked away, leaving Emma alone with the weight of her thoughts.

The penthouse was dark when Emma arrived, the city skyline stretching out in glittering brilliance beyond the floor-to-ceiling windows. Jack was at the bar, pouring himself a drink, his posture rigid. He turned at the sound of the door, his eyes narrowing slightly as he took in her tense expression.

"What's wrong?"

Emma took a slow breath and stepped forward, placing the folder on the counter between them. "Richard Holloway came to see me."

Jack's jaw tightened, his fingers wrapping around his glass. "I see."

She searched his face for any flicker of guilt or hesitation. "Is it true? Were you investigated for fraud?"

Jack's lips pressed into a thin line. He set his drink down with deliberate care. "It's not what you think."

"Then tell me what it is." Her voice wavered slightly, but she held her ground.

Jack exhaled slowly, running a hand through his hair. "Years ago, there were accusations. A former business partner—someone I trusted—manipulated company funds and tried to pin it on me when everything collapsed. I fought the allegations, and eventually, the case disappeared because there was no proof against me."

Emma's heart pounded. "So, you were innocent?"

Jack's gaze met hers, steady and unwavering. "I didn't commit fraud, Emma. But I did make mistakes. I trusted the wrong people. I let myself get too close to the fire."

Emma's fingers curled into fists. "And you never thought to tell me?"

His expression softened. "Because it was over. I put it behind me. I didn't want it tainting what we have."

Emma let out a slow, shuddering breath. She wanted to believe him. Desperately. But something about Richard's warning still clung to her, an unease she couldn't shake.

Jack stepped closer, his hands sliding to her waist. "Emma, I need you to trust me."

She looked up at him, her mind warring with her heart. Then, finally, she whispered, "I don't know if I can."

A flash of pain crossed his features, but he masked it quickly. "Then let me prove it to you."

His hands slid up her arms, his touch firm, grounding her. His lips brushed against hers, hesitant at first, as if waiting for permission. But when she didn't pull away, he deepened the kiss, pouring silent promises into it.

Emma melted into him, the taste of whiskey lingering on his tongue. She wanted to lose herself in him, to let his touch erase the doubts in her mind. His hands roamed her body, igniting a fire that momentarily drowned out everything else.

But as he carried her to the bedroom, she couldn't silence the voice whispering at the back of her mind.

What if Victoria and Richard were right?

Chapter 90: Fading Walls

"The walls we build around us to keep sadness out also keeps out the joy." —Jim Rohn

The morning sun had barely broken through the heavy clouds when Emma arrived at Jack's penthouse. The city was still wrapped in a cloak of mist, the sounds of the bustling streets muffled by the early fog. She felt a familiar knot in her stomach, one that had been slowly building over the past few days. The past wasn't something Emma usually dwelled on, but after Richard's visit yesterday, and the sudden revelations, she couldn't help but wonder if she truly knew Jack at all.

The door swung open before she could even reach for the handle. Jack's silhouette stood in the doorway, his frame blocking the light from the hallway behind him. He looked tired, his face drawn with an expression that Emma couldn't quite place. When their eyes met, he gave a faint smile, but it didn't reach his eyes.

"Hey," he greeted, his voice low and rough. "Come on in."

Emma stepped inside, the warmth of the penthouse immediately wrapping around her. She stood for a moment, taking in the space that had once felt so comforting, so secure. Now, it felt like a place where secrets lingered, where truths were hidden beneath polished surfaces.

"Is everything okay?" she asked, her voice quieter than she intended.

Jack hesitated, rubbing his jaw as if trying to gather his thoughts. He gestured for her to sit on the plush sofa, but Emma remained standing, her instincts screaming at her that something was off.

"I've been thinking a lot," Jack began slowly. "About us... about everything. I need to be honest with you, Emma. You deserve that."

Emma's heart rate quickened. She could sense the weight in his words, the hesitation that had never been there before. She crossed her arms, suddenly feeling the coldness of the room seep into her skin. "What do you mean? What's going on, Jack?"

His eyes flickered to the floor before meeting hers again. "Yesterday, when you saw Richard, it wasn't just a coincidence. He didn't come to you out of the blue. He was hired."

Emma's brow furrowed, confusion clouding her thoughts. "Hired? Hired by who?"

"By me," he admitted, his voice barely a whisper. "I asked him to investigate my past."

The words hit Emma like a physical blow. Her legs nearly gave out beneath her, but she steadied herself by gripping the back of the sofa. "Why?" she asked, barely managing to force the word from her lips.

"I wanted to make sure that when I brought you into my world, you had all the facts," Jack replied, his gaze unwavering. "I didn't want there to be any surprises, Emma. I didn't want you to be blindsided the way Victoria was."

Emma's mind raced. "And what did he find? What's in the files?"

Jack's eyes clouded with something between guilt and regret. "There's a lot in there that I regret. Things I did—things I said—that I can never take back. The woman I was with before you, Victoria, she... she wasn't the person I thought she was. She was manipulative, controlling, and when I realized that, I ended things. But I never explained it to her, never gave her the closure she needed."

Jack's voice faltered, and Emma could hear the pain in his words, the rawness of his confession. She felt a pang of sympathy, but it was quickly swallowed by the storm of emotions swirling inside her.

"And what does that have to do with me?" Emma asked, her throat tight.

"Because, Emma," Jack replied, his voice now steady, "I don't want you to ever feel like you're just another chapter in my past. I don't want you to feel abandoned or discarded when things get hard."

Emma looked at him, really looked at him, trying to understand the man standing before her. The man who had made her feel things she hadn't even known she was capable of feeling. The man who had made her feel cherished and wanted, even if only for a fleeting moment.

"And you think I will?" she asked, her voice small. "That I'll just walk away like Victoria did?"

Jack's expression softened. "No, I don't. I just need you to know that there are things about me, things that are painful, that might change the way you look at me."

"I don't know if I can handle that," Emma admitted, her voice breaking. "I don't know if I can keep going without knowing everything. Without knowing who you really are."

Jack closed the distance between them, his hands reaching for hers. He held them gently, as though he were afraid she might slip through his fingers if he gripped too tightly. "I'll tell you everything, Emma.

Every single thing. But I need you to understand that it won't be easy. And it might hurt you. It might hurt both of us."

Emma stared at their intertwined hands, feeling a flood of conflicting emotions. She wanted to trust him. She wanted to believe that everything he was saying was true. But the fear of the unknown, the fear of being hurt again, gnawed at her.

"I'm not sure I'm strong enough for that," she whispered, her chest tightening.

Jack's thumb brushed over her skin in slow, soothing circles. "You are stronger than you think. I know you are."

The tenderness in his voice, the way he held her, made her want to believe him. But there were so many questions still left unanswered. So many things she didn't know.

"Maybe we should take a step back," Emma suggested, her voice barely audible. "Maybe we need some time to think."

Jack nodded, his face darkening with a mixture of regret and determination. "I can't force you to stay, Emma. But I want you to know that I'm not going anywhere. Not unless you tell me to leave."

Emma stood there, frozen, as the reality of the situation settled over her. She had always prided herself on her independence, her ability to handle things on her own. But with Jack, everything was different. The connection they shared was powerful, intoxicating, and she wasn't sure if she was ready to let go.

"I don't want you to go," she whispered, her voice thick with emotion. "But I need time to process everything. To understand if I can handle this... if I can handle all the pieces of you that I don't know yet."

Jack's eyes softened, and he stepped closer to her, placing a gentle kiss on her forehead. "Take all the time you need, Emma. I'm here for you. Always."

And as Emma stood there, caught between the promise of everything she could have with Jack and the weight of the unknown, she couldn't help but wonder if their love would be enough to overcome the shadows of the past.

Chapter 91: The Final Reckoning

"The heart was made to be broken." — Oscar Wilde

The morning after their difficult conversation, Emma awoke to the quiet stillness of Jack's penthouse. She lay in the bed they had shared the night before, the sheets tangled around her legs, her mind swirling with a mixture of confusion, fear, and longing. She had barely slept, too restless to shut out the questions that had taken root during her conversation with Jack. Every word he had spoken, every confession he had made, seemed to echo in her mind.

The last few weeks had been a whirlwind of emotions, of passion and desire, of vulnerabilities and dreams. Yet now, with the weight of the secrets he had been holding on to, she felt like she was standing at a precipice, unsure of what was on the other side. Could she truly move forward with Jack, knowing the darkness that lurked in his past? Could she trust him enough to face whatever else he had yet to reveal?

As Emma sat up in bed, the soft light of dawn filtered through the windows, casting a golden glow over the penthouse. She could hear Jack moving around in the kitchen, the sound of coffee brewing and the quiet rustle of papers.

With a sigh, she swung her legs over the edge of the bed, feeling the coolness of the hardwood floor beneath her bare feet. The apartment was quiet, almost too quiet. For a moment, she considered calling off everything—running away, disappearing, leaving behind the man who had so thoroughly ensnared her heart. But even as the thought crossed her mind, she knew it wasn't an option. She was already too far in. Her heart, her soul, was tied to Jack in ways she couldn't explain.

Pushing those thoughts aside, she dressed in the clothes she had worn the day before and made her way to the kitchen. Jack was at the counter, his back turned as he poured coffee into two mugs. He hadn't heard her enter, but as she stood in the doorway, he must have sensed her presence. He turned, offering her a small but genuine smile.

"Morning," he greeted, his voice softer than usual.

Emma managed a faint smile in return, though her heart felt heavy. "Morning."

Jack set one of the mugs on the counter in front of her and then leaned against the counter, watching her with an intensity that made her heart skip a beat. But she couldn't bring herself to look at him, not fully—not when there was so much left unsaid between them.

She wrapped her hands around the warm mug, savoring the familiar comfort of the coffee, though it did little to ease the uncertainty clawing at her insides. "So," she began carefully, her voice tight, "about last night... I need to know more, Jack. If we're going to keep going, if we're going to be honest with each other, I need you to tell me everything. No more secrets. No more hiding."

Jack's expression darkened at her words, and he pushed away from the counter, his hands running through his disheveled hair. "Emma, I told you everything I could. I don't want to hurt you, but my past is complicated. I never wanted to drag you into it. I wanted you to see me for who I am now, not who I was."

"But I can't do that," Emma replied, her voice shaking with frustration. "I can't be with someone when I don't know everything about them. When there are pieces of their life that they're holding back, even from me. I need to understand why you're so scared to show me the real you."

Jack looked at her, his eyes filled with conflict. "I'm not scared, Emma. I just... I don't want to lose you. You mean everything to me."

The sincerity in his words was almost enough to break her, but she held firm, unwilling to let him off the hook so easily. "Then show me, Jack. Show me everything. I don't care about your past mistakes—I care about you. But if you're not willing to face the darkness with me, I can't do this."

For a moment, there was only silence between them. The air in the room felt thick with tension, both of them standing on the edge of something they weren't sure they were ready to face. Emma's heart was racing, her pulse pounding in her ears as she stared at Jack, waiting for him to respond.

Finally, after what felt like an eternity, Jack took a deep breath. He stepped closer to her, his hands reaching for hers, his touch gentle but firm. "I want to be with you, Emma. More than anything. But I'm not sure I can give you everything you want. Not right now."

Emma's breath hitched in her throat as she looked into his eyes. There was pain there, a depth of sorrow and regret that she hadn't seen before. "Why not? What's holding you back?"

Jack hesitated, his lips pressed together in a hard line. "I've made a lot of mistakes in my life, Emma. Some of them, I don't think I can ever atone for. But you deserve better than someone like me."

Emma's heart ached at the raw vulnerability in his voice. She wanted to reach out to him, to hold him and tell him that it didn't matter—that she was willing to take him as he was. But something held her back. Something told her that if she didn't hear the full truth now, if she didn't face whatever demons Jack was hiding, she might lose him forever.

"Jack," she began softly, "I need to understand. I need to know why you're afraid of the truth. Why you're afraid to let me in completely. You can't keep running from it."

He closed his eyes, as if bracing himself for the words he was about to say. "It's not that I'm afraid, Emma. It's that the things I've done... they'll change the way you see me. And I'm not sure I can bear it if you look at me the same way Victoria did. Like I'm some kind of monster."

Emma's heart skipped a beat as she absorbed his words. "What did you do, Jack?" she whispered, her voice breaking with the weight of her question.

Jack took a step back, his face suddenly hardening, the walls he had carefully built around himself rising once more. "I don't want to go there, Emma. Not yet."

But Emma wasn't about to let him retreat again. She reached out, grabbing his arm, her fingers pressing into his skin with the force of her desperation. "I need to know, Jack. I need to understand you—every part of you. You can't keep this from me."

For a moment, Jack didn't respond. His body stiffened under her touch, but then he sighed heavily, as if surrendering to the inevitable. He turned away from her, walking toward the windows, his gaze fixed on the distant horizon.

"I'll tell you," he said quietly, his voice strained. "But not today. Not yet."

Emma's heart sank as she watched him. She could feel the weight of his silence pressing down on her, and for a moment, she wondered if she was asking too much. But she couldn't help it—she needed to know. She needed to understand the man she was falling for, completely, without any more half-truths or shadows hanging over them.

Chapter 92: Into the Abyss

"You don't drown by falling in the water. You drown by staying there." — Ed Cole

The tension in the penthouse was palpable, hanging heavy between them like a thick, suffocating fog. Emma couldn't shake the feeling that something had shifted, that they had reached a point where their relationship would either flourish or crumble beneath the weight of their secrets. Jack's cryptic words, his reluctance to open up, had planted a seed of doubt in her mind that she couldn't ignore, no matter how much she wanted to.

She watched him from the kitchen, his broad back turned to her as he stared out the floor-to-ceiling windows. The soft morning light illuminated the lines of his face, casting shadows that seemed to deepen the mystery of who he really was. She had seen the man he was now—the passionate, attentive lover, the ambitious entrepreneur, the man who had made her feel more alive than she ever thought possible.

But who was he before? What had he done to make him so guarded, so afraid to let anyone too close?

Emma took a deep breath, gathering the courage to break the silence. She could feel her heart pounding in her chest as she walked towards him, her footsteps light on the polished wood floor. The space between them seemed infinite, as though every inch was filled with unspoken words and unresolved tension.

"Jack," she said softly, her voice almost a whisper. "I need to know the truth. Not just bits and pieces. All of it."

Jack turned to face her, his eyes dark with a mixture of sadness and guilt. His jaw clenched, and for a moment, he looked as though he were struggling to find the right words. The silence stretched between them, thick and suffocating, before he finally spoke.

"I've never been proud of the things I've done in the past, Emma," Jack began, his voice low, raw. "I've made decisions—decisions that hurt people, that left scars. I... I thought I was doing what was best for me, for my future, but in the process, I destroyed the trust of the people I cared about most. And now, every time I look at you, I fear that I'll do the same thing to you."

Emma's heart tightened in her chest at his words. She could feel the pain in his voice, the weight of the guilt he carried with him. She stepped closer to him, reaching out for his hand, hoping to offer some semblance of comfort. But Jack pulled away, his hands fisting at his sides.

"Jack, please..." she whispered, her voice trembling. "I need to understand. I can't keep living in this limbo, wondering what you're hiding. I love you, but I can't love you fully if I don't know all of you. I can't be with someone who isn't willing to face the truth—who isn't willing to be vulnerable with me."

Jack's expression softened, and for a moment, Emma saw a flicker of the man she had fallen for—the man who wasn't afraid to love, to be open. But then the walls went up again, the distance between them becoming even greater.

"I know it's hard, Emma," Jack said, his voice thick with emotion. "I don't want to hurt you. But the truth, the whole truth, is something I've carried for so long, and I'm afraid of what it'll do to us. I don't want to see the disgust in your eyes when you hear it. I don't want to watch you walk away from me because of the man I used to be."

Emma's throat tightened as she fought back tears. She had never seen Jack like this—so vulnerable, so raw. It tore at her heart to see him in so much pain, but she couldn't back down now. She couldn't let him continue to hide behind his guilt, behind his fear.

"Jack," she said, her voice steady but filled with determination. "I'm not going anywhere. I need you to trust me. I need you to believe that no matter what you've done in the past, it won't change how I feel about you now. I'm here, and I'm not leaving. But you have to let me in. You have to stop pushing me away."

Jack closed his eyes, a deep sigh escaping his lips. He rubbed the back of his neck, clearly torn. Emma's heart ached as she watched him struggle with his demons, wishing more than anything that she could ease his burden.

"I don't want to lose you," Jack whispered, his voice cracking.

"I'm not going anywhere," Emma repeated softly, taking a step forward, her hand resting gently on his arm. "But I need the whole truth, Jack. I need to know everything, even if it scares me."

For a long moment, Jack stood there, his body tense as he fought with himself. Then, with a deep breath, he finally nodded.

"Okay," he said quietly. "I'll tell you everything. But it's not going to be easy."

Emma nodded, her heart racing as she braced herself for what was to come. She had no idea what Jack was about to reveal, but she knew she was ready. She had to be.

Jack turned and walked toward the living room, motioning for her to follow. Emma's pulse quickened as she stepped into the spacious area, her eyes never leaving him. She couldn't help but wonder what kind of past he was about to unveil—what kind of dark secrets he had buried so deep that even now, they threatened to break free.

"Sit down," Jack said softly, gesturing to the leather sofa. "I need to start from the beginning."

Emma did as he asked, her heart pounding in her chest as she sat down. She crossed her legs beneath her, her hands resting nervously in her lap as she waited for him to speak.

Jack took a deep breath and then began, his voice low but steady. "I grew up in a world that wasn't kind. My family was... complicated. My father, especially, was someone I couldn't please no matter what I did. He pushed me to be something I wasn't, to follow a path that was never mine to walk. I spent years trying to live up to his expectations, trying to prove myself. But nothing was ever enough."

Emma's heart ached as she listened to Jack's words. She had known there was more to his story, but hearing it from his lips made it all the more real. The weight of his past, the pain he had carried for so long, was like a heavy anchor, keeping him chained to a version of himself that he could never escape.

"I got caught up in all of it—the pressure, the anger, the fear. I made choices that I'm not proud of, Emma. I hurt people. I used people. And when it all came crashing down, when I lost everything, I realized that I'd destroyed the only thing that had ever mattered to me—trust. And it's taken me years to rebuild that, but now, with you... I don't want to lose it again."

Emma's breath caught in her throat as she listened to Jack's story. Her heart was heavy, but it also swelled with compassion for the man before her. He had carried this burden alone for so long, and now, for the first time, he was opening up to her.

Jack looked up at her, his eyes filled with vulnerability. "I never wanted to hurt you, Emma. But I'm afraid that my past is too much to overcome. That one day, you'll see me the way others have—like a failure, like someone who's too broken to be loved."

Emma stood up and walked towards him, her heart aching with every step. She reached for his hand, squeezing it gently as she looked into his eyes.

"You are not broken," she said softly. "And I won't ever see you that way. I love you, Jack. All of you."

A tear slipped down Jack's cheek, and he pulled her into his arms, holding her tightly as if he were afraid she would slip away. For the first time, Emma felt like they were truly connected—like the walls had come down and they were standing together, ready to face whatever came next.

And for the first time, Emma believed that no matter what the future held, they would be able to face it together.

Chapter 93: The Weight of Silence

"Sometimes the questions are complicated, and the answers are simple." — Dr. Seuss

The days after Jack's revelation were a blur, the weight of his past still lingering between them but no longer suffocating. Emma found herself wrapped in a sense of understanding she hadn't expected. The walls Jack had built so meticulously had come crashing down, and though the cracks were still visible, something new was growing in the space between them.

The next few days passed in a strange but comforting rhythm. They shared moments of tenderness and passion, their bond growing stronger with each passing hour. But Emma couldn't shake the feeling that there was more to uncover, more layers to Jack's story that he hadn't shared yet. He had been open with her, yes, but there was still a shadow of doubt that hung over his past, one that he had yet to fully illuminate.

Despite this, she didn't want to push him. She knew the weight of his confession had been difficult for him, and she didn't want to break the fragile peace they had found. But at the same time, she couldn't ignore the nagging curiosity that burned inside her. She had to know everything, to truly understand who Jack was, and why he still seemed so haunted by the things he had done.

It was late in the evening when she decided to confront him again. Jack was working, his focus absorbed in his laptop as he sat at the kitchen counter, a glass of whiskey resting beside him. His concentration was fierce, his brow furrowed as he typed away, and Emma hesitated for a moment, watching him from the doorway. She could feel the familiar pull of desire, the heat in her chest as her eyes traced his strong frame, but tonight, she had something else in mind.

"Jack," she called softly, her voice cutting through the quiet.

He looked up at her, a flicker of surprise crossing his features before he masked it with a calm expression. "Emma," he greeted, his voice deep, rich with the quiet intensity that always seemed to surround him. "What's on your mind?"

She crossed the room slowly, her footsteps measured, deliberate. When she reached him, she stood just out of reach, her hands resting lightly on the counter as she studied him. There was a tension in the air, a feeling of inevitability that made her pulse quicken.

"I've been thinking," she began, her voice steady but soft, "about everything you said. And I'm not angry with you. I'm not disappointed. But I need to ask... Is there more to your past? I need to know everything, Jack. I want to understand you fully, and I can't do that if you keep holding back."

Jack's eyes darkened, and for a moment, Emma thought he might retreat again, but instead, he leaned back in his chair, a long sigh escaping his lips. He placed the whiskey glass down with a soft clink, his eyes not leaving hers.

"You want to know the rest of it, don't you?" he asked quietly, his voice barely above a whisper. It wasn't an accusation, but an observation—one that made Emma's chest tighten.

"I do," she admitted, her breath hitching as she took a step closer to him. "I can't move forward if I don't know the full picture. I need to know who you really are, Jack. All of you."

He stared at her for a long moment, as if weighing her words, and then finally, he nodded. Slowly, he stood and walked towards the window, his broad back to her. The silence between them felt heavier than ever, but Emma stood her ground, not willing to back down.

Jack turned around, his face etched with the same raw vulnerability that had marked their previous conversations. "There's more, Emma. A lot more. And it's not something I'm proud of. But I'll tell you, because you deserve to know the truth."

Emma's heart raced, her pulse pounding in her ears as she waited for him to continue. She wasn't sure if she was prepared for whatever he was about to reveal, but she couldn't pull away now.

"When I was younger, I got involved with some people I shouldn't have," Jack began, his voice steady but tinged with regret. "People who weren't interested in playing by the rules. I wasn't a criminal, but I wasn't exactly a saint either. I made deals, got in over my head, and found myself trapped in a world where loyalty meant everything—and trust was in short supply. There were times when I had to do things I'm not proud of, just to survive."

Emma's breath caught in her throat, her mind racing to process his words. She had always known there were dark parts of his past, but hearing him speak so openly about it was something else entirely.

She had imagined the worst, but she hadn't expected this level of vulnerability from him.

"But that's not all," Jack continued, his voice lowering as he seemed to relive the memories. "The worst part wasn't the deals or the lies. It was the betrayal. The people I trusted... they used me. And when I realized what had happened, I was already too far in to back out. I ended up being the one who paid the price."

Emma moved closer, her heart aching for him as she saw the pain in his eyes. She reached for him, her hands brushing against his arm, and he flinched slightly before meeting her gaze.

"I can't change what happened, Emma," he said softly, his voice strained with emotion. "But I'm not that man anymore. I've spent years trying to atone for my mistakes, trying to build a life that's better than the one I had before. And I've been afraid—afraid that if you knew, you wouldn't see me the way you do now."

Emma's chest tightened as she stepped forward, her hands reaching for his face, cupping it gently. "I see you, Jack," she whispered, her voice soft but unwavering. "I see the man you are now. And that's the man I love."

Jack's eyes softened at her words, the hardness in his expression melting away as he closed the distance between them. He cupped her face in his hands, his thumb brushing lightly across her cheek. The moment was charged with an intensity that neither of them could deny.

"I'm not perfect," he whispered, his voice hoarse. "But I'm willing to fight for you. For us."

Emma's heart swelled with emotion as she stood on her tiptoes, pressing her lips to his. The kiss was slow, tender, a promise between them—a promise that despite the pain of the past, they would move forward together. And for the first time in what felt like forever, Emma felt like she was exactly where she was meant to be.

As the kiss deepened, the world outside their bubble seemed to disappear. There were no more secrets, no more doubts. There was only the two of them, tangled in each other's arms, breaking down the walls that had held them apart for so long.

Emma knew there would still be challenges ahead. She knew that Jack's past would continue to haunt him in ways he couldn't fully escape. But as long as they were together, as long as they continued to face the darkness side by side, she believed they could overcome anything.

Chapter 94: The Cost of Truth

"The truth will set you free, but first it will make you miserable." —James A. Garfield

The morning after their heartfelt conversation, Emma woke with a sense of clarity she hadn't felt in days. There was something about Jack's honesty, the way he laid his past bare before her, that made everything feel lighter. Yes, there were still shadows in his past, things that would never go away, but Emma knew one thing for certain now—Jack had changed. He was not the man he once was, and whatever darkness had followed him into their relationship, they would face it together.

As the sun filtered through the curtains, Emma stretched, her body still humming from the passion they had shared the night before. She rolled over to find Jack still asleep beside her, his features softened in the quiet of the morning. She couldn't help but smile at the sight.

There was a tenderness to him now that had been missing when they first met—a gentleness that made her feel cherished, wanted.

She wanted to stay in that moment, wrapped up in the warmth of their connection, but there was still a lingering feeling deep inside her. The feeling that something was just beyond her reach, something she had yet to understand. And as much as she wanted to ignore it, she knew she couldn't. Not now, not after everything they had shared.

Gently, she slipped out of bed and made her way to the kitchen, the cool marble beneath her feet a welcome contrast to the warmth of the sheets. She started brewing coffee, trying to calm the restless thoughts that churned in her mind. She needed to focus, to stay grounded. But as the minutes ticked by, her mind wandered back to the conversation they'd had last night.

The way Jack had confessed his past, the rawness in his voice—it was still so fresh in her mind. She could feel the weight of it pressing on her chest, a constant reminder of the depth of what they were navigating. Jack's past was not something she could just brush aside, and neither could he. It was a part of him, something that shaped the man he was today. But what about her? Where did that leave her in all of this?

She hadn't expected the ease with which Jack had accepted her questioning. She hadn't expected his openness, his willingness to bare it all for her. But even now, after all the trust they had built, Emma still found herself wondering—could he ever fully let go of that past? Or would it always be a shadow, lurking in the background of their relationship?

She shook her head, willing herself not to go down that path again. She didn't want to doubt him. Not now. Not when they had come so far.

Just as she poured herself a cup of coffee, the sound of Jack's footsteps reached her ears. She turned to find him standing in the doorway, his eyes still heavy with sleep but fixed on her with an intensity that made her heart flutter.

"Morning," he murmured, his voice low and raspy from the sleep he'd just woken from.

"Morning," she replied, her voice soft as she smiled at him.

He took a step toward her, his eyes never leaving hers, and before she knew it, he had closed the distance between them, wrapping his arms around her waist. The feeling of his embrace, warm and protective, made the doubts inside her dissipate for just a moment. She rested her head against his chest, breathing in the scent of him—the mix of cologne, warmth, and something uniquely Jack.

"Everything okay?" he asked, his voice almost a whisper.

Emma hesitated, but only for a moment. She wasn't going to hold back. Not anymore. "I'm just thinking," she said, pulling back to look him in the eye. "About last night. About everything we've shared. And... about us."

Jack's brow furrowed, his concern deepening. "What about us?"

She took a deep breath, searching for the right words. "I want to move forward with you, Jack. I do. But I also need to know if you're really ready to let go of everything that happened before. I don't want to be a part of your life just for the good parts. I want all of you. Even the parts that scare you."

Jack stood there in silence for a moment, his eyes searching hers, as if weighing her words. Then, slowly, he nodded, his lips pulling into a gentle smile. "I am ready," he said, his voice firm. "I've been ready for a while now. And I don't want to lose you. I don't want to lose us."

Emma felt a wave of emotion wash over her, a mixture of relief and something deeper, something that made her heart swell with love for this man. She stepped closer, her hand gently brushing his jaw, and kissed him softly, a tender promise in that single touch.

But as the kiss deepened, Emma felt the familiar pull of desire between them. The need for connection, for intimacy, for something more. She pulled back, her breath catching as she met his eyes again. There was a hunger there, a hunger they both shared, but it was tempered by something else now. Understanding. Trust.

"Are you sure?" she asked, her voice barely above a whisper.

Jack nodded, his hands moving to her waist as he pulled her closer. "I've never been more sure of anything in my life."

His lips found hers again, and this time, there was no holding back. No lingering doubts. No hesitations. Just the raw, undeniable connection that had been building between them since the very beginning. The kiss was slow at first, teasing, but soon it deepened, becoming more urgent, more desperate. Their hands roamed, pulling each other closer, desperate for the comfort of touch, for the reassurance that they were real, that this was real.

Emma's body hummed with anticipation as Jack's lips trailed down her neck, his hands moving beneath the hem of her shirt. Every touch sent shivers down her spine, every kiss igniting a fire inside her that she hadn't realized was smoldering. She could feel the heat between them building, and her mind was consumed by the desire to be closer, to feel every inch of him.

But as much as the passion between them consumed her, Emma couldn't shake the thoughts that lingered at the edges of her mind. There were still pieces of Jack's past that needed to be dealt with, pieces that could either strengthen or break them. She didn't want to push him, but she couldn't ignore the questions that still haunted her.

As Jack pulled her toward the bed, she let herself be swept away in the moment, pushing her doubts aside for now. She would face the rest of their journey together, but for tonight, she would simply let herself be with him, wholly and completely.

For in that moment, Emma knew one thing for sure: whatever challenges lay ahead, whatever secrets might still come to light, they would face it together. They would be stronger for it. Together, they would break through the boundaries of their pasts and create something new—something that belonged only to them.

Chapter 95: Through the Fire

"The best way out is always through." — Robert Frost

The days that followed their intimate connection were full of change—change that neither Emma nor Jack had expected. While their bond had deepened, both emotionally and physically, the unspoken tension that had once been present seemed to dissipate, replaced by an unsteady sense of balance. They had faced their fears, shared their secrets, and for once, they stood on equal ground.

But Emma knew that balance was fleeting. The past had a way of creeping in when you least expected it, like the shadows that clung to the walls of their worlds. She had witnessed it firsthand in Jack's eyes—a flicker of doubt, of something unresolved. And she knew, deep down, that there were still questions that needed answers, no matter how much they had both tried to pretend they didn't exist.

It was late afternoon when she found herself pacing the length of the penthouse. The view outside was breathtaking, as it always was, the city sprawling below her in a perfect blend of modern luxury and chaos. But it wasn't the view she was focused on. No, her mind was consumed with the conversation she needed to have with Jack.

The sound of the elevator doors opening echoed through the apartment, and Emma paused, listening. She didn't need to turn to know it was Jack. His presence always made the air shift, as if everything within her universe aligned when he entered a room.

"Hey," Jack called from the hallway, his voice a little hoarse but steady. "How's your day been?"

She turned, meeting his gaze, and for a moment, the uncertainty that had been building between them threatened to spill over. She wanted to feel at ease with him, to let go of the tension that had slowly built since their last conversation, but the truth was, things still felt... unfinished. She had a nagging feeling that something was off.

"It's been alright," she replied, trying to sound casual. She plastered on a smile but felt it falter at the edges. "But I've been thinking..."

Jack's brow furrowed in concern. "About?"

"About us," she said quietly. "About everything we've been through."

Jack walked into the room, his usual confidence tempered by something softer now. "I thought we were doing okay. Aren't we?"

Emma hesitated. She didn't want to admit the unease she'd been feeling, but she couldn't pretend anymore. "I don't know, Jack. I feel like we're still holding something back. Both of us."

Jack's expression hardened slightly, though his eyes softened as he stepped closer to her. "I'm not holding anything back from you, Emma. I told you everything. You know about my past. You know where I stand."

She nodded, but her voice wavered. "I know, but sometimes... I feel like there's more. Like there's something you haven't told me. Or maybe something you're afraid to face."

Jack took a step back, running a hand through his hair in frustration. "I don't know what you want from me, Emma. I've already told you everything I can. The rest of it—" He stopped himself, his jaw tightening. "The rest of it is just... noise. It doesn't matter anymore."

"But it does matter!" Emma insisted, stepping toward him. "If you really want to move forward with me, we need to face everything, Jack. I can't build something with you if there are pieces of your past still left in the dark."

Jack met her gaze, and for a long moment, they stood in silence. She could feel the weight of the tension between them, the unspoken words that neither of them seemed to want to say. The walls that had been built around both of them, both protecting and suffocating.

Finally, Jack exhaled, his shoulders sagging. "I know. I just—"

"Jack..." Emma's voice softened. She reached out, placing a hand on his chest. "I need you to trust me, just like I trust you. I want to understand, not because I doubt you, but because I want to be a part of your whole world. All of it. I can't live in the shadows anymore, pretending like we're not carrying ghosts."

Jack closed his eyes, his features hardening. "There's nothing in the past that I want to bring into this, Emma. I've been trying to bury it, to leave it behind. It's not easy... but for you, I'll try."

Emma felt a pang of guilt, her heart aching for him. She knew Jack didn't want to go back, to dredge up old wounds, but sometimes, the only way to heal was to face them. "You don't have to go through it alone. But you have to let me in, Jack. You have to let me help you carry that burden."

A long silence passed between them, the weight of their conversation hanging heavily in the air. Jack looked at her, his eyes filled with both fear and relief. Slowly, he nodded, taking her hands in his.

"Alright," he said, his voice low but steady. "I'll tell you everything. The good, the bad... everything. But I need you to promise me something."

"What?" she asked, her heart racing with anticipation.

"That you won't walk away from me," he said, his voice raw with emotion. "I need to know that whatever I say... it won't change how you feel about me. No matter how ugly it might get."

Emma's heart swelled with affection for this man who had been so guarded, so protective of himself, and yet now stood before her, vulnerable and willing to trust. She cupped his face gently, meeting his eyes with unwavering resolve.

"I promise," she whispered. "Nothing will change how I feel about you. I'm in this, Jack. All of it. No matter what."

Jack's lips found hers in a kiss that was more tender than any they had shared before. It was a kiss that held promises, shared fears, and silent assurances. When they finally pulled apart, they were both breathless, their foreheads resting together as they stood in the quiet of the room.

"I won't hold anything back from you again, Emma," Jack murmured. "I promise."

Emma smiled softly, her heart full of hope for what was to come. "I know. And we'll get through it, together."

As the night unfolded, the weight of their conversation lingered in the air, but there was something different now. The walls that had once kept them apart seemed to be crumbling, piece by piece. And with each passing moment, Emma knew that they were both building something stronger—something that could weather whatever storms lay ahead.

Together, they could face anything.

Chapter 96: Flames of Desire

"Desire is a fire that burns unseen." — Luis de León

The silence that followed their conversation was almost deafening. Emma's heart raced, her pulse still hammering in her ears as she processed the promise Jack had just made. There was something intimate in the vulnerability he had shown, a willingness to expose parts of himself he had long buried. For the first time in their relationship, Emma could feel the weight of what Jack had endured—his past, his fears, his regrets—and how it all shaped the man standing in front of her.

But despite the rawness of the moment, Emma couldn't shake the lingering feeling that there was more. That, somewhere deep within him, there were things he hadn't said, things he wasn't ready to face yet. And that knowledge gnawed at her, a quiet whisper that she couldn't ignore.

As the night wore on, they both tried to return to a semblance of normalcy. Dinner was a quiet affair—neither of them particularly hungry, but still going through the motions. Jack's usual easy charm seemed to have faded, replaced by a more introspective mood. Emma could see the conflict in his eyes as they lingered over their wine glasses, the question of what came next hanging between them.

Finally, it was Jack who broke the silence.

"Tomorrow," he said, his voice soft but firm. "Tomorrow, I'll tell you everything. No more hiding."

Emma met his gaze, her heart tightening. "Are you sure you're ready for that? I don't want to push you."

Jack took a deep breath, running his hand through his hair. "I have to be. This—whatever this is between us—can't survive if I keep holding back. I can't keep pretending that it doesn't matter."

Emma nodded, swallowing the lump that had formed in her throat. "And I'll be here, Jack. No matter what you have to say."

For the first time in a long while, Emma felt an undercurrent of hope. The promise of honesty, of real connection, was something she hadn't realized she'd been craving. But there was still an unspoken fear—what if the truth was too much? What if, despite all the assurances, the walls that had been torn down could never truly be rebuilt?

The night passed slowly, the heavy weight of their conversation lingering between them. Jack didn't make a move toward her when they retired to bed, but Emma understood. The distance wasn't emotional—it was necessary, as if they were both bracing themselves for something monumental.

The next morning, Emma woke early, the city still cloaked in darkness. The first light of dawn seeped through the curtains, casting a soft glow on the room. She turned, her eyes finding Jack still asleep beside her, his face relaxed in the rare moment of peace. She studied him for a moment, taking in the lines of his jaw, the way his dark hair fell across his forehead, the soft rise and fall of his chest.

She had never seen him like this before—so vulnerable, so at ease. But the storm of yesterday still hung between them, threatening to disrupt the fragile equilibrium they had found.

With a quiet sigh, Emma slipped from the bed, careful not to disturb Jack. She padded softly to the kitchen, the quiet of the apartment a stark contrast to the turmoil swirling in her mind. She needed a moment—time to clear her thoughts before they faced whatever was coming.

She poured herself a cup of coffee, the steam rising in delicate tendrils. The rich aroma filled the space, grounding her as she stared out the window, the world outside still shrouded in morning mist. Her thoughts were a swirl of confusion—questions she hadn't dared ask, things she didn't want to know but had to. Could she handle the truth? Could she really accept whatever Jack was going to tell her?

The sound of footsteps behind her broke her reverie. She didn't need to turn to know it was Jack. His presence in the room felt different today—heavier, laden with the weight of his unspoken truth.

"Morning," he said quietly, his voice hoarse with sleep.

Emma turned, offering him a small smile. "Morning. Coffee?"

He nodded, moving toward her with the fluidity of someone who had done this dance before. There was a tension in the air now, an electric charge that hummed between them as if both were waiting for something to shift.

She handed him the cup, their fingers brushing for a brief moment. The simple touch sent a shiver down her spine, reminding her of how easily their connection could shift from peaceful to charged.

Jack took a sip, then set the cup down on the counter with deliberate care. His gaze met hers, and she could see the storm behind his eyes. It was there, lingering, waiting to break free.

"I'm ready to tell you," he said, his voice barely above a whisper. "But you need to know that it's not going to be easy. I've been running from this for a long time, and I'm afraid—"

Emma stepped toward him, closing the distance between them. "Jack, whatever it is, I can handle it. I'm not going anywhere."

His eyes searched hers, as if looking for some sign that she was truly ready. Then, slowly, almost hesitantly, he nodded.

"Alright," he said softly. "But first, I need you to understand why I did what I did. Why I pushed so hard to bury everything."

Emma's heart thudded in her chest. She nodded, her voice a mere whisper. "I'm listening."

Jack exhaled, his gaze drifting to the floor as he seemed to collect his thoughts. "It wasn't always like this. I didn't start out wanting to shut myself off from the world. But life has a way of shaping you—of forcing you into corners you don't know how to get out of. And sometimes, the only way to survive is to build walls so high that no one can get in. I did that with Victoria. I did that with everyone who ever tried to get close to me."

He paused, as if weighing his next words. "When I met you, Emma, I felt everything shift. For the first time in years, I was willing to tear down the walls, to let someone in. But I couldn't do that without confronting my past. And my past... it's not pretty."

Emma could see the guilt in his eyes, the weight of his admission heavy in the air between them. She stepped closer, gently cupping his cheek. "You don't have to carry this alone, Jack. Whatever happened, we'll face it together."

For a moment, he didn't respond. He just closed his eyes and leaned into her touch, as if letting himself finally feel the weight of his own vulnerability. And in that moment, Emma realized something—Jack had been fighting himself all this time. He hadn't been running from her. He had been running from the pain of his past.

"Let me in," she whispered. "I'm here for you, Jack. Always."

He opened his eyes, his gaze softening as he took her hand in his. "Alright," he said, his voice steady now. "It's time."

And so, they stood there, two people on the edge of something deeper, something raw, ready to face the shadows of the past and the promise of what lay ahead.

Chapter 97: In the Heat of the Moment

"In the end, we will remember not the words of our enemies, but the silence of our friends." — Martin Luther King Jr.

The tension in the apartment was palpable, the air thick with anticipation. Emma could feel her heart pounding in her chest, every beat thudding in her ears. Jack had promised to tell her everything, and now, with the weight of his words hanging between them, she found herself grappling with the uncertainty of what was about to unfold.

She stood there, in the dim light of the kitchen, watching Jack as he stood across from her. His hands were clenched at his sides, a subtle sign of the inner turmoil he was fighting. She could see the battle in his eyes, the war between his desire to protect her and the necessity of being honest.

Jack had always been a man of control, of composure, but tonight—this morning—it was different. He was unguarded, vulnerable in a way that Emma hadn't seen before. The walls he had carefully constructed over the years were beginning to crack, and it scared him. It scared her too.

"You're shaking," Jack's voice was soft, a note of concern breaking through the tension. He took a step toward her, his eyes softening with the kind of tenderness that made her heart ache.

Emma swallowed hard, trying to steady her breath. "I just... I need to know, Jack. I need you to tell me everything."

He nodded, and for a moment, they just stood there, locked in a gaze that was full of unsaid words. Then, with a deep sigh, Jack took a step back, running his hands through his hair in frustration.

"I don't want to do this, Emma," he admitted, his voice thick with emotion. "But I know I have to. You deserve the truth."

Emma felt a knot form in her stomach. "I can't keep living in the dark, Jack. I can't keep wondering what's really going on. If you're hiding things from me, I need to know."

Jack's expression hardened slightly, and for a moment, Emma thought he might back away, retreat into his usual cold, distant self. But instead, he took another deep breath and finally spoke.

"My father," he began, his voice low. "He wasn't the man you think he was. He wasn't the kind of man who cared about family, about loyalty, about anything except his own gain."

Emma felt a chill run down her spine. Jack had never spoken about his father, and hearing him speak the words with such bitterness unsettled her.

"He was a businessman, ruthless and cold. He built an empire from nothing, but he did it by stepping on anyone who got in his way. And I was just another pawn in his game."

Emma stepped closer to him, her hand brushing against his arm. "Jack, I'm so sorry. I had no idea—"

Jack raised a hand, stopping her before she could finish. "It gets worse. Much worse."

His voice faltered, and Emma could see the pain in his eyes. She wanted to reach out, to hold him, but she understood that he needed to say this in his own time. The truth had to come out, but the weight of it was suffocating.

"When I was young, I thought that if I followed his rules, if I played his game, I'd finally get his approval. But it never happened. He just kept pushing me further, demanding more, expecting more. I became someone I didn't recognize. Someone I hated."

Emma felt a pang of sorrow in her chest. She had known Jack's past was complicated, but she hadn't realized just how deep the wounds ran. The man standing before her, the man she had come to care for, had been shaped by a darkness she couldn't even begin to comprehend.

"And then there was Victoria," Jack continued, his voice cracking slightly. "I met her when I was at my lowest. She was beautiful, charming, everything I thought I wanted. And she played the part—perfectly. But she wasn't real. None of it was. It was all just a game."

He paused, his eyes searching her face as if gauging her reaction. Emma didn't know what to say, so she just nodded, her heart breaking for the boy Jack must have been—lost, desperate for love and validation in a world that had never shown him kindness.

"I thought I loved her," Jack whispered, his voice barely audible. "I thought I could fix everything. But I couldn't. She didn't want to be fixed. She just wanted control."

Emma reached out, placing a hand on his chest. The warmth of his body under her touch was a stark contrast to the cold, harsh reality of his words. She could feel the tension in his body, the way his muscles coiled beneath her hand.

"Jack, you don't have to carry all of this alone," she said softly. "You don't have to keep punishing yourself for things that weren't your fault."

Jack shook his head, his jaw tightening. "I wasn't innocent in all of it. I made mistakes, too. I let her in when I shouldn't have. I let my father's expectations control me for too long. And when I finally broke free, I didn't know how to be the person I needed to be."

Emma felt a surge of empathy for him. She had known Jack was complicated, but she hadn't realized just how deeply his past had scarred him. The man who stood before her, the one she had fallen for, was a man who had been broken—by his father, by Victoria, by his own decisions.

She pulled him toward her, pressing her lips gently to his. The kiss was tender at first, a reassurance that she was here for him, that she wouldn't turn away. But as she felt the heat of his lips on hers, something shifted. The kiss deepened, becoming more urgent, as if they both needed something to anchor them in this moment—something to hold on to in the face of everything they had just shared.

When they finally pulled away, Jack's forehead rested against hers, his breath coming in shallow gasps. He closed his eyes for a moment, as if trying to gather himself.

"Emma," he murmured, his voice thick with emotion. "I need you to know that I'm not running from you. I'm not running from this. I'm just... trying to find myself. I've been lost for so long."

Emma cupped his face, lifting his chin so their eyes met. "And I'll be here, Jack. Every step of the way. I'm not going anywhere."

The words felt true, deeper than anything she had said before. She wasn't just telling him she was there for him. She was making a promise—to stand by him, no matter the weight of the past, no matter the darkness that still clung to him.

Jack's eyes softened, a flicker of something she couldn't quite name passing through them. It was hope, perhaps, or the beginning of trust. But in that moment, Emma knew that they were both ready to face whatever came next, together.

Chapter 98: The Breaking Point

"The only way to deal with this life meaninglessly is to find it meaningful." — Friedrich Nietzsche

The day had barely begun, yet the weight of everything Jack had confessed still lingered heavily on Emma's chest. She had spent the morning trying to focus on work, but each time her mind wandered, it returned to the raw conversation they'd shared. Jack's vulnerability had shaken her, and though she wanted to believe in him, in them, doubts lingered like a shadow in her thoughts.

The past was always a complicated thing to confront, but it was clear now that Jack's was far darker than she had imagined. His father's cruelty, Victoria's manipulation—he had been suffocated by both for so long. It was no wonder he had built such walls around himself.

But Emma knew, deep down, that breaking those walls would be no easy task. She had to be patient, let him open up at his own pace. Yet there was a part of her that couldn't help but feel the need to push forward, to bridge the gap between them. It wasn't enough to simply stand by him; she needed to understand the man he truly was, not just the man he had been.

She was sitting at her desk in her office, sketching out some new design concepts when the sharp knock on her door snapped her out of her thoughts.

"Come in," she called, brushing her hair behind her ear as she glanced up.

The door creaked open, and Richard Holloway stepped inside. He looked slightly more disheveled than usual, his salt-and-pepper hair more tousled, his brow furrowed in concentration.

"Emma," he greeted her, his tone businesslike but with an underlying tension that didn't escape her notice. "I need to talk to you."

Her heart skipped a beat. She had not expected to see him so soon, not after the folder he had left on her desk. The contents of that folder had been haunting her thoughts ever since, and she knew this conversation would only stir the pot further.

"Richard, what is it?" she asked, keeping her voice steady.

He closed the door behind him and took a step forward, his gaze intense as he met hers. "It's about Jack," he said, his tone lowering. "There's more you need to know."

Emma's breath caught in her throat. "More?" She had a sinking feeling she wasn't ready to hear what he was about to say. "What now?"

Richard hesitated before speaking, clearly choosing his words carefully. "I know you've seen the documents I left with you. But there are some things that aren't on paper, things that can't be easily proven." He leaned in slightly, his eyes darkening with something Emma couldn't quite place. "Jack isn't who he appears to be. His past is... messier than he's letting on."

Emma's chest tightened. "You've already told me a lot," she said, her voice firm. "I don't need to hear more accusations, Richard."

He held up a hand, as if to calm her. "This isn't about accusations, Emma. This is about truth. And the truth is, Jack's involvement in his family business—his father's company—isn't just about bad decisions or misguided loyalty. There's more at stake here. His connections run deeper than you think. I'm not just talking about money or power. This is about something much darker. His father wasn't just ruthless; he was involved in things that go far beyond the scope of what you know. And Jack? He was right there beside him, involved in some of it."

Emma felt the world tilt on its axis, her mind reeling as she processed his words. "You're saying Jack—" She couldn't bring herself to finish the sentence.

Richard's jaw tightened. "I'm saying that Jack wasn't just a pawn in his father's game. He was part of it, a willing participant. And that means there's a side to Jack you haven't seen, a side that's been buried under layers of guilt and shame."

Emma stood up abruptly, her chair scraping against the floor. Her mind was racing, her thoughts in a whirl of confusion and betrayal. She didn't know what to believe. Jack had always painted his past as a series of mistakes, things he had learned from, things he wanted to move beyond. But now Richard was telling her that there was a far more sinister truth lurking beneath the surface.

"Why are you telling me this?" Emma asked, her voice trembling despite her best efforts to remain composed. "What do you want from me?"

Richard's eyes darkened, his gaze unwavering. "I want you to understand what you're getting into, Emma. I want you to see the full picture before you go any further with him. Jack is dangerous, not in the way you think, but in the way that his past can come back to haunt both of you. You can't ignore this, no matter how much you care about him."

The words stung like a slap to the face, but there was truth in them. Emma felt the weight of his warning settle deep in her chest, a cold dread creeping through her veins.

"I care about him more than I've cared about anyone," she whispered, her voice barely audible. "But I don't know what to believe anymore."

Richard took a step closer to her, his tone softening for the first time. "I'm not trying to hurt you, Emma. But you need to be cautious. Jack has a lot of demons, and I'm afraid that if you get too close, they'll drag you down with him."

Her pulse quickened as his words sunk in. Could she really afford to keep falling deeper for a man whose past was so entwined with danger and lies? Could she trust him, or was she simply setting herself up for heartbreak?

"I'll make my own decisions," Emma said, her voice steady despite the turmoil swirling inside her. "Thank you for the warning, Richard. But I have to figure this out on my own."

Richard nodded, his eyes filled with something unreadable. "Just be careful, Emma."

With that, he turned and walked out, leaving Emma standing alone in her office, the weight of his words hanging heavily in the air. She didn't know what to believe anymore, but one thing was certain: she couldn't walk away from Jack, not without facing the full extent of his past.

Chapter 99: The Depth of Revelation

"You can never cross the ocean until you have the courage to lose sight of the shore." — Christopher Columbus

Emma stood at the edge of the balcony, the city lights of Sydney casting a shimmering glow in the distance. She could feel the cool evening breeze against her skin, but it did little to quench the fire that had been steadily burning inside her for the past few days. The uncertainty that had clouded her mind was slowly turning into something darker—something dangerous.

Her thoughts swirled around Jack, his mysterious past, the cryptic words from Victoria, and now Richard's ominous warning. She could still feel the weight of the folder in her hand, though she had yet to open it. It was as if the very act of looking through the documents would shatter the fragile illusion she had built around her relationship with Jack. And yet, the temptation to know everything gnawed at her insides, pushing her closer to a breaking point.

She heard the soft click of the door behind her, followed by the smooth, familiar voice she had come to crave. "Emma."

She didn't turn around, afraid of what she might see on his face, the unreadable expression that seemed to hide something important. "Jack," she responded softly, her voice betraying a hint of vulnerability.

He stepped closer, his presence filling the space, and gently touched her shoulder. "What's wrong?"

She let out a shaky breath, finally turning to face him. His eyes were filled with concern, but there was something else there, something she couldn't quite place. "I don't know if I can do this anymore, Jack."

His face tightened, and he reached for her hand, drawing her closer. "Do what?"

"Live in the dark," she whispered, her heart hammering in her chest. "I need to know the truth. All of it."

Jack exhaled sharply, the muscles in his jaw tensing. He looked down for a moment, as if contemplating how to respond. When he finally met her gaze again, there was an undeniable sorrow in his eyes.

"Emma," he began softly, "there's so much you don't understand about me, about the life I've led. I never wanted you to be caught up in it."

"Then why didn't you tell me, Jack?" she asked, the frustration and pain evident in her voice. "Why didn't you trust me enough to share your past with me?"

"I was trying to protect you," he confessed, his voice low. "But now I see that I only built a wall between us. And I hate that."

Her throat tightened as she absorbed his words. She wanted to reach out, to forgive him, but something inside her wouldn't let go of the nagging doubt. "Do you love me, Jack?" she asked, her voice barely a whisper.

He looked at her for a long moment, his eyes searching hers. Slowly, he stepped forward, cupping her face in his hands. "More than you'll ever know."

The sincerity in his words caused her heart to flutter, but the lingering questions remained. Was love enough to overcome the lies? Was she willing to dive deeper into the unknown?

Before she could respond, Jack leaned in, capturing her lips with his in a kiss that was both tender and urgent. It was a kiss that spoke of years of unspoken longing, of moments lost in time, and of a deep, raw connection that neither of them could escape.

Emma closed her eyes, surrendering to the intensity of his touch. His hands slid down her back, pulling her closer, his body pressing against hers in a way that made her pulse race. The kiss deepened, becoming more heated as their desires collided, their boundaries blurring.

She could feel the heat between them intensify, the electricity of their connection almost palpable. Every inch of her skin seemed to hum with anticipation, her body responding instinctively to the need that pulsed between them. His hands roamed to her waist, tugging at the fabric of her dress, eager to feel the warmth of her skin beneath his fingertips.

"Jack," she breathed against his lips, her hands slipping into his hair, tugging him closer.

But he pulled back just enough to meet her gaze, his breath coming in shallow gasps. "Are you sure, Emma?"

She could see the hesitation in his eyes, the conflict he was feeling. But in that moment, her own uncertainty faded. She didn't need all the answers right now. What mattered was the way he made her feel, the way his presence made her feel alive, consumed by the intensity of their connection.

"I'm sure," she whispered, her voice low and full of desire. "Show me everything, Jack. Show me what it means to love me."

And with that, he closed the distance once more, his lips claiming hers as he guided them both toward a deeper place of passion and surrender.

The night stretched on, their bodies entwined in a dance of love and longing. The world outside seemed to fade away, leaving only the two of them, lost in each other's embrace. Every touch, every kiss, every breath shared between them felt like a promise—an unspoken vow to face whatever challenges lay ahead, together.

But as the first light of dawn began to break over the horizon, Emma knew that their journey was far from over. There were still secrets to uncover, truths to confront, and wounds to heal. And no matter how deep their connection ran, she couldn't ignore the shadow that lingered over them.

The shadow of doubt.

Chapter 100: Tangled Hearts

"Sometimes, the most dangerous thing is not knowing what you want." — Unknown

Emma woke to the sound of soft rain tapping against the windows. The early morning light filtered through the curtains, casting a pale glow over the room. She turned over, her eyes immediately landing on Jack, who was still asleep beside her. His face was relaxed in peaceful slumber, his breath steady. For a moment, everything felt perfect—like nothing in the world could touch them, like they were untouchable in their own little bubble of safety.

But that wasn't true, was it?

She could feel the weight of the world pressing in on her chest. The truth about Jack's past, the revelations that still loomed over them, was like a shadow that refused to be shaken. It had been hours since they'd fallen asleep, wrapped in each other's arms, but the doubt, the unresolved tension, had not left her. She lay there, her fingers tracing the faint lines of his jaw, trying to reconcile the man beside her with the man she'd heard about from others.

The warmth of his skin beneath her fingertips made her heart race, but even as she longed to be closer, to feel more, she knew she needed to confront what was left unsaid.

Slowly, she slipped out of bed, careful not to wake him. She wrapped herself in the soft blanket, her thoughts swirling with everything that had happened in the past few days. The folder Richard had left on her desk, the cryptic messages, Victoria's warnings—they were all pieces of a puzzle that didn't quite fit, and she wasn't sure if she even wanted to try and make them.

Emma stood in front of the window, gazing out at the rain-soaked city, her mind racing. She had to know. She had to understand what Jack was hiding, even if it meant tearing apart everything they had built.

She was just about to turn away when she heard the sound of footsteps behind her. Jack's voice, deep and groggy from sleep, cut through the quiet. "You're up early."

She didn't turn to face him. She couldn't bring herself to do it, not yet. "I couldn't sleep."

There was a pause before he spoke again, and she could hear the concern in his tone. "Emma, what's wrong?"

She didn't answer immediately, and for a long moment, she was lost in the rhythm of the rain and the quiet, uncertain ache in her chest. It was then that she knew. She couldn't keep hiding from the truth, from what she had to face in order to move forward.

"I met someone yesterday," she finally said, her voice steady, but her heart racing.

Jack's footsteps approached, and his hand rested lightly on her shoulder. "Who?"

"Richard," she said quietly. "He said your past isn't as clean as you've made it seem."

Jack froze, and Emma could feel the tension in his body as he processed her words. He didn't speak for a moment, and Emma took a shaky breath, willing herself to stay calm, to not let the doubts she was trying to suppress take over.

"What did he tell you?" Jack finally asked, his voice tight.

"He said you've got a lot of secrets, things you haven't told me," Emma replied, her throat tight. "He said I needed to know the truth before I got too deep."

Jack let out a slow breath, and she could hear him moving closer. His hand slid around her waist, and she felt the heat of his body against hers, his presence grounding her in the moment. "I'm not proud of everything in my past, Emma," he admitted softly. "But the man I am now—the one standing in front of you—is not the same person I was before. I've made mistakes, but none of them change what we have."

Emma swallowed hard, still not turning to face him. "But I need to know, Jack. I need to understand what I'm really dealing with. What if all this time I've been living in a lie?"

Jack was silent for a long time, and Emma could feel his hesitation, his inner battle. When he finally spoke, his voice was low, tinged with a sadness that sent a chill down her spine. "I never wanted you to find out this way. I was trying to protect you."

She closed her eyes, shaking her head. "From what? The truth?"

He exhaled sharply. "I didn't want to drag you into a world you couldn't handle. A world that's full of darkness, regret, and danger."

Emma turned to face him then, her eyes searching his. "What kind of world, Jack? What are you really hiding?"

For the first time, she saw it—raw vulnerability. The façade he'd so carefully built around himself was cracking, and she could see the fear in his eyes. "A world I thought I could leave behind. A world of dangerous people, secrets I buried deep... and a past that I wish I could forget."

Her heart clenched. She had always known that Jack had a complicated past, but hearing it from his own lips—seeing the pain in his eyes—made it real in a way she hadn't expected. She didn't know whether she was more afraid of the darkness in his past or of what it meant for their future.

"Is that who you are now, Jack?" she asked softly. "The man standing in front of me? Or are you still that person from your past?"

Jack's eyes darkened with emotion, but his voice was steady. "I'm not that person anymore, Emma. I left that world behind. But I can't erase what I've done. And I can't protect you from the fallout if it ever comes back."

Her mind raced with all the possibilities, all the risks. But there was something in his voice, something in the way he looked at her, that made her believe him. She wanted to trust him. She had to.

"I'm not asking you to erase your past, Jack," she said, her voice firm. "I just want to know who you are now. The man I'm with. The man I'm falling for."

He stepped closer, his hand cupping her cheek. His touch was gentle, but the weight of his words hung heavily between them. "I'm still that man, Emma. And I'll do whatever it takes to prove it to you."

In that moment, Emma knew that they were standing on the edge of something—something that could either break them or bind them together forever. The uncertainty that had been clouding her thoughts was still there, but for the first time in a long while, she felt like she could breathe again.

Jack's lips brushed against hers, a soft, lingering kiss that held a promise. A promise that no matter what happened next, they would face it together. And for the first time in days, Emma felt a flicker of hope, a spark of belief that maybe, just maybe, they could overcome the storm brewing on the horizon.

But as the kiss deepened, she knew that their journey was far from over. The road ahead was uncertain, filled with shadows and unanswered questions. And the truth—whatever it was—would have to come out eventually. She just hoped they could make it through.

Chapter 101: Shattered Illusions

"In the labyrinth of desire, the truth often slips through the cracks." — Anonymous

Emma sat in her office, the faint hum of the city outside her window doing little to quiet the chaos brewing in her mind. The rain from the night before had passed, but the storm of emotions and questions still lingered, thick and heavy in the air. Her fingers hovered over her keyboard as she tried to focus on the design work in front of her, but all she could think about was Jack.

The conversation from that morning kept replaying in her mind. She could still feel the warmth of his touch, the sincerity in his eyes, and yet... there was still so much she didn't know. She wanted to believe him. She truly did. But the nagging feeling that there was more—so much more—just beneath the surface, kept her awake at night.

She let out a sigh and closed her eyes for a moment, trying to center herself. She needed a distraction, something to take her mind off the whirlwind of thoughts that consumed her every waking hour. Her phone buzzed on the desk, and she glanced at the screen to see a message from her best friend, Sarah.

Sarah: *How's everything with you and Jack?*

Emma hesitated, her finger hovering over the keys. She wanted to tell Sarah everything, to confide in her and seek reassurance. But she couldn't bring herself to share the doubts swirling in her head. Instead, she typed back a simple reply.

Emma: *Good. Just a little... complicated.*

She hit send, then leaned back in her chair, staring out the window. The sky was a pale blue now, the sun attempting to break through the clouds. But Emma knew the calm wouldn't last forever. The storm was still coming, and it was only a matter of time before it hit.

The sound of her office door opening snapped her out of her thoughts, and she turned to see Richard, the investigator from the other day, standing in the doorway. His sharp eyes met hers, and she felt a chill run down her spine.

"Richard," she said, her voice steady despite the rush of anxiety flooding her chest. "What are you doing here?"

He stepped inside, closing the door behind him with a quiet click. "I need to talk to you," he said, his tone serious. "About Jack."

Emma stood up, her pulse quickening. "What is it? What else is there?"

Richard hesitated for a moment, then walked over to her desk, setting a folder down on the surface. "This," he said simply, "is a warning."

Emma's heart skipped a beat as she glanced down at the folder. It was thick, the edges worn as though it had been handled many times before. She looked up at Richard, her brows furrowing. "A warning? What do you mean?"

Richard's eyes were intense, his voice low. "Jack's past is more dangerous than you think. It's not just about bad decisions or old relationships. There are people involved—dangerous people—and they don't forget easily."

Emma felt a wave of nausea wash over her. She couldn't shake the feeling that the ground beneath her feet was shifting, becoming unstable. "I don't want to hear this," she said, shaking her head. "I trust Jack."

Richard's gaze softened, but his words were unwavering. "You need to understand what you're getting into, Emma. The truth isn't always pretty. You deserve to know what's at stake."

She took a step back, her hands trembling slightly. She had no idea what to do with this new information. The doubts, the uncertainties, they were consuming her. "I don't want to believe you," she whispered. "I want to believe in him."

Richard gave her a long, searching look. "I'm not here to tear you apart, Emma. I'm here to help you see the whole picture. You can ignore the truth, but it doesn't go away."

Emma swallowed hard, her mind racing. She wanted to turn away, to pretend none of this was happening. But the nagging voice in her head told her that wasn't an option. Not anymore. "What's in the folder?" she asked, her voice barely above a whisper.

Richard pushed the folder toward her, his eyes never leaving hers. "Open it. The truth is in there."

Emma's hand hesitated for a moment before she finally reached for the folder. She pulled it closer, her fingers brushing against the edges of the papers inside. She could feel the weight of what she was about to discover pressing down on her chest. Slowly, she opened the folder, revealing a collection of documents, photos, and handwritten notes.

As she flipped through the pages, her eyes scanned the contents, each piece of information more unsettling than the last. There were financial records, transactions that didn't make sense, and photographs of Jack with people she didn't recognize. And then, there was a file with a name that made her blood run cold.

Victor DeMarco.

Emma's hands shook as she read the name, her stomach tightening. The photograph accompanying the name showed a man with a sharp jawline, dark eyes, and a cold, calculating expression. She had no idea who he was, but the fact that his name was linked to Jack's past made her feel sick to her core.

"Who is he?" she asked, her voice trembling.

Richard leaned forward slightly. "Victor DeMarco is someone Jack's been involved with for years. A man with ties to some very dangerous organizations. You don't get out of that world without making enemies. And Jack... he's been trying to leave that life behind, but the people he's crossed—people like DeMarco—they don't forget."

Emma's heart raced. "What does this mean for me? For us?"

Richard's eyes were grave. "It means Jack is in deeper than you realize. He might not be able to protect you from the fallout of his past, no matter how hard he tries."

She felt the weight of his words sinking in, threatening to crush her. Was she really prepared for this? Could she handle the storm that was coming?

Emma stood there, frozen, her mind a whirlwind of confusion and fear. She wanted to walk away, to pretend none of this was happening. But she knew that wasn't an option. Not anymore.

"I need to talk to him," she said finally, her voice firm, though her hands still shook. "I need to know everything."

Richard nodded, his expression softening slightly. "I'll leave you to it. But remember, Emma, the truth isn't always what it seems."

As Richard turned to leave, Emma stood there, staring at the contents of the folder. Her mind raced with questions, her heart heavy with uncertainty. But one thing was clear: no matter what happened next, she had to face the truth. She had to confront the past if she wanted a future with Jack.

And she wasn't sure if she was ready for what that would mean.

Chapter 102: Whispers in the Dark

"The darkest nights produce the brightest stars." — Unknown

Emma sat on the edge of her bed, the contents of the folder spread out before her. Each page seemed to weigh more heavily on her chest than the last. Her eyes scanned the documents again, her mind racing, desperately trying to make sense of what she had learned. She couldn't believe it. Or at least, she didn't want to.

Victor DeMarco. A name that now haunted her every thought. The cold, calculating man who seemed to have ties to everything and everyone in Jack's past. The criminal world Jack had worked so hard to escape, yet it still held its grip on him, unwilling to let go.

The photographs—those cold, incriminating images—felt like they were burning into her memory. Jack, standing with people she didn't know, looking so different than the man she loved. The man who had held her in his arms, kissed her like he could never get enough, and whispered sweet nothings into her ear. That man was so far removed from the world these photographs revealed.

Her phone buzzed on the bed beside her, snapping her out of her reverie. It was a text from Jack.

Jack: *Can we talk tonight?*

She stared at the screen, her thumb hovering over the reply button. What was there left to say? What could he possibly say that would make all of this go away? She didn't know if she could look at him the same way after what she had seen. The lies, the secrets. Everything felt tainted.

But she also knew that avoiding him wouldn't help either. She had to confront him. She needed answers, even if they were painful. She owed it to herself—and to their relationship—to know the truth.

Emma: *Yes. Come to my place.*

Her heart pounded in her chest as she sent the message. There was no turning back now. She needed to hear the truth from Jack, no matter how hard it was to swallow.

The hours passed like minutes, the weight of the impending conversation pressing down on her. Emma tried to keep herself busy, tidying up the apartment, making tea, but nothing could distract her from the thoughts swirling in her mind. What if he couldn't explain? What if everything she had built with him, everything they had shared, was a lie?

The sound of a knock at the door jolted her from her thoughts, and she stood quickly, her legs almost giving out beneath her. She walked to the door, taking a deep breath before opening it to reveal Jack standing there, his face unreadable.

For a moment, they just stared at each other. She saw the flicker of concern in his eyes, the way he was studying her, but there was no warmth, no comfort. He looked just as tense as she felt.

"Emma," he said softly, stepping inside without waiting for an invitation. He closed the door behind him and took a step toward her, his eyes scanning her face. "You wanted to talk."

Emma nodded, her throat tight. She didn't know where to begin. The words felt like they were stuck in her chest, suffocating her. How did you even begin to address the overwhelming sense of betrayal that was swirling inside her?

"I met with Richard today," she said finally, her voice barely above a whisper. "He showed me the folder."

Jack's face paled, and she could see the tension in his shoulders as he took a slow, deliberate breath. "Emma, I—"

"Who is Victor DeMarco?" she interrupted, her voice sharper than she intended.

Jack froze, his eyes widening. For a split second, he looked like a man who had been caught in a lie, his carefully constructed facade cracking. He opened his mouth to speak, but the words seemed to fail him. He closed his eyes briefly, then looked back at her, his expression filled with regret.

"I never wanted you to find out about that part of my life," he said, his voice low. "I was trying to protect you."

"Protect me?" Emma scoffed, her voice trembling. "By lying to me? By keeping secrets from me? By letting me fall in love with someone who—" She stopped, her words choking her. She didn't want to say it. She didn't want to believe it. But the truth was there, staring her in the face.

Jack's eyes were filled with guilt. "I should have told you, I know. But I was afraid. Afraid of losing you. Afraid of what you'd think of me when you found out the truth. But I swear to you, Emma, I'm not that person anymore. I haven't been for a long time."

She shook her head, tears welling in her eyes. "Then why didn't you just tell me? Why keep me in the dark?"

He stepped closer, reaching out for her hand, but she pulled away before he could touch her. "I didn't want to lose you," he said, his voice breaking. "I thought if you knew what I'd done, what I was involved in, you wouldn't be able to look at me the same way."

Emma swallowed hard, the lump in her throat making it difficult to speak. "What did you do, Jack? What are you hiding?"

Jack's gaze faltered, his eyes darting to the floor as if he couldn't bring himself to meet her gaze. "I was part of a world that I shouldn't have been," he admitted, his voice barely above a whisper. "I got involved with people who didn't play by the rules. People like DeMarco... they use you, they manipulate you, and they don't care who they hurt in the process."

Emma felt her heart shatter. "And you think I can just forgive you for that? You think I can just forget everything you've done and trust you?"

Jack stepped back, his hands clenching at his sides. "No. I don't expect you to forget. But I need you to understand. I didn't do this for me. I did it for you—for us. I wanted to get out of that world. I wanted to build something real with you."

Tears streamed down Emma's face as she turned away from him, unable to look at him any longer. She was torn, her heart pulled in two different directions. She wanted to believe him. She wanted to believe that everything they had shared was real. But the truth was too overwhelming, too painful to ignore.

"I don't know what to believe anymore," she whispered, her voice breaking. "I don't know if I can keep doing this." Jack's voice softened as he took a step closer. "Emma, please. I love you. I'll do whatever it takes to prove it to you. Just... don't walk away from us. Don't walk away from me."

Emma turned to face him, her heart aching. She could see the desperation in his eyes, the fear of losing her, and for a moment, she felt the pull of that love. But the weight of the past, of the lies, of the secrets—how could she ever truly trust him again?

"I need time," she said, her voice barely audible. "I need time to think."

Jack nodded, his face falling. "I understand. I'll wait. I'll wait as long as you need."

He turned to leave, but before he reached the door, he stopped. "I love you, Emma," he said quietly, his voice filled with raw emotion.

Emma closed her eyes, the words sinking deep into her heart. She loved him too. But love... love wasn't always enough.

Chapter 103: The Final Confrontation

"There are no secrets that time does not reveal." — Jean Racine

The silence between them was deafening. Emma sat on her bed, her mind whirling as she stared at the empty space where Jack had been moments before. His words echoed in her mind, haunting her with the weight of truth she hadn't been prepared for. Love was never meant to come with such a heavy price.

She glanced at her phone, still sitting on the bedside table, the screen dark. Jack's text earlier was still fresh in her mind—his pleading tone, his promise to wait. But what was she supposed to do with that? How could she reconcile the man she loved with the one who had kept so many secrets? The man who had pulled her into his world, only to reveal the dangers lurking beneath the surface.

The room felt too small. The walls seemed to close in on her as she paced back and forth, trying to sort through the chaos of emotions crashing inside her. She had always prided herself on being strong, independent. But now? Now, she felt as though she was teetering on the edge of something she couldn't control.

The knock at the door startled her from her thoughts. She froze, her heart racing, before slowly walking to the door. Who could it be? She had just seen Jack leave, his face a mask of sorrow and regret. Had he come back?

When she opened the door, it wasn't Jack who stood there.

"Victoria," Emma said, her voice laced with surprise. She hadn't expected to see her, not tonight. Not after everything.

Victoria stood in front of her, looking every bit the image of elegance and control, but there was something in her eyes—a glimmer of understanding, of knowing. She wasn't here to make amends, and Emma knew that. She had her own reasons for coming.

"I need to talk to you," Victoria said, her voice calm but firm.

Emma hesitated. What could Victoria possibly want to talk about after everything that had happened between them? What was left to say?

"I don't know if now's the right time—" Emma started, but Victoria cut her off, stepping past her into the apartment.

"Let me in, Emma. I promise you, I'm not here to cause trouble," Victoria said, her tone laced with something that felt oddly sincere.

Emma sighed, her shoulders slumping in exhaustion. She stepped back, allowing Victoria to enter.

"I'm listening," Emma said, crossing her arms over her chest. She wasn't sure what Victoria was playing at, but she couldn't deny the pull to hear what she had to say.

Victoria sat down on the couch without waiting for an invitation, her posture straight, her eyes locked onto Emma. "I know you're confused," she began, her gaze softening slightly. "I know you don't know who to trust right now."

Emma's heart skipped a beat. She had been hoping, praying, that someone—anyone—would give her some clarity in this mess.

"Jack isn't the man you think he is," Victoria continued. "Not because he's evil, but because he's hiding things from you that could hurt you. Things that you won't be able to ignore once you know the whole truth."

Emma's breath caught. She swallowed hard, trying to steady herself. "I know about the past," she said, her voice trembling. "I know about Victor DeMarco."

Victoria raised an eyebrow. "You think that's all there is to it?" she asked, almost with a hint of a laugh. "That's just the beginning. Trust me when I say there's so much more."

"Why are you telling me this?" Emma asked, her voice a little more forceful now. She was done with secrets, done with half-truths.

Victoria's expression darkened, her lips pressing into a thin line. "Because I've been where you are. I've loved him, too. And I know how this ends if you don't open your eyes. You think you're in control, but you're not. Jack is the one in control. And he's always going to keep you at arm's length."

Emma's pulse quickened. "You think he's using me?"

Victoria shook her head slowly. "No. Not using you. But you're in danger of becoming just another casualty in his war with himself. He's never going to let anyone close enough to truly see him. And that's a dangerous game to play."

Emma was quiet for a long moment, the words sinking deep into her chest. She didn't want to believe them. She didn't want to believe that everything she had built with Jack could be a lie.

But then again, how could she ignore what Victoria was saying? How many times had Jack pushed her away when things got too real?

How many times had he withdrawn, leaving her standing there, alone, wondering if he was hiding something from her?

"I don't know what to do with this information," Emma said finally, her voice cracking. She felt so small, so helpless.

Victoria's gaze softened. "I'm not here to give you answers, Emma. I'm here to show you the truth. You deserve the truth. And right now, that truth is this: Jack isn't the man you think he is. But that doesn't mean he doesn't love you. It just means that love, in his world, comes with a cost."

Emma felt the weight of her words, the gravity of everything she had just learned pressing down on her. She didn't know what the right answer was. All she knew was that she couldn't keep living in this uncertainty. She had to find out for herself what Jack's secrets truly meant.

Later that night, Emma stood on the balcony, the cool breeze against her skin offering little relief from the storm inside her. The city lights flickered in the distance, but all she could see was Jack's face—his eyes, filled with love and desperation, his touch that had once felt like home

.

But now? Now, it felt like a lie.

She didn't know how much more of this she could take. Every step she took with Jack seemed to bring her closer to a cliff she couldn't see but knew was there. And the further she fell, the more it felt like there was no way back.

A knock at the door. A familiar sound, one that she had been dreading and waiting for all at once.

It was Jack.

She closed her eyes, taking a deep breath before turning to face the door. Her heart pounded in her chest as she opened it, her eyes locking with his. There was so much she wanted to say, so much she needed to know, but all she could do was stand there, frozen in place.

Jack's face softened when he saw her, and he stepped forward, reaching out for her. But Emma couldn't let him touch her. Not yet.

"I need answers, Jack," she said quietly, her voice steady despite the turmoil inside her. "And I need them now."

Jack's expression faltered, but he didn't pull away. He just nodded, his eyes filled with something—guilt, fear, regret. "I'll tell you everything, Emma. Everything you need to know. But I need you to trust me ."

Emma swallowed hard, her heart torn in two. She wanted to trust him. She wanted to believe that their love could survive this. But the truth, as painful as it was, was too heavy to ignore.

"I don't know if I can," she whispered, her voice breaking.

Jack's eyes closed for a brief moment before he looked at her again. "I'll do whatever it takes to make this right. Just... don't walk away. Not yet."

Emma's heart ached. "I'm not walking away, Jack. But I can't keep living in the dark."

Chapter 104: Unbreakable Bonds

"Love does not consist in gazing at each other, but in looking outward together in the same direction." — Antoine de Saint-Exupéry

The tension in the air was thick as Emma stood in front of Jack, her heart pounding in her chest. His eyes, usually so confident, now held a vulnerability she had never seen before. He wasn't the man she thought she knew. The man standing before her was full of shadows, full of secrets—and she had a sinking feeling that the truth she was about to hear would shatter everything she had come to believe.

Jack's hands were at his sides, clenched into fists, his face tense as he looked at her, waiting for her to speak. She could feel the weight of his gaze, like it was pressing into her very soul. He was waiting for her to say something, anything, but the words didn't come. Instead, she felt the silence stretch between them, thick and suffocating.

"Emma, I—" Jack started, his voice low and strained. But he didn't finish. Instead, he seemed to retreat into himself, as though he was searching for the right words, or perhaps the courage, to say what had been haunting him for so long.

"Jack," she whispered, stepping closer, her voice barely audible. "Please. I can't keep living in this unknown. I need to understand what's been happening—what's been going on in your life. Why are you keeping these secrets from me?"

Jack's eyes closed, his jaw tightening, and for a moment, he didn't speak. The silence stretched on, and Emma could feel her heart breaking, piece by piece. She had never imagined that the love they shared would come with such a heavy price, and yet here she was, standing on the precipice of something that might destroy everything they had built together.

Finally, Jack exhaled slowly and opened his eyes, meeting her gaze. "I never meant for it to get this far, Emma. I never meant to hurt you. But you're right. I've been hiding things. I've been running from the truth, from my past, from everything that's followed me."

Emma's stomach twisted. She felt like she was about to hear something that would change the course of her life forever. But she needed to hear it. She needed to know what had been lurking beneath the surface of their relationship.

"Tell me, Jack," she whispered, her voice trembling with the weight of her own emotions. "Tell me everything."

Jack took a deep breath, stepping back to sit on the couch, his hands resting on his knees. He seemed to gather his thoughts, his eyes unfocused as if he was reliving something painful, something he wished he could forget.

"I've made a lot of mistakes, Emma. A lot of mistakes that I can't undo. I've been involved in things... things I can't walk away from. People who won't let me forget. And I thought I could leave it all behind when I came to you. I thought I could be the man you deserved—the man you saw in me. But I can't escape my past. Not completely."

Emma's heart raced, her mind struggling to process the weight of his words. Her body felt as though it was in freefall, as if she was standing on the edge of a cliff with no way to stop herself from tumbling down.

"What kind of things?" she asked, her voice barely a whisper.

Jack's eyes met hers again, a flicker of regret passing over his face. "I've been involved in dangerous situations, Emma. People I've worked with—people who expect things from me. And I've been running from them for a long time. But I can't run anymore."

Her breath caught in her throat as the realization hit her like a freight train. "What are you saying? Are you in danger?"

Jack looked away, his gaze distant. "Yes. I've been trying to protect you from it. Trying to keep you safe. But it's impossible. And the longer I keep you in the dark, the more I put you at risk."

Emma's mind reeled. Her thoughts scrambled as she tried to make sense of everything. "What kind of danger are we talking about, Jack? Who are these people?"

Jack stood up, his body tense. "They're connected to the business I used to be involved with. I've tried to get out, but it's not that easy. There are people who don't like to let go, and they'll do anything to make sure I stay in the game."

Emma felt a chill run through her as the words sank in. "You're telling me that you've been involved with criminals? With people who could hurt you... and me?"

Jack didn't answer right away, but the look in his eyes said everything she needed to know. She could feel her world crumbling around her, and she didn't know if she could hold on.

"I never wanted this to touch you, Emma," Jack said, his voice low, raw with emotion. "But I'm telling you now because I can't keep running. And I can't keep pretending that everything's fine. It's not fair to you. It's not fair to either of us."

Emma stood there, her mind spinning, her heart torn between the love she had for Jack and the fear that was starting to seep into her every thought. The man she had fallen for—this strong, confident, passionate man—was hiding a life so dangerous, so filled with shadows, that it threatened to swallow them both.

"I don't know if I can handle this, Jack," she whispered, her voice cracking. "I don't know if I can trust you anymore. You've kept so much from me."

"I know. And I'm sorry," he said, his voice thick with regret. "But I swear to you, Emma, I'm doing this for us. I'm doing this because I love you."

Emma looked at him, her chest tight with emotion. She wanted to believe him. She wanted to believe that love could be enough to overcome all of this. But the doubt was gnawing at her, and the fear was suffocating.

She took a step back, the distance between them growing. "I don't know if I can trust you anymore, Jack. I don't know if I can keep living in this world of secrets."

Jack's face fell, his eyes pleading with her. "Emma, please. I need you. I need you to believe in me. You're the only good thing I have left."

But Emma didn't know if she could keep living in the shadows of Jack's past. She didn't know if she could be the woman standing beside him as he fought battles she couldn't even begin to understand.

As the silence between them deepened, Emma knew that something had shifted. They were no longer the couple they had once been. The walls between them had been built high, and she wasn't sure if either of them could climb over them.

"I need time, Jack," she said, her voice shaking. "I need time to think."

Jack didn't protest, though his expression was filled with pain. He nodded slowly, as if he had expected this answer, but the hurt in his eyes was still palpable.

"Take all the time you need," he said softly. "I'll be here when you're ready."

Emma nodded, her heart heavy as she turned away from him, the weight of his words pressing down on her. She didn't know if she could come back from this. She didn't know if their love could survive the darkness of his past.

But for now, she had no other choice but to try.

Chapter 105: A Future Together

*"T*he future belongs to those who believe in the beauty of their dreams." — Eleanor Roosevelt

The night was still young, but Emma felt as though time had stopped. The events of the day—the truth Jack had revealed to her—hung heavily in the air, a weight she wasn't sure she could shake off. But even with the confusion swirling in her mind, her body craved something else. Something deep. Something primal.

As she walked through the penthouse, her thoughts clashed in a chaotic battle. Her heart wanted to give Jack the benefit of the doubt, to believe in him, in their connection. But every time she closed her eyes, she saw the darkness he had tried so hard to protect her from. His past was a labyrinth, and she wasn't sure she had the strength to navigate its maze.

But then again, her body was telling her something different. The ache inside her had only grown more intense since that fateful night when their lips first touched. The passion between them was undeniable, burning brighter than anything she had ever known. And in the moments of quiet between them, when the world seemed to fade away, she could feel it—the raw connection that had ignited so fiercely between them.

She needed him. That much was clear. But could she still trust him?

The sound of Jack's voice startled her, breaking through her thoughts. She turned to find him standing at the doorway, his eyes dark with a mixture of longing and uncertainty. His hands were shoved deep in his pockets, his posture stiff, as if he, too, was struggling with the emotions tearing at him.

"Emma..." His voice was soft, almost hesitant.

Her heart twisted at the vulnerability in his tone. She had always known him to be confident, assured in everything he did. But right now, he was lost. Just like her.

"Jack," she replied, her voice a mix of uncertainty and desire. "I don't know what to say."

He stepped closer, closing the distance between them. His eyes never left hers, as if searching for something, anything that would bring them back from the edge they were teetering on.

"You don't have to say anything," he murmured, his fingers brushing against her arm. "I just need you to know that I'm here. I'm not going anywhere."

Her breath hitched at the heat of his touch. She could feel the pull between them, magnetic and irresistible. Despite everything, she wanted him. She had wanted him from the very first moment their bodies had come together. And as his fingers traced a path down her arm, she felt the familiar surge of desire flood her veins.

Without thinking, she closed the space between them, pressing her lips to his in a kiss that was equal parts tender and desperate. Jack's hands roamed to her back, pulling her closer, his body rigid with restraint, as though he was struggling to hold back.

Emma deepened the kiss, her hands threading through his hair, tugging him closer. The kiss was no longer just a kiss. It was an unspoken promise—a promise to leave the past behind, if only for a few moments. A promise to give in to the heat, the rawness of the connection that had always existed between them.

Jack's hands moved lower, tracing the curve of her waist, his touch sending a shiver down her spine. She felt the weight of his desire pressing against her, and it ignited something primal deep inside her.

"Are you sure about this?" Jack pulled back just slightly, his voice rough, like it took all his strength to speak.

"Don't stop," she breathed, her words laced with urgency. "I need you."

He didn't need any more encouragement. His hands slid to the back of her thighs, lifting her effortlessly, and she wrapped her legs around him, the world fading away as his lips crashed against hers once more. They moved toward the couch, their lips never parting, their bodies hungry for each other in a way that neither of them could deny.

Jack lowered her to the soft cushions, his body coming down over hers with a weight that felt both comforting and thrilling. His hands explored her body with a newfound urgency, as if he needed to reassure himself that she was really here, really with him.

As his lips traveled down her neck, Emma's pulse quickened. She arched into him, every nerve in her body alive with anticipation. She had felt this before—this craving, this need that went beyond the physical. It was more than just lust. It was something deeper, something she couldn't explain.

"Jack..." she whispered, her fingers trailing over the hard lines of his chest. "I want you."

He kissed her again, this time slow and deliberate, his lips brushing hers with a tenderness that made her ache. She could feel the weight of his emotions in every kiss, every touch. But the desire between them was undeniable, and for a moment, it was enough to drown out all the doubts.

Jack's hands moved to the button of her dress, undoing it with practiced ease. She gasped as the fabric slid off her shoulders, leaving her exposed to him, vulnerable, yet craving the intimacy only he could give her. She wasn't afraid. Not anymore. With Jack, she felt safe—more than safe. She felt wanted, desired in a way that made her feel alive.

He paused for a moment, his eyes scanning her body, taking in every inch of her. The heat in his gaze made her skin flush, her chest rising and falling with each breath. "You're perfect," he whispered, his voice raw with admiration.

Emma's fingers dug into the back of his neck, pulling him closer. "No more talking," she said with a playful smile, her lips curving into a wicked grin.

Jack chuckled darkly, and without another word, he lowered his lips to her neck, kissing a trail down to her chest, his hands exploring her body with a hunger that matched her own. She moaned softly, her hands gripping the back of his head, urging him closer.

The intensity of the moment was overwhelming. Each touch, each kiss, felt like a promise—a promise to forget the world around them, to forget the pain and the secrets. It was just them. Just this. And for the first time in a long time, Emma allowed herself to fully surrender to the passion that had always existed between them.

Jack's lips moved lower, his hands sliding beneath her, lifting her slightly as he kissed his way down to the curve of her waist. She shivered, the anticipation almost unbearable as he slowly kissed his way back up, his lips teasing her skin.

"Jack…" she gasped, her voice a breathless plea.

He paused, his lips just a hair's breadth away from her most intimate places. "Tell me what you want, Emma."

Her mind was a blur of desire, her body humming with need. "I want you inside me," she whispered, her voice low, seductive.

Without hesitation, Jack positioned himself above her, his body pressing into hers, his lips capturing hers in a fierce kiss. As he entered her, Emma's world exploded into sensation—fire, heat, and longing.

Their bodies moved together in a rhythmic dance, the tension between them building with each passing second. Emma's nails dug into his back, urging him on, her breath coming in ragged gasps as she gave herself over to him completely.

Jack's name escaped her lips in a breathless whisper, and in that moment, all the doubt, all the fear, faded away. There was no past, no future—there was only the two of them, locked in an embrace that was as wild as it was intimate.

Their connection was electric, raw, and unyielding, and for the first time in a long time, Emma felt like she was truly alive—caught in a moment where nothing else mattered, where the rest of the world could burn and it wouldn't matter, because she was with Jack. And that was enough.

Chapter 106: The Truth Comes Out

The days following their passionate encounter were a blur for Emma. She woke each morning with Jack beside her, their bodies tangled together in the warmth of the sheets, a constant reminder of the night they shared. Despite the intensity of their physical connection, the emotional weight remained, lingering in the space between them.

Jack was different after that night—more present, more attentive, but Emma could sense the underlying tension in his actions. It was as though he was still trying to prove something to her, to prove that he was worthy of her trust, even though he had already given her everything.

And her heart, despite all the chaos and uncertainty, was willing to follow him down this path. She had never known anyone like him before. He was a force of nature, a man who took what he wanted with a quiet intensity that left her breathless. But he was also a man with shadows in his past, and those shadows had begun to creep into their present.

One afternoon, while she was at the office, Jack called. The sound of his voice was like a balm to her soul, and for a moment, she allowed herself to forget the doubts that had been eating at her for weeks.

"Emma," Jack said, his voice thick with emotion. "I need to see you."

Her heart fluttered in her chest. "I'm working right now, Jack. Can't it wait?"

"I don't think it can," he replied. There was something urgent in his tone, a note of desperation she had never heard before. "Please. It's important."

The urgency in his voice made her stomach tighten with both concern and anticipation. She didn't hesitate to leave her desk, grabbing her bag and heading out of the office. Whatever Jack had to say, she knew it couldn't be avoided. The way things were between them now, every moment seemed to matter, every word, every touch.

When she arrived at his penthouse, the door was already open, and Jack stood in the living room, facing the floor-to-ceiling windows. The city lights gleamed below, but he was lost in thought, his back rigid and his hands clenched into fists at his sides.

"Jack?" Emma's voice was soft, almost tentative as she approached him.

He turned, and she saw the strain in his expression, the exhaustion in his eyes that made her heart ache. "Emma," he whispered, his voice barely above a breath. "I've made some decisions. Things... things I should have told you a long time ago."

Her pulse quickened as she stepped closer, feeling the familiar pull between them, but this time, it wasn't just desire she felt. It was fear—fear of what he might say, what truth he was about to reveal.

"Jack, you're scaring me," she said, her voice trembling with the weight of her own emotions. "What's going on?"

He walked toward her, his footsteps heavy with a sense of finality. "I don't want to lose you, Emma. You mean everything to me, but I'm not sure I can give you what you need. What you deserve."

Emma's breath caught in her throat. "What are you talking about?" She reached out, grabbing his hand and pulling him closer, her body a sudden contradiction of tension and yearning.

"I've been lying to you," Jack admitted, his voice cracking with raw honesty. "Not in the way you think. But I've been holding parts of myself back, parts of my past, because I was afraid it would push you away."

"Jack..." Her heart raced, panic rising in her chest. "What are you trying to say?"

He took a deep breath, gathering himself before speaking again. "I've been involved in things, Emma. Things that go far beyond just business or a broken relationship. People—dangerous people—are still involved in my life. And I've been trying to protect you from it. I never wanted you to know. But I don't think I can keep lying to you anymore."

The words hit her like a ton of bricks, and for a moment, she couldn't breathe. "You're... involved in something dangerous?" she whispered, the disbelief in her voice clear.

Jack's eyes met hers, his expression filled with regret. "Yes. And I'm not sure how much longer I can keep you safe."

Emma stumbled back a step, the weight of his confession sinking in. Her mind raced, her thoughts a blur of confusion and fear. Jack wasn't the man she thought he was. She had known that on some level, but hearing it out loud made it real—too real.

For a long moment, neither of them spoke. Emma's heart pounded in her chest as the tension between them grew unbearable. She could feel the distance between them widening, the walls of doubt rising higher with every passing second.

But then, despite everything, she reached for him. Her hand trembling as she placed it gently against his chest, feeling the steady thrum of his heartbeat beneath her fingertips.

"I can't lose you, Jack," she said, her voice raw and vulnerable. "Not now. Not when I've given so much of myself to you. I don't care about your past. I care about who you are now. I care about us."

Jack closed his eyes for a moment, a mixture of pain and longing crossing his face. "Emma," he whispered, his voice hoarse. "I don't deserve you."

She shook her head, stepping closer, her hand reaching for his. "No, Jack. You do. I know you do."

His lips crashed against hers in a kiss that was all consuming, a desperate, heated kiss that carried with it the weight of their emotions. They pulled each other closer, needing each other in ways that words couldn't express.

Jack's hands moved to her back, sliding under the fabric of her dress, the heat of his touch setting her skin on fire. She gasped as his lips moved to her neck, her body arching toward him, wanting, needing mo re.

But in the back of her mind, the words he had spoken kept echoing. His past, the danger, the people he was still tied to—it was all so much to process. Yet in that moment, none of it mattered. Not when he kissed her like that, like he couldn't get enough of her. Not when his touch made her feel more alive than she had ever felt before.

"I won't let you go," Jack murmured against her lips, his hands moving with urgency now. "Not now. Not ever."

She nodded, her breath ragged, as their bodies intertwined in a dance as old as time. Whatever Jack's past held, whatever shadows lingered, they were together now. And nothing else mattered.

Chapter 107: The Choice

"There is no remedy for love but to love more." — Henry David Thoreau

The days that followed were filled with a mixture of passion and uncertainty. Emma couldn't shake the feeling that she was standing on the edge of something dangerous—something that could pull her under if she wasn't careful. Jack's confession about his past lingered in her thoughts, an ever-present weight on her chest. She couldn't help but wonder what else he was hiding, what other secrets he might be keeping from her.

Yet, despite the questions that burned in her mind, her body craved him. Every glance, every touch, sent a spark of desire racing through her veins. Jack was like a drug, and the more she tried to resist, the more she found herself falling deeper into him.

They spent the next few days in a haze of stolen moments—shared glances, lingering touches, whispered confessions in the quiet of the night. Jack was present, more than he had been in weeks, but Emma could still feel the underlying tension between them. He was trying, she could tell, trying to make things right, but she couldn't shake the feeling that something was about to break.

One evening, after a quiet dinner in his penthouse, Jack took her hand and led her out onto the balcony. The city sprawled beneath them, the lights twinkling like a thousand stars. The night air was cool against her skin, but it didn't diminish the heat between them.

"Emma," Jack began, his voice low, almost hesitant. "I want you to understand something. My past... it's not just a shadow that follows me around. It's more than that. There are people who would do anything to tear us apart."

She turned to face him, her heart pounding in her chest. His expression was serious, the light from the city casting shadows across his face. She wanted to reach out and touch him, reassure him, but there was a part of her that was afraid of what he might say next.

"What do you mean?" she asked, her voice barely above a whisper.

Jack took a deep breath, his eyes searching hers as if weighing how much to reveal. "There are things in my life that I can't control, Emma. Things I never wanted to be a part of, but I was pulled in anyway. There are people who know my every move, people who want to make sure I stay in line. And you... you're in danger because of me."

Emma's stomach twisted with unease, but she refused to pull away. She reached for his hand, holding it tightly in hers. "I'm not afraid of your past, Jack. I'm afraid of losing you."

His gaze softened, and for a moment, he just looked at her—his blue eyes filled with a mixture of longing and regret. "I don't want to lose you either. But I can't keep you in the dark anymore. I have to protect you, Emma. I can't lose you. Not now. Not after everything we've shared."

She felt the sincerity in his words, but the weight of what he was saying hung heavy in the air. The danger, the secrecy, the people who wanted to pull them apart—it was all too much to process. And yet, she couldn't walk away. Not when every fiber of her being was drawn to him.

"I don't care about the danger, Jack," she whispered, her voice thick with emotion. "I want to be with you. I'm not afraid of your past. I'm afraid of living without you."

His lips found hers in a kiss that was tender at first, slow and deliberate, as if he was savoring the moment. But as their mouths melded together, the kiss deepened, becoming more urgent, more passionate. His hands slid to her back, pulling her closer, his body pressing against hers with an intensity that made her heart race.

Jack's kiss was a promise, a pledge that no matter the danger, no matter the shadows in his past, he would always find a way back to her. And she would do the same for him.

They stood there, wrapped in each other's arms, for what felt like an eternity. The city around them faded away, and in that moment, it was just the two of them. No past, no secrets, just the heat of their connection.

But the reality of their situation soon came rushing back. As they pulled away from the kiss, Emma noticed the shadow in Jack's eyes once again—the same one that had haunted him for days. The same shadow that kept him from fully letting go.

"I don't want to pressure you," Emma said softly, her voice barely audible over the sounds of the city. "But I need to know the truth, Jack. What's going on? What's really happening with your past?"

Jack's jaw tightened, and for a moment, he said nothing. His gaze drifted to the horizon, as if searching for the right words. Finally, he spoke, his voice low and filled with emotion.

"I'm tangled up in something I can't get out of. People who won't let me go, no matter how much I try to distance myself. It's not just business anymore, Emma. It's personal."

Emma's heart skipped a beat, a cold shiver running down her spine. "Personal? What do you mean by that?"

He turned back to her, his eyes filled with regret. "There are people who will use you to get to me, Emma. People who won't hesitate to hurt you, to make you suffer, just to make sure I stay in line."

Her mind raced, the implications of his words sinking in. "What do we do?" she asked, her voice trembling with fear.

Jack took a deep breath, his grip on her hand tightening. "We fight. Together."

As the night wore on, Emma couldn't help but feel the weight of the decision ahead of them. Jack's past was more dangerous than she had ever imagined, but she knew one thing for sure—she wasn't going to let him face it alone.

They stood there on the balcony, the world below them dark and indifferent, but in that moment, they were united in a way they had never been before. Together, they would face whatever came their way.

Chapter 108: A New Beginning

"The best thing to hold onto in life is each other." — Audrey Hepburn

The days that followed were a blur of tension, decisions, and undeniable passion. Jack and Emma were walking a tightrope, balancing between the impending danger that threatened their world and the intensity of their connection. Each moment they shared was laden with unspoken promises and desires that burned brightly in the quiet spaces between them.

Jack's confession about his past had only deepened Emma's feelings, even as it pulled her into a vortex of uncertainty. She couldn't deny the gravity of the situation—danger was closing in, and they both felt it—but at the same time, she couldn't turn away from him. Not now. Not when every fiber of her being ached for him.

Their nights had become a sanctuary, a place where they could escape the looming threats and lose themselves in each other. Every kiss, every touch, every whisper of desire seemed to drive the growing connection between them to new heights. Yet beneath it all, Emma knew that things were changing. They were no longer just two people caught in a whirlwind of passion; they were two people who had been thrown into a storm of chaos, and only time would tell if they could weather it together.

One evening, as the sun dipped below the horizon, casting the city in a soft, golden glow, Emma found herself sitting on the edge of Jack's bed, a glass of wine in hand, her thoughts a swirl of confusion and longing. Jack was in the bathroom, getting ready for their dinner date, but she couldn't help but think about everything that had happened.

She had never been one to shy away from challenges, but this—this was different. This wasn't just about love; it was about survival. Jack's world was filled with shadows that reached out and threatened to pull her under, and she couldn't pretend to be naïve to the dangers any longer.

Yet, when Jack stepped out of the bathroom, his hair damp and his eyes dark with desire, the questions that plagued her mind seemed to melt away. He was a force, and in that moment, Emma couldn't deny the pull he had on her.

His eyes locked onto hers, and she felt a shiver of anticipation race through her. "You're beautiful," he murmured, his voice thick with desire.

She smiled, setting the wineglass down and standing to meet him. "I'm not the one who needs to be told that."

His lips curved into a smirk as he reached for her, his hands brushing against her waist. "It's not just about how you look, Emma. It's how you make me feel."

She could feel her pulse quicken at the intensity of his gaze, the heat between them palpable. "And how is that?" she asked, her voice a mix of teasing and sincerity.

"Like I can't breathe without you," Jack replied, his lips brushing against her ear as he spoke, sending a wave of goosebumps down her spine.

Before she could respond, Jack's lips crashed into hers, demanding, urgent. The kiss was electric, sparking a fire in her chest that spread like wildfire. She let out a soft moan as his hands slid down her back, pulling her closer to him until their bodies were flush against one another. Her hands tangled in his hair, deepening the kiss, losing herself in the moment, in the connection they shared.

The world outside their bubble faded away, and for a brief, fleeting moment, there was no danger, no past, no uncertainty. There was only the heat of their bodies pressing together, the rhythm of their breaths syncing in perfect harmony.

Jack pulled back slightly, his hands lingering on her hips, his eyes dark with longing. "Emma," he whispered, his voice rough, "I need y ou."

Her heart pounded in her chest as she met his gaze. "I'm here," she whispered back, her hands tracing the lines of his jaw, memorizing the feel of him under her touch. She had never wanted anyone the way she wanted him.

Jack's lips found hers again, this time slower, more deliberate, as if savoring each moment. His hands skimmed down her body, pausing only to tug at the hem of her dress, lifting it over her head in one smooth motion. Emma didn't hesitate; she reached for his shirt, pulling it over his head, the fabric sliding effortlessly off his muscular fra me.

The tension between them was almost unbearable, but there was no turning back now. She needed him—needed to feel him—and it wasn't just a desire. It was something deeper, something that had been building ever since they met, something that had now reached a fever pitch.

Jack's hands found the clasp of her bra, undoing it with practiced ease, his fingers grazing her skin as he slid it off her shoulders. Emma's breath hitched, her body trembling as his lips traced a path down her neck, across her collarbone, and to the sensitive curve of her breast. Her head fell back as he teased her, his tongue flicking across her skin, sending jolts of electricity through her body.

"You feel so good," Jack murmured against her skin, his hands worshiping her, mapping every inch of her body. "I've never wanted anything more than I want you right now."

Emma's hands roamed to his pants, undoing the buckle with a sense of urgency that mirrored her own desperation. She needed him, needed the connection, the escape from everything that weighed on them.

They moved together with an urgency that only heightened the passion between them, a desperation that was driven by the uncertainty of their situation. As they made love, it wasn't just about pleasure; it was about reaffirming the bond they shared, the trust they had in each other despite the looming danger.

In the heat of the moment, they were more than just two people lost in desire. They were a force, unstoppable and undeniable, and nothing—not even the shadows of Jack's past—could tear them apart.

As their bodies moved together in perfect rhythm, Emma could feel the tension in her body unraveling, her mind going blank as she gave herself completely to the experience. She was lost in him, in the heat of their connection, and for the first time in what felt like forever, she didn't think about the danger that threatened them. She only thought about him—about them.

When they finally collapsed together, breathless and spent, Emma buried her face in Jack's chest, her fingers tracing the lines of his muscles, feeling the steady thrum of his heart beneath her palm. For a moment, she felt safe. For a moment, they were free.

But she knew that this peace would be fleeting. There were still shadows looming over them, secrets that needed to be uncovered, and enemies they hadn't yet faced. But for now, in this moment, they had each other.

And that was enough.

Chapter 109: Ever After

"It's not about finding someone to live with. It's about finding someone you can't imagine living without." — Rafael Ortiz

The morning light seeped through the curtains, casting a soft glow over the penthouse. Emma woke with Jack's arm draped around her, his steady breathing the only sound filling the room. She stayed there for a moment, listening to the beat of his heart beneath her ear, feeling the warmth of his skin against hers. It was a moment of peace—a brief interlude in the chaos that had become their lives.

But that peace was fragile. The danger they faced, the secrets Jack kept buried, it all still lingered, just below the surface. And Emma could feel it, like an invisible weight pressing down on her chest.

She shifted slightly, careful not to disturb Jack's rest, and eased herself out of bed. Her feet landed softly on the cool hardwood floor, and she wrapped herself in one of Jack's shirts that she had carelessly discarded the night before. As she moved towards the kitchen, she took a deep breath, trying to clear her mind. She needed to focus, needed to regain control of the situation. The past few days had been a whirlwind of emotions, physical desire, and an underlying tension that refused to let go.

She poured herself a glass of water, staring at the reflection of the city skyline in the window, her thoughts swirling. Jack had become more than just a lover. He was a force, an enigma that she was helplessly drawn to. But as much as she cared for him, she couldn't ignore the nagging feeling that there were still parts of him she didn't know—parts he was keeping hidden, perhaps even from himself. And Victoria's warning echoed in her mind, a constant reminder that there were truths yet to be revealed.

Her phone buzzed on the counter, breaking her from her thoughts. She glanced at the screen, her heart skipping a beat when she saw the name. It was Richard Holloway—the investigator who had appeared at her office with disturbing information about Jack's past. She had tried to push the thought of him out of her mind, but now it seemed impossible to escape.

Without thinking, Emma picked up the phone and answered. "Richard," she said, her voice a little sharper than she intended.

"Ms. Carter," Richard's voice was calm, almost too calm. "I trust you've had time to think about what we discussed."

Emma's stomach tightened. "I've been thinking," she admitted. "But I'm not sure what you want from me."

"I'm not here to cause trouble," Richard replied, though his words didn't exactly reassure her. "But I do think you should know the full story. There's more to Jack Sullivan than he's let on."

"I'm listening," Emma said, her voice tight.

Richard paused, as if weighing his words carefully. "Jack's ties to the criminal underworld go deeper than he's willing to admit. There are people involved who aren't just after him—they're after anyone close to him. Including you."

Emma felt a chill run down her spine. "What are you saying?"

"I'm saying that Jack has made enemies," Richard continued, his tone colder now. "And if you stay involved with him, you'll be dragged into it. Whether you like it or not."

The silence between them stretched out, the weight of his words sinking in. Emma's pulse quickened as she thought about everything she had learned about Jack—the secrets he had shared, the ones he hadn't. She had always known there was darkness in his past, but hearing it so bluntly made it feel all too real.

"I don't need to hear any more of this," she said, her voice trembling despite her best efforts to sound firm. "I trust Jack."

"Then you're making a mistake," Richard said, his voice firm, almost like a warning. "But the choice is yours."

Before she could respond, the line went dead.

Emma stood there, holding the phone in her hand, her mind racing. She felt sick. Everything she had believed, everything she had trusted, was now under question. Was Jack truly the man she thought he was, or had she been blinded by desire and lust?

She had been so consumed by the chemistry between them, by the emotional and physical connection, that she had failed to fully consider the consequences of getting involved with him. But Richard's words were impossible to ignore. What if Jack's past really was as dangerous as he made it sound? What if he was hiding things from her for a reason?

The sound of the shower turning on interrupted her thoughts, and she glanced toward the bathroom. Jack would be awake soon, and she would have to face him. She couldn't keep ignoring the questions that haunted her. But did she have the strength to confront him? Could she handle the truth, whatever it might be?

Her hand trembled as she set the phone down, trying to steady herself. She needed to talk to Jack, needed to understand what he had gotten himself into. But at the same time, part of her was terrified of what she might uncover.

Before she could come to any decision, the bathroom door opened, and Jack stepped out, his damp hair falling in soft waves around his face. His eyes locked onto hers, and for a moment, they simply stared at each other, as if time had slowed.

"Good morning," he said, his voice low and husky, his gaze sweeping over her.

"Good morning," she replied, forcing a smile despite the storm raging inside her.

Jack didn't seem to notice her internal struggle. He walked towards her, his arms reaching out to pull her close, but Emma hesitated, stepping back slightly. She needed to say something, needed to confront him, but the words wouldn't come. Instead, she just stared at him, her heart pounding in her chest.

Jack frowned slightly, his brows furrowing in concern. "Emma, what's wrong?"

"I... I need to ask you something," she said, her voice barely above a whisper. "About your past."

He sighed, the tension in his shoulders tightening. "I told you everything."

"Did you?" Emma asked, her gaze locking onto his. "Richard Holloway came to see me yesterday. He said things about you, about your past... things you haven't told me."

Jack's face tightened at the mention of Richard's name, and Emma saw something flash in his eyes—a flicker of discomfort. "What did he tell you?"

"That you're involved with people from the criminal underworld. That you've made enemies who will stop at nothing to get to you—and to anyone you care about."

Jack's silence spoke volumes. Emma's heart sank as she waited for him to speak. Finally, he exhaled sharply, running a hand through his hair.

"I didn't want you to be involved in this," he said, his voice strained. "It's not something I can just walk away from. It's too dangerous. But I thought... I thought you should be safe, not dragged into it."

"And now?" Emma asked softly. "What happens now, Jack?"

He stepped closer to her, his eyes full of regret and raw emotion. "Now... I don't want to lose you. I'll do whatever it takes to keep you safe. But I need you to understand—this is my fight, not yours."

Emma's heart wavered as she looked into his eyes, seeing the conflict within him. She had always known Jack was hiding something, but now she was faced with a choice that could change everything.

Could she really stay by his side, knowing the dangers he was bringing into her life?

Or was it time to walk away, before it was too late?

Chapter 110: The Calm Before The Storm

"The best way to predict the future is to create it." — Abraham Lincoln

The tension between Emma and Jack was palpable. As much as she wanted to trust him, as much as she wanted to believe in their future together, she couldn't ignore the weight of the secrets he was still keeping. Every conversation seemed to deepen the divide between them, pulling them further apart despite the intensity of their attraction.

Jack had always been the kind of man who lived in the shadows, elusive and impossible to pin down. But now, it felt like the walls were closing in. Richard Holloway's words lingered in Emma's mind, like a shadow she couldn't outrun.

Was it possible to love someone and still fear them?

As the days passed, Emma's internal struggle grew. She wanted to confront Jack, to demand the truth about his past, but a part of her feared that doing so would tear everything apart. She had already seen the cracks forming between them, and the last thing she wanted was for him to shut her out completely.

The phone rang, pulling Emma out of her spiraling thoughts. She glanced at the screen, her heart skipping a beat when she saw the name.

It was Richard Holloway.

Against her better judgment, she picked up the phone.

"Richard," she said, her voice guarded.

"Ms. Carter, I'm sorry to disturb you," Richard's voice was calm, but there was an edge to it that Emma couldn't ignore. "I thought you should know that things are escalating. Jack's enemies... they're getting closer."

Emma's stomach dropped. "What do you mean, 'getting closer'?"

"I've had some intel," Richard continued, his tone grave. "There are people looking for him, people who aren't afraid to get their hands dirty. And now, they know about you."

Emma felt a chill run down her spine. "What do they want from me?"

"I don't know," Richard replied. "But it's only a matter of time before they come for you. And when they do, I'm afraid you won't be able to protect yourself. You're in way over your head, Emma."

Her grip on the phone tightened, her pulse quickening. "I don't need your warnings, Richard."

"I'm just trying to keep you safe," he said, the urgency in his voice escalating. "Jack can't protect you from everything. You need to get out of this before it's too late."

Before Emma could respond, the line went dead.

Her mind raced as she stood there, staring at the phone in her hand. The man she loved, the man she had fallen for, was tangled up in a world of danger and deceit that she could never truly understand. And now, she was caught in the middle of it, no matter how hard she tried to distance herself.

The sound of Jack's voice from the doorway startled her.

"Emma?"

She turned to see him standing there, looking concerned. His expression softened when he saw the look on her face.

"What's going on?" he asked, stepping closer.

Emma swallowed hard, trying to push down the flood of emotions threatening to overwhelm her. "Richard called. He said things are escalating. That they know about me."

Jack's face hardened, his jaw clenching. "I told you, I don't want you involved in this."

"I never asked for this," Emma replied, her voice shaking. "I didn't ask to be dragged into your mess, Jack. But now I'm here, and I can't just walk away from it."

Jack closed the distance between them, his hands gently taking hers in his. "You don't have to be a part of this. You don't have to stay. I can make sure you're safe."

"But you can't," Emma whispered, her heart breaking. "You can't protect me from everything. And I can't live like this, constantly wondering when it'll all come crashing down."

Jack's eyes darkened, a flicker of pain flashing across his features. "I don't want to lose you, Emma. But I can't walk away from this. It's who I am. I can't just erase my past."

"I know you can't," Emma said softly. "But I don't want to lose myself in it, Jack. I don't want to become part of this world. I can't handle the fear, the constant danger, the secrets. I need something real, something that isn't built on lies."

The words hung heavy between them, the silence stretching for what felt like an eternity. Emma could see the conflict in Jack's eyes—the battle between his love for her and the dark world that had always been a part of him.

"I don't want to be the person who drags you down," Jack finally said, his voice barely above a whisper. "I never wanted this for you."

"I don't want to be the person who drags you down either," Emma replied, tears welling in her eyes. "But we can't keep pretending everything is fine. It's not. And if you really love me, you'll let me go."

Jack's expression faltered, his hand reaching out to gently cup her cheek. "I can't let you go, Emma."

But Emma knew, deep down, that it wasn't a question of whether he could or couldn't. It was a question of whether he would.

The days that followed were a blur. Emma tried to throw herself into work, to ignore the constant unease gnawing at her. But every time she closed her eyes, she saw Jack's face—torn between love and guilt, a man who had been broken by the choices he had made long before she came into his life.

And the more she thought about it, the more she realized that she couldn't change him. She couldn't make him let go of his past any more than he could make her forget who she was. They were from two different worlds, and no matter how much passion they shared, no matter how much chemistry there was between them, they were still divided by an unbridgeable chasm.

One night, as Emma stood by the window, watching the city lights flicker in the distance, she heard a soft knock at the door. Her heart skipped a beat, and she knew, without looking, that it was Jack.

She opened the door, her breath catching when she saw him standing there. His eyes were filled with something she couldn't quite name—something raw, something desperate.

"I can't lose you, Emma," he said, his voice hoarse.

Emma took a deep breath, her mind racing. "You already have."

With those words, Emma stepped back, closing the door between them. And as the sound of his footsteps faded down the hallway, she knew that it was over. She had made her choice, and the truth was, she couldn't be part of Jack's world anymore.

The love they had shared would always remain, but she couldn't stay. Not with the constant fear, the secrets, the lies.

She wasn't afraid of him—she was afraid of what she was becoming.

Chapter 111: The Tipping Point

"When you stand at the edge, you have two choices: jump or step back." — Unknown

The morning light filtered softly through the curtains, casting a warm glow across the room. Emma sat at the small kitchen table, her hands wrapped around a mug of coffee that had gone cold long ago. The silence in the apartment was deafening. There was no sound of Jack's footsteps, no soft murmur of his voice, no comforting presence beside her. It felt as though an entire world had crumbled in the wake of their last conversation.

She hadn't expected things to end this way—so abruptly, so painfully. But now that it had, there was a strange sense of finality settling into her bones. She had made the decision, and though it hurt, she knew it was the right one. Jack's world, his past, his tangled web of secrets—it was too much.

As much as she had loved him, the fear of losing herself had begun to outweigh everything else. She couldn't continue walking this tightrope between love and danger. Something had to give, and she had let go.

Her phone buzzed across the table, pulling her out of her thoughts. With a deep sigh, she picked it up, already knowing who it was. Jack.

She stared at the screen for a long moment, her thumb hovering over the 'answer' button. Part of her wanted to pick up, to hear his voice, to feel his hands on her again. But another part of her—the part that had been pushed to the edge—knew that this was the moment. She had to let go.

Reluctantly, she pressed 'decline.'

The phone buzzed again almost immediately. This time, she didn't even look at it. She let it ring, her heart hammering in her chest.

Minutes passed, and the ringing stopped. But instead of feeling relief, Emma felt a growing emptiness inside. The silence between them had stretched too far, and it was starting to suffocate her. She was alone, and it was terrifying.

But that terror was nothing compared to what Jack must have been feeling. She could only imagine the conflict and pain he was going through, but she couldn't fix it anymore. He had to fix it himself.

The clock on the wall ticked steadily, each second dragging on as if mocking her. She tried to focus, to distract herself with something, anything, but the memories of Jack, of their nights together, flooded her mind. The heated kisses, the passionate embraces, the promises made in the dark—it all felt like a lifetime ago.

Her thoughts were interrupted by another knock at the door.

This time, her heart skipped a beat. She didn't need to guess who it was. She stood, her legs shaky as she moved toward the door. There was no turning back now.

Emma opened it slowly, almost hesitantly, and Jack stood there, his figure silhouetted against the dim hallway light. His face was drawn, his eyes tired and full of emotion. His gaze met hers, and for a moment, neither of them spoke.

He took a step forward, and she instinctively stepped back. The tension between them was unbearable, thick in the air like a storm waiting to break.

"Emma," he said, his voice quiet but filled with rawness. "Please... I need to talk to you."

She swallowed hard, her throat tight. "There's nothing more to say, Jack."

"Don't do this," he pleaded, his voice cracking. "Don't walk away from me. I can't... I can't lose you."

She shook her head, her chest tightening with each word. "You're not the only one with something to lose. I'm not the one who chose this life. I never asked for any of this."

"I didn't choose it either," Jack's words came out almost like a confession. "But I've been living with it for so long, I didn't think about the cost until it was too late. Until you... until us."

Emma's heart ached at the sincerity in his voice, but it wasn't enough. Not anymore. She had to protect herself. She had to protect her heart.

"I'm not like you, Jack," she whispered, her voice trembling. "I can't live in the shadows, constantly looking over my shoulder, wondering who's going to come after us next. I can't keep pretending that everything will be okay."

Jack stepped forward again, his hands reaching for her, but she held up her palms, stopping him.

"Please, just listen," Emma said, her breath shaky. "I love you. God, I love you. But I'm drowning in all of this. And I don't think I can breathe anymore."

Jack's face crumpled, his hands falling to his sides in defeat. "I never wanted to put you in this position, Emma. I never wanted to hurt you."

"I know you didn't," she whispered. "But the pain is still there. And I can't keep ignoring it. I need space. I need time to figure out who I am without you."

The silence stretched between them, suffocating and thick. Jack didn't say anything for a long time. He simply stood there, staring at her as if trying to find something—an answer, a reason to keep fighting.

Finally, he spoke, his voice hoarse. "I understand. But if you change your mind... if you ever need me, I'll be here."

Emma didn't know what to say. The words caught in her throat, and she could feel the ache in her chest deepening. But she nodded, her eyes brimming with unshed tears.

"Goodbye, Jack."

She closed the door softly, the sound of it clicking shut echoing in her ears.

And with that, she let go.

The days that followed were quieter than Emma had expected. She spent the first few days in a haze of emotions—grief, anger, regret. But eventually, the noise began to fade, replaced by a strange sense of peace. She still missed him, still felt the ache of his absence in every corner of her life. But she also felt a growing sense of freedom.

The freedom to live her life on her own terms. The freedom to rediscover who she was before Jack, before the chaos and the danger.

It wasn't easy, and it wasn't without its moments of doubt. But it was hers.

And that, for now, was enough.

Chapter 112: The Final Showdown

"Sometimes, the only way to win is to walk away. But sometimes, the only way to survive is to fight." — Unknown

The atmosphere in Jack's penthouse had shifted, a subtle but undeniable tension hanging in the air. Emma stood by the large windows overlooking the city, the cool night breeze brushing her skin as she watched the lights flicker below. The weight of the last few days—the secrets, the uncertainty—pressed heavily on her chest. She could feel the walls closing in, yet Jack remained close, his presence both comforting and unsettling at once.

It was hard to ignore the way things had shifted between them. Every kiss now carried a layer of desperation, every touch laden with unspoken questions. Their connection had always been intense, but now it was like a dangerous dance, where each step was calculated, each word carefully chosen, and every silence filled with anticipation.

"Emma," Jack's voice came from behind her, low and steady, but she could hear the strain in it. She turned, her gaze meeting his. He had that familiar look in his eyes, the one that made her feel like he was reading her every thought.

"What is it?" she asked softly, though the words felt hollow in the stillness.

"I don't want to do this anymore," Jack confessed, stepping closer to her. His eyes were dark, almost unreadable, but there was a vulnerability there that she hadn't seen in a long time. "I don't want to keep pretending."

Emma's heart skipped a beat. Pretending? "What do you mean?"

Jack took another step, closing the distance between them. His hand reached for hers, his fingers gently brushing against her palm before he entwined them together. "I've spent so much time trying to protect you from my past, from the things I've done, that I've forgotten what it means to just be with you in the present. To be real."

Emma's breath hitched. She knew there was more. She could feel it in the way he held her hand, the way he looked at her like she was something sacred and irreparably flawed at the same time.

"I need you to trust me," Jack continued, his voice barely a whisper now, a breath against her ear. "I know I've failed you before. I can't change that. But what I can do is fight for us. Fight for you."

Emma's mind was spinning. Was this a turning point, or another empty promise that would eventually fall apart? She had to be honest with herself: her heart wanted to believe him, but her mind was still tangled in the web of lies and doubts.

"You say that, Jack," she murmured, looking down at their hands, still tightly clasped together. "But how do I know that it's real? How do I know that you won't just walk away again, like you did before?"

Jack's thumb gently stroked the back of her hand, a soothing motion that didn't quite mask the underlying tension. "I don't know, Emma. But I'm not asking for you to have all the answers. I'm asking you to take a leap of faith with me. For us."

Her pulse quickened. Was he asking for too much? She wasn't sure. She had always been a fighter, someone who believed in love despite the odds. But this... this was different. The stakes felt higher, the risks greater. Yet, in that moment, standing in front of him, with the weight of their past hanging between them, she realised she didn't want to walk away. Not without giving it one last chance.

"Okay," she said finally, her voice trembling just slightly, but with determination. "Okay, Jack. I'll try. I'll try to trust you again."

Relief washed over his face, and his lips curved into the faintest smile. But it was the look in his eyes that spoke louder than anything else. She saw the vulnerability there, the longing, and the hope. He wasn't asking for a perfect relationship. He was asking for a chance.

Without another word, Jack closed the gap between them, his lips capturing hers in a kiss that was desperate and tender, fiery and gentle all at once. Emma's heart raced as she kissed him back, her hands finding their way to his chest, feeling the rapid beat of his heart under her fingertips. The intensity of their connection was overwhelming, like they were both drowning in the depth of their emotions, yet still clinging to each other, desperate not to let go.

As their kiss deepened, Emma's body responded to him instinctively, the heat between them growing, the world around them fading away until there was nothing but the two of them, entangled in each other's arms. She could feel his breath on her skin, the roughness of his touch, and the way he held her like she was the only thing that mattered. For the first time in what felt like forever, the doubts and fears that had clouded her mind seemed to dissipate, replaced by the raw intensity of the moment.

She pulled back just enough to catch her breath, her chest heaving with the force of her emotions. Jack's hand slid down to her waist, pulling her closer, his lips brushing against her ear as he whispered, "I'm not letting you go, Emma. Not again."

Her heart pounded in her chest as she looked up at him, her mind racing with all the possibilities that still lay ahead. Was this the beginning of something new, or just another fleeting moment that would eventually fall apart?

There was no way to know. But for now, in this moment, she chose to believe. She chose to trust him.

And as his lips met hers again, this time with a gentleness that only seemed to intensify the passion, Emma knew that whatever happened next, they would face it together. They were tangled, their hearts intertwined, and she wasn't ready to untangle them just yet.

Chapter 113: Fractured Illusions

"The cracks in the foundation are often the places where the light shines through." — Unknown

The night was heavy with expectation as Emma made her way down the hallway toward the penthouse. Every step seemed to resonate in her mind, each one dragging her further into a maze of uncertainty. She had felt Jack's absence the moment she left his side earlier that day. Despite the tension that loomed over them after their conversation, her desire for him burned with an intensity that matched the conflicted emotions swirling inside her.

As she entered the penthouse, the familiar scent of cedarwood and citrus greeted her. The lights were dim, casting long shadows across the open space. She could hear the soft hum of the city below, but tonight, it felt distant, as though the world had faded away, leaving only the quiet ache in her chest and the racing of her heart.

Jack was there, leaning against the kitchen counter, his eyes locked on her the moment she stepped inside. His expression was unreadable, yet something in his gaze held an unspoken apology, a silent plea for understanding.

"Emma," he said her name softly, his voice low but thick with emotion. "We need to talk."

She closed the door behind her, her eyes not leaving his. The weight of his words hung in the air like a delicate thread, ready to snap under the smallest tug. She could feel the heat rising between them, an invisible barrier she was reluctant to cross.

"What do we need to talk about, Jack?" Emma's voice was steady, but her mind raced with questions she wasn't sure she was ready to ask. "Is it about Victoria? Or the secrets you've been keeping from me?"

Jack pushed away from the counter, his movements slow and deliberate, as though he were carefully considering every step. When he finally spoke, his voice was filled with a quiet intensity. "It's about us, Emma. About what we have and where we're headed. I can't keep pretending that everything is as it seems, not when you deserve the truth."

Emma swallowed hard, feeling the heat rise to her cheeks. The truth. It was the one thing she had been craving from him all along, but now, in the face of it, she wasn't sure if she was ready to hear it. She had already allowed herself to be swept away by him—his charm, his passion, his promises. But now, that beautiful illusion seemed to be crumbling, and she was left wondering if anything he had told her was ever real.

"I don't want to lose you, Emma," Jack continued, his voice barely above a whisper as he took a step closer. "But I need you to understand something. I'm not the man you think I am. And I never have been."

Emma felt the ground beneath her shift, her heart racing as she processed his words. "What are you saying?" she asked, her voice trembling slightly.

Jack's hand found hers, his touch warm and grounding, but the look in his eyes told her that whatever he was about to say would change everything. "I've been living a lie," he confessed, his thumb brushing over her knuckles. "Not just with you, but with everyone. My life isn't the fairytale you've imagined. It's a maze of choices I've made, some good, some bad, and some I'll regret forever."

The confession hung in the air between them, thick and heavy. Emma could feel her chest tightening, the rush of emotions nearly suffocating her as she tried to make sense of what he was saying. She wanted to pull away, to retreat into the safety of the unknown, but her body betrayed her. The pull she felt toward him was magnetic, and despite the storm brewing inside her, she couldn't look away.

"Jack..." she began, but her voice faltered as she tried to find the right words. "Why didn't you tell me? Why hide everything from me?"

Jack's gaze softened, a flicker of guilt flashing in his eyes. "I thought I was protecting you. From my past, from the darkness that's always followed me. I thought if I kept it buried, I could give us something better. But I've been fooling myself." He paused, swallowing hard before continuing. "You deserve more than that, Emma. You deserve the truth, even if it shatters everything we've built."

Her heart ached, the weight of his confession pressing down on her chest. She had known there was more to Jack than he had let on, but hearing him admit it out loud made it all the more real. The walls that had once seemed so impenetrable between them now seemed fragile, as though one wrong move could bring them both crashing down.

"I want to know the truth, Jack," she whispered, her voice breaking with the intensity of her emotions. "Even if it scares me."

Jack closed the distance between them, his hands cupping her face gently. "You won't like it," he said softly, his thumb brushing across her lower lip. "But I'll tell you everything. All of it."

Emma felt her breath catch in her throat as she stared into his eyes, searching for the man she had fallen for, the man she still wanted to believe in. But the man before her was a stranger in many ways, and the truth he was about to reveal could shatter everything.

"Tell me," she urged, her voice barely above a whisper, her pulse quickening with anticipation.

Jack hesitated for a moment, as though weighing the consequences of his words. "I wasn't always this...successful," he began, his voice laced with regret. "There was a time when I was deep in the world of organized crime. I was involved in things I'm not proud of—things that still haunt me. The money, the power, the influence—it all came at a cost. I thought I could escape it, but it's never really gone away. And when I met you, Emma, I thought I could leave it behind for good."

The confession was like a blow to the stomach. Emma felt the air leave her lungs as she processed his words, the magnitude of what he was saying sinking in. "You were... involved in that world?" she whispered, her voice trembling.

Jack nodded, his eyes never leaving hers. "I've made a lot of mistakes, Emma. I've hurt people. I've done things I wish I could take back. But I don't want that life anymore. I want you. And I'll do whatever it takes to make sure that past stays buried. But I can't protect you from it forever."

Emma felt her knees go weak, her body trembling with a mixture of shock and confusion. She had never imagined Jack's past could be so dark, so dangerous. But even as fear bubbled to the surface, something inside her stirred—something fierce and defiant. She wasn't going to let him go without a fight. Not when the pull between them was still so undeniable.

"I don't know what to say," she murmured, her voice barely audible. "This is... a lot."

Jack stepped closer, his body pressed against hers, and for a moment, they were both silent, letting the weight of the moment settle over them. He could feel her heart racing, hear the shakiness in her breath as she tried to process what he had just revealed.

"I know," he said softly. "But no matter what, Emma, I'm not giving up on us. On you. I can't."

Her gaze locked with his, and for a fleeting moment, all the chaos seemed to fade away. It was just the two of them—tangled in their desires, in their pasts, in the fragile thread of hope that held them together.

"I'm not going anywhere, Jack," she whispered, her voice filled with determination. "I'll fight for us. For you. For this."

And in that moment, despite the uncertainty, despite the weight of the truth hanging between them, Emma knew one thing for certain: they were both in this together, for better or for worse.

Chapter 114: The Breaking Point

"We are all fragile. All of us, hanging by a thread." — Jodi Picoult

Emma's eyes flickered open to the soft light of early morning. The sun had just begun its ascent, spilling delicate golden rays across the penthouse. The air, still cool and fresh, clung to her skin, a contrast to the heated tension that had been building between her and Jack for what seemed like forever. Her thoughts were swirling, and the unresolved knot in her chest tightened with every passing second.

She glanced beside her at Jack, his chest rising and falling steadily in his sleep. For all the raw passion that existed between them, it felt like something was still missing. A connection that wasn't quite complete. Was it the lingering doubts she had about their future? The secrets buried deep within Jack's past? Or was it her own fears, rising up to meet her when she allowed herself to truly feel?

She lay there for a few moments, the weight of her own thoughts heavy in the air. She wanted nothing more than to ignore it all. To dive deeper into the intense physical connection they had, to lose herself in the heat of his touch. But a small part of her wanted answers—answers that she wasn't sure if Jack could provide.

The sound of a phone vibrating on the nightstand broke the silence, causing Emma to jump slightly. She turned her head to look at Jack, but he remained oblivious, his body turned away from her. She sighed, reaching over to grab the phone and glanced at the screen. It was a message from an unknown number.

"We need to talk."

Her stomach dropped. The words were simple, but they felt like a threat. Who could this be? Who knew about her and Jack, and why would they want to talk?

Curiosity gnawed at her. As much as she wanted to toss the phone aside and forget about it, she couldn't. She felt the pull of the mystery—of what it could mean for everything that had been building between her and Jack.

She slid out of bed carefully, trying not to disturb him, and padded barefoot to the living room. Her mind was racing, and her pulse quickened as she sat on the plush sofa, staring at the message.

Her fingers hovered over the screen, wondering if she should respond or simply ignore it. But the pull of the unknown, of what this could reveal, kept her from walking away. She hesitated for a moment before typing a quick reply.

"Who is this?"

It didn't take long for the reply to come through.

"Someone who knows the truth."

The answer sent a chill down her spine. Truth? What truth?

She stood up, pacing the room, trying to steady the trembling in her hands. Her mind was swirling with a thousand questions—about Jack, about herself, about everything that had led them to this point. She had always thought she could trust him. But now? Doubt had crept into her heart like an uninvited guest.

As if on cue, Jack entered the room, his hair tousled, a faint stubble darkening his jaw. His gaze swept over her with concern, noticing immediately that something was off.

"Everything okay?" he asked, his voice still thick with sleep.

Emma quickly shoved the phone into her pocket, forcing a smile that didn't quite reach her eyes. "Yeah, just... thinking."

He nodded slowly, stepping closer to her. His eyes softened as he cupped her cheek, a gentle caress that had the power to ground her, even if just for a moment. But she couldn't shake the feeling that something was off. The tension between them had never felt this heavy.

"Emma," he said, his voice low, "I know you have doubts. I see it in your eyes. And I don't blame you. I've never been the easiest person to trust."

She swallowed, his words cutting deeper than she expected. Her own doubts were bubbling to the surface, but she didn't want to admit them aloud. Not yet. She needed to be sure—sure of herself, sure of him.

"You don't have to explain yourself, Jack," she said quietly, meeting his gaze. "But I need to understand... everything. Not just the surface, but the things you've been keeping from me."

His expression faltered, and for the first time, Emma saw a crack in his carefully constructed exterior. She could feel the weight of his past pressing on him, and for the first time, she felt the distance that had always existed between them.

"I want to tell you," Jack whispered, his voice strained, "but some things... they're not easy to say."

The vulnerability in his eyes sent a sharp pang through Emma's chest. Her heart ached for him, for the man he was, and for the man she wasn't sure she could trust completely. She reached up to touch his face, her fingers tracing his jawline with tenderness.

"You don't have to carry this alone, Jack," she murmured, her voice thick with emotion. "Whatever it is... I want to be there for you."

The words hung in the air between them, heavy with unspoken promises. He didn't respond immediately. Instead, he leaned down and kissed her softly, a kiss that spoke volumes—a kiss that told her that, in that moment, they could forget everything else.

But as they pulled apart, the phone buzzed again.

Emma's heart skipped a beat, and Jack's eyes flickered to the screen.

"What is it?" he asked, his expression guarded.

With a deep breath, she pulled the phone from her pocket and handed it to him. "It's a message. From someone who knows something I don't."

Jack's eyes scanned the message, and his face went pale. For a split second, Emma could see the shift in him—a quiet panic that he had been holding at bay.

"This isn't good," he muttered, his jaw tight.

"What isn't good?" Emma demanded, stepping closer, her anxiety mounting.

He didn't look at her immediately, but when he finally met her gaze, there was a weight in his eyes that she had never seen before.

"It's about my past," Jack said quietly. "Things I thought I left behind."

Emma stood frozen, her mind spinning. For all the passion, the heat, the intimacy they had shared, was it all a lie? Was there something darker lurking in Jack's past that could destroy everything they had?

The world around her seemed to shrink, the room growing colder as her pulse quickened. What truth had Jack been hiding? And how much of it was she willing to face?

As the tension between them thickened, Emma realized one thing: their future was about to change. The question was whether they could survive the storm that was coming, or if the past would finally tear them apart.

Chapter 115: Shattered Dreams

"The truth is rarely pure and never simple." — Oscar Wilde

The silence between Emma and Jack seemed to stretch for an eternity. As she watched him, her mind reeled from his cryptic words. His past—whatever it was—was now crashing into their present, threatening to tear apart everything they had fought so hard to build. The love, the passion, the deep connection they shared—all of it now felt fragile.

"Jack," she whispered, her voice breaking the silence, "you need to tell me what's going on. I can't keep dancing around this. Not anymore."

He stood motionless, his eyes darkening with the weight of unspoken truths. For a long time, he didn't say anything. Instead, he looked down at his hands, as if searching for the right words—or perhaps avoiding them altogether. Emma's heart clenched. She could feel his hesitation, but she could also sense his internal battle. The wall he had so carefully constructed between his past and present was crumbling, piece by piece.

Finally, he sighed deeply, the sound heavy with resignation. "I never wanted to drag you into this, Emma," Jack muttered, his voice low. "But you're already in it. I can't protect you from the truth anymore."

Emma took a step closer, her heart racing with both fear and anticipation. "What truth, Jack?"

He hesitated again, his gaze flicking briefly to the phone in her hand. "The person messaging you... they know things about me. About my past. Things that I've kept hidden for a long time."

The air in the room seemed to thicken, and Emma felt her stomach tighten. "What kind of things?" she asked, her voice trembling, but she couldn't help it. The unknown, the dark secrets Jack had been carrying, were like a storm brewing in the distance, ready to break.

He turned away, pacing a few steps before stopping, running a hand through his hair. "Things I did—people I hurt. I was involved in some dangerous business before we met, Emma. People who don't forget easily." His voice dropped to a whisper. "And now, they're trying to drag me back into it."

Emma's mind reeled. "You've been involved in something criminal?"

Jack nodded slowly, his jaw tightening. "Yes. I tried to leave it behind. I thought I was free. But now... I think I might be wrong. Whoever this person is, they're trying to get something from me—something I thought I'd left in the past."

Emma's breath caught in her throat. "Jack... why didn't you tell me?"

He met her gaze, his eyes full of regret and something else—fear, vulnerability. "I couldn't. I wanted to protect you. I didn't want to bring that darkness into your life. You deserve better than this."

Emma took a deep breath, feeling the weight of the decision ahead. She had always known that Jack was complicated—his past, his secrets, the things he kept hidden from the world. But this? This was something she hadn't prepared for.

"I love you," she said softly, her voice trembling with emotion. "And I want to help you, Jack. But you need to let me in. We can't keep running from this. We need to face whatever's coming together."

Jack's eyes softened at her words, and for a moment, she saw the real him—vulnerable, scared, and raw. "I don't know how to let you in, Emma. I've built walls for so long, it's hard to break them down."

Emma reached for him, her fingers brushing his arm gently. "It's okay. We'll figure it out together. You don't have to do this alone."

Jack's gaze dropped to her lips, and in that moment, she could see the conflict within him. He was torn between the need to protect her and the overwhelming desire to pull her closer. To feel her warmth, her love. To lose himself in the one thing he could trust.

Without another word, he kissed her—deep and slow, as if to savor the moment before everything changed. The kiss was a silent promise, a declaration that despite the storm brewing around them, they would stand together.

As they pulled apart, the phone buzzed again. This time, it was a message from the mysterious contact.

"Meet me tonight. I'm sending someone to your location. Don't bring anyone else. It's time to settle the score."

Jack's face hardened as he read the message. "They're not wasting any time," he muttered under his breath. "I think they're going to make their move tonight."

Emma's heart pounded in her chest. The sense of danger, of impending doom, was thick in the air. But she refused to be afraid. Not now, not with Jack. Whatever was waiting for them, they would face it head-on.

"We'll deal with it, together," she said, her voice steady.

Jack nodded, his expression resolute. "I'm not going to let them hurt you, Emma. Whatever it takes."

Her pulse quickened at the intensity in his voice. For all the fear she felt, there was something undeniably thrilling about standing by his side, about facing the unknown with him. The uncertainty of it all heightened the desire, the tension that pulsed between them. But there was no turning back now. Whatever Jack's past held, they would confront it—and hopefully, come out stronger on the other side.

As the evening drew closer, Emma and Jack prepared themselves for whatever lay ahead. The evening promised to be pivotal. The future, uncertain and fraught with danger, lay in the shadows, waiting for them to step into it.

They shared one last, lingering kiss before Jack grabbed his jacket, and Emma, with a sense of both anticipation and dread, followed him out the door.

Chapter 116: Fleeting Moments

The night air clung to Emma's skin like a weight, a tangible reminder of the storm that was brewing. Her steps were slow as she followed Jack through the dimly lit streets, the tension between them thick and palpable. The city, once a place of freedom and escape, now felt more like a labyrinth with no exit.

Jack had always been the one to protect her, to keep her in the dark when it came to the dangers surrounding him. But now, as they walked side by side, she could feel the heaviness of the truth settling between them, threatening to tear them apart. She had asked him for honesty, for clarity, and now, as they approached the meeting point, Emma could feel the rawness of everything he had kept hidden.

"Jack," she said quietly, her voice barely a whisper against the cool breeze. "Are you sure this is the right thing to do?"

Jack's grip on her hand tightened. "I don't know anymore, Emma. But we don't have a choice. They're coming for me, and if they're coming for me, they're coming for you too." His voice was low, strained, as though the words were slipping out of him like water through his fingers.

Emma's stomach tightened at the thought. She had always known there was more to Jack's story, more to the man who had swept her off her feet with his charm and intensity. But nothing had prepared her for the reality of his past, or the price they would both pay for the secrets he had kept buried.

They reached a narrow alley, the shadows stretching long and deep, obscuring the world beyond. Emma felt the hairs on the back of her neck rise as Jack led her deeper into the darkness, his face grim. The air felt heavy here, oppressive, as though the weight of everything that had led them to this moment was pressing down on her chest.

The silence was broken by the sound of footsteps. They weren't alone.

A man stepped into the alley, his figure tall and imposing, his face obscured by the hood of his jacket. Emma instinctively reached for Jack's hand, her fingers trembling. Jack didn't flinch. He stood tall, his expression unreadable as the man approached them.

"You're late," Jack said, his voice sharp, but with an edge of something darker beneath it.

The man didn't respond at first. Instead, he pulled out a small device from his pocket and pressed a button. The sound of a door opening echoed through the alley. Jack nodded toward the door, his eyes still locked on the stranger. "After you," he said, his voice cold.

Without another word, the man turned and walked toward the entrance, Jack and Emma following close behind. The door closed silently behind them, sealing them into the dimly lit room.

The interior was stark—concrete walls, a single light hanging overhead, casting harsh shadows on the floor. In the center of the room stood a man Emma had only heard about but never met: Viktor, the name Jack had mentioned in hushed tones. A man whose reach seemed to extend far beyond anything Emma had imagined.

Viktor didn't waste time with pleasantries. His cold, calculating gaze swept over Emma before landing on Jack. "You're late," he said simply, his voice devoid of emotion.

"I said we'd be here," Jack replied evenly, his hand still tightly clutching Emma's. "What do you want?"

Viktor's lips curled into a smile, though there was nothing warm about it. "What I want, Jack, is for you to make good on your promises. The ones you've been running from. The ones you've been hiding from everyone, including her." His gaze flicked briefly to Emma, and her stomach twisted.

Jack's expression remained impassive, but Emma could see the tension in his jaw, the barely contained fury simmering beneath the surface.

"We're done here, Viktor," Jack said, his voice firm. "I've paid my dues. You know that. I'm not going back."

Viktor's eyes narrowed. "I don't think you understand, Jack. There are consequences for running away from your debts. You think you can just walk away from this life? You think you can just walk away from *me*?"

Emma's pulse quickened at the venom in Viktor's voice, but she stayed silent, her eyes darting between the two men. This was it—the truth of Jack's past, right here in front of her. The confrontation she had feared, the one that would change everything between them.

Jack took a step forward, his voice dropping to a dangerous low. "I made it clear, Viktor. I'm done. You want your money? Take it. But you don't get to control me anymore."

Viktor laughed, a harsh, mocking sound. "You think it's that simple? No, Jack. You're not leaving here with your freedom intact. You owe me more than money. You owe me your loyalty, your trust. And you're going to give me that, one way or another."

Emma felt a chill run down her spine. The air around them crackled with tension, and she could feel the weight of Viktor's words sinking in. Jack had been running, hiding, and now it seemed like there was no way out.

Jack's hand squeezed hers, a silent promise that he would protect her no matter what. "I'm not giving you anything, Viktor," he said, his voice unwavering. "I've paid my price. And I'm done. You don't get to dictate my life anymore."

Viktor's eyes flicked to Emma again, and a knowing smile tugged at the corners of his lips. "We'll see about that. You can run, Jack. But the past always catches up."

He turned and motioned toward the door. "I'll give you one more chance to make things right. But remember—there's a price for everything."

With that, he was gone, leaving Jack and Emma standing in the cold, empty room, the weight of the confrontation settling like a storm cloud between them.

Emma turned to Jack, her heart racing. "What does he mean, Jack? What's going to happen now?"

Jack's face was unreadable as he walked toward the door. "It's not over, Emma. Not by a long shot."

Chapter 117: A Reckoning of the Heart

"Sometimes, the hardest thing and the right thing are the same."
— The Fray

The silence in the room was suffocating. Every corner seemed to press in on Emma as she stood, still gripping Jack's hand, her mind swirling with questions and fears she hadn't yet voiced. Viktor's words echoed in her mind, repeating like a broken record. No matter how many times she tried to push them away, they lingered, threatening to unravel everything she thought she knew about Jack and the life they were trying to build together.

Jack had always been her rock, a man who had the answers to everything, a man who made her feel invincible. But standing here now, in this dimly lit room with the weight of Viktor's threats hanging heavily between them, Emma wasn't so sure of anything anymore.

Jack's jaw was clenched, his body tense with the raw energy of a man who had already fought too many battles. His eyes were dark, distant, as though he was somewhere far away, reliving moments from a past he would never fully escape.

"Jack..." Emma's voice trembled slightly, but she steadied herself. This was it—the moment she needed to know everything. "What is it with you and Viktor? Why does he want so much from you?"

Jack turned toward her slowly, his eyes meeting hers with a look she could barely decipher. "I didn't want you to find out like this. I didn't want you to see me like this." His voice cracked at the end, a vulnerable crack in the otherwise impenetrable façade he had built around himself.

Emma took a step toward him, her heart breaking at the sorrow and guilt she saw in his eyes. "You don't have to protect me anymore, Jack. I'm not going to leave you just because of your past. But you have to let me in. I need to know what's going on, what's really happening."

Jack ran a hand through his hair, pacing in the small, oppressive space of the room. He opened his mouth to speak, but no words came out at first. He was struggling with something deep inside him, something he had never shared with anyone before.

"I made a deal with Viktor years ago," Jack finally said, his voice low and filled with regret. "It wasn't supposed to get this complicated. I thought I could handle it, thought I could control it. But then... then things spiraled. And now he wants more than just the money I owe him. He wants power. And he's willing to use whatever he can to get it."

Emma's heart skipped a beat. "What do you mean, power? What does he want from you, Jack?"

Jack met her gaze, his eyes dark and full of the secrets he had been carrying for so long. "He wants control over me, Emma. Control over my future, my decisions. Everything I've built—everything I've worked for—he's threatening to take it all away if I don't give him what he wants. And he's using you to get it."

Emma's breath caught in her throat. "Me? How?"

Jack's eyes softened, but the intensity in them remained. "He knows you're important to me. He knows that you're the one thing I'll fight for, the one thing I won't let go of. He's using that against me. If I don't comply with his demands, he'll hurt you, Emma. He'll make you pay for the choices I've made."

Tears welled in Emma's eyes as the weight of Jack's words sank in. "But you said you're done with him. You promised me you're done with this life."

"I am," Jack said, his voice firm, though the uncertainty in his eyes was hard to miss. "But the past doesn't let you go so easily. Viktor has a hold on me, on everything I've worked for. And he won't let go without a fight."

Emma's mind reeled, trying to process everything she was hearing. Jack had never been anything but open with her, and yet, here he was, revealing a side of himself she hadn't known existed—one filled with darkness and danger.

"What are you going to do?" she asked, her voice barely above a whisper.

"I don't know," Jack admitted, the weight of his words hanging in the air. "I've been running from this for so long, Emma. I thought if I could just get away from him, get away from that life, everything would be fine. But now... now it's all crashing down around me."

A wave of sadness washed over Emma, mingling with the fear she had been trying so hard to suppress. Jack was strong, resilient, but even he had limits. And she could see it now, the toll this past was taking on h im.

"Jack, you don't have to face this alone," Emma said, her voice trembling with a mixture of fear and determination. She stepped closer, closing the distance between them. "I'm here. I'm not going anywhere. We'll figure this out together."

For the first time in a long while, Jack's face softened, and a small, broken smile tugged at the corner of his lips. He reached for her, pulling her into his arms, and Emma let herself fall against him, allowing herself to draw strength from his warmth, even if it was only temporary.

But just as quickly, the moment of solace slipped away. Jack pulled back slightly, his hands gripping her shoulders as he looked into her eyes. "You need to be careful, Emma. You need to understand that this doesn't just affect me—it affects you too. If Viktor gets to you, if he threatens you, I'll do whatever it takes to protect you. But it won't be easy. I won't let him win."

Emma nodded, the gravity of the situation weighing heavily on her heart. She had asked for the truth, and now she had it. The question was: could she handle it? Could she stand by Jack as his past came crashing into their lives, threatening everything they had built?

"I'm not afraid, Jack," Emma said, her voice steady despite the storm raging in her chest. "We'll face this together. We'll fight. And we'll win."

Chapter 118: The Final Embrace

"Love is not something you look for. Love is something you become." — Wayne Dyer

The air in the apartment was thick with unspoken words, the kind that twisted in the chest, making it difficult to breathe. Emma sat on the edge of the couch, her hands clasped tightly in her lap, as Jack paced across the room. His movements were sharp, almost frantic, as if he was fighting against the encroaching pressure of his past threatening to break free and ruin everything he had worked for.

Every second that passed felt like a ticking clock, and Emma could see the weight of the situation pressing down on him. She had always known Jack to be confident, unshakable in his resolve, but now... now he was unraveling, bit by bit.

Emma's heart ached for him, but at the same time, she couldn't ignore the gnawing fear in her stomach—the fear of what Viktor's involvement meant for their future. The shadows of doubt that had been slowly creeping into her mind over the last few days were now impossible to ignore. Viktor wasn't just some fleeting threat—he was a force, and one that seemed to have the power to destroy everything Jack had built, including the love they had.

"I can't keep running, Emma," Jack said, his voice rough, as though each word carried the weight of a thousand regrets. He stopped pacing and turned to face her, his eyes dark with both determination and fear. "I've tried to shut him out, but it's not enough. Viktor's never going to let go. And the longer I fight him, the more I put you at risk."

Emma stood, her heart racing in her chest as she moved closer to him. "We can fight this together, Jack. We've made it this far, haven't we? You don't have to do it alone."

Jack's gaze softened, but the weariness in his eyes didn't fade. "I've made mistakes, Emma. Big ones. And I thought I could leave that life behind, that I could keep you safe. But now it feels like it's all slipping through my fingers."

He took a step toward her, his voice quieter now, almost like a confession. "The worst part is, I don't know if I'm strong enough to face him again. I don't know if I can protect you from the chaos he's about to bring."

Her heart clenched as she reached out, cupping his face in her hands, forcing him to meet her gaze. "You've already protected me, Jack. You've been there for me through everything. And I know you'll keep fighting. But you don't have to do it alone. I'm not going any-where."

Jack's jaw tightened, and for a moment, it seemed like he was going to pull away. But then, something changed in his eyes—something raw, vulnerable—and he closed the distance between them, his lips capturing hers in a kiss that spoke of fear, desperation, and an unspo-ken promise.

Emma kissed him back with equal urgency, as if their very lives depended on it. She felt the tension in his body, the way his hands gripped her waist as though he feared she might slip away from him. She ran her hands through his hair, pulling him closer, letting him know that she wasn't going anywhere. Not now. Not ever.

They broke apart only for a moment, both breathless, their faces inches apart. "I can't lose you, Emma," Jack whispered, his voice hoarse with emotion. "You're everything to me."

"I'm not going anywhere," she reassured him, her words firm. "We're in this together."

Jack let out a heavy breath, leaning his forehead against hers. The silence between them was filled with the weight of everything unsaid—the past they both carried, the fear of the future, and the undeniable pull they had toward each other. But despite the uncertainty, Emma knew one thing for sure: she would not let him face this alone. Whatever Viktor was planning, whatever darkness lay ahead, they would face it as one.

Just then, a soft knock at the door broke the tension. Both Emma and Jack froze, their senses heightened, as if they both instinctively knew that whoever stood on the other side of that door would change everything.

"Who the hell is that?" Jack muttered under his breath, a flash of concern passing through his eyes.

Emma felt the knot of anxiety tighten in her stomach. "I don't know. But we can't ignore it."

Jack's expression hardened, his body tensing as he moved toward the door. "Stay behind me," he ordered, his voice low but commanding.

Emma nodded, stepping back, her pulse quickening with the anticipation of what might come next. She knew Jack was ready for a fight, but she wasn't sure if either of them were prepared for the storm that was about to break.

When Jack opened the door, the last person Emma expected to see stood there—Viktor. His presence was like a shadow, tall and imposing, his cold eyes scanning the room before locking onto Jack with an unreadable expression.

"Jack," Viktor said, his voice smooth but laced with a threat that made the hairs on the back of Emma's neck stand on end. "We need to talk."

Emma's heart skipped a beat as she watched Jack's posture shift, every muscle in his body becoming taut. She could see the storm brewing between them—the history, the resentment, and the shared tension that could only be the result of years of bad blood.

"What do you want, Viktor?" Jack's voice was low, icy, but there was an underlying tension that Emma could feel in her very bones.

Viktor's lips curled into a smile, though it held no warmth. "I think you know why I'm here. It's time to settle the score."

Emma swallowed hard, fear creeping into her chest as Viktor stepped inside, his gaze never leaving Jack. The moment had arrived, and Emma could feel the tension between them grow thick, electric with the promise of a confrontation that could change everything.

Chapter 119: A Heart Reclaimed

"The deepest love is often born in the most unlikely of places."
— Unknown

The tension in the room could have been cut with a knife. Viktor's presence seemed to suck the air out of the space, leaving Emma feeling like she was trapped in a storm of uncertainty. Jack's body was rigid, his eyes narrowed with the kind of cold fury that only someone with a deeply complicated history could understand. But even in the face of Viktor's imposing presence, Emma could see the flicker of vulnerability in Jack's gaze—something that made her heart ache for him.

She had never seen him like this—fighting not just for his love for her, but against his past. It was as if Viktor was the embodiment of all the demons Jack had been running from. And now, that darkness had finally caught up with him.

Viktor stepped further into the apartment, his gaze sweeping the room with calculated precision. He was like a predator, and Emma couldn't shake the feeling that they were both the prey. His gaze landed on her, a flicker of amusement in his eyes as if he knew something she didn't.

"You're brave, Emma," Viktor said, his voice smooth and taunting. "But you're also naïve. You really think you can protect him from what's coming? From me?"

Emma straightened, feeling the heat of his words, the weight of his challenge. She wasn't going to back down, not now. Not when everything she had built with Jack was at risk.

"I'm not afraid of you," she said, her voice steady despite the turmoil inside. "We're not running. We've made it this far. Jack and I, we're in this together. And no one—especially not you—can tear us apart."

Viktor's lips twitched in amusement, but there was no mirth in his expression. "You really don't know what you're up against, do you? You think this is some kind of game? That love can fix everything?"

Jack's voice cut through the tension like a blade. "This is not a game, Viktor. And you're right—love can't fix everything. But it's enough to make me stand here, face you, and end this."

Emma watched as Jack stepped forward, the air between them crackling with the intensity of their past, their history, and the force of their emotions. She could see the storm building within him, the fight that was about to break free, and for the first time, she was certain that Jack wasn't just fighting for himself—he was fighting for her.

The words Viktor spoke next were as cold as ice, the danger in his voice unmistakable. "You've always been a fool, Jack. And this time, you'll see just how costly your mistakes are. No one escapes me."

With that, Viktor's gaze shifted to Emma, locking onto her with a look that made her stomach churn. "And you, Emma. You think you're safe? You've made your choice. But the cost of that choice will be greater than you ever imagined."

A chill ran through her as his words hung in the air, sharp and dangerous. She had always known Viktor was capable of cruelty, but hearing it directed at her—at their love—made her blood run cold.

Jack's response was swift, his voice low but filled with a dark promise. "You'll regret this, Viktor. You've underestimated me. Underestimated us."

There was a flash of something dangerous in Viktor's eyes, and for a moment, Emma feared he might lash out physically. But instead, Viktor gave a low chuckle, his posture shifting from one of aggression to something far more sinister—a kind of twisted amusement.

"You think you've won, Jack? That you've conquered me?" Viktor's voice dropped to a chilling whisper. "This isn't over. Not by a long shot."

Before Emma could react, Viktor turned, heading for the door with a final glance over his shoulder. "We'll see each other again soon," he said with a smirk, his tone dripping with menace.

As the door clicked shut behind him, the room was plunged back into silence. Jack stood motionless, his back to her, his hands clenched into fists at his sides. She could feel the intensity of his emotions, the depth of his struggle, but she knew—knew in her bones—that the battle wasn't over. Not yet.

"Jack," she whispered, her voice trembling slightly. She moved toward him, placing a hand on his arm. "What now?"

He turned to face her, his expression hardened but softening the moment he saw the concern in her eyes. He reached out, pulling her into his arms as if the weight of the world was too much to carry alone. And in that moment, Emma knew that whatever Viktor was planning, she and Jack would face it together. No matter the danger. No matter the cost.

For the first time in days, she allowed herself to breathe, to hold on to the solace of his touch, knowing that this was where she belonged. In his arms. Safe.

Jack's voice was barely a whisper as he held her close. "We'll get through this, Emma. I'll make sure of it. No one's going to tear us apart."

She nodded, the heat of his promise sinking into her chest. She wanted to believe him—God, how she wanted to believe him. But a part of her, the part that had been trained by too many years of disappointment, couldn't shake the feeling that this was just the calm before the storm. That Viktor wasn't done with them yet.

But for now, all she could do was hold on. Hold on to Jack. Hold on to their love. Because no matter what came next, it was the one thing that was hers to protect.

Chapter 120: The Cost of Love

"Love is an endless act of forgiveness. Forgiveness is the key to action and freedom." — *Maya Angelou*

The night was heavy with tension. The air was thick with the unspoken words that still lingered between them, the jagged edges of Viktor's threats gnawing at Emma's mind. She couldn't sleep—not after what had just happened. Not after the way Jack had stood tall in the face of Viktor, defiant and yet vulnerable, like a man who knew that the battle was far from over.

Emma couldn't help but feel the weight of it all, pressing against her chest, making it hard to breathe. She had been so sure, so confident in her belief that love could protect them from the past. But now, she was beginning to see the cracks in that illusion. The past was never just the past. It had a way of creeping back in, forcing its way into the present, threatening everything they had built together.

Jack hadn't said much after Viktor's departure. He had pulled her into his arms, kissed her with a desperation that spoke volumes, but the silence that had followed was deafening. She could feel him, but he was distant. There was something he wasn't telling her, something about Viktor and his past that made her stomach twist with uncertainty.

She sat on the edge of the bed, her fingers tracing the edge of the sheets. The cool, silk fabric felt foreign beneath her touch, as if the comfort of their home had suddenly become a trap. Everything was changing. The future they had dreamed of—together, in love, free from the shadows of the past—seemed further out of reach with every passing moment.

Her thoughts were interrupted by the sound of footsteps in the hallway. Jack appeared in the doorway, his silhouette framed by the soft glow of the lamp behind him. He was dressed in black jeans and a dark shirt, looking every bit the man she had fallen in love with. But tonight, there was something different about him. Something guarded.

"Emma," he said softly, his voice carrying a weight that made her heart ache. "Can we talk?"

She nodded, her heart pounding in her chest. She didn't know what to expect, but she knew it was time. The silence between them had stretched on long enough.

He moved closer, sitting next to her on the bed. His hand brushed against hers, and for a moment, she thought he might pull away, but he didn't. His fingers twined with hers, the warmth of his touch grounding her in a way that nothing else could.

"I know I've been distant," Jack began, his gaze never leaving hers. "But there's something I need to tell you. Something about Viktor... about why he's come after me."

Emma's breath caught in her throat. She had known there was more to the story, but she hadn't expected this. "What do you mean?" she asked, her voice barely a whisper.

Jack sighed, his chest rising and falling with the weight of whatever was coming. "Viktor isn't just some former lover. He's... he's someone from my past. Someone I've been trying to escape for a long time."

Emma felt a chill wash over her as the pieces began to fall into place. Viktor's coldness, his threats—everything about him felt personal. "You've been running from him?" she asked, her voice trembling.

"Not just running," Jack admitted, his eyes darkening with the burden of the past. "I made mistakes. Mistakes that I thought I could bury. I thought I could outrun them. But Viktor is relentless. And he's not going to stop until he's gotten what he wants."

"What does he want, Jack?" she asked, her heart racing. She wasn't sure if she was more afraid of the answers he might give or the fact that she already knew some of them.

Jack hesitated, as though the weight of his words was too much to bear. "He wants control. Power. He's always had a hold on me, Emma. A way of making me believe that I owe him—owe him for everything he's done for me, for the way he's shaped my life. I was weak. I didn't see it back then, but I know it now."

Emma squeezed his hand, her heart aching for him. She wanted to reach into his soul and erase the pain, but she knew she couldn't. Not yet.

"You don't owe him anything, Jack," she said softly, her voice firm. "You've made your own choices. You've built your own life. Viktor may have been part of your past, but he doesn't control you anymore."

Jack's eyes flickered with uncertainty, but then he nodded, as though her words had given him a sense of clarity. "I know. But he doesn't see it that way. He's determined to make me pay for leaving him, for breaking away. And now he's targeting you, Emma. Because he knows the one thing that scares me—the one thing that could break me—is losing you."

Emma's heart swelled with emotion. "You won't lose me," she said, her voice steady despite the rising panic inside her. "Not now, not ever. We're in this together, Jack. Whatever happens, we face it together."

He nodded, a flicker of gratitude passing through his eyes. But Emma could see the fear beneath it, the fear of losing her, of not being strong enough to protect her from the past that still haunted him.

"I'll do whatever it takes to keep you safe," Jack said, his voice rough with emotion. "I swear it."

She pulled him close, pressing her lips to his, needing to feel the strength of their connection, the heat of their love. The kiss deepened, the urgency building between them, as if their bodies knew that this was a fleeting moment in time—a moment when nothing else mattered but the two of them. The kiss was a promise, a vow that they would survive whatever came their way.

But even as they kissed, Emma knew that their battle wasn't over. Viktor was still out there, watching, waiting. And she couldn't shake the feeling that things were about to get even more dangerous.

But for now, all she could do was hold on to Jack, knowing that their love was strong enough to weather whatever storm was coming.

Chapter 121: The Path Forward

"The future belongs to those who believe in the beauty of their dreams." — Eleanor Roosevelt

Emma's thoughts spiraled as she stood in the middle of the penthouse, the cool breeze sweeping through the open balcony doors. Jack was somewhere in the other room, his presence almost a tangible force, pulling her in and repelling her at the same time. She had known, deep down, that this moment would come, but now that it was here, she couldn't escape the weight of it.

Jack had done everything he could to reassure her, to prove his sincerity. But the more she tried to convince herself, the more doubt crept in, curling like a dark shadow, refusing to let go.

Victoria's words still echoed in her mind, taunting her, feeding the uncertainty. "You think you know him, but you don't. You never will."

The words of the investigator, Richard Holloway, only added more fuel to the fire. What if everything Jack had told her was a lie? What if there was more to his past, something that he had never shared with her?

She took a deep breath and walked towards the living room, where Jack was sitting on the edge of the couch, his fingers drumming lightly against the coffee table. His eyes lifted when she entered, a mixture of anticipation and anxiety clouding his gaze.

"Emma," he said softly, his voice low, yet steady.

She hesitated before speaking. "I don't know if I can do this anymore, Jack."

His expression faltered, his shoulders tightening as if he were bracing for impact. "What do you mean?"

"I mean... I don't know if I can trust you," she confessed, her voice cracking slightly as the words escaped her. "You've told me so many things, but now I don't know what to believe."

Jack stood up, his expression intense. "Emma, please—"

"No," she interrupted, holding up a hand. "You don't get to say anything just yet. I need to know everything. Every part of you that you've hidden from me. I need to know the truth—no more secrets."

He didn't speak immediately, and for a long moment, all that could be heard was the sound of the wind rustling outside, the tension between them thick enough to cut through.

Finally, Jack walked towards her, his eyes dark with something she couldn't quite name. He reached out, his fingers brushing her cheek in the gentlest of touches, a gesture that sent a shiver through her body.

"I've told you everything that matters," he said, his voice almost pleading. "But if you want the truth... if you want to know it all, then you have to be ready. Because it's not just me you'll have to confront—it's everything I've done, everything I've been."

Emma swallowed, her heart pounding in her chest. This was it. She could feel the weight of the decision pressing down on her, and yet, she couldn't bring herself to walk away.

"I'm ready," she said quietly, her voice barely above a whisper.

Without another word, Jack took her hand, leading her to the bedroom. The air between them was thick with anticipation, and as they entered the room, the world outside ceased to exist. Everything was just them, and the truth that would change everything.

As Jack closed the door behind them, the tension was palpable, the atmosphere heavy with the promise of what was to come. He turned to face her, his hands trembling slightly as he reached for the buttons of his shirt. One by one, they were undone, revealing the sculpted muscles beneath, the remnants of the man she had come to know—and the stranger she was about to meet.

"Are you sure?" he asked, his voice tight with emotion. "Once you know, there's no going back."

Emma nodded, her breath catching in her throat. This was the moment. The moment that would define them. She needed this, needed the truth, no matter how dark or twisted it might be.

Jack pulled her towards him, his lips capturing hers in a kiss that was both desperate and tender. His hands roamed over her body, igniting a fire within her that burned brighter than before. She responded in kind, her own hands pulling at the fabric of his shirt, eager to feel the warmth of his skin beneath her fingertips.

As their kiss deepened, the world outside faded into oblivion. They were no longer in a penthouse overlooking the city—they were in a universe of their own, one where nothing existed but the overwhelming desire to connect.

When they finally broke apart, their breaths ragged, Jack's gaze held hers, the depth of his emotions clear in his eyes. "You asked for the truth," he said, his voice a low murmur. "Now you'll have it."

Emma swallowed hard, her heart racing. This was it. She could feel it—the moment that would either bring them closer together or tear them apart.

Without another word, Jack led her to the bed, the final step in this journey of discovery. And as they lay together, the secrets of his past were laid bare, their passion more intense than ever before.

Chapter 122: The Light Beyond the Darkness

"Sometimes, the things we cannot change end up changing us." — Unknown

The moonlight poured in through the sheer curtains, casting long shadows across the floor of the penthouse. Emma lay in Jack's arms, her head resting on his chest, feeling the steady rhythm of his heartbeat beneath her ear. The intimacy of the moment was almost overwhelming, the silence between them both comfortable and suffocating in its weight. She had asked for the truth, and now she was reeling from the consequences of that request.

The secrets Jack had revealed were more than she could have imagined. They weren't just about a past filled with shadowy figures and unspeakable choices, but they were about the very essence of the man she had fallen for—the dark corners of his soul that he had kept hidden from her. She wasn't sure if she could carry the burden of knowing them, but one thing was certain: she couldn't turn away from him now.

Emma shifted slightly, her fingers tracing small circles on his chest as she tried to process the revelations. "Jack, I..." She faltered, unsure of how to start. The words tangled in her throat, caught between the love and fear that had taken root inside her.

Jack's voice cut through the stillness, his words low but firm. "I know what you're thinking." He turned his head to face her, his eyes searching hers with a tenderness that made her heart ache. "I never wanted to hurt you, Emma. But I had to be honest with you. No more lies. No more hiding."

She swallowed hard, her heart pounding in her chest. "I need time." she whispered, the weight of the truth settling deeper into her soul. "I just... need time to process everything."

Jack nodded, understanding. "I'll give you all the time you need. But I won't let you go. I won't walk away from you."

His words were like a balm on her raw emotions, soothing the uncertainty that had taken root in her heart. He had been vulnerable with her, shown her a side of himself that he had kept locked away for so long. And now, despite the fear and confusion that lingered, she couldn't bring herself to pull away.

"Jack," she said quietly, her voice trembling slightly, "I don't know if I can handle everything. Your past, your secrets, they're so much. It's hard to believe that someone like you—someone so full of darkness—could want me."

He sat up slightly, propping himself up on his elbow as he looked down at her, his expression fierce yet tender. "You think my past defines me?" he asked softly, a note of disbelief in his voice. "Emma, what we have is real. The connection we share, the love—it's not tied to the mistakes I've made or the things I've done. What matters is who I am now, who I am with you."

His words struck deep, piercing through her doubts like a hot knife through butter. He was right. It wasn't the man he had been that she loved. It was the man he had become—the one who held her in his arms like she was the most precious thing in the world.

"But your past..." Emma trailed off, her words hesitant. "It's so dark. You've done things, hurt people—"

"Yes," Jack interrupted, his voice sharp but not defensive. "I've made mistakes. I've hurt people. And I'll regret those things for the rest of my life. But they don't define me. Not anymore."

Emma's heart ached as she reached up to touch his face, her fingers brushing against his stubble, feeling the roughness of his skin beneath her fingertips. He was so close, so real, and yet the distance between them felt immense at times. She wanted to believe him, to let go of her fear and fully embrace what they shared. But the scars of his past lingered, haunting her like ghosts.

"I just don't want to be hurt," she whispered, her voice barely audible.

Jack's eyes softened, his expression filled with an intensity that made her breath catch in her throat. He leaned down, kissing her forehead gently before pulling her into a tight embrace. "You won't be hurt by me," he murmured into her hair. "I swear it. All I want is to give you everything I have, to make you feel loved, safe, and cherished."

Emma closed her eyes, allowing herself to sink into his warmth, feeling the weight of his promise settle deep within her. His touch was everything she had ever wanted—comforting, passionate, and fiercely protective. But she also knew that the road ahead wouldn't be easy. The darkness of his past would always be there, lurking in the background, threatening to tear them apart.

She shifted in his arms, pulling away just enough to look into his eyes. "I want to believe you, Jack. But I don't know how to shake this feeling... like I'm walking into something I can't escape."

Jack's expression grew serious, his gaze unwavering as he met her eyes. "Emma, you're not walking into something you can't escape. You're walking into something real. A love that's been built on trust, honesty, and vulnerability. We're not perfect. We've both made mistakes. But together, we can make this work."

Emma's breath caught in her throat as she looked up at him. The rawness of his words stirred something deep within her—a longing, a hope, and a fear all wrapped together. She wasn't sure what the future held, but she knew one thing for certain: she wasn't ready to walk away from him. Not yet.

"I don't know what to do," she whispered, her voice barely audible as she gazed up at him, feeling a mix of love and doubt swirl inside her.

Jack cupped her face in his hands, his thumb brushing over her lower lip. "All we can do is keep moving forward, Emma. One step at a time. And if we fall, we fall together. But I'll never stop fighting for us."

His words struck a chord deep within her, and in that moment, Emma made a choice. She chose him. She chose to face the unknown, to embrace the love that had already consumed her heart. No matter what lay ahead, she wouldn't let go.

As Jack kissed her gently, the world outside seemed to fade into the background, leaving only the two of them and the intensity of their connection. She was no longer afraid. Whatever came next, she would face it with him, side by side.

Chapter 123: A Journey to Wholeness

"What we are is God's gift to us. What we become is our gift to God." — Eleanor Powell

The days had blurred together for Emma, a strange mix of moments where everything felt normal, and others where the weight of Jack's revelations threatened to break her. She had tried to carry on as usual, burying herself in work and distracting herself with the mundane tasks of life, but she knew the truth now. Nothing could ever be the same. Her connection with Jack had been irrevocably altered by the secrets he had shared, by the darkness that still lingered in the corners of their love.

She stood at the window of the penthouse, gazing out over the glittering lights of the city, the pulse of Sydney beating below her. The view was magnificent, but it did little to soothe the storm swirling inside her. The city felt both close and far, a reflection of her own internal conflict.

The moment Jack walked into the room, Emma felt a jolt of electricity. Her body responded to his presence before her mind had time to catch up. Even after everything that had happened, even after the uncertainty and the fear, her heart still raced at the sight of him. He was the man she had fallen in love with, but he was also a stranger in some ways—the man with secrets, the man who had hurt others, the man who had fought for their love but whose past would never fully let him go.

"Emma," Jack said, his voice low, a hint of apprehension in it. He stepped toward her, but she didn't turn to face him. She wasn't sure if she could look at him without seeing the things she had learned. The truth about his past—the mistakes he had made, the people he had hurt—was a bitter pill to swallow. She had been naive to think that love could erase all that. She had been naive to think that they could outrun the darkness that followed him.

"Emma?" Jack repeated, his voice softer now, like he was trying to coax her back from a distance she had created between them. "Please look at me."

She turned slowly, her eyes locking with his. She could see the exhaustion in his face, the lines etched deeper than before. His eyes held the same love for her that had always been there, but now it was tinged with something else—something darker. Guilt? Regret?

"Why didn't you tell me sooner?" she asked, her voice hoarse with emotion. "Why did you wait so long to tell me the truth, Jack?"

He flinched, his shoulders tightening at her words. "I didn't want to lose you," he said quietly, his gaze falling to the floor. "I thought if I told you, you would leave. I couldn't bear the thought of losing you. So I kept it from you. I thought I could protect you from the truth."

Emma's heart twisted at his words. She could see the pain in his eyes, the vulnerability that he tried so hard to hide. She knew that, in his own way, Jack had tried to shield her from the ugliness of his past, but now that the truth was out, they had to face it together. They couldn't keep pretending it didn't exist.

"You didn't protect me, Jack," she said softly, stepping closer to him. "You just made it harder for us. The lies... the secrets... they've put a wall between us that I don't know how to tear down."

He reached for her, his fingers trembling as he cupped her face, forcing her to look into his eyes. "I never wanted to hurt you," he whispered. "I never wanted to hurt anyone. But I've done things that I can't undo. I've made choices that I regret more than anything. All I can do now is be honest with you. All I can do is show you who I am today, and hope that you can see past the mistakes of my past."

Emma felt the warmth of his touch, the sincerity in his words. She wanted to believe him, wanted to throw herself into his arms and forget everything else. But the reality was that the past would never fully disappear. The shadow of his previous life would always be there, lingering at the edge of their relationship, reminding them of what had come before.

"I don't know if I can forget it, Jack," she whispered, the pain evident in her voice. "But I want to move forward. I don't want to let it tear us apart."

Jack's lips parted as if he were about to speak, but before he could say anything, Emma took a deep breath and continued.

"I don't know if I can forgive everything. I don't know if I can be the person who heals you. But I can be the person who stands by you. I can love you for who you are now. I can give you all of me, if you'll promise me one thing."

Jack's brow furrowed, his eyes searching hers, desperate for some kind of clarity. "What do you want me to promise?"

"Promise me that you'll never shut me out again," she said, her voice steady despite the emotions swirling inside her. "Promise me that, no matter how dark it gets, we will face it together. No more secrets. No more lies."

Jack nodded, a look of determination crossing his face. "I promise you, Emma. No more lies. No more secrets. We face everything together from here on out."

Emma allowed herself to believe him, her heart swelling with love and hope. It wasn't going to be easy, but maybe, just maybe, they could rebuild what had been broken. Maybe the love they shared could withstand even the darkest of truths.

He kissed her then, a slow, deep kiss that was filled with the weight of everything they had gone through. It was a kiss of reconciliation, of understanding, and of trust. For the first time in what felt like an eternity, Emma let herself truly feel what she had been too afraid to admit to herself. She loved him—she always had. And she wasn't ready to let go.

Chapter 124: In the Eye of the Storm

"The only way out is through." — Robert Frost

The warmth of the early morning sun streamed through the windows, casting a golden hue across the penthouse. Emma lay awake, her body tangled in the soft sheets, her mind racing. The night had been unlike any other — a fusion of passion, revelations, and secrets. But now, as the daylight crept in, so did the gnawing uncertainty.

She reached for her phone on the nightstand, her fingers hesitating over the screen as memories of the evening before flooded her senses. Jack's touch, his declarations, the way he made her feel — alive, seen, desired. But behind it all, she knew the truths they had uncovered couldn't be ignored.

There was a reckoning that was coming, and she couldn't push it away any longer.

Sitting up slowly, Emma ran her fingers through her disheveled hair and let out a quiet sigh. The love between them was undeniable. The connection was electric, drawing them closer with each passing day. But there was also a storm on the horizon, and it loomed large in her mind.

The unresolved threads of Jack's past, the lingering shadows of betrayal, the things left unsaid — it was a weight that threatened to pull them apart.

But Jack had insisted on honesty. He'd said that nothing would come between them, that they had the strength to weather any storm. Yet, the doubt still clung to her heart.

As she moved to get out of bed, the sound of a door creaking open made her pause. Jack's figure appeared in the doorway, a silhouette of desire and vulnerability.

"You're up early," he said, his voice low and husky with sleep.

Emma turned towards him, her heart skipping a beat at the sight of him. There was something about the way he looked at her — like she was the only thing that mattered in the world. And for a moment, she let herself believe it.

But the question still hung in the air between them.

"Jack..." Her voice was shaky, uncertain. "We need to talk."

He stepped forward, concern flashing across his features. "What is it?"

She swallowed, the words feeling heavy in her throat. "About everything. About us, about what's coming. The future."

The tension in his jaw was immediate. He moved to sit next to her on the bed, his hand finding hers. "Emma, you know I'm not hiding anything from you. Whatever happens, we face it together."

But Emma couldn't shake the feeling that something was still lurking, something Jack hadn't fully shared.

"I don't want to lose you," she whispered, the rawness of the admission surprising even herself.

Jack's gaze softened, his thumb gently caressing the back of her hand. "You won't lose me, Emma. I'm here. I always will be."

But as his words echoed in the room, Emma couldn't ignore the niggling thought at the back of her mind. What if he wasn't telling her everything? What if there were things in his past that could tear them apart, secrets too dark to share?

Before she could voice her concerns, her phone buzzed on the nightstand, cutting through the moment.

Jack's eyes flickered towards it, and for a split second, Emma saw the flash of unease in his expression. It was enough to make her stomach twist.

She grabbed her phone, glancing at the screen, and her heart sank. It was a message from an unknown number. The message was short, but its impact was anything but.

"You don't know the whole story. Be careful. There's more you need to learn about Jack."

Her hand shook as she read the words again. Her mind raced. Could it be someone from Jack's past? Someone who knew the secrets he'd yet to reveal?

"What is it?" Jack asked, his voice now tight with concern.

Emma hesitated, looking at the phone in her hand, torn between confronting him and keeping the trust they'd built.

"Who was it?" Jack pressed, his tone urgent.

She took a deep breath, her gaze meeting his. "A message. From someone I don't know. It says there's more I need to know about you."

Jack's face tightened, a flash of tension crossing his features. "What do they mean?"

Emma didn't answer immediately, her thoughts swirling in a whirlwind of fear and confusion. "Jack, what aren't you telling me?"

His jaw clenched, and he looked away for a moment before turning back to face her. His voice was quieter now, as though he was weighing his words carefully.

"Emma..." he started, then paused, as if searching for the right thing to say. "There are things in my past that I've tried to leave behind. Things I didn't want to bring into this—into us."

"Like what?" she demanded, her pulse quickening. "What are you hiding from me, Jack?"

For a moment, he said nothing, his gaze dropping to their joined hands. His fingers curled slightly around hers before he finally spoke again, his voice low and tinged with regret.

"I don't want to hurt you," he said, the weight of his words heavy in the room. "But if this person knows things they shouldn't, I have no choice but to tell you."

Emma's heart raced, her breath shallow as she waited for him to continue.

"Before I met you," Jack began, his voice almost inaudible, "I was involved in something—something dangerous. People I got mixed up with. I thought I could control it, but it spiraled out of my hands. And when I met you, I promised myself that I'd leave it behind, that I'd protect you from it."

Emma sat back, the shock of his words sinking in. She had always known there was something about him — a darkness that he kept hidden, but hearing it out loud was something else entirely.

"Jack... what are you saying?" she asked, her voice barely a whisper.

He closed his eyes for a moment, as though preparing himself for the storm that was coming. "There are people who want to pull me back into that life. People I've wronged, and now they want to make me pay."

Emma's heart pounded, her thoughts a chaotic mess. "Is that what this is? What this message is about?"

Jack nodded. "They want something from me, and they think you can be used to get it."

Fear flooded her chest, but she fought to keep her composure. "What do they want from you, Jack?"

"The truth," he said quietly, his voice filled with regret. "They want me to betray everything I've worked for, everything we've built. They want to use you to force me into their world again."

Emma felt a chill run through her as the weight of his words settled into her bones. "What do we do now?" she asked, her voice shaking.

Jack's expression hardened with determination. "We fight. Together."

But Emma couldn't shake the feeling that their fight was only beginning.

As the tension between them deepened, one thing was certain: the love they shared would be tested in ways neither of them could have imagined. And only time would tell if they could survive the storm on the horizon.

Chapter 125: The Final Reckoning

"The heart was made to be broken." — Oscar Wilde

Emma stood at the edge of the balcony, her eyes fixed on the sprawling city below. Sydney's skyline glittered in the distance, the night air cool against her skin. The weight of the past few days sat heavily on her shoulders, and her heart raced as she replayed the events in her mind. The undeniable tension between her and Jack, the undeniable pull, but also the shadows of doubt that had begun to cloud her thoughts.

The confrontation with Victoria still echoed in her mind, a constant hum in her consciousness. Could she truly trust Jack? Or was she destined to repeat the mistakes of the past, falling for someone who would ultimately let her down?

A soft rustle of fabric behind her broke the silence. She turned to see Jack, his presence steady and grounding, even as the air between them seemed charged with unspoken words. His gaze was intense, but there was no trace of the usual confidence. His vulnerability was laid bare, raw and unguarded.

"Emma," he said, his voice low, steady. "We need to talk."

Her pulse quickened at the tone, a mix of trepidation and yearning. She nodded, stepping aside to let him join her on the balcony.

They stood together, gazing out over the city, both lost in their own thoughts.

"I've been thinking about us," Jack began, his words measured. "About everything that's happened and everything that's still to come."

Emma turned to him, her heart in her throat. She could feel the intensity of the moment, the weight of their shared history, and the uncertainty of their future.

"I know I haven't always been open with you, Emma," Jack continued, his eyes searching hers. "There's a lot I've kept from you. But I need you to know that you're everything to me. This... whatever this is between us, it's more real than anything I've ever experienced."

Emma's breath caught in her throat. Her mind raced, the walls she had carefully built around her heart beginning to crumble. "Jack," she whispered, her voice a fragile thread. "I need to know the truth. All of it. No more secrets."

Jack hesitated for a moment, his gaze dropping to the floor. Then, with a deep breath, he met her eyes again. "I've never been good at trusting people," he admitted. "Not after everything I've been through. But with you, it's different. I've never felt this way about anyone before. You're not just another woman to me, Emma. You're everything. And I don't want to lose that."

The words hung in the air between them, heavy with meaning. Emma could feel her heart beginning to race, the raw honesty in his voice stirring something deep within her. Could she trust him? Could she let go of the fear and the doubt that had taken root in her heart?

Before she could respond, Jack closed the distance between them, his hand gently cupping her face. His touch was warm, grounding, and Emma leaned into it, feeling the heat of his skin against hers.

"You don't have to say anything, Emma," Jack murmured, his lips brushing against her ear. "I just need you to know that I'm here. I'm not going anywhere."

The tension between them was palpable, the unspoken desire hanging in the air like a promise. Jack's lips found hers, slow at first, tentative, as if testing the waters. But the moment their mouths met, everything else faded away. The world outside ceased to exist. There was only the heat of his kiss, the undeniable chemistry between them, and the overwhelming need for closeness, for connection.

As the kiss deepened, Emma's body responded instinctively. Her hands threaded through Jack's hair, pulling him closer, wanting more. She could feel his heart pounding in his chest, matching the frantic beat of her own.

"Jack," she whispered against his lips, her voice trembling with desire. "I don't know if I can trust you, but I want to. I want to believe in us."

Jack pulled back slightly, his eyes searching hers with a mixture of longing and sincerity. "I don't expect you to trust me right away. But I'm here, Emma. And I'll do whatever it takes to show you that I'm worth it."

The vulnerability in his voice, the sincerity in his eyes, made Emma's heart swell. She could feel the walls around her heart starting to crumble, piece by piece. She wanted to trust him. She wanted to believe in the possibility of something more, something real.

Without another word, Jack kissed her again, more urgently this time. His hands slid down her back, pulling her closer as their bodies pressed together. Emma's breath hitched as she felt the heat of his body, the undeniable pull between them growing stronger with each passing second.

Their kiss grew more passionate, more insistent, as if they were both trying to convey everything they had kept locked inside. Emma's hands roamed over Jack's chest, feeling the steady thud of his heartbeat beneath her fingertips. She had always been drawn to him, to his intensity, to the fire that burned in his soul.

But now, in this moment, she felt something deeper. Something more real than she had ever experienced before. A connection that went beyond the physical, beyond the passion that had always been at the forefront of their relationship. It was the beginning of something more—something that had the potential to change everything.

Jack's hands slid under her shirt, his touch sending a jolt of electricity through her body. Emma gasped, her skin tingling as he trailed his fingers over her spine. Her body arched instinctively toward him, craving the closeness, the connection. She could feel his desire, his need, and it mirrored her own.

The kiss broke, both of them breathless, their faces inches apart. "Are you sure about this?" Jack asked, his voice raw with emotion.

Emma's heart raced as she looked into his eyes, searching for any sign of doubt. But all she saw was sincerity. And desire. And something more.

"I'm sure," she whispered.

With that, they were lost in each other again, the rest of the world fading into oblivion as their bodies became one, their hearts beating in time. There was no turning back now, no more fear, no more hesitation. Only the undeniable connection between them, the passion that surged through their veins, and the promise of a future together—if they were willing to fight for it.

Chapter 126. Where Love Leads

"*Sometimes, you have to let go of the life you planned to make room for the life that's waiting for you.*" —*Joseph Campbell*

The morning light filtered through the curtains, casting a soft glow across the room. Emma lay in Jack's arms, tangled in the sheets, the events of the night before still fresh in her mind. Every inch of her body felt alive with the aftereffects of their passion, and yet, there was a sense of uncertainty that lingered at the edges of her thoughts. The walls she had spent so long building were crumbling, piece by piece, and with each passing second, she could feel herself falling deeper into this connection with him.

Jack stirred beside her, his arm still draped around her waist. She could feel the steady rise and fall of his chest against her back as he breathed in sync with her. His presence, so solid, so secure, was both a comfort and a reminder of everything that had been left unsaid between them.

She turned in his arms, her gaze meeting his. His eyes were still heavy with sleep, but there was a softness to them that she hadn't seen before—a vulnerability that made her heart flutter.

"Good morning," Jack murmured, his voice hoarse from the night's passion.

Emma smiled faintly, her fingers tracing the outline of his jaw. "Good morning," she replied, her voice just as quiet, as though the weight of the moment required no further words.

For a few moments, they simply lay there, tangled together in the quiet comfort of each other's presence. Emma's thoughts were a swirling mix of emotions—desire, love, fear, and doubt. She had allowed herself to fall into this, into him, and now she was left wondering what it all meant. Was it truly possible to trust him, to trust herself, after everything that had come before?

But before she could fully unravel her thoughts, Jack's hand found hers, his fingers gently threading through hers, as though he was grounding her in the present moment. "Emma," he said softly, his voice almost a whisper, "I need to be honest with you. There's something I've been holding back."

Her heart skipped a beat at his words. It was as if the world around them shifted, and suddenly, every breath she took seemed to hang in the balance. "What is it?" she asked, her voice tight with a mixture of anticipation and trepidation.

Jack hesitated, his thumb running along the back of her hand in soothing motions. "You deserve to know everything. No more secrets, no more lies."

Emma's pulse quickened, but she remained still, waiting for him to continue.

"I haven't always been... the man I am now," he began, his gaze searching her face for any sign of judgment. "I've done things—things

I'm not proud of. And I know that's not an easy thing to hear, but you need to know that I'm not the same person I was before. I've changed, Emma. And I'm trying to be better. For you. For us."

Her heart pounded in her chest as she processed his words. The vulnerability in his voice, the sincerity that laced his confession, was enough to make her stomach twist in knots. She could see the pain in his eyes, the weight of his past threatening to pull him back.

"Jack..." Emma whispered, her voice trembling. She wanted to reach out, to pull him closer, but a part of her was frozen in place, unsure of what to say, unsure of how to react. His past—whatever it was—was still a mystery to her, and that uncertainty made her anxious.

"I'm not asking you to forgive me for things I've done," Jack continued, his voice thick with emotion. "But I need you to understand that who I am now is nothing like who I used to be. And I'll spend the rest of my life proving that to you."

Emma's mind raced. Could she really forgive him for something she didn't even know? Was she ready to take that leap, to trust him completely? Part of her wanted to pull away, to shield herself from the fear that crept into her heart. But another part of her—the part that had let go of everything last night—wanted to believe him.

"I don't know what happened before, Jack," Emma said slowly, her eyes locking with his. "But I do know what's happening now. And right now, all I want is to be with you. No secrets, no walls between us. Just... us."

Jack exhaled, as though a weight had been lifted from his chest. He brought her hand to his lips, pressing a soft kiss to her knuckles. "You're everything to me, Emma. And I won't take that for granted."

For a moment, they simply lay there, wrapped in each other's arms, the unspoken understanding between them more powerful than any words could convey. The storm of emotions that had been swirling inside Emma began to settle, replaced by a sense of calm. She didn't have all the answers yet, but for the first time in a long time, she felt like she might be able to find them. With Jack, she felt safe enough to explore the unknown.

After a while, Emma broke the silence, her voice a soft murmur. "Do you think we're ready for what comes next?"

Jack's lips curved into a smile, a hint of playfulness in his gaze. "I think we're ready for whatever we choose, Emma."

Her heart skipped a beat, the truth of his words sinking in. Whatever happened next, they would face it together. No more secrets, no more hiding. Just them, learning and growing in the wake of everything they had experienced.

And with that thought, the rest of the world seemed to fade away, leaving only the two of them, bound by a connection deeper than either of them had anticipated.

Chapter 127: The Heart's Truth

"The truth will set you free, but first it will make you miserable."
—James A. Garfield

The days that followed Jack's confession were a whirlwind of emotions, a mix of clarity and doubt, passion and hesitation. Emma had thrown herself into her work, trying to maintain a sense of normalcy, but every glance toward Jack, every touch, only deepened the questions swirling inside her.

It wasn't that she didn't trust him. In fact, her trust in him had only grown since their conversation, but the weight of his past was like an invisible shadow, lingering between them. She could feel it, feel the history that Jack was so desperate to leave behind, but which still tugged at him—at them.

It was the night after their long discussion, when the sky was painted in the deepest shades of twilight, that the next step in their journey began to unfold. Jack was late. He had promised to meet her at the restaurant, but when he hadn't shown up by the time her meal had arrived, unease settled over her. She knew something was off; her instincts never failed her.

A soft buzz of her phone on the table interrupted her spiraling thoughts. She glanced at the screen—Jack's name flashing.

Her heart skipped a beat. She answered immediately. "Jack?"

"Emma," his voice crackled over the line, but something was wrong—there was a strange tremor in his tone. "I need you to come. Now."

"Where are you?" she asked, her voice shaking with the urgency in his words.

"I'll send you the address. Just... please hurry." His voice dropped to a whisper. "I love you, Emma. Please come."

Before she could respond, the line went dead. Panic seized her chest, her heart racing as she quickly gathered her things and ran out the door. Her mind raced through possibilities—what could be happening? Why was he so desperate, so afraid?

The address he had sent her led to an area she didn't recognize, a series of narrow, dimly lit alleyways near the city's edge. As she stepped out of her car and into the chilling night air, the sounds of the city seemed distant, muffled, swallowed by the weight of the moment.

She made her way down the alley, her pulse thundering in her ears, her steps quick and uneven. When she finally reached the address, she saw him standing there, near the entrance of an old building. His silhouette was illuminated only by the faint light of a single streetlamp.

"Jack?" she called out, her voice hoarse with anxiety.

He turned sharply at the sound of her voice, his eyes wide with an emotion she couldn't quite place. He looked frantic, almost unrecognizable in his distress.

"Emma," he breathed, taking a step toward her. "You shouldn't have come here."

"Why? What's going on?" she asked, her hand reaching for him instinctively. "What is this?"

Jack took a deep breath, running a hand through his hair. He looked around, as though he were checking for anyone else before speaking. "I had to come here," he began, his voice barely above a whisper. "There are things... things I've never told you, Emma. I didn't want you to know. I didn't want to hurt you."

Her heart pounded harder in her chest. "Jack... please, just tell me what's going on."

"I—" Jack faltered, then shook his head. He seemed to gather himself before continuing. "You've been asking about my past, about the things I did... well, the truth is, I've been hiding something from you. Something bigger than I ever realized. There are people from my past, people who won't let me go."

Emma's breath caught in her throat. "What do you mean? Who are they?"

Jack stepped closer, his hands grabbing her shoulders gently but firmly. His eyes locked onto hers. "I was involved in things I shouldn't have been. Dangerous things. I tried to walk away, but not everyone I was involved with is willing to let me go that easily. They've been watching me, watching us."

Her mind reeled as his words sank in. She could feel the weight of the situation settle around them. "Are you in danger?" she asked, her voice trembling.

"I don't know," Jack replied, his face pale. "But I think I'm about to find out."

Before she could ask him anything more, the sound of footsteps echoed through the alley. She turned sharply, her body tense, only to see a group of men approaching. They were dressed in dark clothing, their faces obscured by shadows. The tension in the air was palpable.

Jack pulled Emma closer, his arm protective around her waist. "Get in the car," he whispered urgently. "Now."

Her heart raced, but she didn't hesitate. She followed Jack's lead, running toward his car parked just down the street. As they slid into the vehicle, the sound of the men's voices grew louder, their footsteps echoing closer.

Jack's hands gripped the steering wheel, his knuckles white. He threw the car into gear and sped off, the tires screeching as they raced through the streets. Emma's breath was shallow, her mind still trying to process what was happening.

"Jack, who are they?" she asked, her voice barely a whisper.

"They're people from my past," Jack answered, his voice thick with tension. "They were part of a business I wanted nothing to do with anymore. But they don't just let go. And now... they know about you, Emma."

Her heart clenched. The danger was real. Jack wasn't just the man she thought he was—he was someone wrapped up in something dark, something dangerous. And now she was caught in the storm.

They drove in silence for what felt like hours, Jack's eyes flicking to the rearview mirror constantly, checking for anyone who might be following them. Emma could feel the weight of the moment, the looming threat hanging between them like a thick fog.

Finally, Jack pulled into a nondescript parking garage and parked in a secluded corner. He turned to Emma, his face drawn with worry and regret. "I never wanted this for you, Emma. I never wanted you to be dragged into this world."

She reached for him, her hand resting on his. "You're not alone in this," she said softly. "We'll face it together. Whatever happens, we'll face it together."

Jack squeezed her hand, his lips pressing into a tight line. "I'm scared, Emma. I'm scared of losing you."

Her heart swelled with love and determination. She leaned in and kissed him gently, her lips lingering on his. "You won't lose me," she whispered. "I'm here. And we're in this together, Jack. We'll fight this together."

For a long moment, they simply held each other, the silence between them filled with understanding. The world outside seemed to cease to exist, leaving only the two of them—caught in the eye of the storm, yet determined to face whatever came next.

Chapter 128: The Depth of Connection

"True love is not about perfection; it's about embracing flaws and finding peace in the chaos." — Unknown

The air between Emma and Jack had thickened with tension. The quiet moments in the penthouse felt louder than ever, filled with the weight of unsaid words and feelings both raw and intense. Jack's eyes never left her as she entered the living room, but he said nothing. His gaze, steady and deep, seemed to pull her closer even without words.

Emma could feel her pulse quicken in response to the silent communication they shared. He was still the man who made her feel like the world could stop spinning, and yet, the uncertainty in her heart clawed at her every time they were alone.

"I think we need to talk," she finally said, her voice steady despite the whirlwind inside her. She perched on the edge of the couch, feeling the cool leather beneath her fingertips.

Jack remained standing, his posture as rigid as his jaw, but his eyes softened. "I know," he said quietly.

Emma inhaled sharply. She wanted to believe him. To believe in them. But doubts still lingered, like shadows cast over their once-perfect connection.

"I know you don't want to revisit the past," she began, her voice a whisper now. "But I can't ignore it anymore. There's too much that's been left unsaid, too much that feels... unfinished."

Jack took a step toward her, his broad form blocking the light from the window. He was close, but the distance between them had never felt wider. "Emma, I—"

"No, Jack," she interrupted, standing to face him now, her resolve stronger than it had ever been. "I need you to be honest with me. About everything. About your past, your fears, your secrets."

His brow furrowed, and for a moment, she thought he might turn away. But then, he did something she hadn't expected. He reached out, cupping her cheek gently in his palm, his thumb brushing over her skin as if he were trying to memorize the feel of her.

"You know I'd never hurt you intentionally," Jack's voice was thick with emotion. "But I've never been good at sharing what's inside. I never thought anyone would understand."

"I'm trying, Jack. I need to understand."

His gaze flickered to the side, his fingers still lingering on her skin. "You want the truth? The whole truth?"

Emma's heart pounded in her chest. "Yes. I need to know. I need to know who you are... and who I am to you."

The silence stretched between them, thick and suffocating. She could see him warring with himself, unsure whether to speak the words that could shatter everything they'd built, or remain silent and let the uncertainty fester.

Finally, he spoke, his voice low and raw. "There are parts of me, Emma, parts of my past, that I've buried. I've been running from them for so long, convinced they wouldn't catch up with me. But you—" He paused, looking into her eyes as if searching for something. "You make me want to face them. You make me want to fight for us."

Her breath caught in her throat, her emotions overwhelming her all at once. She reached up, her fingers tracing the line of his jaw, the stubble rough under her touch.

"I don't know what you're hiding, Jack," she murmured, "But I need to trust you."

"You can," he said with a certainty that grounded her, pulling her closer. "Whatever it is, we'll face it together."

The words seemed to hang in the air between them, charged with something unspoken but undeniable. Jack's hands found her waist, drawing her in until their bodies were flush against each other. The heat between them was instant, like the flickering of a flame, dangerous and consuming.

For a moment, neither of them spoke. Their lips met in a kiss that was slow at first, tentative, as if testing the waters of something deeper. But soon, the kiss deepened, becoming more urgent, more passionate. Emma's hands slid up to his chest, feeling the steady beat of his heart beneath her palm.

As their bodies moved together, Emma felt the weight of their connection—of their history, of everything they had yet to face. She could feel the raw desire pulsing between them, stronger than ever, but it was tempered by something deeper, something that felt like love. A love that was messy and complicated, but real.

Jack's hands moved to her back, pulling her even closer, his lips trailing down her neck, finding the sensitive spots that made her shiver with pleasure. Her breath caught in her throat as he kissed her there, the intensity of their connection intensifying with each passing second.

"I need you, Emma," Jack murmured against her skin, his voice thick with desire. "I've always needed you."

The words sent a shock through her, a realization that everything they had shared wasn't just fleeting. It wasn't just about passion or lust. It was about something deeper, something that couldn't be ignored anymore.

"I need you too, Jack," she whispered, her hands moving to the buttons of his shirt, her fingers trembling as she worked them open. "Now more than ever."

As the last button came undone, Jack's hands moved to her dress, pushing it off her shoulders, his eyes never leaving hers. The hunger in his gaze was unmistakable, but so was the tenderness with which he undressed her. He wasn't rushing. He was savoring every moment, every touch.

And in that moment, Emma realized that this was more than just passion. It was a connection forged in the deepest parts of themselves. It was trust. It was love. It was raw, unfiltered, and real.

With a deep breath, she allowed herself to let go, to give in to the moment, to the man who had captivated her from the very beginning. Their bodies came together, and everything else faded away. There was only the two of them, lost in the heat of the moment, and the promise of something more to come.

But as they moved together, Emma knew that their journey was far from over. There were still shadows lurking in the corners of their love story, and they would have to face them—together.

Chapter 129: The Final Choice

"There is no remedy for love but to love more." — Henry David Thoreau

Emma stood at the edge of the penthouse balcony, looking out over the city lights twinkling below. The cool breeze tousled her hair, and yet, the weight of uncertainty and the storm of emotions she had carried with her for so long threatened to crush her spirit. Tonight had been the culmination of everything—the passion, the betrayal, the secrets, and now, the final choice that would define her future.

The past few days had been a whirlwind. The truths she had uncovered, the emotions she had battled, had left her breathless and shaken. Victoria's warnings, Richard's investigation, Jack's elusive responses—it all hung in the air like a suffocating fog. And yet, despite the fear and doubt, Emma had never been more sure of one thing: she was done hiding from her own heart.

Her fingers gently traced the edge of the glass, a tangible connection to the world outside. She had always wanted control—over her choices, over her heart—but as she stood there now, all she wanted was to feel. To surrender, to experience the fire that had burned between her and Jack. She had been holding back, not just from him but from herself.

Behind her, the soft sound of footsteps broke her reverie. She didn't need to turn to know it was Jack. His presence had become a constant, a force that she could feel even when he wasn't around. She felt his gaze before he spoke.

"You're thinking too much," he said softly, his voice deep with knowing. "I can see it. You've always been a thinker, Emma. But sometimes, you just need to stop thinking and feel."

She swallowed, the knot in her throat tightening. His words were both a balm and a burn, reminding her of everything she wanted, everything she feared. She finally turned to face him, her breath catching in her chest at the intensity in his eyes. They had been through so much, and yet, she could see it now—what they had was undeniable.

"I'm not sure I can," she whispered. "There's so much I don't know, Jack. So much I can't unsee."

His expression softened, and for the first time in what felt like forever, he closed the distance between them. His hand reached up, brushing a strand of hair from her face before cupping her cheek. The warmth of his touch grounded her, and for the first time, she let herself lean into it, surrendering to the heat that had always existed between them.

"You don't need to know everything, Emma," he said quietly. "You just need to trust me. Trust what we've built. Trust what we are."

Her heart raced as she searched his eyes for any trace of doubt. But all she found was sincerity. And something deeper—something raw.

He wasn't asking for forgiveness. He wasn't asking for anything except her trust.

"I do trust you," she breathed, her voice barely audible. But it was the truth. She had to trust him. She had to trust herself.

Without another word, Jack leaned in, his lips capturing hers in a kiss that sent sparks racing through her veins. It wasn't gentle or hesitant. It was everything—passion, need, desire, and the unspoken promise of what was to come. She responded without hesitation, her body pressing into his, as if they were two pieces that had always belonged together.

The kiss deepened, and Emma's hands found their way to his chest, feeling the steady beat of his heart beneath the fabric of his shirt. She could taste the salt on his skin, the taste of everything they had shared. She could feel the weight of their past, their struggles, but it didn't matter anymore. In this moment, all that mattered was them. The connection that neither of them had been able to sever, no matter the circumstances.

Jack pulled back just enough to look at her, his breath ragged. "Are you sure about this?" he asked, his voice hoarse. "Because I don't want to rush you. I want you to be sure."

Emma's chest tightened, but it wasn't from fear—it was from the intensity of what they were about to embark on. "I'm sure," she whispered, her lips curling into a smile. "I'm more sure than I've ever been about anything in my life."

Without another word, Jack took her hand and led her inside. The lights were dim, the air thick with anticipation, as they moved to the bedroom. The door closed behind them with a soft click, sealing them in their own world. A world where the past couldn't touch them and the future was uncertain, but where the present—this moment—was theirs to claim.

The clothes they had been wearing moments before were discarded with haste, as if each piece was holding them back from what they both needed. Emma's skin flushed under his gaze, the warmth of his touch sending waves of electricity through her body. The way he looked at her, with a hunger and a tenderness that seemed to pull her apart, made her heart race.

"Are you sure, Emma?" he asked again, his voice a low growl. But this time, it wasn't out of hesitation—it was out of a desire to ensure that she was ready, that she knew what she was about to step into.

"I'm sure," she replied, her voice steady despite the storm of emotions swirling inside her. "Let's just do it."

And with that, they came together again, their bodies merging in a frenzy of passion and desire. There were no words needed between them, only the shared understanding of what they both wanted—each other. Completely.

Chapter 130: The Journey Continues

"Every ending is just the beginning of something new." — Unknown

The air in the penthouse felt different now. Less heavy, less burdened with the weight of unspoken words. Emma's heart still pounded in her chest, but now, it was not out of fear or confusion. It was anticipation. The night they had shared had been everything she had ever dreamed of—intense, electric, raw. But as the first light of dawn began to seep through the curtains, she knew that the journey they were on was far from over.

She lay beside Jack, his steady breathing a comforting presence in the otherwise silent room. The bond between them had shifted, deepened, and now, there was nothing between them except the truth. The truth that they had both carried for so long, locked away in their hearts, but now released.

Emma traced her fingers over his chest, the strong, steady beat of his heart grounding her. She had known passion before, had felt the rush of lust and desire, but with Jack, it had been different. It was more than just chemistry—it was a connection that went beyond the physical. It was as if every part of her had been attuned to his, and the moment they had come together, the world had faded away.

But the past was still there. It loomed over them like a shadow, a reminder of the secrets and the lies. Emma knew that the road ahead would not be without its struggles. They still had obstacles to face, demons to confront. But for the first time, she felt ready to face them.

Jack stirred beside her, his hand reaching for hers in the dim morning light. His eyes opened slowly, a smile tugging at the corners of his lips as he met her gaze.

"Good morning," he murmured, his voice rough from sleep.

"Good morning," Emma replied, her voice soft but filled with emotion. She didn't need to say anything more. The look in his eyes told her everything she needed to know. They had crossed a threshold last night, one that they couldn't go back from.

He pulled her closer, his lips brushing against her forehead in a gesture so tender it made her chest tighten. "Are you okay?" he asked, his voice low, almost hesitant. As if he was still afraid of pushing her too far.

"I'm more than okay," she whispered, her fingers threading through his hair as she pulled him into a kiss. It was gentle at first, a slow melding of lips, but the hunger between them quickly reignited. There was no turning back now. Not for either of them.

Jack deepened the kiss, his hands sliding down her back to pull her closer. The heat between them was undeniable, a physical manifestation of everything they had just shared. And yet, it was more than that. It was trust, it was understanding, and it was the promise of more.

When they finally broke apart, Emma's breath was shallow, her body still aching for him. She looked up at him, her hand resting on his chest, her thumb brushing over the rise and fall of his heart. There was no uncertainty now. No lingering doubts. She was all in.

"I know what you're thinking," Jack said, his voice low and thoughtful. "We've come a long way, and there's still so much we need to work through. But Emma, I'm not going anywhere. I promise you, I won't let go. Not now, not ever."

The sincerity in his words settled deep within her. He was right. The path they had walked had been rocky, filled with doubts and fear, but they had made it this far. They had faced everything together and come out stronger.

"I know," she said softly, her voice filled with emotion. "And I'm not going anywhere either."

Jack's hand slid to the back of her neck, his fingers threading into her hair as he brought her into another kiss. This time, there was no hesitation. No reservations. Just the raw need to be together. To continue this journey. To leave the past behind and move forward into whatever came next.

But as they kissed, the world outside seemed to return to them—its noise, its chaos, its uncertainty. The shadows that had once seemed so distant were now creeping back into their lives, threatening to pull them apart again. But this time, Emma wasn't afraid. She was ready to face whatever came. With Jack by her side, she knew they could conquer anything.

When they finally pulled apart, the room felt different. Lighter. As if a weight had been lifted from their shoulders. There was no more pretending, no more hiding from what they felt. The truth had been laid bare between them, and nothing could change that now.

Emma stood, stretching her arms above her head as she looked out the window, the city sprawling below them. She could feel the change in the air, the promise of something new on the horizon. Their journey together wasn't over. It was just beginning.

"Where do we go from here?" she asked softly, her voice filled with both hope and uncertainty.

Jack rose from the bed and walked over to stand beside her, his hand resting gently on her shoulder. "We go wherever we want to go," he said, his voice filled with conviction. "Together."

For the first time in a long time, Emma felt the weight of the world slip from her shoulders. The fear, the doubts, the unresolved questions—they no longer had power over her. With Jack by her side, she could face anything.

And as the sun began to rise, casting a warm glow over the city, Emma knew that this was only the beginning.

Chapter 131: Awakening the Soul

"Sometimes, the most dangerous thing is not knowing what you want." — Unknown

The morning light streamed through the windows, casting long, soft shadows across the penthouse. Emma sat at the edge of the bed, gazing out over the city that had become the backdrop to their journey—a city that had seen both their greatest triumphs and their deepest fears. There was an unfamiliar weight in the air today, a feeling that things were shifting, that something was coming to a head.

Jack was in the other room, his presence a constant source of both comfort and tension. They had come so far together, but the past still lingered—those unspoken words, those hidden truths, and the questions that neither of them had fully answered. It was time to face them, to strip away the last of the doubts and fears, and confront the future they had built together.

She stood, walking toward the window, her gaze locked on the skyline. It felt as though they were standing on the edge of something monumental, something that would change everything. But what exactly was that change? What would the next step look like for them? For her?

The sound of footsteps behind her broke her reverie, and she turned to see Jack standing in the doorway. He was dressed casually, his shirt unbuttoned just slightly at the collar, his hair still tousled from sleep. He had that familiar, magnetic presence that made her heart race, but there was something different in his eyes today—a hint of resolve, of finality.

"You okay?" Jack asked, his voice low, his tone laced with concern.

Emma nodded, offering him a soft smile. "I'm okay. Just thinking about everything."

Jack walked toward her, his gaze never leaving hers, and when he reached her, he placed a hand on her shoulder. "I've been thinking too. About us. About everything we've been through." His eyes were intense, searching, and she could see the storm of emotions swirling behind them. "I know we've had our ups and downs, but I don't want to lose you, Emma. I can't lose you."

The sincerity in his words hit her like a wave, and for a moment, she found herself speechless. The weight of everything they had been through, all the obstacles they had overcome, felt overwhelming. But even with all of it, all the fear, all the complications, she knew the truth—she didn't want to lose him either.

"I don't want to lose you either," she whispered, stepping closer to him. The warmth of his touch, the steady beat of his heart beneath her fingers—it was everything she had ever wanted. But there was still one thing standing between them. One last thing they needed to face before they could move forward.

Jack seemed to sense it, his eyes searching hers as if he could see straight through to the heart of her fears. "Emma," he began softly, his voice almost a whisper. "I know there's something more we need to talk about. Something that's been hanging over us for a while. We've both kept parts of ourselves hidden. But I can't keep running from it. Not anymore."

Emma's pulse quickened. She had known this conversation was coming. She had known that the truth, all of it, had to come out. But the thought of it—of everything being laid bare between them—felt terrifying.

"What do you mean?" she asked, her voice small.

Jack took a deep breath, his hand sliding down her arm, his touch gentle but firm. "I'm talking about my past. About what I've been hiding from you. There's more to me than you know, Emma. There are things I've never told you, things that I'm afraid to share because I don't want to lose you."

Emma's heart skipped a beat, and a knot tightened in her chest. "Jack—"

He placed a finger against her lips, silencing her. "No, listen to me first." His voice was steady, but she could hear the vulnerability beneath it. "You deserve the truth, all of it. You've given me so much of yourself, and I've kept pieces of me locked away. But not anymore."

He stepped back, running a hand through his hair, as if gathering his thoughts. "I've made mistakes, Emma. Big ones. Things I regret. People I've hurt. I've been running from my past for so long, thinking that if I could bury it deep enough, it would just disappear. But it hasn't. And it's not fair to you that I've kept it hidden. So, I need to tell you. I need you to understand what I've done and why it matters."

The weight of his words hung in the air, thick with anticipation. Emma felt her breath catch, but she nodded, her heart pounding in her chest. She knew this was the moment. The moment that everything could change. The truth, no matter how painful, would be the key to everything.

Jack's eyes darkened as he looked at her, his voice quiet but filled with emotion. "I hurt someone I loved. I made choices that tore lives apart. And I've spent so long running from it that I didn't realize how much it was eating me up inside. I've built a life with you, Emma. A beautiful, messy, perfect life. But I've been haunted by my past. By the things I've done."

Emma's mind raced, but she remained silent, waiting for him to continue. She had never seen him like this—raw, vulnerable, torn. It made her heart ache for him. And yet, she couldn't help but feel a little afraid. The truth was heavy, and it carried the weight of everything they had worked so hard to build.

But then, Jack took a step toward her, his eyes softening, his voice filled with determination. "I've hurt people, Emma. But not you. You are everything I've been searching for. You are the one thing in my life that I can't afford to lose. And I will fight for you. For us."

Her breath caught in her throat as the weight of his words settled over her like a blanket. She had known there were things he hadn't shared, but this—this was the rawest, most painful confession he could have given. And yet, despite the heaviness, Emma felt something else rising within her. Understanding. Compassion. A fierce love for the man standing before her.

"I don't want you to carry this alone anymore," she said softly, her voice breaking with emotion. "We're in this together, Jack. Whatever you've done, whatever you're running from—it doesn't matter to me. What matters is that we're here. And we're not going anywhere."

Jack's eyes filled with gratitude, and he pulled her into his arms, holding her tightly as though he was afraid to let go. As though the weight of the world was finally lifting from his shoulders.

"I love you," he whispered, his voice thick with emotion.

Emma's heart soared as she whispered back, "I love you too."

They stood there, wrapped in each other's arms, as the world outside seemed to fade away. For the first time in so long, the past was no longer a shadow over them. They had faced it. They had confronted it. And now, there was nothing left but the future—together.

Chapter 132: The Weight of Silence

"Sometimes the questions are complicated, and the answers are simple." — Dr. Seuss

Emma lay awake in the dark, the warmth of Jack's body beside hers comforting, yet there was an undeniable tension lingering in the air. It was the kind of silence that spoke volumes, not of distance, but of the weight of everything they had been through. They had fought, they had loved, and now, they were standing on the edge of something new, something unknown, and the anticipation was almost overwhelming.

Jack stirred beside her, his hand moving across the sheets to find hers. His touch was gentle, soothing, but there was something in his grip that betrayed the same uncertainty that Emma felt.

"Are we really here?" Emma whispered, her voice soft, barely more than a breath. "Is this it, Jack?"

He didn't immediately respond, as if the question hung in the air like a fragile thread, one tug away from breaking. Instead, he turned his body towards hers, his face coming into the dim light that filtered through the curtains. His eyes were intense, deep with emotion, yet there was a softness there—a tenderness that made Emma's heart ache in the best way.

"You mean this," he said, his voice thick with emotion. "You and me, everything we've been through... Is this really happening?"

Emma nodded, swallowing the lump in her throat. "I think we've already made it happen, haven't we? We've built something from the ashes of our pasts. We've torn down walls and rebuilt each other, piece by piece."

Jack's thumb brushed over her knuckles, the simple touch grounding her, and in that moment, she felt the deep connection they shared. The fear that had once plagued her, that voice telling her it could all slip away, began to quiet. This was real. What they had was real.

"You know," Jack murmured, pulling her closer until their bodies were flush against each other. "I've never felt this way about anyone. Not with her, not with anyone. You're different, Emma. You've made me see myself in a way no one else ever could."

His lips brushed against her forehead, and Emma felt her pulse quicken. It wasn't just his words; it was the sincerity in them, the vulnerability that made her feel like she had been stripped bare. He was giving her something she hadn't asked for but had desperately needed: his heart, his trust, his love.

The air between them was thick with unspoken promises, the kind that could only be forged in the most intimate of moments. The world outside seemed so distant, so irrelevant. There was only them now, in this space, in this time.

Jack's lips found hers, not with the urgency of their past encounters, but with a slow, lingering pressure that left Emma breathless. It wasn't just passion; it was connection, a melding of two souls finally understanding that the storms they had weathered had led them to this.

She kissed him back, her hands threading through his hair, pulling him closer as if she could never be close enough. She wanted him, needed him, but more than that, she needed this moment with him—one where the world outside faded away and there was nothing left but the two of them, their hearts in perfect rhythm.

Jack moved above her, his body hovering just inches from hers, and for a moment, Emma thought time had slowed down. He was everything to her—her past, her present, her future—and with each touch, each caress, they were building something that went beyond mere physicality. They were weaving a tapestry of trust, love, and d esire.

Her hands roamed over his chest, feeling the steady beat of his heart beneath her fingertips. It was the same heart that had been through so much, the same heart that had known loss and pain, yet now it was hers. And she was his, in every sense of the word.

With a soft sigh, Jack lowered himself onto her, his lips capturing hers in a kiss that deepened as the world around them seemed to dissolve. They were two people who had fought through the storms, and now, they were here—together.

The intensity of their connection left them breathless, their bodies moving in sync, each touch sparking a fire that burned hotter with every passing second. Emma's hands slid down to his back, urging him closer, wanting more of him, needing to lose herself in the sensation of being with him, completely and entirely.

Jack's hand slid between them, his touch a whisper against her skin as he explored her with a gentleness that made her heart swell. Every caress, every kiss, every breath they shared was a promise—a promise that no matter the battles they had fought or the ones they still faced, they would always come back to each other.

As the intensity of their passion built, Emma felt as though she was falling, tumbling into something greater than herself, something she had never known existed. The world around them ceased to exist as they became nothing but the sensations, the feelings, the connection that bound them together.

Jack's name slipped from her lips in a breathless moan, and he responded with a soft groan of his own. The rhythm of their bodies, the heat between them, was all-consuming, and in that moment, they both knew that this was it—the culmination of everything they had worked for, everything they had fought through.

With a final, shuddering breath, they came together, the world around them spinning as they held onto each other, savoring the intensity of their connection. It wasn't just physical; it was emotional, spiritual—it was everything they had ever wanted, everything they had ever needed.

And when the world finally slowed down, when the heat between them subsided, they held each other close, their hearts still racing in unison. There were no more questions, no more doubts. There was only love, pure and unyielding, and the promise that they would always find their way back to each other, no matter what.

"I love you," Emma whispered, her voice thick with emotion.

"I love you, too," Jack replied, his voice full of conviction. "And nothing will ever change that."

In that moment, as they lay in the quiet aftermath, Emma knew that they had both finally found their place, their peace, and their love. It had been a journey of passion, of fire, of heartache and healing, but it had led them to this—a love that was as strong as it was endless.

And as they drifted off to sleep in each other's arms, the future stretched out before them, full of possibilities, full of hope. Together, they were unstoppable.

Chapter 133: Fading Walls

"The walls we build around us to keep sadness out also keeps out the joy." —Jim Rohn

The air between them crackled with unspoken words. Emma lay in Jack's arms, her thoughts racing as she tried to digest the magnitude of what had just happened. They had reached a point where every touch, every kiss, carried more weight than before. Their bodies were tangled, but so were their hearts—worn raw by past battles, yet stronger because of them.

Jack's fingertips lightly traced patterns on her skin, slow and deliberate, as if he were memorising the very essence of her being. She shivered under his touch, but not from cold; it was the electric current of vulnerability and connection that ran deep between them.

"I've never known anything like this before," Jack murmured, his breath warm against her ear. "Not just the passion, but everything. With you, it's more than I ever imagined."

Emma shifted slightly, propping herself up on one elbow to look into his eyes. "It's the same for me. I never thought I could let someone in again, but here we are. This feels right, Jack. It feels... like I'm finally home."

He brushed a strand of hair away from her face, his expression soft, almost reverent. His eyes were dark with desire, but there was something deeper, something more—love, maybe, or the kind of connection that transcends mere emotion. It was something permanent, something real.

"We've been through so much," Jack continued, his voice almost a whisper. "But now, I'm not afraid anymore. Not of you. Not of what's to come. We've made it this far, and I'll do whatever it takes to make sure this... this thing we have, this love, doesn't fade."

Emma's heart swelled in her chest. He spoke with such raw honesty, and it left her breathless. She had never known this kind of certainty, and it made her feel weightless, as if the very ground beneath them had been removed. All that remained was him, her, and the undeniable force between them.

"I won't let it fade either," she whispered, leaning in to kiss him. This kiss was different—softer, deeper, a promise. The kind of kiss that conveyed everything words could not express.

When they finally broke apart, their breaths were shallow, but their eyes held something that no one else could see. They were on the precipice of something bigger, something more profound. Emma could feel it in every fiber of her being.

Jack lifted her chin, his touch tender yet insistent. "I want this, Emma. More than anything. I want us, the way we are now, but forever. I want to build something lasting, something that doesn't fade like the rest of the world."

Her heart raced as the weight of his words sank in. "And I want that too, Jack. But we both know that building something like that takes more than love. It takes trust, commitment, and the willingness to fight for each other—even when things get hard."

Jack nodded, his gaze unwavering. "I'm ready for that. No more running. No more doubts. It's you and me, Emma. Always."

The intensity in his voice set her soul on fire. She had known love before, but never like this. It wasn't just the heat of passion; it was the steadiness, the certainty, the security that only came from knowing you were truly seen by someone else.

They had both been broken, had both stumbled through life, questioning what it meant to be truly loved, to be enough. But in this moment, as they lay in each other's arms, Emma knew they had found the answer. It wasn't about perfection or certainty; it was about the willingness to continue, to try, to trust—even when the path ahead seemed unclear.

"I'm scared too," Emma admitted softly, her voice a mere breath. "But not of you. I'm scared of everything else, of what the world could throw at us, of what could go wrong. But with you, I think I can handle it. Because I trust you, Jack. And I believe in us."

Jack's thumb caressed her cheek gently, his eyes searching hers. "I know. I'm scared of the same things. But as long as we're together, I believe we can face anything."

A heavy silence fell between them, but it was a comfortable silence, one filled with understanding. Their love had survived the trials of their pasts—betrayal, heartache, and fear—and now, as they stood on the edge of this new chapter, it felt as though they were both holding their breath, waiting for the leap into the unknown.

Emma wrapped her arms around him tightly, pressing her body closer to his. "Let's not wait anymore, Jack. Let's take that leap."

Jack's lips found hers once more, this time with an urgency that matched the wild rhythm of their hearts. It was as though every kiss, every touch, was a reaffirmation of the commitment they had made, the love they had chosen to build.

They moved together once more, not just out of passion, but out of a need to be closer, to prove to each other that they could weather whatever storms might come. The world outside faded into nothingness, and all that remained was the intimacy between them, the promise of tomorrow, and the deep, burning connection they shared.

As the night stretched on, Emma felt herself surrendering fully to the moment, to Jack, to their future. There was no fear left—only the certainty that they were meant for this, meant for each other.

When morning came, and the first rays of sunlight broke through the blinds, they lay entwined, their bodies still humming with the remnants of the night. Emma's head rested on Jack's chest, her heart still racing with the intensity of everything they had shared.

And as they lay there, wrapped in the warmth of each other, they both knew that this was just the beginning. Whatever came next, they would face it together, with love, with strength, and with the unshakable belief that they were enough.

Chapter 134: Into the Light

"Sometimes, the greatest act of love is the courage to face the truth, no matter how painful." — Unknown

The city was quiet when Emma woke up, the soft hum of the morning settling over the skyline of Sydney. The gentle light from the rising sun streamed through the windows, casting a warm glow across the room. She shifted slightly, her body still entwined with Jack's, the comfort of his presence a stark contrast to the storm of emotions that had swirled in her chest over the past few days.

Jack's steady breathing was a rhythmic lullaby that had helped calm the chaos of her mind. But now, as the morning light grew stronger, Emma couldn't help but wonder—what would the day bring? They had come so far, but there were still so many questions, so many things left unsaid.

The softest touch of Jack's lips brushed against the back of her neck, his warmth seeping into her skin. "Good morning," he murmured, his voice husky with sleep.

She smiled, turning slightly to meet his eyes. "Morning," she whispered back, her voice still thick with the remnants of the night. Her fingers traced the line of his jaw, still marveling at the way he made her feel—like she was both grounded and free, both loved and independent.

Jack's hand slid over her back, pulling her closer, as though he could hold her tighter and keep her safe from whatever doubts lingered in her mind. "Are you okay?" he asked, his voice serious, a slight edge of concern in his tone. "You've been quiet this morning."

Emma hesitated, her eyes drifting to the window, watching the world outside slowly come to life. She had been quiet, yes. But it wasn't because she didn't want to talk—it was because she didn't know how. She wasn't sure how to articulate everything she was feeling. How could she explain the swirl of emotions inside her, the mixture of hope and fear, of love and uncertainty?

"I'm just... thinking," she admitted, her fingers still playing with the fabric of the sheets. "I'm not sure what comes next, Jack. We've come so far, but the world doesn't stop just because we've decided to take a leap. There are still things we need to figure out."

Jack's eyes softened, and he lifted his hand to gently cup her face, guiding her gaze back to his. "You don't have to have all the answers right now, Emma. Not everything needs to be figured out. All I know is that I'm here, and I want to be with you. Whatever that means, we'll figure it out together."

She could see the sincerity in his eyes, the depth of his words, and for the first time in a long while, Emma felt a sense of peace settle within her. It wasn't about having everything neatly planned out—it was about moving forward, together. It was about trusting that, no matter what, they could face anything.

"Together," she repeated, a smile tugging at the corners of her lips.

Jack kissed her then, slow and deep, a kiss that spoke of promises made and of the future they would build. It was a kiss that made her forget about the world outside, made her forget about anything that could go wrong. In that moment, all that mattered was the two of them, and the bond they had created.

The sound of Emma's phone buzzing on the nightstand interrupted their moment. She sighed, reluctantly pulling away from Jack. "I should probably check that," she murmured.

Jack groaned, clearly not ready to leave the sanctuary of their shared intimacy. "Can't it wait?"

Emma smiled and reached over to grab her phone. "It's probably work," she said, half-expecting it to be another update from the design team.

But as she unlocked the screen, her eyes widened at the message on the display. It wasn't work—it was from someone she hadn't heard from in a while.

"Emma, I need to see you. We need to talk. – Victoria."

Her heart skipped a beat, and she felt a cold rush of dread settle in her chest. The last time she had heard from Victoria, it had been a conversation full of venom, bitterness, and warning. What could she want now? And more importantly, what did this mean for her and Jack?

Jack noticed the change in her expression immediately, sitting up slightly as he watched her intently. "What is it?" he asked, his voice laced with concern.

Emma hesitated for a moment, unsure of how to explain. She showed him the message, and his face darkened as he read it.

"I thought we were done with her," Jack muttered, frustration clouding his tone. "I thought we'd moved past that."

"We have," Emma said quickly, but she couldn't shake the feeling of unease that had settled deep within her. "But I don't know what this is about. She hasn't reached out in weeks."

Jack ran a hand through his hair, his usual calm demeanor slipping. "I don't like this, Emma. If she's trying to stir something up, we don't need to give her any power over us. We've worked too hard to get where we are."

"I know," Emma said, swallowing her fear. "But I need to understand. I can't just ignore it."

Jack exhaled sharply, clearly frustrated but understanding. "Then let's go together. Whatever she wants, we'll face it together."

Emma nodded, her heart heavy with the weight of what was to come. She had come so far with Jack, and she wasn't about to let Victoria, or anyone, tear them apart. But there was still a nagging doubt in her mind, a question she couldn't quite silence: Was this a test of their love? Or was there something more to it?

Jack stood up, pulling on his shirt and jeans, determination in his every movement. "Let's get this over with. We'll put an end to whatever it is, once and for all."

Emma quickly dressed as well, her mind racing with a million possibilities. But as she caught a glimpse of herself in the mirror, something inside her settled. No matter what happened, she knew one thing for certain—she had Jack by her side, and that was all that truly mattered.

Together, they would face whatever came next. Together, they would find the answers.

Chapter 135: Beyond the Horizon

"The heart has its reasons which reason knows not." — Blaise Pascal

The tension in the air was palpable as Emma and Jack drove toward the small café on the outskirts of the city. The message from Victoria still lingered on Emma's mind, the words echoing with a sense of dread and uncertainty. She couldn't shake the feeling that this meeting would be more than just a simple conversation. Whatever Victoria wanted, Emma was determined to face it head-on, no matter the cost.

Jack's grip on the steering wheel was firm, his jaw set in determination. He glanced at Emma, his eyes darkened with concern. "Are you sure about this?" he asked quietly, his voice steady but edged with worry. "We don't need to do this, you know."

Emma exhaled slowly, her fingers tracing the edge of her phone. She had to admit, a part of her was scared. Scared of what Victoria might reveal, scared of the emotions that had been stirred up in the past. But she knew deep down that she needed closure. She couldn't let Victoria's shadow hang over her relationship with Jack any longer.

"I need to know," she said, her voice quiet but resolute. "I need to understand what this is about. If we're going to move forward, I can't keep ignoring the past."

Jack nodded, his eyes back on the road. "I'm with you, Emma. No matter what, we'll handle this together."

As they neared the café, Emma's heart began to race. The small building stood in the corner of a quiet street, the windows offering a glimpse of the few early customers enjoying their morning coffee. They parked the car and walked inside, the bell above the door ringing softly as they entered.

Victoria was already there, sitting at a corner table, her posture stiff and tense. She looked up as they entered, her gaze meeting Emma's with a mixture of guilt and resolve. The air between them was charged, and Emma could feel the weight of unspoken words pressing down on her.

She took a deep breath and walked over to the table, Jack following closely behind her. Victoria's eyes flickered to him briefly, but she didn't acknowledge him directly. Instead, she focused entirely on Emma, her face a mask of carefully controlled emotions.

"Sit down, Emma," Victoria said, her voice low and slightly strained. "We need to talk."

Emma took a seat, Jack standing slightly behind her, his presence a comforting anchor. She didn't look away from Victoria, her posture firm. "What is it, Victoria? What do you want from me?"

Victoria exhaled, her gaze briefly dropping to the table. "I know this isn't easy for you," she began, her voice thick with something Emma couldn't quite place. "But I need you to listen. There's something you need to know about Jack. About his past."

Emma's heart skipped a beat, but she didn't flinch. "You've already said everything there is to say. I know about your history. I know about what happened between you."

Victoria shook her head, a bitter smile curling on her lips. "It's not what you think. It's not the whole story, Emma. There's more—so much more—about Jack's past that he's never told you."

Emma's breath caught in her throat. She could feel Jack tense behind her, but she didn't dare turn to look at him. Her eyes were locked on Victoria, searching for any hint of truth in her words.

"More?" Emma asked, her voice barely above a whisper. "What are you talking about?"

Victoria leaned forward, her eyes narrowed with a mixture of regret and something darker. "Jack hasn't been honest with you, Emma. About who he really is. About what he's done."

Emma felt the world shift beneath her feet. Her pulse quickened, and her mind raced to make sense of the words Victoria was saying. She could feel Jack's presence behind her, but the distance between them suddenly felt vast, as if an ocean separated them.

"You're lying," Jack's voice broke in, low and commanding. He stepped forward, his expression hard. "I've told Emma everything. There's nothing left for you to twist."

Victoria's gaze flickered to Jack, a flash of something—anger, perhaps—crossing her face. "You've told her everything?" she repeated, her voice rising. "You think she knows the truth? The whole truth?"

Jack's eyes darkened, and Emma could feel the tension in his body. "Enough, Victoria," he said, his tone sharp. "This ends now. Whatever game you think you're playing, it's over."

Victoria laughed bitterly, her eyes glinting with something cold. "Is it? Is it really over, Jack? Do you really think she knows everything? Do you really think she knows what you did to me?"

Emma's stomach churned as the words hit her like a physical blow. She wanted to shut them out, to stop the conversation, but something inside her wouldn't let her. She needed to know. She needed to understand the truth, no matter how painful it was.

"What did he do to you?" Emma asked, her voice a mixture of anger and confusion. She wasn't sure she was ready for the answer, but she had to ask. She couldn't let Victoria's words hang in the air, unanswered.

Victoria's eyes locked onto hers, her voice steady now, as though she were relishing the moment. "He made me believe in him. He made me think I was the only one, that he was my world. And then one day, without warning, he left. Just like that. No explanation. No apology."

Emma felt the world tilt, her mind spinning with the weight of Victoria's words. She wanted to scream, to demand that this be a lie, but deep down, she knew that Jack's past was more complicated than he had ever let on.

Jack's voice cut through the tension, calm but cold. "You know why I left, Victoria. You know why it ended."

But Victoria wasn't finished. "Do you really think she'll be different, Jack? Do you really think you'll be able to walk away from her, just like you did with me?"

Emma turned sharply to face Jack, her heart hammering in her chest. She needed to hear him say it. She needed to hear that he was committed, that he wouldn't leave her like he had left Victoria.

Jack took a deep breath, his eyes meeting hers with unwavering intensity. "Emma, I love you. I'm not going anywhere. This isn't about what happened in the past. It's about what we have now. And I won't let anyone—no matter who they are—destroy that."

The words settled in her chest like a balm, easing the tension that had built up over the past few days. For the first time in a long while, Emma felt like the storm inside her had calmed.

Victoria's expression flickered for a moment, a hint of doubt creeping into her eyes, but she quickly masked it. "Fine," she said, standing up. "You'll see, Jack. You'll see that things don't end so easily."

With that, Victoria turned and left, her exit as abrupt as her arrival. The silence in the café was deafening as Emma and Jack sat there, the weight of the conversation still hanging heavily between them.

Emma turned to Jack, her heart still racing. "Is it true? Is everything she said true?"

Jack's hand found hers, and he squeezed it gently. "No, Emma. She's twisting things, trying to hurt you. I've made mistakes, yes, but I would never do that to you."

Emma searched his face, her eyes searching for any hint of dishonesty, but all she saw was the man she loved. "I believe you," she said softly. "I just... I need time to process all of this."

Jack nodded, his eyes softening. "Take all the time you need. But know that I'm here. Always."

For the first time in a long while, Emma felt a sense of clarity wash over her. She didn't have all the answers, but one thing was certain—she and Jack would face whatever came next together.

Chapter 136: The Final Embrace

"*In your arms, I find my world, and in your kiss, I lose it all.*" — *Unknown*

The days following Victoria's confrontation passed in a blur of emotions, uncertainties, and moments of quiet resolve. Emma and Jack spent more time together, drawing closer with each passing hour. Yet, beneath their growing connection, a sense of unease still lingered. Emma knew the past was never truly gone; it could still creep into their lives when they least expected it.

But they were stronger now, together. They'd weathered storms before, and this would not be any different. As Jack held her in the quiet moments of the night, she could feel the tension slowly unspooling from her body. His presence was the anchor she needed. No matter the chaos of the world around them, when he was near, she felt safe.

They were sitting in their favourite café, sipping their coffee in silence, the city's hum drifting through the large windows. The rain outside had begun to fall in gentle sheets, blurring the outlines of the world beyond. Emma rested her head against Jack's shoulder, the warmth of his body radiating against her skin.

"I've been thinking," she said softly, breaking the comfortable silence.

Jack turned his head toward her, his eyes warm. "About what?"

"About everything," she said, her voice a mixture of vulnerability and determination. "The past... the things we've been through. It's all part of who we are, right? But I don't want to keep looking over my shoulder anymore."

Jack's hand found hers, their fingers intertwining. "We don't need to, Emma. You and me... we have a future. We're writing our own story now. The past doesn't have a hold on us."

Her heart swelled with affection, but a part of her still worried. She had always believed in the power of love, in the idea that love could overcome anything. But what if that wasn't enough? What if their love was not as unbreakable as she hoped?

"I want to believe that," Emma said, her voice just above a whisper. "But there's so much to carry, Jack. You've been through so much... and I've had my own battles. We can't just pretend everything's perfect. We have to face things. We need to heal."

Jack squeezed her hand gently, his thumb brushing over her skin. "We will. Together. Every step of the way."

Their conversation drifted to lighter topics, but the weight of their earlier exchange still lingered. Emma knew deep down that they were on the right path, but she couldn't ignore the unsettling thought in her mind—that they were just a few wrong choices away from everything falling apart.

Later that afternoon, as they made their way back to Jack's apartment, Emma couldn't help but feel the tension in the air. It was as if the world were holding its breath, waiting for something to give. She had her doubts, her worries, but she couldn't let that stop her. Jack was right. They were in this together, and they had the power to change the course of their future.

They walked inside, and as soon as the door closed behind them, Jack turned to her, his eyes intense and filled with something Emma couldn't name. The silence between them was thick with expectation.

"I need to ask you something," Jack said, his voice low.

Emma looked up at him, her heart pounding in her chest. "What is it?"

He hesitated for a moment before stepping closer, his hand gently cupping her face. "Are you ready for this? Are you ready to leave the past behind, to make something new with me? Because I'm ready, Emma. I'm ready to do this. All of it. For you. For us."

She could feel the sincerity in his words, in every touch, every glance. She had seen his vulnerability, his fears, and she knew what this meant. It wasn't just about love—it was about trust. About opening herself up completely to him, to the future they could build together.

"I am," she said, her voice filled with conviction. "I want this. I want you. And I'm ready to face whatever comes next, as long as we're together."

Jack's lips met hers in a kiss that was tender and passionate all at once. The storm that had raged inside her calmed, replaced by a fierce desire to move forward, to embrace the unknown. Whatever challenges lay ahead, they would face them side by side.

As their kiss deepened, Emma felt the weight of the world lift from her shoulders. She knew that they had their struggles, that things wouldn't always be easy. But she also knew that love was worth fighting for, worth sacrificing for. And this—this feeling of connection, of unity—was something she wouldn't let go of.

Jack pulled back slightly, his breath heavy as he gazed at her. "Are you sure? Because I don't want you to have any doubts. This is everything, Emma."

"I'm sure," she said, her voice firm. "I want all of you, Jack. I'm all in."

With a satisfied smile, Jack kissed her again, this time with a sense of urgency, as if the world outside could wait. The future could wait. For now, all that mattered was the two of them, and the love they had found in each other.

And in that moment, Emma felt an overwhelming sense of peace. The past, with all its shadows and uncertainties, no longer held any power over her. She was free. They were free. Together.

Chapter 137: A Future Together

"*The future belongs to those who believe in the beauty of their dreams." — Eleanor Roosevelt*

The weeks that followed felt like a blur of emotions. Every day was a step closer to something new, something more than either of them had ever imagined. Emma and Jack were building something real, something that felt solid, unshakable. Despite the doubts that had once clouded her mind, Emma could now see the horizon in front of them—an exciting, unpredictable future where love and trust would be their guiding stars.

But life, as it always does, had a way of throwing curveballs when you least expected them.

It had been a quiet evening when Emma received the call. She was sitting in the living room of their shared apartment, flipping through a design portfolio when the phone rang. The number was unfamiliar, but she answered anyway.

"Hello?"

"Emma Carter?"

Her pulse quickened. The voice on the other end was familiar, but she couldn't place it. "Yes, this is Emma."

"It's Richard Holloway. I'm sorry to bother you, but there's something important I need to discuss."

Emma's stomach tightened. Richard was the investigator who had approached her months ago, with the folder full of unsettling documents. She hadn't heard from him since, but the memory of that day still haunted her. She glanced over at Jack, who was in the kitchen, preparing dinner.

"I'm listening," Emma said, trying to keep her voice steady.

"I think it's time we talk about Jack's past. There are things he hasn't shared with you, things I think you need to know if you're truly going to move forward with him," Richard said, his voice low and serious.

Emma's heart skipped a beat. Her initial instinct was to hang up the phone, to shut it all out, but something inside her stopped her. She needed to know. She had to know if there was more she didn't understand about Jack's past.

"I'm listening," she repeated, her voice barely above a whisper.

"I'll meet you tomorrow," Richard said. "I think you deserve the truth."

With that, he hung up, leaving Emma standing in stunned silence. The silence was deafening, and all she could do was stare at the phone in her hand, the weight of his words hanging heavily in the air.

The next day, Emma found herself sitting in a small, dimly lit café, waiting for Richard. Her heart was pounding in her chest, her thoughts spinning. Jack's past—what more could there be? She had seen the fragments of it, the brief glimpses of the man he used to be, but she hadn't expected any more surprises. She had believed in him. She still did.

But now, she wasn't so sure.

Richard walked in a few minutes later, his expression unreadable. He spotted her immediately and made his way over, sitting down across from her without a word. He pulled out a manila envelope, setting it gently on the table.

"Jack has a history, Emma," Richard said, his voice low. "A history he hasn't shared with you. And while I don't expect you to believe everything I'm about to show you, I think you need to see it."

Emma hesitated. She wanted to tell him she was fine, that she didn't need to know, that it didn't matter. But she couldn't bring herself to lie. She had to know.

Richard opened the envelope and slid a few photographs across the table. Emma's breath caught in her throat as she looked at the images in front of her. They were of Jack, but not the Jack she knew. These photos showed a different man—darker, colder, more dangerous. There were images of him with people she didn't recognise, in places she couldn't imagine. The evidence was damning, yet she refused to let herself jump to conclusions.

"Do you recognise these people?" Richard asked.

Emma shook her head slowly, her mind struggling to process the pictures. "No... who are they?"

"People from Jack's past. People he's tried to bury," Richard said. "But you can't escape the past, not when it's this ugly."

Emma's hands shook as she reached for one of the photographs. Her mind raced with a thousand questions, but she couldn't seem to make sense of it. Was this the man she had fallen for? The man she had trusted with everything?

"I know this is a lot to take in," Richard said, his voice softer now. "But you need to understand what you're getting into. Jack's past isn't clean, and there are things that could still come back to haunt you both."

Emma stared at the photograph in her hand, her thoughts a whirlwind. Her heart screamed for the Jack she had come to love—the man who had opened his heart to her, the man who had shared his vulnerabilities and fears. This... this wasn't the Jack she knew.

But as she looked at Richard, something inside her snapped. She couldn't let fear and doubt control her anymore. She couldn't let the past dictate their future.

"Thank you for showing me this," Emma said, her voice steady. She stood up, collecting the photographs and the envelope, slipping them into her bag. "But I need to talk to Jack. I need to hear it from him."

Richard seemed taken aback, but he didn't argue. "Just remember what I've told you, Emma. The truth has a way of coming to light, whether you're ready for it or not."

Emma nodded, leaving the café without looking back.

She barely made it through the door before Jack was there, concern etched into his features. "Emma? What's wrong?"

"Jack," she said softly, her voice trembling with emotions she couldn't yet name. "We need to talk."

Chapter 138 – Ever After

"*It's not about finding someone to live with. It's about finding someone you can't imagine living without.*" — *Rafael Ortiz*

The weight of the world seemed to hang heavy in the air as Emma stepped into the apartment. Jack's eyes never left her, his concern for her etched into every line of his face. The moment she walked through the door, he could sense something had shifted, something profound, and his heart skipped a beat at the thought of what it could mean.

He closed the distance between them, his hands reaching for hers. But Emma pulled back slightly, taking a deep breath, her mind a whirlwind of conflicting emotions. The time for silence was over. The time for facing the truth had arrived.

"Jack, we need to talk," she said, her voice soft yet firm.

"Of course," he replied, his brow furrowing. "What's going on?"

Emma exhaled slowly. She had never been afraid of confronting the truth, but what she had to say now felt like a mountain she wasn't sure she could climb. But she would do it for them—for the future they had dreamed about, for the love they shared.

"I met with Richard Holloway," Emma began, her gaze never wavering from his. "He showed me things. Things about your past."

Jack's eyes flickered with a mix of emotions—surprise, guilt, but also a quiet resignation. He had known this moment would come. He had hoped it would never arrive, but he knew better than to hide from it

.

"Emma, I—" He began, but Emma held up her hand, stopping him.

"I'm not here to accuse you," she said, her voice steady but thick with emotion. "I'm not here to judge you either. I just... I need to understand. I need to know what happened. I need to hear it from you."

Jack looked down, as though gathering the strength to say the words. The silence stretched between them, heavy and thick with the weight of their shared history. He had carried the burden of his past for so long, and now, it was time to share it.

"It's true," he began, his voice barely a whisper. "My past... it's not something I'm proud of. I've done things I regret. Things that I wish I could take back. But those things, those people—they're gone. And I've spent so many years trying to outrun it, to be someone else. But it's never easy to outrun your past."

Emma swallowed, her heart pounding in her chest as she absorbed his words. "I need to know everything, Jack. No more secrets. I need to know who you were before I can fully trust who you are now."

Jack nodded slowly. He took a step back, running his hand through his hair as he processed her words. There were so many things he wished he could undo, things he wished he could erase from his past, but now, there was no escaping them.

"I grew up in a world of wealth and power," Jack began, his voice heavy with the memories. "My father was a businessman—ruthless, controlling. He taught me that success meant everything, and he taught me that you could achieve anything, no matter the cost. I was molded into someone who thought he could have it all. And I did. But I paid the price."

He paused, his eyes clouded with the ghosts of the past. "I got involved with people who didn't care about anything but power. And I did things—things that hurt people. People I loved. People I lost."

Emma stood still, her breath caught in her throat as she listened to him. She had always sensed that Jack had a side to him that he kept hidden, but hearing it from him directly was something else entirely. It was raw. It was honest. It was painful.

"Why didn't you tell me any of this before?" Emma asked, her voice trembling slightly.

"I was ashamed," Jack admitted, his voice hoarse. "I didn't want you to see me as the man I used to be. I didn't want to carry that baggage into our relationship, into what we had. I wanted to be someone you could love without hesitation, without the fear of my past tainting it."

Emma's heart ached for him, for the burden he had carried all these years. She understood why he had kept his secrets, but the weight of it was still heavy.

"Jack, I love you. And I don't want your past to define you," she said, her voice steady now, full of conviction. "But I need you to understand something. You can't keep parts of yourself hidden from me. Not if we're going to make this work. Not if we're going to have a future together."

Jack nodded, his eyes full of emotion. "I know. And I'm ready to face it, all of it. For you. For us."

The tension in the room seemed to dissipate as they stood there, facing each other, two people who had been through so much but who still found their way back to each other.

"I want a future with you, Jack. A future that's built on trust and honesty," Emma said, her voice trembling as she reached for his hand. "We can't keep living in the shadows. Not anymore."

Jack's gaze softened, his fingers interlacing with hers. "I know. And I want that too. I'll do whatever it takes to make things right."

In that moment, Emma realized that love wasn't just about passion and excitement—it was about facing the hard truths, supporting each other through the storms, and never letting go. She wasn't sure what the future would hold, but one thing was clear: as long as they were together, they could face anything.

Chapter 139: Unbreakable Bonds

"*Love does not consist in gazing at each other, but in looking outward together in the same direction.*" — *Antoine de Saint-Exupéry*

The weight of the decision pressed down on Emma's chest as she sat on the edge of the bed, her thoughts swirling in every direction. Jack's words echoed in her mind, over and over. He had finally confessed everything—the good, the bad, and the ugly of his past. And while the truth had been difficult to hear, it was exactly what she had needed.

They had talked long into the night, hashing out the details of his past life and the things he had done. But there was one thing they hadn't discussed yet—the future. What would it look like? Was it even possible for them to move forward, knowing everything now?

Her phone buzzed on the nightstand, breaking the silence. Emma reached for it, her heart skipping a beat when she saw the name on the screen.

It was Jack.

She hesitated for a moment before answering, pressing the phone to her ear.

"Emma," Jack's voice was low, but there was an undeniable urgency to it. "I need to see you. Now."

Her pulse quickened. "What's going on?"

"I can't explain over the phone. Please, just trust me."

His words sent a shiver through her. She had never heard him sound so serious, so desperate. Something was wrong.

Without thinking twice, she grabbed her jacket and rushed out the door, not even bothering to lock it behind her. Her mind raced as she made her way to the car, her heart pounding in her chest. She knew whatever was coming, it was going to change everything.

When she arrived at Jack's apartment, she was met by his tense expression. He stood in the doorway, his eyes searching hers, as if looking for something. Or perhaps waiting for something.

"Jack, what's going on?" Emma asked, her voice tinged with concern.

He stepped aside to let her in, but his gaze never left hers. "I don't know how to say this, but... I'm leaving."

Emma froze. "What do you mean, leaving?"

"I've made a decision," Jack said, his voice hoarse. "I've decided I need to go. For good."

Her heart clenched in her chest, the words he spoke making no sense. "You're leaving? But... why?"

"I thought I could be the man you needed me to be. I thought I could outrun my past, but I can't. It's catching up to me, Emma. It's going to destroy everything, and I can't let that happen. Not to you."

Tears welled in Emma's eyes as she took a step toward him, her hands trembling. "Jack, please don't. We've fought so hard for this. We've been through so much. We can get through this too. We don't have to run away from it."

"I'm not running away," Jack replied, his voice breaking. "I'm trying to protect you. From me. From my past. From the things I've done."

Emma reached for him, her fingers brushing against his cheek. "Jack, I love you. I want to be with you. We'll face it together. Whatever it is, we can face it."

Jack's eyes softened, but there was a sadness in them that tore at her heart. "I don't know if that's enough anymore. I don't know if we can overcome everything."

"I don't care about your past, Jack," Emma said, her voice strong now. "I care about who you are now. Who you've become. I care about us, about what we've built together."

The silence between them stretched on, a heavy weight of unspoken words and unresolved feelings. Jack looked torn, caught between his desire to protect her and his desire to hold onto the love they shared.

"Emma," he said, his voice barely above a whisper. "I've made so many mistakes. But the one thing I know is that I don't want to lose you. You mean more to me than anything. I never thought I'd find someone like you."

She stepped closer, closing the distance between them. "Then stay. Stay and fight for us, Jack. We're not done yet. We've only just begun."

For a long moment, Jack remained silent, his eyes locked on hers, as if searching for the right words. Finally, he spoke, his voice filled with determination.

"Okay. I'll stay. We'll figure this out. Together."The night felt different now, heavy with anticipation, the kind of tension that always preceded something monumental. Emma's heart still raced from the conversation with Jack, her body humming with the possibility of what was to come. It was as if the world had slowed down around them, leaving only the two of them in their own universe, ready to write the next chapter.

They had spent hours together, talking—really talking—in a way they hadn't before. The raw honesty of the conversation had stripped them both bare, exposing their vulnerabilities. But it was more than just confessions and shared truths. It was the understanding that they had the power to choose their future together. That their love could be stronger than any past mistakes.

Now, as Jack stood in front of her, his face inches from hers, Emma could feel the promise of that future in every brush of his breath against her skin, every whisper of his words that trembled on the edge of something more.

He reached out, gently cupping her face in his hands. His eyes searched hers, as if looking for the final affirmation of what they both knew to be true—that their love wasn't a fleeting thing, but something that could withstand whatever storms life threw their way.

"Are you sure about this?" Jack asked, his voice low, almost a whisper.

Emma nodded, her lips trembling as she answered, "I've never been more sure of anything in my life."

His lips met hers then, soft but insistent, and all the tension that had built between them over the last few days melted away. The kiss deepened, their hands wandering to places they'd both longed to touch. Emma's fingers tangled in Jack's hair, pulling him closer as if trying to fuse their bodies together. The heat between them, the longing, it had been building for far too long.

She had always known that when Jack finally let go of his past, he would be hers. And now that he had, she would never let him slip away again.

Jack's hands roamed down her back, pulling her tightly against him. Emma could feel the hardness of his chest beneath her fingers, the rapid beat of his heart matching the pounding of her own. She had longed for this, for him, for the intimacy they shared. They had fought so hard for this moment—fought through doubts, fears, and insecurities. And now, they had reached the point of no return.

He pulled away for a moment, his chest heaving with the effort of controlling his breathing. His voice was strained with desire. "Are you sure this is what you want?"

Emma's eyes were dark with emotion as she replied, "I want you, Jack. All of you. I want every part of you—your past, your present, and your future. I want it all."

Jack's breath caught, his gaze never leaving hers. Slowly, he leaned down to kiss her again, but this time, it was different. There was an urgency to it now, a hunger that had been building ever since they first met. Their bodies moved in perfect harmony, as if they had been made for this moment. Emma's hands traced the lines of his chest, memorizing every inch of him, while Jack's lips trailed down her neck, leaving a trail of fire in their wake.

The passion between them flared hotter with each touch, each kiss. There was no holding back now. They were both lost in the moment, consumed by the desire and the love they had fought so hard to find.

Finally, they found their way to the bed, their clothes falling away in a frenzy of need. The heat between them was all-consuming, overwhelming in the best way. Emma felt Jack's hands on her body, his touch sending sparks of electricity through her skin. Every kiss, every caress, was a promise—a promise that they would never let go of each other again.

As they moved together, their bodies perfectly in sync, Emma felt a sense of freedom she had never known before. It wasn't just about the physical pleasure. It was the emotional connection—the way their hearts beat in unison, the way their souls intertwined with each other.

And as the intensity of their love reached its peak, Emma knew that this was it. This was the moment that would define them, the moment they would remember for the rest of their lives. Because in this moment, nothing else mattered. They had found each other in a world that was often uncertain, and they had chosen each other. And nothing, not even the past, could take that away from them.

When the storm of passion finally began to settle, Emma lay in Jack's arms, her body still trembling from the intensity of their connection. Jack held her tightly, his lips brushing against her forehead as they both tried to catch their breath.

"You're everything to me," Jack whispered, his voice filled with a tenderness that made Emma's heart swell.

"I love you," she whispered back, her fingers tracing the lines of his jaw, as if imprinting the moment on her memory forever.

And in that moment, they both knew that they had crossed a threshold. The past was behind them, and the future stretched out before them, full of possibilities. Together, they could face anything.

The sun rose over the horizon, its warm golden light spilling into the penthouse, casting long shadows across the room. The soft sounds of the city waking up were barely audible, a reminder that life continued, even after everything they had been through. But for Emma, nothing else mattered now. She had everything she needed right here, in this moment, with Jack.

Her hand rested gently on his chest, feeling the steady rhythm of his heartbeat beneath her fingers. He was still asleep beside her, his arm draped over her waist, his breath soft and even. She smiled to herself, feeling a deep sense of peace settle in her heart. This was the life she had always dreamed of, the life she had fought for. And now, with Jack by her side, it was real.

Slowly, she sat up, careful not to disturb him, and gazed out the window. The view of Sydney was breathtaking, the skyline bathed in the soft glow of dawn. It was a city full of promise, a city that had witnessed their struggles, their triumphs, and everything in between. And now, it would be the backdrop for their new beginning.

Turning back to the bed, Emma's eyes lingered on Jack. He looked so peaceful, so content, and she couldn't help but feel a deep sense of gratitude. The journey they had taken together hadn't been easy. They had both made mistakes, hurt each other, and faced countless challenges. But in the end, they had come through it all stronger, more certain of their love than ever before.

As if sensing her gaze, Jack stirred and slowly opened his eyes, meeting her gaze with a soft, sleepy smile. "Morning," he murmured, his voice rough with sleep.

Emma's heart fluttered at the sight of him—his eyes warm with affection, the faintest trace of stubble on his jaw. He was everything to her.

"Good morning," she replied, her voice barely above a whisper. She leaned down to kiss him softly, the kiss lingering, a promise of everything that was yet to come.

Jack's hand cupped her face, his thumb brushing gently over her cheek. "You're beautiful," he said, his voice thick with emotion.

She smiled, feeling a warmth spread through her chest. "I'm just happy, Jack. Happy to be here. Happy with you."

He pulled her closer, his lips pressing against her forehead. "We've been through so much, haven't we? But we made it. And now, we get to write our own story."

Emma nodded, her eyes shining with unshed tears. "The story isn't over yet, Jack. It's just beginning."

For a long moment, they simply held each other, wrapped in the quiet of the morning. Emma's thoughts drifted to everything they had overcome—every doubt, every fear, every moment of hesitation. They had made it through it all, and now, nothing would tear them apart. They were ready for whatever came next, together.

Eventually, they rose from the bed, the promise of a new day filling the air. Jack slipped into the kitchen to make them both coffee, and Emma watched him, feeling a deep sense of fulfillment. They had come so far, and yet, she knew they still had so much more to experience. There would be challenges, of course, but she had no doubt they would face them head-on, just as they always had.

As Jack handed her a cup of coffee, their fingers brushed, sending a spark of electricity between them. She smiled at him, her heart full. "We've built something beautiful here, Jack. And I know we'll keep building, keep growing."

Jack smiled back, his eyes shining with a mix of love and determination. "We're in this for the long haul, Emma. Nothing can change that."

The words hung in the air, heavy with meaning. Emma felt the weight of them settle in her chest, but it wasn't a burden. It was a promise, a commitment to each other that no one could break.

And as they stood there, sipping their coffee and exchanging quiet smiles, Emma knew that their journey wasn't over. It had only just begun.

There would be more adventures, more discoveries, more moments of passion and intimacy. But no matter where the path took them, one thing was certain: they had each other. And that, she knew, was all they needed.

The city outside continued its rhythm, the world spinning on as it always did. But Emma and Jack, in their own little corner of the world, had everything they ever needed. And they were ready to face whatever came next—together.

www.ingramcontent.com/pod-product-compliance
Lightning Source LLC
Chambersburg PA
CBHW070332170726
48291CB00001B/28